THE FINAL STAND

A COLONIAL FLEET NOVEL

NEXUS HOUSE BOOK 1

RICK CAMPBELL

SEVERN RIVER PUBLISHING

Severn River Publishing
www.SevernRiverBooks.com

ISBN: 978-1-64875-637-5 (Paperback)

ALSO BY RICK CAMPBELL

MAIN CHARACTERS

A complete cast of characters is provided in the addendum

NEXUS HOUSE
Rhea Sidener Ten (Placidia) / the Nexus One (The One)
Noah Ronan Nine (Primus)
Jina Hong Eight (Primus)
Dewan Channing Eight (Deinde)
Regina Caine Eight / 1st Fleet Guide
Angeline Del Rio Eight / 3rd Fleet Guide
Chen Wei Seven (Primus)

COLONIAL COUNCIL
Morel Alperi Inner Realm Regent / Director of Personnel
Lijuan Xiang Terran (Earth) Regent / Director of Material

COLONIAL FLEET
Nanci Fitzgerald Fleet Admiral / Fleet Commander
Liam Carroll Admiral / Deputy Fleet Commander
Jon McCarthy Admiral / 1st Fleet Commander
James Denton Admiral / 2nd Fleet Commander

Nesrine Rajhi Captain / Battleship *Athens* Commanding Officer
Gynt Salukas Captain / Battleship *Sparta* Commanding Officer
Jeff Townsend Captain / Battleship *Europe* Commanding Officer

OTHER CHARACTERS
Lara Anderson Grief Counselor – Camden Colonial Hospital

To my father, Jack Campbell — I hope you would have enjoyed the world I've created and the stories told within it.

PROLOGUE

3,043 Ad

Almost eleven centuries after man first walked on the moon, humans have colonized over one hundred planets. For the last thirty years, Earth and its colonies have been engaged in a bitter war for survival—one they have been steadily losing, their star bases destroyed and planets razed. Only Earth and one colony remain as humanity prepares for its final stand against the Korilian Empire.

PROLOGUE

1

As the battle in the Ritalis planetary system entered its third day, Regina Caine stood beside Admiral Jon McCarthy on the bridge of the 1st Fleet command ship, assessing the deteriorating situation. She pushed the hood of her blue robe behind her head as she examined the five tiers of consoles in front of her, manned by fifty men and women wearing the crimson-and-burgundy uniform of the Colonial Navy.

Shifting her gaze to the displays along the curved front of the starship bridge, Regina surveyed the Korilian armada's onslaught against 1st and 2nd Fleets. She focused on what remained of 1st Fleet's four hundred starships, absorbing the brunt of the Korilian attack, then turned her attention to 2nd Fleet, forming a cylindrical flank wrapping back toward the fifth planet in the Ritalis star system.

Through the bridge windows above the displays, yellow flashes lit up the darkness as red pulses impacted starship energy shields. A burst of yellow light illuminated the bridge, announcing the collapse of a nearby shield. Regina's eyes were drawn to the battleship. As its shield disintegrated, the pulse carved into the starship, its compartments brightening as explosions cascaded inside the crippled vessel. Scattered throughout 1st Fleet's defensive formation, the dark hulks of destroyed cruisers and battleships spiraled slowly in space.

Surrounding the command ship was a squadron of twelve Atlantis-class battleships, the newest and most powerful warships in the Colonial Navy, their energy shields extended outward, forming a protective bubble augmenting the command ship's own shields. The battleships' pulse generators were charged, ready to destroy any Korilian warships that jumped to within weapon range before their shields had time to form.

Standing beside Regina, Admiral McCarthy manipulated a three-dimensional display of 1st Fleet ships, his hands rapidly sending commands to his ships. As the battle entered its waning moments, she could tell the strain had taken a toll; beads of sweat had formed on his face. Not even stamina pills could overcome the exhaustion of fifty straight hours of battle.

Thankfully, the evacuation of Ritalis was almost complete; the last dozen troop transports were being loaded with civilians, each ship jumping to safety after escaping the planet's gravitational pull. Behind the command ship, 1st Fleet's carriers had begun retrieving what was left of their single-pilot vipers. As Regina watched the latest troop transport disappear in a flash of light, her skin began to tingle.

She closed her eyes and opened her mind to the carnage around her. 1st Fleet, arranged in a flat, layered defensive formation, had no reserves remaining, but there was no indication of a pending Korilian breakthrough. The colors in her mind told the tale, a mosaic of green and yellow splotches representing the various sectors in the defense grid. As she turned her mind to the cylindrical flank formed by 2nd Fleet, the reason for the foreboding premonition became apparent. There was a red patch in the nine o'clock, forward region.

Regina opened her eyes and turned to Admiral McCarthy. "Sector one-nine."

The admiral glanced at the applicable monitor, attempting to determine how long before Korilian starships began pouring through a hole in the collapsing sector. His eyes shifted to a console in front of him, tracking the status of the remaining troop transports. Only eleven more to go. Regina sensed the tension as McCarthy evaluated the two timelines.

He turned to an officer manning a console in the tier below him. "Operations officer, order all ships to jump at time seven-two-four. Inform Second Fleet of my direction."

The order was acknowledged, then relayed to 1st and 2nd Fleets. Yellow starship symbols appeared on his display, their color shifting to red or green, indicating the status of their jump drives. Finally, only three yellow symbols remained.

The operations officer reported, "All operational ships are ready to jump with the exception of *Helena*, *Athens*, and *Sparta*, which have not acknowledged. All disabled ships are prepared to self-destruct at the jump."

Admiral McCarthy pressed a touch screen symbol on his console, and one of the displays at the front of the bridge shifted to a different sector. In the middle of the screen was the battleship *Helena*. She was in dire straits; one of her port shields was down, and a Korilian pulse had melted a gaping hole through the battleship. Arcs of electricity sizzled across the open wound. *Athens* and *Sparta* were positioned close to *Helena*, shielding her vulnerable port side while they traded pulses with four dreadnoughts, the Korilian version of Colonial Navy battleships. *Athens*'s and *Sparta*'s shields were weakening, with the battleships on the wrong side of a four-on-two battle.

McCarthy turned to another officer in the tier below. "What is *Helena*'s status?"

After a few taps on her display, the officer replied, "*Helena* has lost number four shield, and the shield generator is damaged. Her jump drive and aft reactor are offline."

"What is the prognosis for her jump drive?"

"Unknown," the officer replied. "I can't hail engineering or the bridge."

McCarthy pressed another symbol on his console, and the captain of *Athens* appeared on screen, her face illuminated by yellow flashes as Korilian pulses pounded her shields.

"This is not a good time, Admiral," she said, her image shaking as a pulse penetrated her ship's weakening shields, impacting the warship's armored hull.

"Are you in communication with *Helena*?" McCarthy asked.

"Yes, sir. They're working on their jump drive and should have it repaired in ten minutes."

"We don't have ten minutes. You will abandon *Helena* and jump at the prescribed time."

"Say again, Admiral," she said. "We're having communication difficulties."

"Abandon *Helena* and jump at time seven-two-four."

Athens's bridge lit up again as another Korilian pulse hit the ship's shields. The starship captain looked to the side for a moment before returning her gaze ahead. "Understood. Jump as soon as *Helena*'s jump drive is repaired. *Athens*, out."

The monitor went black, and McCarthy locked eyes with Regina, searching for guidance. She had none. After hesitating a moment, McCarthy turned to the three-dimensional display in front of him, sending commands to warships near *Athens* and *Sparta*, directing them to assist. He examined the collapsing sector again, then gave a new jump order, giving *Helena* additional time.

"Operations officer, reset the jump to time seven-three-one."

McCarthy was pushing 1st Fleet to the limit, but Regina had confidence in him. She had been McCarthy's prescient guide for five years, assigned to him when he took command of the Normandy battle group. The move had been unprecedented; guides with the necessary talent were rare, assigned only to admirals in charge of an entire fleet. But Fleet Admiral Fitzgerald had realized McCarthy's potential, and Regina and McCarthy had honed their skills for three years in *Normandy*, followed by two years leading 1st Fleet. After five years together, she could finish the orders he began, knew where to focus her attention without asking.

Regina's vision was suddenly bathed in a red hue. She braced herself on the edge of McCarthy's console, attempting to make sense of the premonition. The color was more intense to the left, and she turned toward the front of the ship. The bridge windows glowed bright red.

"Shut the shield doors!" she shouted.

McCarthy looked toward the windows as blinding white flashes illuminated the bridge. As the light faded, ten Korilian dreadnoughts appeared, located ahead of and pointed directly at the 1st Fleet command ship.

The shield supervisor called out, "Shut the bridge shield doors!"

Heavy metal doors slid quickly across the bridge windows, but not before six of the Korilian ships exploded as the command ship's protective battleship screen opened fire. The remaining four dreadnoughts fired simultaneously, their pulses converging on the same spot in the command ship's protective outer shield. The four pulses penetrated the outer bubble, impacting the command ship's bow shield, collapsing it in a blinding yellow light.

The shield absorbed most of the pulse energy, but enough bled through to shatter the windows just before the metal doors sealed the bridge. Shards of transparent Kevlar—as strong as steel but clear like glass—were hurled across the bridge, impaling equipment and personnel. Pain pierced Regina's body, and she watched in horror as a Kevlar dagger stabbed into the admiral's chest.

McCarthy stood motionless at his console as he examined the protruding shard. Blood spread from the wound, soaking his uniform as it blended into the crimson-and-burgundy fabric. Slowly, he reached up and extracted the fragment, dropping it to the deck. When he turned to Regina, a shocked expression replaced his calm composure.

Regina followed his eyes to her abdomen, where a six-inch-long shard protruded from her stomach, blood running off the end in a thin stream. She felt behind her, slicing her fingers on the other end of the shard jutting out from her back. Her knees went weak, and McCarthy caught her as she collapsed, calling for a medic as he lowered her slowly to the deck.

He knelt beside her, cradling her head in his lap, brushing a lock of hair away from her face. As she lay on her side, she felt her strength ebbing, her arms and legs turning cold. The voices around her became faint, disconnected, as she listened to the admiral and supervisors give orders and receive reports. A medic arrived, assessing the admiral's wound before shifting his attention to Regina. The two men exchanged glances, and when she looked up at McCarthy, his eyes could not conceal her fate.

Her vision began to cloud, darkness creeping in from the periphery. She reached up and touched McCarthy's face. "I'm so sorry," she said. "I failed you."

"No," McCarthy replied. "I failed *you*."

She caressed the side of his face for a moment, leaving a bloody smear on his cheek, until she no longer had the strength to hold her arm up. As her hand fell away, McCarthy pulled her close.

The operations officer approached. "All ships report ready to jump, Admiral."

As Regina's vision faded to black, McCarthy gave the order.

"Jump!"

2

At the spaceport on the outskirts of the Ritalian capital, Lara Anderson tightened her grip on her backpack straps as she stood in line with the last group of civilians boarding the troop transports. Time was running out. She sensed the urgency in the Army troops as they quickly guided the last four thousand men, women, and children toward the remaining ships, which would take them to Earth. With her eyes toward the night sky, Lara had watched the multicolored flashes as the battle grew more intense and closer to Ritalis; the Korilians were pressing their attack, and the two Colonial fleets had contracted their protective formation.

Lara evaluated the wisdom of her earlier decision, giving up her seat on one of yesterday's transports to a woman with a newborn child who had been left off the evacuation registry. With the woman cradling her son in her arms as she pleaded with an Army officer, Lara had offered the woman her seat. Unfortunately, since the woman had no seat to trade, Lara had been reassigned to the last transport.

Hundreds of bright white flashes illuminated the dark sky, announcing the departure of the Colonial Navy. The flashes were met with silence for a few seconds as those left on Ritalis processed the implication. Without the Fleet shielding the troop transports as they left the planet's surface, the transports would be destroyed before they could jump to safety.

They were stranded on Ritalis.

A death sentence.

It wouldn't be long before Korilian ground troops began their assault, and the outcome would be the same as on every other planet. The Korilians took no prisoners, left no one alive.

As the realization washed over the men and women in line, some lifted their hands skyward, begging the Fleet to return and complete the evacuation. Others raised their fists in anger, cursing the Fleet for its cowardly departure. Others pulled their loved ones close as they shed tears in silence. Lara's chest tightened and her pulse began to race as she tried to contain the emotions swirling inside her: fear, anger, and desperation. As a child, she hadn't imagined her life would end this way, holed up in a bunker somewhere until the Korilians exterminated her.

Lara shuddered as she imagined coming face-to-face with a Korilian: ten-foot-tall, black insect-like creatures with red multifaceted eyes, sharp fangs, and six limbs with razor-sharp edges that sliced through human flesh and bone with ease. As a counselor at Camden Colonial Hospital, interfacing with grieving families, she had seen firsthand the devastating effects of the Korilian War, especially the injuries incurred in close combat. Wounded Army troops were easily healed, assuming their limbs were retrieved; the clean cuts facilitated easy reattachment of their extremities. Fleet personnel were not so lucky, their injuries received as Korilian pulses carved through starships. The burned and maimed personnel were eventually transferred from Fleet hospital ships to planet-side facilities on Earth and its remaining colonies.

Lara was pulled from her thoughts as soldiers turned the line around, directing them back into the spaceport terminal. A sergeant approached, explaining the plan.

"Transportation is being arranged to take you to the nearest military fortification." He pointed toward the mountains in the distance. "You'll be safe there."

Despite the man's reassuring words, the despair in his eyes betrayed the truth. Like the remaining civilians, the ten million troops assigned to defend Ritalis had been handed a death sentence.

Lara wondered what the final days would be like as they withstood the

Korilian assault; the sergeant had undoubtedly been briefed or had gleaned what would happen from the hundred-plus planets that had fallen to the Korilian Empire. Lara was tempted to touch the man's bare skin, using her ability to look into his mind. However, her mother had warned her to use her gift—the Touch, she called it—sparingly. *Looking into someone's mind is perilous; you might not like what you find.*

Instead, she focused on the extended stay in an Army bunker instead of a quick evacuation. She had packed lightly, expecting a two-jump trip to Earth, arriving twelve hours after departing Ritalis. Looking at several weeks in an Army bunker instead, she considered heading home for additional items.

"Do I have time to return to the city to pack a few more things?"

The sergeant nodded. "Military shuttles will run from the spaceport to our defensive positions, picking up any stragglers until just before the assault begins."

"How long do I have?"

"The first wave of Korilian ground troops are in a jump hold in the Valderian planetary system. We expect them to make the jump to Ritalis in six to ten hours, with the ground assault beginning an hour after their arrival."

"Thanks, Sergeant."

Lara's apartment was a forty-minute ride away, so she'd have plenty of time. She tapped an icon on her wristlet, sending a transportation request. The automated city transports were still operating, and a hover-car assigned to her was already at the spaceport, bay 23.

As she looked around, determining the quickest route to the transport bays, the sergeant added, "Keep your eyes skyward. Once you see the flashes, you'll have one hour."

3

Inside the Colonial Fleet command center on Earth, with six rows of consoles stretching into the distance, the lights were dim, imparting a feeling of twilight in the underground facility. A blue glow from the consoles illuminated the faces of the personnel manning them, while various colored symbols appeared on the large displays mounted on the front wall.

At the back of the command center, Fleet Admiral Nanci Fitzgerald studied the screens. 1st and 2nd Fleets were engaged at Ritalis, 3rd Fleet was defending the jump point at Lohiri, and 4th Fleet was positioned at Areanis. Her eyes shifted to the display portraying the status of 5th and 6th Fleets. They were refitting in Earth's orbit, receiving replacement starships, supplies, and pulse-generator fuel cells. It would be at least five days before either fleet was ready for battle.

Fitzgerald's attention was drawn to the screen displaying the battle at Ritalis. The 1st and 2nd Fleet symbols vanished, and the watch captain announced the obvious.

"Ma'am, First and Second Fleets have departed Ritalis, en route to—" The captain halted his report, placing a hand to his earpiece. His face paled, then he continued. "First Fleet reports damage to their command ship. Their guide is dead, and Admiral McCarthy is seriously wounded."

Fitzgerald's acknowledgment stuck in her throat. Regina was their most experienced guide, and her replacement would not be as capable. If McCarthy died, however, all was lost.

Admiral Liam Carroll, the deputy fleet commander, overheard the report and stopped beside Fitzgerald, turning his attention to the displays. With his eyes on the Ritalis sector, he said, "First and Second Fleets are en route to Citani. Without McCarthy..." His voice trailed off.

They were in a serious predicament. Aside from the injury to McCarthy and death of his guide, Ritalis had gone as planned. Most of the civilians had been evacuated, and enough troops landed on the planet to keep the Korilians busy for a few weeks. However, 1st and 2nd Fleets were now supposed to hold the crucial jump point at Citani. Her eyes shifted to one of the nearby consoles, assessing the strength of both fleets. 2nd Fleet had been ravaged, losing over half its starships, while 1st Fleet remained in good shape, still at eighty-five percent. However, without McCarthy in charge, they could not hold Citani if the Korilians pressed the attack.

"I intend to pull all fleets back to Earth," Fitzgerald said. "Comments?"

Carroll replied sharply, "If we abandon the jump points at Lohiri, Areanis, and Citani, the Korilians will be one jump away from Earth. There will be nowhere to retreat to."

"We cannot risk having Third and Fourth Fleets cut off," she replied. "We need to pull them back now while we still control Citani."

Carroll turned back to the displays, searching for a solution.

Fitzgerald added, "We knew it would come to this. It was only a matter of time."

Admiral Carroll stared into the distance for a while, then offered a solemn nod. "I concur."

Fitzgerald gave the order to the watch captain, who relayed it to the supervisors. A hush fell over the command center as the operators at their control consoles grew silent. There was nowhere else to fight now.

Before retreating to her quarters, Fitzgerald directed the watch captain, "Inform me if there is any change in McCarthy's status."

4

Lara Anderson leaned over her eighty-fifth-story balcony, dangling an empty crystal glass in her right hand. Far below, the deserted streets were illuminated by blinking neon cafe signs, which had energized automatically at dusk. The rest of the city's nighttime advertisements had also activated: videos gracing the facades of towering skyscrapers and holograms hovering in the air above the abandoned city. Weeks ago, as Lara looked down upon the crowded streets, she had sensed the desperation and fear from the men and women as they carried on their daily routines, hoping the Korilians would be stopped before they reached Ritalis.

Hold on.

She said it again tonight, only this time to an empty city, as if her words could somehow help humanity hang onto an existence that was slipping away.

A thousand years after man first walked on the moon, humans had populated over one hundred planets. Humanity's expansion throughout the galaxy had been slow for the first five centuries after Neil Armstrong's historic step onto the moon's surface, with progress limited to Mars and the asteroids in Earth's solar system. However, the invention of the hyper-jump drive, which allowed starships to fold time and space, traveling great distances in only seconds, had enabled the rapid colonization of planets capable of supporting human life.

Now, however, humanity was on the brink of extinction. Thirty years after humans had finally answered the question that had captivated their thoughts for millennia—did other life exist in the universe—after a space exploration ship had encountered a Korilian warship beyond the Fringe Worlds, all of Earth's colonies except for Ritalis had been destroyed.

As Lara's thoughts dwelled on the Korilian War, she searched the dark sky again. Only the faint twinkle of distant stars was visible. Without shields flaring from pulse impacts, the hundreds of Korilian warships in orbit were invisible. That was good news, however. There had been no white flashes announcing the arrival of transports carrying Korilian combat troops.

A sparkle in the corner of her vision drew her eyes to the ring she still wore on her left hand; the city lights reflected off the solitaire diamond. As she stared at the glittering gem, her thoughts shifted from humanity's despair to one more personal, and it wasn't long before tears began flowing. She examined her wedding ring for a moment, then stepped back from the railing and flung her glass across the balcony.

The glass shattered against the far wall, the fragments ricocheting across the red terrazzo floor toward her, some of the shards coming to rest just inches from her feet. She wiped away the tears and stared at her ring again, struggling to muster the resolve to finally remove it. She imagined placing it in a dark container and closing the lid in a symbolic gesture that would force her anguish to retreat into the dim recesses of her mind. Instead, she left the ring on her finger, where it had remained for the last three years since Gary's death aboard a Colonial starship in the Tindal solar system.

Lara slumped into a lounge chair on the balcony, leaning back into the thick cushion as tears began to flow again. She covered her face with her hands, waiting for the tightness in her chest to fade, for the tears to end. As she struggled through the despair, she almost laughed at the irony. She was a joke. A grief counselor unable to deal with her own anguish. She wondered if the Colonial Council had tasked her appropriately, perhaps incorrectly assessing her abilities. However, she had to admit she had a unique talent—the ability to sense people's emotions and the drivers behind them.

The pain eventually eased, and she wiped the tears away again. As she stared at the stars, childhood memories flooded back: sitting on her mother's lap on their front porch searching the sky each night, hoping to catch the return of one of the fleets, hoping even more it was 6th Fleet and that her cheek would soon be pressed against her dad's chest, his strong arms delivering a long-awaited hug.

As a child, Lara had counted the bright flashes, each one announcing the return of one of the immense starships from battle. Each time a fleet returned, however, she stopped counting on a lower number. She hadn't understood the implication—that fewer and fewer starships survived each battle. Gazing into the night sky in wonder, she hadn't realized that her mother's eyes were filled instead with fear.

They were losing.

Once the Korilians controlled Ritalis, they would jump into Earth's solar system, where there would be one final battle—humankind's last, desperate struggle for survival. The six fleets would be marshaled together, making a final stand against the Korilian armada, and the outcome would determine humanity's fate.

Lara still harbored hope that they would somehow defeat the Korilians —the Fleet continued to fight, and the shipyards in Earth's orbit worked relentlessly, building new starships and repairing damaged ones. The factories across Earth hummed nonstop, churning out equipment to support the war. The Colonial Defense Forces worked day and night, fortifying cities and mountain ranges across the continents.

At least now there was a glimmer of hope, where none had existed two years ago. Admiral Jon McCarthy had taken command of 1st Fleet, and since then, 1st Fleet had not lost a battle. There had suddenly been hope the tide would turn.

But it hadn't.

1st Fleet could not be everywhere, and while 1st Fleet won or fought to a draw, the other fleets lost. Fleet Command rarely combined more than two fleets for battle due to the unpredictability of Korilian jumps, unwilling to send the entire Fleet into battle and leave other sectors and even Earth itself undefended. But when the Korilians reached Earth, the six fleets would fight together, and Admiral McCarthy would somehow lead them to victory.

Not that it would help Lara. She was stranded on Ritalis and wouldn't live long enough to learn humanity's fate. Lying on the lounge chair staring into space, she debated whether to head to an Army bunker, extending the inevitable for a few weeks, or await her fate at home. She was tired from a long day and emotionally drained from the decades-long war, and it wasn't a hard decision. She would remain at home, where she had spent the few years she'd had with Gary.

Lara closed her eyes, and not long thereafter, her body relaxed and her breathing slowed. She drifted into an uneasy sleep, her dreams haunted by images of Gary's starship being destroyed, of assault vehicles landing on Ritalis, and of Korilian combat troops streaming forth to exterminate all humans who remained.

5

Carved from the eastern side of Earth's Ural Mountains, the two-hundred-foot-high granite walls, with snowcapped peaks jutting skyward behind them, stretched for more than two miles. Bearing the jagged scars of ambition and hatred, the ramparts had been guarded for three millennia, breached only once in its turbulent history. Complementing the imposing granite escarpment, two towering rock sentinels flanked a narrow, winding path leading toward the main entrance into Domus Praesidium, the primary stronghold of the Nexus House.

Beneath gray overcast skies, a blue-and-white executive transport, its navigation lights blinking in the encroaching darkness, descended toward a narrow ridge, its top sliced away centuries ago to create an artificial plateau. As the transport slowed to a hover above the landing pad, the light snow blanketing the plateau swirled in small vortices created by the transport's engine exhaust.

The hovercraft touched down, and a door slid open. Five blue-robed figures emerged, hoods over their heads, moving quickly down the ramp onto the mountain surface. The lead individual was small and slender, the four on the flanks broader and taller. They formed a human triangle, their blue robes flowing behind them as they proceeded briskly up the winding path toward the guarded gate.

Recessed deep between the watchtowers, two heavy metal doors, each ten feet wide by forty feet high, swung slowly inward, a deep rumbling reverberating off the steep granite walls. The five individuals swept into a lofty, domed rotunda, moving across a floor of transparent quartz imprisoning spidery veins of gold. Ten stories overhead, supported by columns of white marble crowned with elaborate Corinthian capitals, the painted ceiling recorded the chaos of a medieval battle.

Evenly spaced along the perimeter of the rotunda were three corridors, each manned by a pair of guards clothed in white-and-blue ceremonial uniforms with swords strapped to their waists. As the five figures curved toward the opening on the right, each guard withdrew his sword and raised it crisply to the center of his chest, blade pointed up at a forty-five-degree angle, rendering honors as The One passed between them.

They entered a long corridor, its blue marble floor worn by centuries of passage. As the group proceeded down the dimly lit passageway, the lead figure pulled the hood of her cloak down around her shoulders, revealing silver hair woven into a circular braid behind her head. The four men on her flanks did likewise, exposing dark, penetrating eyes.

After a five-minute walk down the corridor, their footsteps echoing off marble walls, Rhea Sidener and her guard approached a man leaning beside a dark opening on the left side of the passageway. Although his short-cropped hair was speckled with gray, his lean, muscular features were evident beneath a thin, form-fitting blue uniform that shimmered in the corridor's faint light. A hand signal from him and the four men continued down the corridor as The One slowed and turned, passing into the dark alcove.

Noah Ronan followed the woman into her small office, its walls lined with beech wood harvested from the Germanic forests twelve centuries ago. Rhea hung her robe in the corner, revealing a dress made of the same blue fabric as Ronan's uniform, complemented by a white sash with gold embroidery tied around her slender waist, then took her seat in a chair behind an ornately carved desk. Behind her, a lamp on the credenza pushed weak yellow light across the room. Tonight, Ronan thought Rhea looked far older than forty-seven. The strain of the last thirty years had taken its toll, and the events of the last few hours seemed to have added years to her appearance.

As head of House Defense, a rather oblique term for his duties, Ronan wondered if his thirty years of service would amount to nothing. For thousands of years, the Nexus House had worked in the background, its members using their psychic abilities to discreetly provide guidance to governments and other institutions that affected humanity's fate.

However, humankind was now on the brink of extinction and the House in its weakest state in millennia, unable to adequately shape the outcome of the Korilian War. McCarthy's near-fatal injury and the death of his guide had brought home that stinging realization all too painfully. Regrettably, Ronan was convinced that their helplessness was due to the woman sitting across from him.

Rhea was only seventeen when she had ascended to stewardship of the Nexus House—the youngest ever anointed to lead them. It was without precedent, but after much deliberation, The Three—the Placidia who ruled the Nexus House—had made their decision; Rhea had all the markers and would eventually complete her development. They weren't sure when, because their views of the future had been blocked for only the second time in the history of the House. The first time, five centuries ago, the Corvads had breached the walls of Domus Praesidium and the Nexus losses had been staggering, the reverberations of that day still felt five hundred years later.

With their prescient views blocked, The Three had decided they had no choice but to strike first. After carefully analyzing the potential outcomes to the best of their abilities, they had spearheaded a final confrontation between the last two major houses: the Nexus House—the last of the six original, true houses—against the Corvad House, the lone survivor of the six renegade, false houses. As thirty centuries of conflict came to a climax, The Three had led the Nexus Legion into battle. Although only Ronan and a handful of others returned, annihilation of the Corvads had been achieved.

But Ronan's relief had been short-lived. After the Nexi had finally vanquished their mortal enemies, the Korilian War erupted only months later. In an effort to assist humanity more effectively, Rhea had brought the

Nexus House out of the shadows, offering guides like Regina—prescient level-eight Nexi—who used their visions to provide guidance to the admiral in charge of each of the six Colonial fleets.

At the same time, in an effort to more efficiently coordinate the galaxy-wide effort to defend Earth and its colonies from the Korilian Empire, the planetary governments had ratified the War Act, establishing a truncated Colonial Council—only twelve regents instead of one per inhabited planet —which now ruled Earth and the colonies with an iron fist. Humankind had traded democracy for survival.

Unfortunately, the Colonial Council believed it had the power to force the Nexus House to obey its commands. The Council should have been put in its place years ago, but Rhea, young and inexperienced, had chosen otherwise. Now, after thirty years of subservience, the Council's authority over the House had solidified. Following Admiral McCarthy's injury, Rhea had been summoned by the Council to explain how years of careful preparation had almost been ruined in an instant. And Rhea had obeyed.

The thought of The One appearing before the Council churned Ronan's stomach. The Nexus House had acquiesced to the Council for far too long, and it was time someone convinced Rhea to rectify that situation. The House could easily bend the Council to its will, show them what absolute power truly was. But that would not occur as long as Rhea was content with the status quo. After three decades, Ronan knew it would be difficult to change her mind, and the tactic he had chosen to accomplish this task was a dangerous one. He could not predict her reaction to his criticism. As he prepared to vent his frustration, he decided to phrase his words carefully, easing his way into his commentary.

"What did the Council want?" he asked.

"They were upset," Rhea replied. "They wanted to know how I could have let this happen."

"What did you say?"

"I reminded them that I'm prescient, not omniscient. I can't follow every timeline into the future, and even if I had followed McCarthy's line, it would have dissolved shortly after the battle began. It was McCarthy's and his guide's responsibility to ensure no harm befell them."

"And the Council's response?"

"They wanted to know if McCarthy will recover and how we will replace Regina."

"What did you tell them?"

"McCarthy will be fine by the time the Korilians arrive, and he will have a replacement guide. That is all that matters."

"That is *not* all that matters," Ronan said sharply. "You defer to the Council too much, and we have suffered as a result. If The Three could see what has become of our House—"

Rhea slammed her hand on her desk. "Enough!"

But Ronan wasn't finished. The House would not end its existence as the Council's obedient dog. He moved forward, stopping at the edge of Rhea's desk. "You prostrate yourself before the Council, and we are *weak* because of it."

Rhea leveled a harsh gaze at Ronan. "I made my decision thirty years ago, and I stand by it today. A strong House is meaningless if the human race becomes extinct. Our resources were requested, and we provided them. I am convinced this is what The Three would have done."

"This is *not* what The Three would have done. You may be master of this House now, but you lack the *wisdom* to lead us." Ronan deliberately let disdain creep into his voice.

Anger flashed in Rhea's eyes, and Ronan realized he had gone too far. He was aware of her power—the ability to end his life with a mere thought. Bowing his head, he stepped back.

"I apologize, Rhea. I have spoken my mind too freely. I'm just frustrated by many things. The Korilians continue to advance, and the House seems powerless to alter the future."

"You don't think I know that!" Frustration bled through her words. "You don't think that's been at the forefront of my mind for the last thirty years!" There was an uneasy silence as she glowered at Ronan.

"We need not worry about the House," she replied, waving away his concern with her hand. "We are the last major house, and you will protect us from even the strongest alliance of minor houses. What is far more important is defeating the Korilians. Yes, we are weak because of it. We have expended our resources as the Council has directed rather than reconstitute our strength. I had no choice. Surely, you see that." She looked up at Ronan, unable to hide her uncertainty behind stern eyes.

Ronan nodded, deciding not to press the issue further. It was clear that the war was the higher priority, but nothing they had done thus far had helped.

The intercom activated, and Jina Hong, the level-eight Primus—in charge of all level-eight Nexi—announced her presence outside The One's office. Rhea acknowledged, and Jina entered.

"You've selected a replacement for McCarthy's guide?" Rhea asked.

Jina hesitated before replying. "There is no suitable replacement. Regina's backup was assigned to the Fleet to gain experience and was killed at Alacron a few weeks ago. The next in line is not ready."

"Who is the next candidate?"

"Siella."

Rhea raised an eyebrow.

"It's unusual," Jina said, "but McCarthy is difficult to match."

"Prepare a simulator," Rhea ordered. "Load the Telemantic scenario."

"Siella will fail," Jina replied.

"I'll be the judge of that."

Jina nodded, then excused herself. As the door closed, Rhea turned to Ronan, addressing his earlier confrontation.

"You will continue your training. *Tonight*." She spoke the last word firmly.

Rhea's tone was not lost on Ronan as she reminded him of the responsibility that was his, and the authority that was hers.

6

Ten minutes later, Rhea approached the entrance to Simulator 3. The double doors whisked open, revealing a replica of a fleet command ship bridge. Already stationed for the simulation was Siella, a woman in her late twenties, who stood near the admiral's command console overlooking five tiers of computer workstations descending to a curved row of monitors below the bridge windows. Next to Siella stood Jina Hong, and on the other side was a static hologram of a four-star admiral standing at his control console. Several dozen more holograms staffed the consoles in front of them, all controlled by the simulator computer.

Rhea entered and stopped a few feet behind Siella, where she could monitor the woman's performance. Siella was nervous, wiping her palms on the shimmery blue Nexus uniform as she waited for the simulation to begin. The inability to control her emotions would normally have earned her a sharp rebuke, but given the short notice and the unusual presence of The One, Rhea decided to let it go. In the next few minutes, Siella would need to settle down and display an ability desperately needed now that McCarthy's guide, plus the backup in training, had been killed.

Jina looked toward Rhea, who nodded her approval to begin. Jina tapped a command on her wristlet, and the holograms of the admiral and other bridge personnel came to life.

Rhea sensed Siella's anxiety skyrocket. She'd had no time to prepare herself mentally and hadn't been briefed on the mission. The rapid commencement of the simulation was part of the test, assessing how well Siella responded to short-fused tasking. She would not be able to control when the Fleet jumped into battle or what they might find when they arrived. She would need to perform well under high-stress scenarios.

The operations officer, in the tier below Siella and the admiral, called out, "One minute to the jump."

Siella took a deep breath and examined the displays mounted across the front of the starship bridge. She was on the 3rd Fleet command ship, one jump away from the Gideon system. Two Korilian battle groups were attempting to destroy the star fortress complex guarding a prized hyper-jump hole, one of the few spots in the galaxy where time folded in a way that enabled enormous jumps across space, up to twenty-five times that of normal jumps.

Her eyes shifted to the other screens, assessing the status of the Colonial Navy. It was weathering a heavy Korilian assault, one of the largest of the war thus far. 1st Fleet was shielding the evacuation of a planet in the Aquari system. 4th and 5th Fleets were heavily engaged in the Paunus system, and 6th Fleet was tied down at Legaria. 2nd Fleet was in reserve, in the middle of a jump hold, its four battle groups in a position to assist as required. Far away from the main action, 3rd Fleet was preparing to jump to Gideon.

There were two key takeaways from the assessment. The good news was that 3rd Fleet would have a two-to-one numerical superiority over the Korilian battle groups at Gideon. The bad news was that if 3rd Fleet required assistance for some reason, the nearest reinforcements were a day's travel away.

Rhea watched Siella closely, attempting to discern whether she recognized her peril. The scenario was thinly disguised, and in a few minutes, Siella should recognize it for what it was. The simulator was recreating the battle that had occurred in the Telemantic planetary system—the only time in the history of the war that an entire Colonial fleet had been annihilated.

The operations officer announced, "Five seconds to the jump."

The time counted down, then the bridge went dark for a few seconds, simulating the brief jump interval, although the simulator could not replicate the physical sensation and debilitating effects of the jump.

"Shields up!" The shield supervisor's voice was the first to be heard as the command ship completed the jump.

Siella's gaze pivoted from screen to screen, assessing the tactical situation. 3rd Fleet was organized in a hollow cylinder attack formation, one of the open ends aimed toward the left flank of the Korilian battle groups, which were focusing their efforts on the nearest star fortress surrounding the hyper-jump hole. The Korilian strategy was clear; they were attempting to destroy the complex one base at a time before Colonial warships arrived.

The six star fortresses were mammoth unmanned star bases preventing Korilian access to the hyper-jump hole. Each fortress was the equivalent of ten battleships, constructed of ten concentric segments atop each other, each section containing a pulse generator capable of rotating independently 360 degrees. Additionally, due to being unmanned, the fortress shields were much stronger than a typical starship's and could take a heavy pounding. All six of the automated fortresses were still in operation, trading pulses with the Korilian starships.

The admiral beside Siella ordered 3rd Fleet into motion. "Ahead flank, all battle groups."

The Korilian forces disengaged the star fortresses, focusing on 3rd Fleet advancing toward them. Korilian dreadnoughts and cruisers moved away from the Colonial starships, attempting to avoid getting trapped within the hollow cylinder formation. But unlike the single-pilot vipers launched by carriers, the massive starships—even cruisers—maneuvered slowly.

3rd Fleet bore down on the Korilians, and the leading edge of the hollow cylinder sliced into the Korilian formation. The Colonial starships focused their attack on the Korilian ships passing through the center of the cylinder, each starship pounding the Korilian ships in succession. With the firepower of an entire fleet focused on only a few dozen ships, the Korilian shields failed. By the time they reached the end of the hollow cylinder, blue pulses had carved the Korilian starships to pieces.

When the 3rd Fleet cylinder exited the other side of the Korilian formation, the admiral turned to Siella. "Another pass, or flare?"

The admiral was evaluating whether to make another pass through the

Korilian formation or flare out and attempt to envelop the Korilian battle groups. Ideally, another pass was preferred, as 3rd Fleet could destroy additional starships, but the Korilians understood the danger and were spreading out to minimize the number of ships trapped within the cylindrical formation.

After a moment of indecision, Siella replied, "Flare."

The admiral responded quickly. "Commence flare."

The operations officer gave the order, and the end of the 3rd Fleet cylinder spread outward and reversed course.

As 3rd Fleet enveloped the Korilian starships like a hand closing around its prey, Siella's body stiffened. Rhea waited as Siella attempted to make sense of her premonition. She turned to the admiral.

"Korilian reinforcements are coming."

"How many?" the admiral asked.

Rhea focused on Siella again. By now, her premonitions should be strong. Disaster was approaching. However, most Nexi had difficulty interpreting premonitions during battle, translating the information into tactical guidance. Those who could were rare and valuable.

"I cannot tell," Siella replied.

The admiral scoured the bridge displays, pulling up a summary of the entire Korilian armada on one of the screens. According to intelligence estimates, the Korilians had no additional reserves. Whatever was on its way could be easily dealt with by 3rd Fleet, which now had a five-to-two advantage.

As 3rd Fleet completed its envelopment of the Korilian warships and began contracting the encapsulating sphere, bright flashes illuminated the darkness through the bridge windows.

The sensor supervisor called out, "Korilian starships! Sector one. Sector three. Sector seven. Sector nine. Over thirty squadrons!"

"That's impossible!" the admiral replied.

Four Korilian battle groups had just jumped into the Gideon system, forming a loose sphere around 3rd Fleet. Before the admiral could redirect efforts against the arriving Korilian starships, their shields formed.

The situation had changed dramatically; 3rd Fleet was now outnumbered.

The 3rd Fleet admiral now had a decision to make. Jump away and abandon the Gideon hyper-jump hole, or stay and fight.

"Recommendation," the admiral asked, turning to Siella.

Siella was silent for a moment before replying, "I have none."

Jina Hong, still standing beside Siella, entered a comment on her wristlet, while on the other side of Siella, the admiral pulled up his three-dimensional control, displaying every ship in 3rd Fleet. His eyes then went to the star fortresses, the equivalent of almost two battle groups.

"I intend to retreat inside the star fortress perimeter and reassess. Comments?"

Siella closed her eyes, then opened them a few seconds later. "I agree."

Another comment went into Jina's wristlet while the admiral gave the required orders.

Even though 3rd Fleet was outnumbered, the Korilian forces surrounding them were spread thin, and 3rd Fleet punched through the Korilian sphere, reaching the star fortresses moments later. Once inside the protective perimeter, 3rd Fleet came to a halt, its battleships and cruisers pointed out toward the Korilian armada.

The Korilians enveloped 3rd Fleet and the star fortresses, slowly contracting their sphere. Through the command ship bridge windows, a constant barrage of blue and red pulses and yellow flashes illuminated the darkness as the two opposing fleets battled. With the additional firepower of the star fortresses, they were on a roughly one-to-one footing with the Korilians.

The admiral announced his decision. "I intend to stay and defend the Gideon hyper-jump hole until reinforcements arrive. Whether those reinforcements are Korilian or Colonial will determine our next move." He ordered his communications officer, "Inform Fleet Command of our situation and request reinforcements."

The operations officer relayed the information to all 3rd Fleet starships and Fleet Command, and it looked like the battle was going to settle into a long, drawn-out affair, when the six star fortresses, which had been trading pulses with Korilian starships, went silent. The Korilian starships did the same.

The admiral turned to Siella, who closed her eyes. A moment later, her body began to tremble, and she opened her eyes. "It's a trap!"

Before the admiral could respond, the star fortresses reactivated. The ten concentric rings on each fortress rotated until their pulse generators faced inward. The fortresses opened fire, each one targeting a Colonial starship. With ten pulses impacting each ship at almost point-blank range, six battleships disintegrated.

"Attempt to override!" the admiral shouted. "Reset the fortresses!"

The operations officer sent the commands, but the star fortresses fired again, destroying another six Colonial ships. The Korilian starships commenced firing as the fortress pulse generators recharged.

Yellow flares lit up the bridge and the command ship shuddered as Korilian pulses impacted the starship's shields. Siella scanned the consoles. Six more ships disintegrated under the star fortress assault, and shields were weakening throughout the fleet as they endured the Korilian onslaught. The battle was lost and the fleet needed to disengage, but under the constant barrage, at what point could the fleet drop shields and jump?

Starships could not jump with their shields up; the energy field interfered with the jump drive. Prior to jumping, shields would be dropped, leaving each starship vulnerable in the few seconds before the jump drive engaged. If enough Korilian warships were in range with their pulse generators charged, the starship could be destroyed. For that reason, Fleet jumps were usually sudden and simultaneous, giving the enemy no time to prepare. The timing was also critical, jumping when the fewest Korilian pulse generators were charged.

"To all ships," the admiral ordered, "prepare to jump."

Siella tensed as she focused on determining the most opportune time for the jump, but was distracted by a report from the operations officer.

"We have a problem, Admiral. The jump drive isn't spinning up. Shield interference from the star fortresses is too high."

The fortress shields, much more powerful than the ones generated by starships, were interfering with the jump drives. Under normal circumstances, a command would be sent and the fortresses would momentarily drop shields to allow the jump.

"Send overrides on all channels," the admiral replied. "Shut down the fortresses!"

The orders went out again, but the fortresses remained in operation. Siella's breathing turned shallow and rapid.

3rd Fleet was trapped.

The admiral turned to Siella. "Recommendation?"

"I...," Siella stammered. "I..."

"I need something," the admiral said. "Reinforcements are a day away, even if they short-cycle their hold times. We need to shut down the fortresses or figure out how to weather the attack until reinforcements arrive." Siella provided no response, so the admiral pressed his Nexus guide. "I need a recommendation!"

Siella's eyes darted between the displays and consoles, frantically searching for a solution. As her panic crested, Rhea felt a cold sensation emanating from Siella.

Rhea hand-signaled Jina Hong. The Primus Eight swiveled toward Siella, backhanding her across the face. Siella's head jolted to the side and she stumbled backward, regaining her balance after a few steps.

Her eyes widened, and the color drained from her face. "I...I'm sorry. If I could only—"

"It is *forbidden!*" Jina replied. "*Never* in the presence of Admiral McCarthy."

Rhea had seen enough. "Terminate the simulation."

The holograms dissolved as Rhea approached Siella. She stared dispassionately at the woman who had failed to predict the Korilian trap. The appropriate premonitions had either not materialized or had been interpreted incorrectly.

After a long moment, Rhea said, "You will never be ready."

Siella sank to her knees, burying her face in her hands as she began crying, muffled sobs escaping between her fingers.

Rhea turned to Jina. "Who is next in line?"

"There is no one else," Jina replied. "You know my hands are tied."

"I didn't ask for excuses," Rhea said. "I asked for another candidate. Find one."

7

An hour later, with Rhea seated behind her desk discussing Siella's future with Ronan, their conversation was interrupted by the door intercom. Rhea acknowledged, and Jina Hong entered, fingering an electronic tablet in her hands.

As Rhea looked up, Jina said, "I've identified a candidate."

"What level?" Rhea asked.

Jina hesitated a few seconds before replying, "She is not a Nexus."

"What?"

Jina handed the tablet to Rhea. "Lara Anderson. She's an Altarian who was resettled on Ritalis during the exodus from the Pleiades cluster ten years ago."

Rhea reviewed the information. "Her test scores are impressive. A rare full spectrum. Why was she not inducted into the House?"

"Read the comment," Jina replied. Her eyes shifted to Ronan, who had retreated to the back of Rhea's office while The One conducted business with her Primus Eight.

Rhea read it aloud. "Age seventeen at time of evaluation." She looked up. "We normally induct children at the age of five, but with latent talent like this, we should have inducted her despite her age."

"It's the next comment," Jina said.

Rhea looked down, and after reading further, she said, "I remember now. She has the Touch."

Ronan, who had been leaning against the wall, stood erect. "Why was I not informed? I would have terminated her immediately."

"*That*," Rhea replied, "is why you were not notified."

Ronan clenched his hands into fists. "How dare you keep this information from me!"

"We have nothing to fear," Rhea said. "The Corvads are destroyed. There is no house to defect to and no one to train her if she did. She poses no threat."

"We never found the remaining fragment of the Krystalis," Ronan replied. "That means there's a Corvad compound we have not discovered."

According to legend, the Krystalis was a gem of immense power. Three millennia ago, on the eve the six original houses split into the six true and six false houses, the Krystalis had been shattered. Throughout the House War, as one house after another was vanquished, the remaining true and false houses strove to obtain the Krystalis fragments.

Rhea replied, "The Corvads were destroyed and the rest of the Krystalis lost forever. We continue to watch over their deserted compounds, and there hasn't been a trace of a Corvad for thirty years. The Three did their work well, and I might remind you that it was *your* official assessment that the Corvad House was destroyed."

Ronan shifted tactics. "For three thousand years, the Touch has been forbidden, and we have eliminated all who possess it. You do not disregard three millennia of precedent lightly."

"I did not dismiss it lightly," Rhea said. "I assessed this woman to be of no risk. Although rare, it's possible to develop the Touch without training. Ten years ago, it was prudent not to induct her, but the situation today is different. With latent ability like this, it's possible she might develop the necessary skills in the short time remaining."

As Ronan bristled with anger, Rhea turned to Jina. "Have this woman assigned to the House, and put the appropriate training support in place. Where is she now?"

Jina tapped several commands into her tablet, then looked up with consternation in her eyes. "The registry says she's still on Ritalis. She was one of four thousand civilians who weren't evacuated."

Rhea leaned back in her chair. "Over one hundred million Ritalians evacuated, and this woman is one of four thousand who didn't make it?"

"It's fate," Ronan interjected. "She was meant to die on Ritalis. We should let her."

"There is no such thing as fate, Ronan. You know that." Rhea evaluated the situation for a moment, then added, "Asking the Fleet to rescue Lara is out of the question. That means if we want her, *we'll* have to get her."

Although Rhea had revealed the existence of the Nexus House to the Council and the Colonial Defense Forces, the Nexus House remained an independent entity. Rhea's only obligations were the two items she had agreed to: provide level-eight fleet guides, who had intermittent prescient visions of the future, and push all excess Nines to the level-ten Test. Level-ten Nexi, like Rhea, could not only view the future—they could evaluate how various actions altered the future, then guide events along the timeline that produced the optimal outcome. As a result, the Council and Colonial Defense Forces had a rabid desire to develop the extremely rare level-ten Nexi—a feat accomplished once per decade on average, but it had been almost twenty years since the feat was last accomplished.

Neither the Council nor the Colonial Defense Forces had an obligation to reciprocate assistance to the Nexi in any way, and considering the Korilian forces massing for the assault on Ritalis, the Fleet would not intervene on the Nexus House's behalf; it was harboring all available warships for the pending assault on Earth. If the Nexus House wanted a woman who was stranded on Ritalis, they'd have to get her themselves.

"An entire Korilian fleet is in orbit around Ritalis," Ronan replied. "Without the Fleet's assistance, rescuing this woman is an impossible task."

During the three-millennia-long House War, the Nexus and other houses had developed robust military capabilities to defend their houses and assault others. House Defense, led by Ronan, comprised an elite legion of ground combat troops and pilots, along with the most technologically advanced military equipment. However, the scale of the Nexus House's military capability was miniscule compared to the Korilian and Colonial Defense Forces engaged in the Korilian War.

The standard Korilian planetary ground assault force numbered one hundred million troops, while the Nexus House's total population was only eighty thousand, with just over one thousand dedicated to House Defense when the legion was at full strength. Additionally, the Nexus House's military capabilities were tailored for combat on Earth's surface—battle on the ground and in the air—with no equipment or experience in space warfare. The Colonial Navy had the immense starships and personnel required to engage the Korilians; the Nexus House did not.

"I agree," Rhea replied. "Rescuing this woman from Ritalis is impossible using our standard military equipment and tactics. What do we have in Engineering Design? What about the jump shuttle we're building for McCarthy?"

Ronan pondered Rhea's idea. "It might work. We'll need to ask Design, though."

Rhea activated a hologram display on her desk, and a miniature version of Dominic Zamora, head of the Nexus Engineering Design Department, appeared. Rhea explained the situation, then asked if the shuttle would give the mission a chance to succeed.

"It's possible," Zamora replied. "As you directed, the jump drive is designed for very short jumps, which gives the shuttle the ability to jump into higher gravity conditions. Conceivably, the jump to Ritalis could place the shuttle inside the ring of Korilian starships. However, there are several issues to consider. The first is that we haven't finished installing the shuttle's artificial intelligence, but that can be overcome with manual control. The more important factor is that the shuttle hasn't been tested yet."

Ronan felt the cool sensation as Rhea followed the relevant timeline into the future.

"It'll work," Rhea said. "The jump to Ritalis will be successful, but the timeline dissolves as the shuttle descends to the surface; there's too much volatility in the outcome. Since the shuttle hasn't been tested yet, let's include our most experienced Design Department troubleshooter on the mission in case there are any hardware glitches or software bugs."

"Yes, One," Zamora replied.

"The timeline dissolves shortly after the jump to Ritalis for a reason," Ronan announced. "The shuttle will have to descend through the atmosphere to the surface, then ascend until gravity is low enough for a return jump. The shuttle won't last more than a few seconds after it arrives at Ritalis. The Korilian starships will vaporize it."

"Leave that to me," Rhea replied. "I'll coordinate the rescue with Army Command."

Ronan folded his arms across his chest, accepting defeat. Rhea was set on a rescue mission for this woman, and it was his job to assist despite his opinion on the matter.

"We'll need a level-nine pilot," he said. "I also recommend you ask Fleet Admiral Fitzgerald to assign a senior starship captain to the mission. Our pilots aren't experienced in combat against the Korilians, and a Fleet captain's insight might prove valuable."

Rhea nodded, then addressed Zamora's hologram. "Have the shuttle ready for departure in thirty minutes. We don't have much time. Once the Korilian ground assault starts, a rescue will be impossible."

8

Lara's eyes flickered open, awakened from her slumber by her wristlet vibrating, informing her of an incoming call. A blinking red light indicated an identity verification had been requested. As she raised the wristlet to her left eye for a retina scan, she wondered who had requested the verification and the reason for it. The wristlet beeped after confirming her identity, and an Army officer appeared on the wristlet's flexible display.

"Miss Anderson," the man said quickly. "Your presence is required at the Tenth Army Command complex. You have received new tasking."

Lara was surprised by the news. Taskings were rarely changed, with each person assigned to their optimal profession upon reaching adulthood. There was no indication she was suitable for anything other than counseling, nor had she received any training outside that field. Additionally, what was the point in changing her tasking while she was stranded on Ritalis, with only a few weeks left alive?

"What is my new tasking?" she asked.

"It's classified."

Lara pondered the unusual response. However, if the man couldn't tell her what her new tasking was, she might glean some insight from her destination. "Where is my new assignment?"

"Also classified," the man replied.

Lara needed to know what to pack. "Hot or cold?" she asked dryly. "Should I pack my thermal underwear or sunscreen?"

"Clothing will be provided upon arrival. You will need only your personal care items."

Lara checked her wristlet. It was still the middle of the night, and she'd need to order transportation. "Where is the Army complex I need to travel to?"

"A military shuttle will arrive at your building in ten minutes," the man said. "Be ready to depart."

The wristlet display went dark.

Precisely ten minutes later, after throwing a few personal items and several changes of clothing into a duffel bag, Lara emerged onto the rooftop as a military transport, its navigation lights blinking in the darkness, slowed to a hover above the building and descended onto the landing pad. As Lara waited, illuminated by the hover pad's perimeter lighting, the transport's engine exhausts buffeted her body and blew her hair out behind her in the darkness. The transport's side hatch opened, and a second lieutenant wearing the green-and-olive uniform of the Colonial Army leaned out and beckoned her to enter.

The officer introduced himself but said nothing else during the fifteen-minute trip, with the shuttle streaking just above the towering skyscrapers. After leaving the city behind and traversing across the flat landscape toward the Army mountain complex, the transport followed the rising terrain until a spaceport appeared in a deep recess between two mountain peaks. The shuttle slowed to a hover above the heavily reinforced spaceport doors, which began retracting. The shuttle descended into the spaceport, and a gentle thump announced the end of Lara's trip.

The shuttle doors opened, and Lara stepped into the busy spaceport, with troops off-loading the last of the supply ships that had arrived before the Colonial Navy had departed. A colonel stepped forward, extending his hand.

"Welcome to Tenth Army Command," he said. His words were friendly and he managed a smile, but Lara detected an icy undertone to his greeting. "You'll wait here," he added. "Additional transportation will arrive shortly."

"Where am I headed?" she asked, hoping the colonel could provide more information than the officer on the initial call.

"Earth," he said.

Lara was stunned by his response. Earth meant safety, but transit off Ritalis was no longer possible with Korilian warships in orbit. She concluded the man had a sadistic sense of humor.

"No, really," Lara said. "Where am I going?"

The colonel elaborated. "A shuttle is being sent for you. A rescue mission."

The news took Lara by surprise. The Fleet hadn't abandoned everyone after all. However, as she looked around the spaceport, there were no other civilians present.

"For how many people?" she asked.

"It's a four-seat shuttle, and three of the seats are already occupied. This rescue mission is just for you." This time, the icy tone of his words came through clearly.

Lara wondered why the Fleet would send a shuttle just for her, and had difficulty comprehending how the shuttle would make it in and out of the Ritalis planetary system without being destroyed. It sounded more like a suicide attempt than a rescue mission, and she considered declining, spending her remaining days at home instead. But there was something in the colonel's demeanor that implied she didn't have a choice. If the shuttle made it to the spaceport, she'd be forced to board it.

"You must be pretty special," the colonel said. "We've been directed to neutralize all Korilian starships in this sector long enough for your extraction."

Lara finally realized the reason for the colonel's resentment. In preparation for the Korilian invasion, in addition to fortified defenses, thousands of artillery batteries had been built, each capable of vaporizing a descending surface assault vehicle with a single pulse. The pulse batteries were immense, with their tyranium coils descending a quarter mile underground. However, each coil provided power for only a few dozen pulses, and there was no way to replace them during battle. 10th Army had been directed to expend pulses to support Lara's rescue, and each pulse fired on Lara's behalf meant an extra Korilian assault vehicle would reach the surface. Each pulse expended for Lara meant the Army troops would meet their fate sooner.

"What now?" Lara asked.

"We wait," the colonel replied. "Your shuttle should arrive in a few minutes."

9

"One minute to shuttle arrival," the colonel announced as he monitored his wristlet.

The spaceport doors above, which had closed after Lara's arrival, slowly opened again. It was still nighttime and the stars were much brighter, the view uncontaminated by the city's lights.

"Fifteen seconds."

The spaceport deck began trembling as the defense batteries began firing. Blue pulses streaked upward, striking dozens of Korilian starships, illuminating their shields in a yellow sizzle. A small white flash in the dark sky announced the shuttle's arrival. After the light faded, Lara lost track of the shuttle, but then she spotted a small, glowing red object streaking toward her. The pulse batteries kept firing, hitting each Korilian starship again just before sizzling arcs from the previous pulse faded.

The shuttle continued its descent, approaching the spaceport with such speed that Lara thought it wouldn't be able to stop in time, crashing into the spaceport instead. But the shuttle quickly slowed, firing its thrusters as it descended into the spaceport bay. A door in the side of the blue-and-white shuttle opened as it touched down, and the colonel guided Lara forward. A man wearing the crimson-and-burgundy uniform of the Colonial Navy leaned out, beckoning her to enter.

"Quickly!" he shouted.

Lara reached the shuttle and was hauled inside by the man. The shuttle lifted off, passing through the spaceport opening as Lara was buckled in and her duffel bag stowed. There was no time for introductions, but Lara read the name tags embroidered on the three men's uniforms. The pilot's name was Eugenio Tabarzadi, beside him sat Captain Jeff Townsend, who had helped her inside, and Harindar Kapur was in the second row with her. Townsend wore a Colonial Navy uniform, but the other two men wore blue uniforms she hadn't seen before. Harindar had eight white stripes around each arm, while Tabarzadi had nine.

Tabarzadi controlled the shuttle with a joystick and throttle while Townsend manipulated a three-dimensional display on the console between them, rotating and turning the image with his hands, examining the location of the Korilian starship icons. Other displays reported a myriad of gravitational, velocity, and speed vectors. There was also a digital clock on the console, currently at two minutes and twenty-three seconds, counting down as they streaked upward. Lara assumed the clock was counting down the time before jump conditions were obtained. Gravity rendered jump drives inoperable, and they'd have to wait until they were a sufficient distance away from the planet's surface before the jump drive could be engaged.

The throttle had been pushed forward to maximum thrust, and the shuttle shook as it rocketed skyward, pressing Lara into her seat. Her stomach began to churn, and she looked out the shuttle window, trying to find something to focus on to help settle her stomach. But all she could see were blue pulses impacting Korilian starships above.

Townsend studied the three-dimensional display while Lara watched in fascination. Red specks began streaming from one of the larger icons on the edge of the display.

"Marauders," Townsend said, "being launched from the nearest unaffected carrier."

"How long before they reach weapon range?" Tabarzadi asked.

"I can't say exactly," Townsend replied. "This shuttle doesn't have adequate sensors. My best guess is about two minutes."

Lara glanced at the clock. It read 1:42.

Her eyes alternated between the clock and the three-dimensional display, watching as several dozen marauders sped toward a symbol in the center, which she assumed was their shuttle. When the clock read 1:00, a ship symbol on the console turned from red to yellow.

"One minute to the jump," Tabarzadi announced.

As the seconds counted down, Townsend looked up from the display, staring through the shuttle window. "There." He pointed toward several dozen red specks, barely visible in the dark sky, streaking toward them. Townsend examined the display again.

"About forty-five seconds to weapon range."

Lara glanced at the clock: 0:32.

She watched the seconds count down, her eyes shifting between the clock and the approaching marauders. Just before the time approached 0:00, the pilot placed his hand above the yellow ship symbol. But when the clock reached 0:00, the symbol remained yellow.

Tabarzadi slammed his fist into the console. "Harindar!"

Harindar leaned forward and examined the console displays, focusing on the gravity, acceleration, and velocity vectors. "The drive should engage," he said. "Initial conditions are met."

"They are obviously *not* met!" Tabarzadi growled.

"We can argue about it later," Townsend said. "Ten seconds to marauder weapon range. Alter course to starboard to buy time."

Tabarzadi complied, and the shuttle veered sharply to the right, throwing Lara against her seat harness. The jump symbol turned red momentarily before returning to yellow as the acceleration and velocity vectors fluctuated before stabilizing.

"The calculations must be off," Harindar said as he studied the displays. "It's been centuries since we took velocity and acceleration parameters into consideration, and jump drives have evolved considerably since then."

"I don't care about your engineering mumbo jumbo," Tabarzadi said. "When will the jump drive engage?"

"I can't say, since the calculations are obviously wrong. Gravity is paramount, so the farther away from the planet's surface we can get, the better. But when incorporating acceleration and velocity into the initial conditions, acceleration is more important."

"Time's up!" Townsend announced as he examined the approaching marauders. The shuttle veered suddenly to the left as a red pulse sped by, narrowly missing them. Tabarzadi had reacted so quickly that it almost seemed he had maneuvered before the pulse had been fired. An instant later, the shuttle jolted up and zigged to starboard, avoiding another red pulse.

"A second marauder will be in range in ten seconds, and a third in five more," Townsend announced. He glanced at the jump-drive indicator, which still glowed yellow, then turned to Harindar. "Any advice?"

Harindar studied the display parameters while Lara prayed he had a solution. As the second marauder closed to within firing range, Harindar said, "Maximum acceleration! Any direction."

Tabarzadi complied, tilting the shuttle up and backward, sending the transport plummeting toward Ritalis. The ship rapidly accelerated, but gravity began to increase. Tabarzadi juked the shuttle sideways again as two red pulses sped by, then the jump-drive indicator turned green. He slammed his hand onto the symbol, and Lara's vision went black.

10

Lara lost track of time as she tumbled head over heels in the darkness. Then she was suddenly sitting aboard the shuttle again as it rested in space not far from a large asteroid. She felt weightless and her hair floated around her. But the turbulent, swirling sensation from the jump didn't cease. Lara felt nauseated and searched for a vomit bag.

Harindar opened a compartment in his chair armrest, retrieving a brown tablet.

"Take this," he said, handing it to her. "It will help with the nausea."

Lara placed the pill on her tongue, where it dissolved, and the nausea quickly faded.

Townsend turned toward Lara. "I'm Captain Jeff Townsend. This is Harindar, and our pilot is Eugenio. We've been assigned to take you to *Mercy*."

"*Mercy*?" Lara was surprised at the mention of a Fleet hospital ship. The Army colonel said she was headed to Earth. Perhaps that was all he'd been told. *Mercy* made sense, though. It appeared she would still be tasked as a grief counselor, only aboard *Mercy* instead of at Camden Colonial Hospital on Ritalis.

"You weren't informed of your destination?" Townsend asked.

"No," she replied. "Just *Earth*. It seems that when the military is involved, everything is shrouded in secrecy."

"That much is true," Townsend replied. "I'd love to explain, but I wasn't provided many details either, other than transportation had been arranged to take you from Ritalis to *Mercy*."

"*Transportation had been arranged*," Lara repeated. "That's a gross over-simplification of what just happened."

"I agree," Townsend replied, adding a grin. "But I just do what I'm told."

"Me too," Harindar said. "I'm just glad this baby held together. I didn't want to mention it to Captain Townsend, but today was the first time we've engaged the jump drive."

Townsend raised an eyebrow. "I'm glad you kept that from me." He turned to Lara. "Jump drives are notoriously fickle. The slightest manufac-turing flaw can result in drive implosion the first time it's engaged. That's why all initial starship jumps are unmanned."

Lara noticed the command insignia embroidered on Townsend's uniform above his right breast. "Which ship is your command?"

"The battleship *Europe*, just out of new construction. She's on her shakedown cruise, and I was on my way to *Mercy* for a medical checkup—I had punctured a lung when my previous battleship was damaged—when Fleet Command assigned me to this mission." Townsend paused, then said, "I have to ask. Why are you so important?"

Lara shrugged. "I'm not. I'm just a grief counselor. I was hoping you would tell me."

Townsend turned to Harindar, who raised his hands in defense. "I just do what I'm told." Townsend glanced at the pilot, and Harindar said, "Eugenio too. We're the lucky ones chosen for this mission."

Lara examined Harindar's and the pilot's unusual uniforms, with a color scheme she hadn't seen before. "What organization are you two from?"

"I'm not at liberty to discuss things," Harindar said. "You'll learn every-thing you need to know aboard *Mercy*. The appropriate personnel are waiting for you."

Lara glanced at the pilot, hoping he'd expound, but he remained silent. She'd have to wait until she boarded *Mercy* to have her questions answered.

Looking out the window at the asteroid beside them, she asked, "What now?"

"We're in a jump hold," Townsend answered. "We need to decompress. The standard hold for starship jumps is twelve hours, but this drive can't jump very far and the physical effects are minor. If pressed, we could jump right away like we did on the way to Ritalis, but the standard hold after jumping on this shuttle is two hours. Colonial starships can make the trip from Ritalis to Earth in two jumps, but our shuttle needs six. So, settle in for the trip."

The blue-and-white shuttle continued its journey, arriving in Earth's solar system on the sixth jump as Townsend predicted. The conversation between jumps had been limited, as Lara slept most of the way. She'd been exhausted from the long day waiting to board an evacuation shuttle on Ritalis and hadn't slept much before being awoken at home by the Army communication on her wristlet. Additionally, the jump effects, although minor according to Townsend, left her nauseated and weary, and the best way to deal with the effects was sleep.

Upon reaching Earth's solar system, Lara perked up. She'd never been to Earth, where humanity had begun. *And might end.*

She looked out the shuttle window. All she could see was darkness lit by the bright pinpricks of distant stars. Then the shuttle tilted as it changed course, and the view was breathtaking. Stretched out as far as she could see were hundreds of gigantic white starships resting in space. Interspersed between them were countless transports flying to and from the starships in a dizzying array of activity.

"First Fleet," Townsend said.

Even after their losses at Ritalis, the 1st Fleet starships were too numerous to count. And this was just one of the six fleets. It was hard for Lara to believe they were losing, driven steadily backward until there was nowhere else to fight. When all six fleets mustered together for their final stand against the Korilians, Lara could barely imagine the carnage as thousands of starships engaged in a duel to the death.

As the shuttle threaded its way through 1st Fleet toward *Mercy*, they passed close to one of the battleships, *Crimea*, its name painted on the side of the ship in black letters. The battleship soon filled Lara's window as the shuttle passed by, and she finally gained an appreciation for the size of the immense starships as their shuttle was dwarfed by the dot atop the "i" in *Crimea*.

They left *Crimea* behind, and one of the battleships they approached had a massive hole through the ship. Electrical arcs sizzled across the opening, and the inside of the ship illuminated periodically as explosions detonated inside the crippled starship. Two other battleships flanked the damaged one, with shuttles speeding back and forth between them, entering through large spaceport doors in the side of each starship.

"That's *Helena*," Captain Townsend said. "She barely made it back. *Athens* and *Sparta* are transferring additional damage control personnel aboard."

As Lara watched the activity, a small gray ship approached *Helena*, then slowed and turned around. A sparkling green beam shot out from behind the gray ship, completely enveloping *Helena*, and the gray ship began accelerating toward Earth with *Helena* in tow.

"She's off to one of the repair yards," Townsend said.

Lara's mind drifted to the coming battle with the Korilians, a battle supposedly only a few weeks away. "Will the ship be repaired in time for the next battle?"

Townsend nodded. "Probably. Our repair yards are very efficient. She'll be good as new in a few weeks." The shuttle banked again, and an odd-looking ship filled the shuttle window. "That's *Mercy*."

Mercy was disk-shaped, with a center saucer sandwiched between five more on top and five on the bottom, each disk smaller in diameter as it moved away from the center. Spaceports dotted the rim of the center disk, with ships arriving and departing *Mercy* in every direction.

The shuttle changed course again as it made its final approach, decelerating as it entered one of *Mercy*'s spaceports, the facility's bright lights illuminating the shuttle cockpit. Lara sank into her seat, and her hair fell onto her shoulders.

"*Mercy* and the other starships have gravity generators," Townsend said, "so you'll be perfectly at home here."

The shuttle slowed to a hover, then settled onto *Mercy*'s deck. The door opened, and Lara exited after Townsend. The spaceport was a frenzy of activity as dozens of ships off-loaded injured personnel, some on hover-gurneys and others ambulatory, assisted by *Mercy*'s crew.

An admiral wearing the purple Medical Corps jumpsuit stood near Lara's shuttle, flanked by an elderly man and a woman about Lara's age, both wearing blue robes, the hoods pushed back behind their heads. The admiral approached, returning Captain Townsend's salute.

"Good evening, Miss Anderson," he said, extending his hand. "Welcome aboard *Mercy*."

11

"I'm David Reynolds," the admiral said, "*Mercy*'s commanding officer. You'll be staying aboard my hospital ship until you're ready for transfer."

"Transfer?" Lara asked as she shook the admiral's hand.

The elderly, blue-robed man stepped forward. "I am Dewan Channing, responsible for the final stages of your training."

"Which—?"

"Begins first thing tomorrow morning," he interjected.

It seemed that Channing didn't want her to reveal that she was clueless as to what was going on. Lara extended her hand. "I'm looking forward to it," she said, forcing a smile.

Channing stared at her hand, but his remained by his side. "This is Angeline," he said, nodding to the woman beside him. "She will be your mentor."

As the woman stepped forward, Lara swung her hand toward her. "It's a pleasure to meet you."

Angeline hesitated a moment, then shook Lara's hand, quickly releasing it. As their hands touched, Lara sensed a genuine friendliness, laced with fear and suspicion.

"Follow me," Admiral Reynolds said, leading them into a passageway exiting the spaceport, briefly explaining the ship's capabilities as they walked. "*Mercy* is a large facility, with over five hundred operating rooms and ten thousand beds."

Lara had heard the statistics before; *Mercy's* size was staggering, and the twenty-to-one ratio of beds to operating rooms indicated the type of care the hospital ship offered. *Mercy* didn't care for patients with the sniffles or other routine maladies. Its crew dealt with trauma victims, many of them requiring immediate surgery.

"*Mercy* was built to operate far from Earth," the admiral continued. "Earlier in the war, when the fleets fought many jumps away, *Mercy* and the other hospital ships would rendezvous with the fleet during its return. That's not necessary now, as the fleets can make it home in a single jump or two, but *Mercy* still has its uses; the injured can be treated on *Mercy* without having to endure the rough descent through the Earth's atmosphere."

After traversing several busy corridors and heading down two levels, the admiral led the group through double doors that slid open, entering the crew's quarters. The sound of the busy hospital ship faded as the doors closed behind them, and the admiral stopped halfway down the hallway.

"This is your berthing. Remember the number." He pointed to 8-5-1051 on the label plate. "Eighth deck, section five, room 1051." He turned to Townsend, gesturing toward the adjacent room. "Captain, your quarters." Turning back to Lara, he added, "If there's anything you need, let me know. Whatever Admiral McCarthy's new guide wants, she gets."

Lara froze. She couldn't possibly have heard the admiral right. There had been rumors of guides assigned to each fleet admiral, supplied by a secretive group of clairvoyants. They were just rumors, of course.

Before Lara could reply, Channing intervened, stepping in front of Lara. "Thank you, Admiral. We'll take it from here." Angeline sidled up to Lara, supporting her with a firm hand on her arm.

The admiral headed down the corridor, and after Captain Townsend bid farewell and entered his quarters, Channing turned toward Lara.

"I apologize. We were going to break the news to you more delicately."

Lara was speechless, finding it difficult to believe psychic guides existed, much less her assignment as one. An impossibility, compounded by absurdity.

"I will see you tomorrow morning," Channing said, then departed.

Angeline slowly released her grip on Lara's arm. "Are you okay?" she asked.

Lara nodded.

Angeline opened the door to Lara's quarters and guided her inside.

The room was small, the accommodations Spartan: a twin bed, a dresser, and one nightstand. Thankfully, there was an adjoining private bathroom, which was uncommon on starships as far as Lara knew. On the corner of the bed were Lara's duffel bag, a stack of shimmery blue uniforms, and two blue robes.

Angeline sat Lara on the edge of the bed, sitting beside her. She waited while Lara collected her thoughts. Finally, Lara spoke.

"What the hell is going on?"

Angeline answered, "Each of the six fleets has a guide assigned, supplied by the Nexus House. These guides have prescient abilities, able to provide critical guidance and recommendations during battle. First Fleet's guide was killed at Ritalis, and we require a replacement. Unfortunately, there is no replacement guide available." Angeline paused for a moment, then said, "Let me rephrase. *You* are the replacement guide."

"Are you crazy?" Lara asked. "I'm not prescient. I can't provide guidance during battle. This is absurd!"

Angeline nodded. "There are some who agree with you. However, The One has decided that you are the most suitable, with the potential to develop the necessary skills before the Korilians arrive."

"The One?"

"She is the head of our House, the most powerful among us."

"Powerful?"

"At the highest level," Angeline replied, "other talents emerge. No one can challenge The One."

"Levels?" The information was coming fast, and Lara was trying to absorb everything.

"There are ten levels within the House. The One is a level-ten Nexus. I'm at level eight, as are the other fleet guides. Each level identifies your prescient capability. Level one is basic intuition, that foreboding feeling one gets when something bad is about to happen. At higher levels, one can place a hand on an object or person and discern something that occurred in the past. Those at level eight have glimpses of the future.

"However, it's much more complicated than that, as prescient ability can manifest in any of the five senses. Clairvoyance—premonitions received as visual images—are the most powerful, as they can impart the most data. But premonitions can also be received via the other senses. Specific smells, voices from the past or future, tingling or other sensations, even unusual tastes can impart knowledge beyond the realm of the present. The challenge in most cases, however, is the interpretation of each premonition. This is most critical in battle, because we do not have control of the type or frequency of the premonitions, and we must be able to translate their meanings into tactical terms.

"That is what you are going to learn," Angeline added. "Channing and I will help you."

"Why you two?"

"Channing is responsible for training all fleet guides. I have been assigned as your mentor because I am the only female guide your age. Also, I knew the guide you are replacing very well; I understood Regina's premonitions and techniques. We are hopeful that your talents will be more like Regina's than the other guides."

"Why is that?"

"Regina was Admiral McCarthy's guide for five years, and her capabilities are what he is used to." Angeline looked into Lara's eyes. "I must warn you. There are many challenges ahead. We must identify and tap into your talents, and we don't have much time. Additionally, McCarthy and Regina were very close, and I fear their relationship will be an obstacle."

Angeline added, "McCarthy can be difficult to work with. He is the youngest fleet admiral ever, fifteen years younger than any other. Very talented, but very high-strung. He has already stated that he does not want a replacement guide."

"Well then, that settles it," Lara said, rubbing her hands on her thighs. "You can send me to Earth."

Angeline smiled. "I take my orders from The One, not McCarthy. You will be trained, and you will become McCarthy's guide." There was a firmness in her voice that told Lara it was pointless to argue.

Angeline glanced at the digital clock on Lara's nightstand. "It's late, and I'm sure your head is swirling right now. Try to get a good night's sleep, and we'll start first thing in the morning. Zero-six-hundred."

"Zero-six-hundred?"

"Sorry. That's military speak for six a.m. Your days will be long; you won't be getting much sleep after tonight."

Lara glanced at the clock. It was almost midnight aboard *Mercy*. If six hours was a good night's sleep...

Angeline stood, placing a hand on Lara's shoulder. "You will do well. I can already tell." She offered a warm smile. "Get some sleep."

The Nexus Eight departed, leaving Lara sitting on the edge of the bed, trying to make sense of what had occurred in the last few hours. Her assignment as a psychic guide to Admiral McCarthy was preposterous, yet she had been rescued from Ritalis and the plan put in motion.

She took a deep breath and let it out slowly, pretending she was lying on her lounge chair, staring at the stars. As the tension eased from her shoulders, she opened her duffel bag and extracted a nightgown. After stripping off her clothes, her eyes went to the stack of shimmery blue uniforms on the edge of the bed, wondering if they were the right size. She slipped one on, and the thin, form-fitting one-piece jumpsuit fit perfectly.

The Nexus House was psychic, indeed.

12

"Rise and shine!"

The lights flicked on as Angeline entered Lara's room. Lara glanced at the clock on her nightstand. It was 5:30 a.m.

"I thought you said six o'clock," Lara said as she sat up in bed, rubbing the sleep from her eyes.

"We *start* at six," Angeline answered. "You have to shower, dress, and eat breakfast."

Lara glanced at the clock again. It normally took her forty-five minutes just to get out the door each morning, not to mention eating breakfast in the hospital cafeteria after she arrived.

"Hop to," Angeline added. "Time's a-wasting."

"You sound like a drill sergeant," Lara said as she slid from bed.

Angeline laughed. "Yeah, I suppose the military has rubbed off on me a bit. They're a very efficient lot."

She sat on the edge of the bed while Lara grabbed her toiletry bag, underwear, and one of the Nexus uniforms and entered the bathroom. She emerged twenty minutes later, her hair still damp from a short blow-drying, plus a quick application of makeup.

Angeline checked her watch. "You should probably ditch the makeup from here on out. There are more important things to spend your time on."

As Angeline spoke, Lara noticed she wasn't wearing her robe this morning, only the same shimmery blue uniform that Lara wore, except for eight white bands around her upper right arm. A glance at her own sleeve, which also had eight white bands.

Angeline followed her eyes. "You'd normally be given a plain blue uniform with no stripes, since you haven't passed any of the level tests. However, this is an unusual circumstance, and we do not want to alert Fleet personnel to your true level, or lack thereof."

"You're going to try to fool them, even Admiral McCarthy?" Lara asked.

"We will not be able to fool McCarthy. Regina trained to be a guide for twelve years, and spent five more with McCarthy. He will recognize you for what you are in an instant."

"A fraud?"

"Let's not be too harsh with the labels," Angeline said. "Let's find out what you're capable of. Hopefully, The One is correct and you will be of use to McCarthy.

"Are you hungry?" Angeline added.

"Not really."

"All right, then. Let's get started."

Angeline led Lara through the maze of *Mercy*'s passageways, with Lara doing her best to remember the way back to her room. As they passed medical and military personnel in the corridors, Lara noticed their reaction. She was an attractive woman, and the form-fitting blue uniform accented her body. There wasn't a man they passed who didn't spend a few seconds eyeing her. She figured she could have been wearing a uniform with zero or twenty white stripes, and no man would have noticed, their eyes going elsewhere.

After a five-minute trek, they entered a small conference room with Channing sitting at the head of a table. He motioned Lara into a seat, and Angeline settled into a chair opposite her.

"Let's start with your background," Channing said as he began a new note in his tablet. Small talk was apparently not his strong suit.

Lara spent the next hour providing the details. She was an only child, born on the planet Altaria, evacuated to Ritalis at the age of seventeen as the Korilian Empire advanced toward the Pleiades star cluster. By then she was an orphan; her dad had been tasked to the Colonial Navy and was killed during the fierce battles keeping the supply lines open to Darian 3, the bloodiest ground battle in the thirty-year Korilian War. Lara was twelve when her mother died, killed in an accident at the starship shield-generator plant she was tasked to. Upon reaching Ritalis, Lara had undergone a battery of tests to determine her talents and was tasked as a grief counselor, spending a few months in training before her assignment at Camden Colonial.

Channing then questioned Lara, attempting to identify any unusual abilities. It wasn't long before Lara mentioned her ability to look into someone's mind by touching his or her skin.

"Would you like me to show you?" Lara asked, reaching for Channing's hand.

He pulled his hand away. "We are already aware of this talent. From this point forward, you will not use it. Is that clear?"

Lara nodded, and Channing spent the next few hours probing for additional abilities, learning that Lara was adept at reading people's emotions. For some reason, however, he wasn't interested. He instead searched for anything unusual that had occurred to her. When she mentioned the premonition she'd had as a child, she caught Channing's attention.

"Go on," he said. "All the details."

Lara collected her thoughts, thinking back to the nightmare she'd had when she was eight years old.

She awoke screaming in bed, jolted to a sitting position, and screamed again. Perspiration dotted her face, and she gripped the edge of her bedsheet in sweaty fists.

Lara's mom rushed into her bedroom, hurrying over to comfort her as Lara reached for her reassuring embrace.

"*They're all dead!*" *Lara shouted.* "*All of them!*"

"*Who?*" *Cheryl sat on the bed and wrapped her arms around her terrified child.*

"*Everyone on the shuttle.*"

"*What shuttle?*"

"*My class. Their shuttle was knocked off a bridge, into the water. They all drowned.*"

"*Now, now. Nothing's happened to them. They're on their way to the zoo. You're just disappointed you couldn't go.*" *Cheryl brushed the damp hair away from her daughter's face.* "*At least your fever's broke. It won't be long before you're feeling better and back in school.*"

"*But it was so real! I watched the shuttle fall into the river, and water poured in from everywhere. They couldn't get out. They were screaming and reaching for me. And I couldn't help them.*"

"*It was just a dream,*" *Cheryl said, rocking Lara gently in her arms.* "*It was just a dream.*"

Lara clung to her mom and closed her eyes tightly, trying to force the vision of her drowning classmates from her mind.

"*How about some breakfast?*" *Cheryl asked.* "*I'll make pancakes. With chocolate chips. How's that sound?*"

Lara looked up and nodded.

"*That's my little girl. Come on.*"

Lara followed her mom into the living room and headed for the video display while Cheryl entered the kitchen and began making pancakes. Lara was flipping through the channels, searching for her favorite cartoon show, when for some reason she stopped on a channel with a reporter on screen and the Altarian capitol building in the background. Cheryl turned her attention from the pancakes to the breaking news story.

"*...horrible tragedy on the 18th Street Bridge. There was a heavy fog this morning, and a school shuttle lost control and crashed through the retaining wall, plummeting forty feet into the frigid waters of the Nuvian River. Initial reports say there were twenty-four children and five adults on board, on a school field trip to the Altarian National Zoo. The name of the school is being withheld pending notification of the children's parents and other next of kin.*"

The milk container slipped from Cheryl's hand, falling onto its side on the kitchen counter. Milk sloshed from the carton, running down the side of the cabinet onto the floor. Cheryl righted the milk container and cleaned up the mess, then headed into the living room toward Lara.

Channing took notes as Lara spoke, looking up as she finished. "What did your mother say?"

Lara thought for a moment, then answered, "I asked her how I could have dreamt what happened, and she told me that I was special and had been chosen by the five gods to do great things."

"The five gods?" Channing said. "Is that an Altarian religion?"

"Not that I know of. My parents weren't religious."

"Then why the reference to five gods?"

Lara replied, "That's not exactly what she said. She said that I was chosen by the five. I always assumed she was referring to deities of some sort."

Channing, who had been scribbling notes in his tablet, stopped suddenly and looked up. "What did your mother say? I need you to repeat it back exactly."

After a moment of reflection, Lara replied, "She said, '*You are a special girl, and you will do great things when you grow up. You have been chosen by the five, and they do not place their faith in someone lightly.*'"

Channing locked eyes with Angeline for a few seconds, then leaned over and whispered in her ear. Angeline pushed back from the table and stepped from the room.

"Let's move on," Channing said. "I'm interested in any other visions or predictions you've had. Anything, even an odd occurrence, something you may have brushed off as irrelevant or coincidence."

Lara searched through her memories, and after additional probing by Channing, realized that she'd had numerous visions she had categorized as dreams or daydreams.

"Is there anything common in these visions?" Channing asked. "Something that always occurs or is always present?"

Lara nodded. "Whenever I have a vision, there's always a cold fog nearby."

Angeline returned to the conference room with an electronic tablet, which she slid across the table to Channing as she took her seat. Channing read the tablet data aloud.

"Your mother was Cheryl Taylor Anderson. Maiden name Jonson. Your father was Matt Damian Anderson." He scrolled through the tablet data. "Both parents migrated to Altaria from Canopus." He looked up. "Your parents were from a Fringe World?"

"They were from Canopus," Lara answered. "What of it?"

"It's unusual," Channing replied. "Migration is normally outward, from the more civilized worlds toward the outer colonies."

"Canopus is quite civilized," Lara said defensively.

"That's debatable," Channing replied. He continued scrolling through the data. "This is interesting. No biological data for either of your parents." As he looked up at Lara, his eyes narrowed.

"What does that mean?" Lara asked.

"It means there is no genetic record of your parents in the Canopus registry."

"Are you saying my parents never existed?" The heat was rising in Lara's cheeks. Why the inquisition about her parents?

"I'm saying," Channing answered, "that the Canopus *registry* doesn't think your parents existed."

Angeline, who had been watching the interchange between Channing and Lara, joined in. "It's probably just an oversight. Those were hectic times, with the Fringe Worlds being the first to be abandoned as the Korilians advanced. Canopus wouldn't be the first registry transferred to Earth with incomplete data."

"This is true," Channing said as he entered a note into the tablet and handed it back to Angeline. "Let's get back to business, shall we?"

Channing explained to Angeline the common element in Lara's visions—a cold fog—then continued probing Lara for another hour before breaking for lunch. Before Channing departed, he said, "Reflect on each of your premonitions, focusing on the fog. Try to distinguish differences in the fog—the thickness, density, temperature. What does the fog do—does it envelope everything, blanket the floor, or flow in unusual patterns?"

Lara nodded as Channing stood, and after he left the conference room, Angeline asked, "Are you hungry?"

"Famished," Lara replied.

"Let's get something from the cafeteria and bring it back here," Angeline said. "We need to talk."

13

Seated across from Angeline in the conference room with a sandwich in her hands, Lara listened as Angeline provided more insight into her role as a guide.

"All of the guides are synesthesians."

"Synthetics?"

"No, synesthesians. We have the ability of synesthesia." Lara gave her a blank stare, so Angeline elaborated. "Synesthesians are rare, because it's an extra ability on top of premonitions. It takes years of training, but the synesthesia helps translate any premonition into a common format. For example, Regina and I are color synesthesians. No matter what type of premonition I receive, it will have a color scheme, and I can interpret the colors rather than attempt to understand the premonition. This is particularly important in battle, because we don't have time to digest the meaning of each premonition—they're almost always different—and we don't always interpret them correctly to begin with. The synesthesia is critical. That's why Channing is focusing on the fog in your visions."

"Why the fog?"

"It's the one common element in your visions. It's possible you might be able to use the fog as your Rosetta Stone. But you first have to *create* the Rosetta Stone, determining what the subtle variations in the fog mean, so that when you see it again, you'll know. Then, of course, it has to mean something in tactical terms. Something the admiral can use to influence his decisions."

Lara placed the half-eaten sandwich on her plate. She'd lost her appetite. What she was being asked to do was overwhelming. Angeline apparently agreed.

"What you've been asked to do normally takes a decade of training. And only if you have the required talent." She reached across the table and was going to put her hand on Lara's, then pulled up short. "Take it one step at a time. That's all you can do."

Noticing Angeline's reluctance to touch her, Lara asked, "What's the deal about you and Channing not wanting to touch me?"

Angeline answered, "You have the Touch."

"So?"

Angeline hesitated, and Lara could tell she was choosing her words carefully. She answered, "Our mortal enemies, the Corvads, all had the Touch. You are not a Corvad, obviously, but you are predisposed to joining their House." After a slight pause, Angeline smiled. "There is nothing to worry about, however. The Corvads have been eliminated, and there is no house for you to defect to. However, the fear of those who have the Touch is ingrained in every Nexus."

Lara mulled Angeline's explanation, concluding she had answered truthfully, but not completely. She was holding something back. Deciding not to press the issue, Lara changed the topic. "Why the third-degree grilling about my parents?"

Angeline replied, "House candidates are normally thoroughly vetted, their backgrounds researched meticulously. We had short notice with you, and Channing is just completing the paperwork."

Another incomplete answer. There was more to Channing's curiosity than routine paperwork. "What about his interest in my mom's reference to the five?"

"Channing can be a bit odd at times. I wouldn't dwell on it if I were you."

This time, Lara knew Angeline was lying. Before she could inquire further, however, Channing entered the room, returning to his seat at the head of the table.

"Our schedule for the rest of the day has been confirmed," he said. "We will have a formal dinner tonight with all guides, here on *Mercy*. Also, our meeting with Admiral McCarthy has been scheduled for five p.m. We'll introduce him to his new guide."

Channing studied Lara for a moment before adding, "I have to warn you. Your meeting with the admiral will not go well."

14

The rest of the afternoon passed quickly, with Channing and Angeline taking turns probing Lara's memories and examining each premonition, no matter how insignificant it seemed. It was now almost five p.m., and Lara, Channing, and Angeline were standing beside the nurse's desk in one of *Mercy*'s wards. Lara had learned from the nurse that Admiral McCarthy had undergone surgery last night following his return from Ritalis. Near the end of the battle, a shard of transparent Kevlar had pierced his chest. He'd been lucky; an inch either way and it would have either punctured his heart or severed an artery.

The admiral seemed to have recovered quickly, though. While Lara waited, a steady stream of Navy captains, tablets in their hands, entered and exited McCarthy's room. Interspersed among the captains, several one- and two-star admirals visited with their aides in tow. The clock struck five p.m., and the flow of personnel in and out of the admiral's room continued unabated. A captain approached, informing Channing that McCarthy was running behind schedule and would see them shortly. The time dragged on, and Lara got the distinct impression their meeting was being intentionally delayed.

It was almost six p.m. when the captain returned, informing Channing that the admiral was ready to see them. Lara felt the tension in

Channing and Angeline rise as the captain led them into McCarthy's room.

They entered a four-patient room that had been modified for a single person, the extra beds removed in exchange for three desks manned by the admiral's aides, busy reviewing data on plasma displays and entering notes into their wristlets. The hospital room was at the end of the passageway, along *Mercy*'s outer hull, and the far wall contained a large window looking into space, the darkness dotted by stars and the hundreds of white starships in 1st Fleet. Instead of resting in bed, the admiral was standing near the window, wearing the crimson and burgundy Fleet uniform, staring into space. He turned as Lara, Channing, and Angeline entered.

Admiral McCarthy addressed his staff. "Leave us."

The three captains acknowledged and departed, and the admiral's eyes scanned the three persons remaining, his eyes settling on Lara until Channing spoke.

True to form, Channing wasted no time with small talk. "We are here to introduce your new guide."

McCarthy replied quickly, "I do not require a new guide. I believe I've made that clear."

"You have, Admiral. However, Fleet Admiral Fitzgerald has directed the House to provide you with a new guide. You do not have a choice in this matter."

"I will clear this up with Admiral Fitzgerald when I get a chance. You are dismissed."

The admiral turned away, gazing through the window again.

Undeterred, Channing continued, "Your new guide is Lara Anderson. I believe you are aware of her limited training?"

McCarthy turned toward Channing. "This conversation is over."

"You're correct, Admiral. The conversation is over. The One has assigned Lara as your new guide. We do not have a choice."

"Do you want to hear what I think of The One's assignments?"

Lara sensed Channing's and Angeline's apprehension spike, as if merely being in the presence of someone blaspheming The One was dangerous. McCarthy added, "Besides, this new guide is untrained. She will only serve as a distraction."

Channing answered, "We will train her as best as possible, and The One is convinced she will be of assistance."

As the two men faced each other in a stalemate, Lara realized she had an ally in Admiral McCarthy. He was the only one who was thinking straight, realizing her assignment as his guide was a huge mistake. At the risk of alienating Channing and Angeline, she jumped to McCarthy's side.

"You're right, Admiral. I don't have a clue as to what I'm doing, and I'd only be a hindrance. It would be best if you—"

"I didn't ask for your opinion," McCarthy said, cutting her off.

Lara snapped her mouth shut, her anger flaring. Her affinity for the admiral transformed instantly into dislike.

As McCarthy turned his attention back to Channing, the tension in the room rising, Lara realized something was amiss. The emotions she sensed were coming from Channing and Angeline. There was nothing from the admiral. His words clearly indicated that he was irritated, yet his tone and body language were calm, completely devoid of emotion. It didn't seem possible that someone could have such control. She focused harder, probing the admiral as he engaged in a heated discussion with Channing.

Nothing. No physical indication of the emotion his words conveyed.

Lara sucked in a sharp breath.

For six centuries, sentient machines had been forbidden. After the 1st and 2nd Cyborg Wars, sentient machines and their cyborg variants—machines covered with human flesh or humans with brain implants—had been banned. There was no more sacred law. However, with humankind on the brink of extinction, had the Council disregarded the law, developing a cyborg in secret? That would explain the admiral's prowess in battle, able to process information more efficiently than humans. But they would have had to begin development years ago; the admiral had been in command of 1st Fleet for two years, and three more as head of the Normandy battle group. And if they had built McCarthy, why stop there?

A silence in the room pulled Lara from her thoughts, and she realized everyone was staring at her.

Channing spoke. "There is more to consider than the assistance she may provide."

"I am aware of that," McCarthy replied, "but my position is firm. I have been somewhat indisposed since returning from Ritalis," he waved a hand across the hospital room, "but I will discuss this with Fleet Admiral Fitzgerald as soon as she is available."

"In the meantime," Channing said, "we will continue Lara's training."

McCarthy stared at Channing for a moment, then replied, "You are dismissed."

15

_____

Lara followed Channing and Angeline from the admiral's hospital room, and she felt the tension dissipate as they exited. Channing let out a deep breath, but Angeline still appeared shaken. Their emotions seemed somewhat out of place, however. McCarthy had simply refused to accept her as his guide. Channing's and Angeline's reactions were more intense than they should have been, as if making up for the admiral's lack of emotion.

Angeline engaged Channing in a conversation Lara couldn't overhear, then dropped back, joining Lara. "You okay?" she asked.

"I'm fine," Lara replied. "I just don't appreciate how he talked to me."

Angeline replied, "That is not the admiral I know. I've never seen him rude like that, and Regina had nothing but glowing things to say about him. I knew they were close, but Regina's death must have affected him more than I expected. He's also waging a battle he will lose. He cannot defy Fleet Admiral Fitzgerald's and The One's commands."

As Angeline spoke, Lara debated whether to discuss her suspicions about McCarthy with her. However, Lara could tell the two Nexi were not being completely honest with her. She wondered if they were complicit in some way, and whether revealing her suspicions about McCarthy would jeopardize her safety. If the Colonial Council had broken the sacred law and built a cyborg, anyone who discovered that fact would be in peril. Lara decided to keep her mouth shut for the time being.

After they reached the end of a long corridor, a door whisked open, and they entered a small dining room containing a circular table. Seated in four of the seven seats were three men and one woman, each wearing the Nexus blue uniform with eight white bands on their sleeves. Three of the guides were very young—still teenagers, sixteen or seventeen years old at best—while the fourth guide was a man closer to Lara's age. Channing took one seat as Lara and Angeline settled into the other two vacant chairs.

Channing led a round of introductions, and Lara learned that the older man was the 2nd Fleet guide, with the younger ones assigned to 4th, 5th, and 6th Fleets, which meant Angeline was the 3rd Fleet guide. The three younger guides shook Lara's hand but pulled theirs back quickly. During the brief touch as their hands met, she sensed a cold hardness that belied their youthful appearance. The older guide, named Arjun, refused to shake Lara's hand, but Lara didn't need to touch his skin to sense the hostility.

Arjun's eyes bored into her as Channing said, "Please make our new guide welcome."

The younger guides seemed friendly, peppering her with questions about her background and how she had been selected as a guide. Perplexed looks were exchanged when they learned that less than twenty-four hours ago, Lara had never even heard of the Nexus House. In turn, Lara learned that each of the guides had been inducted into the Nexus House at the age of five.

Servers entered the dining room from an adjoining galley, bringing the first course of the meal—salad. As the conversation drifted between topics, Lara wondered about the significant age difference between the six guides, with three of them being ten years younger than Arjun and Angeline.

As Lara and the others dug into their salads, Lara asked, "Why is there such an age difference between the guides?"

The forks stopped moving, and there was an uneasy silence until Channing replied, "On occasion, replacement guides are required. The Korilians target our command ships when possible. Arjun and Angeline have defied the odds."

Lara considered his response. Angeline and Arjun appeared to be in their mid-twenties. If living to their mid-twenties defied the odds...

"What is the average life expectancy of a guide?"

Channing seemed reluctant to answer but finally said, "About two years."

Lara put down her fork.

She felt Angeline's hand on her forearm as she said reassuringly, "But there's only one more battle."

Arjun, who had been silent until now, added, "That's right. The most important battle of the war. Its outcome will determine humanity's fate, and a clueless commoner has been assigned as guide to the most important fleet." He slammed his fists on the table, causing the silverware to jump. "What is The One thinking?" He glared at Lara. "She's completely untrained." Glancing at the stripes on Lara's sleeve, he added, "She's not an Eight. She's a zero!"

He stood, throwing his napkin on his plate. "This is lunacy!"

Arjun stormed from the dining room, leaving another uneasy silence until Angeline spoke, directing her words at Channing. "You asked me how Arjun was taking his fleet's beating at Ritalis. You have your answer."

Channing nodded, then waved his hand across the table. "Eat. This may be the last time we dine together. Enjoy each other's company." After a moment of reflection, he stood. "Excuse me," he said, then exited the dining room.

Conversation between Lara and the other four guides resumed, but the three younger ones soon drifted off into a separate discussion. The ten-year age difference was notable, as well as their unique backgrounds. They had spent almost their entire lives in either the Nexus House or assigned to the military and used acronyms and terms Lara didn't understand. They'd occasionally break into laughter after one of them made a reference that Lara couldn't follow.

Lara turned to Angeline as the guide said, "You'll have to excuse Arjun. He's been under a lot of stress, with First and Second Fleets engaged in battle almost nonstop these last few months, and he has not taken the outcome at Ritalis well. First Fleet absorbed the brunt of the Korilian attack and escaped relatively unscathed, while Second Fleet almost collapsed, losing over half of its ships. His pride has been wounded. Couple that with Regina's death...the three of us were close."

"You seem to be doing okay," Lara replied.

"On the outside, yes. But I share Arjun's concerns. However, I have been tasked to assist you, and assist you I will. If you enter battle as McCarthy's guide, every bit of preparation will be critical."

Lara reflected on Arjun's outburst. "Why did he say First Fleet is the most important fleet? Aren't the fleets the same?"

"They are, but First Fleet is different because Admiral McCarthy is in charge; there is no better tactician. When the Korilians arrive, our battle plan will somehow hinge on First Fleet." Angeline smiled. "How well you perform might make the difference."

"Assuming Admiral McCarthy accepts me as his guide."

"Well, there's that." Angeline glanced at the door through which Arjun and Channing had departed. "I suspect a few things are in the process of being rectified."

16

After dinner, Lara and Angeline returned to the conference room, where Channing was waiting. His probing questions continued, and it was not long before the topic of her husband's death came up. Channing homed in on it immediately, and Lara's face became flush as she admitted her inability to deal with her own grief and move past Gary's death. Channing took notes as the evening dragged on, and as the time approached midnight, it appeared the examination of her background and experiences was drawing to a close. Her training would begin tomorrow.

Angeline escorted Lara to crew berthing, leaving her at the end of the corridor leading to her room as Angeline headed toward hers. It was late and the lighting was dim, simulating nighttime to keep everyone's biological rhythms in sync with the artificial twenty-four-hour day. As Lara approached her room, the day's events swirled through her head: Admiral McCarthy's refusal to accept her as his guide, plus the long sessions with Channing and Angeline, which helped her realize that throughout her life, she'd had prescient glimpses of the past and future. However, her thoughts kept returning to the encounter with McCarthy and his lack of emotion. She was almost certain he was a cyborg, but how could she prove it, and what would she do with the information once convinced?

Lara was about to enter her room when she noticed light leaking under

Captain Townsend's door. During their brief interaction, she had sensed a calm confidence and, more important, an honesty she failed to detect from Channing and Angeline. He'd been in the Fleet for many years. Perhaps he knew McCarthy and could shed light on her suspicion.

She approached Townsend's door and knocked firmly. A few seconds later, Townsend opened the door, wearing a gray sweat suit.

"Evening, Lara," he said. "Can I help you with something?"

"Maybe," Lara replied, searching for a way to ask the desired questions without giving her suspicion away. "As Admiral Reynolds mentioned last night, I've been assigned as Admiral McCarthy's new guide, and I'd like to learn as much about him as possible. How well do you know McCarthy?"

"You happen to be in luck. There's probably no one, aside from Fleet Admiral Fitzgerald, who knows him better than I do."

Lara overrode the urge to raise an eyebrow. *What a coincidence.*

Townsend checked his wristlet. It was just past midnight. "Why don't we get a cup of coffee? Decaffeinated."

A few minutes later, Lara was sitting in a small alcove across the table from Townsend, who had donned his Fleet uniform before escorting her to the nearest coffee shop.

"I met with Admiral McCarthy today," Lara said.

"How did things go?"

"McCarthy thinks I'm inadequately trained and would only be a distraction. He refused to accept me as his new guide." As she spoke the words, she realized there was disappointment in her voice. McCarthy's position was appropriate and one she should have been happy with. But for some reason, his rejection troubled her.

"Jon will come around," Townsend said. "He and Regina were close, and it will take time."

Admiral McCarthy's relationship with Regina had come up several times, and Lara wondered how close they had been. "Were they in a relationship?"

Townsend shook his head. "God, no. Jon learned his lesson with..." He stopped, his mood turning somber.

"They were just friends?"

Townsend nodded. "Engaging in battle together creates a strong bond, and with the weight of responsibility placed on Jon's and Regina's shoulders, it's easy to understand how close they became. I feel it as a starship captain. I can only imagine the burden Jon feels, being in charge of an entire fleet."

As the conversation continued, Lara found the information interesting and Townsend's friendship with McCarthy reassuring, but she wasn't obtaining the information she desired. If McCarthy was a cyborg, it would be glaringly obvious once you pulled the string; cyborgs didn't age.

"How long have you known McCarthy?"

Townsend took a sip of coffee. "Almost twenty years. Eighteen to be exact."

"Eighteen years?" McCarthy looked like he was in his early thirties. That would make him a teenager when he and Townsend first met. "So he was sixteen, seventeen when you first met?"

"Sixteen. I was twenty-two when we were both assigned to the battleship *Tulaga*. Jon was a midshipman, and I was a newly reporting ensign. I knew instantly that he was destined for great things. In only a few months, he was on the bridge offering advice to one of the most seasoned captains in the Fleet."

"Has he...aged much since you met him?"

Townsend placed his coffee cup on the table, and Lara flinched inwardly as his eyes probed her. She'd blown it, her question too far from the norm. Townsend asked, "What do you really want to know?"

Lara hesitated, assessing whether she could trust Townsend with her suspicion. Her gut told her he was honest, someone she could confide in without risk.

"As you know," Lara replied, "Admiral McCarthy's prowess in battle is unrivaled. Some are better than others, I suppose." She felt Townsend's stare as she skirted the issue. As he took another long sip of coffee, she blurted it out. "I think McCarthy might be a cyborg."

Coffee almost came out of Townsend's nose as he slammed the cup on the table, alternating between coughing and laughing.

When the spasms subsided, he leaned forward, a smile on his face. "That's the best one I've heard yet."

Undeterred, Lara backed up her assertion. "It would explain everything. His exceptional tactical ability. Plus, when I met him today, he was devoid of emotion. I can sense people's emotions," Lara added, attempting to add credence to her observation. "Every person I've met emits emotion. He does not. Explain that."

Townsend leaned back in his chair, retrieving his cup and swirling the coffee inside as he contemplated his response. "For starters," he said, "unless they've developed cyborgs that can develop acne as a teenager, then grow three inches, Jon's no cyborg. Regarding his lack of emotion, that's a casualty of the trade. Emotion can override logic in the heat of battle, costing the lives of others and also your own. Jon has always been cool under stress, and the losses he has endured, both professional and personal, have no doubt hardened him. You will learn," Townsend added, "that there is no place in battle for emotion."

He leaned forward again, all hint of humor gone from his face. "Every decision Jon makes costs lives. He holds the fate of every man and woman in his fleet in his hands, and with every command he issues, he sentences some to death while letting others live. In that endeavor, there is no place for emotion—only cold analytical calculations, unencumbered by regret or guilt."

Townsend took one final sip of coffee, checking his watch. "It's past my bedtime, and I suspect yours as well. I meet with Admiral McCarthy in the morning, then depart for *Europe*."

At the mention of Townsend's new starship, Lara recalled his punctured lung, and her eyes went to his chest.

He gave her a thumbs-up. "Good to go." He smiled and stood, offering his hand to assist her. After dealing with the Nexi's reluctance to touch her, she welcomed the gesture. She looked into his mind during the brief time their hands touched. Townsend was being honest. As far as he was concerned, McCarthy was not a cyborg.

As Townsend escorted Lara back to crew berthing, Lara described her encounter with McCarthy, and Townsend agreed with Angeline that his behavior was not characteristic of the man he knew.

"You'll have to forgive Jon," Townsend said. "I'm sure Regina's death has affected him, plus he hasn't taken a day off in the last two years, refitting First Fleet as quickly as possible after each battle. More than one fleet has been saved by the last-second arrival of First Fleet, returning to battle more quickly than anticipated."

Townsend's respect for McCarthy was evident in his voice. Additionally, Lara had met many of the men and women who served under McCarthy, interfacing with them at Camden Colonial as they healed from injuries, and she was impressed by their admiration for him. They seemed indebted to McCarthy, realizing they'd probably be dead if they had been assigned to one of the other five fleets.

They walked in silence for a moment before Townsend continued. "You have no idea of the terror that struck First Fleet when he was injured at Ritalis. We believe we are invincible as long as he leads us into battle, that we will defeat the Korilians or at worst fight them to a draw. If he had died, First Fleet would have been demoralized, our combat effectiveness reduced at a time we can ill afford it. It wouldn't matter who would have taken command of First Fleet. Belief in someone is not something that can be conferred by adding a fourth star to his or her collar.

"That's the problem with the other five fleets," Townsend added. "Don't get me wrong. They fight hard. And they're led by capable admirals. But the other fleets don't believe in their admirals the same way we believe in Jon. That belief can mean the difference between victory and defeat. And in this next battle, the difference between survival and extinction."

Captain Townsend's grim words reassured Lara for some reason. He openly discussed the upcoming battle—their final stand against the Korilian Empire—without the resignation that permeated the population on Ritalis. He spoke as if he believed they could defeat the Korilians when it really mattered, that the outcome wasn't predetermined.

"Do you really think we can defeat them?" Lara asked.

"I'll admit, it doesn't look good," Townsend replied. "But this time the Fleet will fight to the last starship. Admiral McCarthy will lead the combined Fleet in this next battle, and that gives us the hope we need."

They arrived at her door a moment later, and she bid Captain Townsend farewell. Lara entered her quarters and prepared for bed, slipping into one of the silk nightgowns she had packed for her trip to *Mercy*. As she stood in front of the mirror, her thoughts shifted from McCarthy to Gary, somberly noting that the nightgown was the one she had worn the last time they were together, the weekend before he left on the deployment he never returned from. She clenched her left hand into a fist, feeling the hardness of her wedding ring as a lump formed in her throat.

Her love for Gary had been intense, and she couldn't imagine sharing her innermost feelings or becoming intimate with anyone else. The mere thought of doing so only made her long for Gary's tender touch. Her fist opened, and she caressed the side of her face, pretending it was Gary's strong, reassuring hand. But that intensified the pain.

She welcomed it.

That was her ritual. She thought about Gary each night, the pain keeping his memory alive, his face vivid in her mind. After a long moment in front of the mirror, she turned off the light and slid under the bedsheets.

17

Even though Lara was exhausted, she slept fitfully, tossing and turning through the night as visions of Gary and McCarthy haunted her dreams. She woke at five a.m., then rolled over, hoping to catch another thirty minutes of sleep, but last night's conversation with Captain Townsend tumbled through her mind. If Townsend was right and McCarthy wasn't a cyborg, then his lack of emotion in light of Regina's death was troubling. If McCarthy was internalizing his grief, he needed help. She had seen first-hand what happened to those who failed to deal with the death of a loved one; it affected their interactions with others and the decisions they made. With humankind's final stand against the Korilians approaching, McCarthy needed a clear mind, unencumbered by grief.

As she lay in bed in the darkness, she realized that maybe she had been selected by the Nexus House not because she'd make a good guide, but to help McCarthy through his grief. What Admiral McCarthy really needed was counseling, and there was no one better than her. She sat up in bed, and for the first time since learning of her new tasking, her confidence returned.

After glancing at the clock, she figured she could spend time with the admiral and still meet Channing and Angeline at six a.m., assuming

McCarthy was awake this early. She decided to stop by the admiral's room, hoping he was an early riser.

Lara took a quick shower and skipped her makeup as Angeline suggested, then hurried through the maze of *Mercy's* passages, eventually reaching the nurse's station not far from McCarthy's room. She asked the nurse if he was awake, and the nurse selected the admiral's room on her monitor. McCarthy was already dressed for the day in his Fleet uniform, resting in bed atop his sheets, his head bent toward an electronic tablet in his hands. His fingers moved quickly, scrolling through the data.

Lara knocked on his door, and she heard the admiral respond, "Enter."

The door slid open, and Lara stepped into his room, locking eyes with McCarthy, who stood as she approached.

"What are you doing here?" he asked.

"There is something we need to discuss."

His eyes narrowed. "There is nothing I need to discuss with *you*."

"I disagree." As Lara spoke, she probed McCarthy, searching for emotion. There was nothing. Although Townsend was convinced he wasn't a cyborg, Lara still wasn't sure. If he was human, however, she would eventually detect the emotions he was controlling. She decided to be aggressive. Considering the admiral's demeanor, she might not have much time.

"My tasking until yesterday was as a grief counselor, and I can sense you're having trouble dealing with Regina's death."

McCarthy didn't respond.

There. A flash of emotion, quickly extinguished.

McCarthy was human after all. And she was on the right track.

Lara continued, "It's normal to grieve when you lose someone you care for. But you can't hold it in. Left unresolved, it will affect you in ways difficult to predict, and not for the better. You have to release it, let it flow from you."

"I don't need your advice on how to deal with Regina's death."

Lara approached McCarthy, stopping an arm's length away. Considering how close he and Regina supposedly were, she should have felt grief radiating from him, like heat from a furnace. But he was cold. His force of will was remarkable. She needed to find a way to break through. Her thoughts

went back to McCarthy's flash of emotion, realizing there had been something else besides grief. Something even more intense. He was hiding
something.

She reached toward McCarthy, touching his hand in a gesture of
comfort, and she looked into his mind. Her vision clouded in a thick fog,
parting quickly from the center out. A starship bridge appeared around her,
and Lara realized she was reliving one of McCarthy's memories.

*He was kneeling on the starship deck, holding Regina's head in the crook of his
arm. Warm blood spread across his chest, but the ache in his heart was for the
woman in his arms, a long shard of glass protruding from her stomach and back.
McCarthy brushed a lock of hair away from Regina's face as she stared up at him.
A medic was soon by his side, assessing McCarthy's wound before turning his
attention to Regina. The medic looked up; there was nothing he could do.
McCarthy looked down at Regina, unable to conceal her fate.*

*Regina reached up and touched his face. "I'm so sorry," she said. "I failed
you."*

"No," McCarthy replied. "I failed you."

*Regina caressed his cheek, and McCarthy felt her warm blood on his face. Her
hand fell away, and he held Regina close until the life faded from her eyes.*

McCarthy pulled his hand away, and the vision dissipated.

"You are dismissed," he said, "and *don't* come back." He headed toward
one of the desks, stopping in front of the computer display, his back toward
her as his fingers tapped on the keyboard.

Dismissed?

Lara's anger smoldered. No one dismissed her. She had come here for a
purpose, and she'd known her task wouldn't be easy. This meeting wasn't
over.

"I know you and Regina were close. It's normal to grieve when something happens to someone you care deeply about. But you have to acknowledge that grief or you will never move past it."

McCarthy spoke over his shoulder, his back still toward her. "I've
reviewed Channing's notes. Do not lecture me about my grief when you
cannot deal with your own."

His comment stabbed into her, slicing into the tender subject of her
inability to move past Gary's death, a grief counselor unable to deal with

her own grief. Pouring salt into the wound, McCarthy added, "The wedding ring you wear is a symbol of your failure."

Lara's rage ignited, and she spotted a half-empty plastic juice bottle on the nightstand by the admiral's bed. She grabbed the bottle, then flung it toward him.

The juice bottle flew over McCarthy's left shoulder, smacking against the wall before clattering onto the floor. Even more infuriating, McCarthy ignored her assault, typing away on the keyboard as if nothing had happened.

That bastard. She had come here to help him, and he had responded by attacking her where she was most vulnerable.

However, her vision of McCarthy holding Regina in his arms had told Lara what she needed to know. She now knew what McCarthy was hiding and how to break through his emotional barrier. Throwing caution to the wind, she went for McCarthy's emotional jugular.

"I might be a failure, but so are you. *You* are responsible for Regina's death."

McCarthy swiveled toward her, and Lara felt and even heard a sharp crack. Emotion surged across the room toward her, like water streaming through fissures in a dam. The emotions were more intense than anything she had felt in ten years of counseling, as if a lifetime of grief, guilt, and rage were breaking through.

McCarthy advanced toward her, his face twisting with anger, and she suddenly realized her peril. McCarthy was over six feet tall, two hundred pounds. Muscular. The cracks in the dam were widening, emotion surging through. When the dam broke, there was no telling what he would do.

She backed up as he approached, stopping when she could retreat no farther, her back hitting the wall. He stopped a foot away. His hands were clenched into fists, the muscles in his neck straining. The heat from his body was suffocating—the dam restraining his emotions, crumbling.

Lara was about to scream for help when the intense heat extinguished. But although the emotions were gone, McCarthy stared at her with cold, hardened eyes, and she felt a chill run down her spine. When he spoke, his voice was low and menacing.

"*Leave.*"

Lara slid away from him, her back against the wall until she was out of arm's reach, then she ran to the door, bursting into the passageway. The nurse at her station looked up as Lara pulled to a halt. Her heart was pounding, her breathing rapid and shallow. She turned back to the admiral's room to verify he hadn't followed her, then placed her hands on her knees and caught her breath.

18

Angeline and Channing turned toward the door as Lara entered the conference room, arriving fifteen minutes late, having gotten lost along the way from Admiral McCarthy's room.

Channing looked up with a disapproving frown. "Where have you been?"

Lara took her seat, outwardly calm but still shaken from her encounter with McCarthy.

"I stopped by Admiral McCarthy's room this morning."

Channing and Angeline exchanged glances as Lara explained the plan she had concocted to help McCarthy deal with Regina's death and how it had backfired. Channing took notes in his tablet as she described the encounter, stopping when Lara mentioned she had lost her temper, throwing a juice bottle at the admiral. Channing said nothing, but Lara saw the concern in his eyes before he looked down and added a few more notes. Given Channing's direction to refrain from using her Touch, Lara skipped the part about looking into McCarthy's mind. However, Channing appeared to pick up on it.

"How did you know McCarthy felt guilty for Regina's death?"

"I've been a counselor for ten years," Lara replied quickly. "It's easy to detect guilt."

Channing replied, "It may be easy to detect the emotion, but not easy to determine the reason for it."

"It's easy for me. It's one of my talents you don't seem interested in."

Channing studied her for a moment before speaking again. "I told you not to use your Touch. If there is one thing you must learn as a Nexus, it is to obey your superiors." He looked down at his tablet again as he entered another comment. "Others are not as lenient as I am, and I cannot protect you."

Finally, Channing finished his notes and looked up. "Visiting Admiral McCarthy this morning was unwise. Given his position on accepting a new guide, I fear you've made the situation worse."

Lara agreed, concluding she had destroyed whatever chance they had of changing his mind. Still, there was a silver lining to it all. Perhaps, once the Nexus House realized she would not become McCarthy's guide, they would send her to Earth. Despite the heartaches involved, her task as a hospital counselor was far more appealing.

Channing seemed to read her mind. "You cannot leave. Once you are inducted into the Nexus House, you are a Nexus for life, subject to the assignments of The One."

Lara was taken aback. "I don't recall signing a contract to join this cult of yours, nor was there any *induction*."

"The normal process has been perturbed," Channing replied, "due to the urgent requirement for your service. Still, you have been tasked to the Nexus House, and not even the Colonial Council can extract you. You are a Nexus now, and when we have time, you will learn about the House, our role protecting humanity from evil, and what the future holds for you."

"Evil?"

"You don't need to worry about that now. Besides, what is evil is subjective, dependent on your point of view."

There was concern in his eyes before he looked down at the message he had drafted on

his tablet, then hit *Send*.

19

The Nexus One strode down the long corridor, rereading the message from Channing on her wristlet. At the end of the passageway, Rhea Sidener entered the Tanum complex, carved from the mountain rock at the end of the south wing of Domus Praesidium. She avoided Tanum—it had been years since she stepped inside the facility where the House trained its personnel for combat. In her youth, the sprawling complex was packed with level-nine praetorians, training around the clock with weapons and honing the important hand-to-hand skills required to defend the House from assault. But now, Tanum stood eerily quiet, only a dozen students working with Ronan, the vast emptiness a painful reminder of her decision to follow the Colonial Council's edict to push all excess Nines to the Test. How many had she lost? The names were too many to count, their faces a blurred mosaic.

Rhea entered one of Tanum's combat arenas, the blue padding on the walls and floors cushioning the impact of moves not properly executed. Twelve teenage students, all at level nine, were assembled in a line facing Ronan, their complexions flush from exertion, perspiration dotting their faces and dampening their uniforms. They caught their breath as they listened to Ronan explain the finer points of Letalis-Tutela, the deadly House martial arts.

Ronan turned to The One as she approached.

She held her arm out to Ronan so he could read her wristlet. "Message from Channing. The situation is more serious than I expected. McCarthy is behaving erratically, at a time we can ill afford it, and there are new concerns about his guide."

Ronan scrolled through the message. "McCarthy is defying you in front of Channing and Angeline. You cannot let this stand."

"I'm aware of that," Rhea replied, dropping her arm.

"As distasteful as it is, you know what you must do."

Rhea didn't reply, evaluating Ronan's assertion.

Ronan added, "And I warned you about this woman. She has the Touch and is an emotional tinderbox. By training her, you're playing with fire. There is only one solution."

Rhea remained quiet, contemplating her options.

After there was no response from The One, Ronan returned to training the new praetorian candidates, and The One's attention was drawn to Siella, called forward for her turn in hand-to-hand combat. Siella was an off-worlder, unusually slender and frail for a Persean. Due to the stronger gravity, Perseans were normally stocky and muscular, but Siella had inherited recessive Terran genes. Her failure to become a guide had eliminated one possible future, and Ronan's reports had not been favorable concerning her potential as a praetorian.

There were other uses for Nines, of course, but all in excess of the minimum requirement would be pushed to the Test, regardless of the probability of passing. Rhea sensed enormous talent in Siella and had delayed her Test, recycling her in the next class of Nines, hoping to find a worthwhile use for her. But the viable options were narrowing.

When Ronan selected Siella's opponent, Rhea scanned the other Nines, her eyes coming to rest on Brandon Dargel. He was the most physically capable of the new Nines, his combat proficiency already surpassing the level of most of his instructors. However, the comments Ronan had entered in his file were unsettling. Dargel was keenly proud of his prowess, showing disdain for those less capable. If he didn't mature and his pride didn't temper, he would be unfit as a praetorian and would most assuredly fail the

Test, becoming yet another Lost One, his mind trapped in an alternate reality.

When Siella's opponent, the next weakest Nine aside from Siella, stepped forward, The One intervened. "No," she said, waving the young man back, then pointed to the tallest, most muscular teenager. "Dargel."

"Me?" Dargel pointed to himself. "Against Siella? You've got to be kidding."

Ronan interjected sternly. "Do as you're told!"

Dargel stepped forward, then faced Siella. The One didn't need to sense Siella's fear—it was evident on her face. She raised her hands to the defensive position and set her stance, one foot ahead of the other, bracing for Dargel's assault.

It was over in less than twenty seconds, ending with Siella sprawled on her back, clutching her chest in pain as Dargel stood proudly over her. Siella pushed herself slowly to her feet, shame and embarrassment on her face as her eyes shifted between The One and Dargel.

As Dargel moved back toward the line of Nines, The One said, "Again."

Dargel returned to a position in front of Siella, who resumed her defensive posture. Dargel didn't even bother to set himself for combat. He moved swiftly, and this time it was over in fifteen seconds, leaving Siella writhing on the floor, the wind knocked out of her, struggling to catch her breath. Dargel stood over her, glaring at his opponent.

"If you know what's good for you," he said. "Stay down."

Siella ignored him, and as her gasps for air subsided, she pushed herself to her feet again, a defiant look on her face. She raised her hands in front of her and set her feet. Dargel turned to The One.

"Again."

Dargel spun instantly, connecting with a solid thrust to Siella's ribs, and The One heard bones crack. Siella stumbled backward, falling to one knee and wincing in pain as she wrapped one arm around her ribs, her other arm still raised in front of her. Dargel advanced toward her.

"Enough," The One said as she stepped forward, stopping in front of Dargel. She looked up at the taller man. "You choose to humiliate your opponent rather than teach her. Why do you not use your skill in a productive manner?"

"Siella is inept. She doesn't have the build or aptitude." He chose not to filter his disdain for the less capable Nine. "It would be a waste of my time."

The One glanced at Siella, who was being helped to her feet by two other Nines. She turned back to Dargel. It was time to teach him an unforgettable lesson. One that would hopefully assist in developing the humility he required to faithfully serve the House.

"Like Siella," The One replied, "I am slender and frail. Perhaps you'd like to test your ability against me."

"You?" Dargel asked, his eyes surveying the small, almost fifty-year-old woman standing before him. He looked to Ronan, wondering if The One was serious.

"If you think you can defend yourself," Ronan said, "accept her challenge. Of course, if you are afraid, that would be understandable."

"I am not afraid," Dargel said quickly.

Ronan replied, "You *should* be."

"What if I accidentally hurt her?"

"It will not be held against you," Ronan answered. "You will not be punished."

Dargel turned back to The One, and his features hardened. Raising his hands in front of him, he set himself in a defensive posture. He had never seen The One in close combat, and he would evaluate her techniques before going on the offensive.

The One began walking in a slow circle around Dargel, his body tensed for action as he turned to face her. The One slid her hands into the sleeves of her robe but made no other gestures, gave no indication she was preparing to assault the young Nine.

"Your lack of insight is alarming," she said.

Dargel didn't reply, instead remaining focused on his opponent, waiting for her to attack.

The One continued, "You prepare for physical combat, not recognizing the true danger." Her eyes hardened as she added, "Not realizing that a mere thought could *freeze* you in place."

There was a hollowness to her voice as she spoke, and Dargel froze. He stood motionless, as still as a statue. Had his muscles been able to obey his mind's commands, his eyes would have widened in surprise.

The One stopped in front of him. "And now, as you attempt to breathe, you realize it's the muscles attached to your ribs that make it possible, pulling the bones outward to expand your lungs, drawing fresh air into your body. You realize that now, unable to breathe, you will be dead in a few minutes."

As The One stood patiently before him, she noticed the terror in his eyes as his skin slowly turned a blue tint, his mind and body screaming for oxygen that was being depleted from his blood. The other Nines cast furtive glances between themselves and at The One and Dargel, wondering what she had done to him and if she would actually let him suffocate to death.

After a long moment, The One spoke again, lowering her voice so that only Dargel could hear. "Humility is a wondrous virtue. One you must master."

She turned and headed toward the exit as Dargel collapsed onto the floor, gasping for air, sucking in huge gulps.

As The One passed by Ronan, she said, "Prepare my shuttle and guard. I depart for *Mercy* in thirty minutes."

20

Sitting across from Channing and Angeline in the small conference room, Lara cleared her mind and tried again. Her training had begun this morning, and with Channing and Angeline's help, Lara was attempting to force a premonition to appear on command. Any type would do for now, and they would then focus on forcing a specific type, depending on what she was predisposed to. Once they had sufficient visions, they would create the Rosetta Stone to allow a quick and accurate interpretation of each premonition.

So far, the results had not been promising. Channing kept offering suggestions, tricks of the trade that triggered premonitions, but nothing worked consistently. Like the visions she had experienced throughout her life, the few premonitions she'd had so far today were random, with no common thread other than the cold fog that was always, and eerily, present. When pressed for a reason a cold fog would permeate her visions, Lara had no answer.

Channing's wristlet vibrated, and a message appeared. As Channing read the message, concern formed on his face. His emotions were normally subdued, but Lara sensed a flare of anxiety. He showed Angeline his wristlet. As she read the message, the color drained from her face, and Lara was buffeted by a swirl of emotions. Angeline looked up and closed her eyes for a moment. When she opened them, her face seemed to pale even further, and one emotion burned stronger than the others.

Fear.

"What's going on?" Lara asked.

Angeline turned to Channing, glancing at Lara in the process. "I don't see her."

Channing looked at her pensively for a moment, then replied, "The future is not set. Prepare her for The One's arrival. I will inform Admiral Reynolds."

Angeline led Lara through *Mercy*'s passageways toward berthing, with Lara hustling to keep up. When they entered Lara's room, Angeline rummaged through Lara's closet, extracting the two blue robes that had been folded on the corner of Lara's bed when she arrived aboard *Mercy*. She tossed one to Lara.

"Put this on."

Lara donned the robe while Angeline, who was about Lara's size, slipped into the second. As her hand came through one of the sleeves, she checked her wristlet, then took a deep breath. Her breathing slowed and her churning emotions subsided, leaving a simmering residue of fear.

"What are you so afraid of?" Lara asked.

"The One is on her way here." As Angeline spoke, her fear spiked.

"Why are you so afraid of her?"

"I am not afraid of her."

"Then why do I sense fear?"

"The One is coming here to assess you."

"So? What's the worst that can happen? She'll realize I'm not the right person for this job and send me on my way."

"You don't understand," Angeline said.

"Then explain it to me," Lara replied, her irritation rising.

"*That,*" Angeline said as she pointed at Lara, "is what is wrong. You must control your emotions."

"Why is it so important to control my emotions?"

"Emotion is the source of all evil," Angeline replied, as if reciting a mantra. "For you to have any chance..." Her voice trailed off.

"Chance at what?"

Angeline placed her hands on Lara's shoulders, pushing her down onto the edge of her bed. "You have the Touch," she said, as if that explained everything.

When Lara looked at her with a blank stare, Angeline continued, "Our mortal enemies, the Corvads, all had the Touch." Angeline paused, then added, "It has been House policy for three thousand years to terminate all who have the Touch."

"Terminate? As in—"

"Yes. The One has broken precedent by letting you live. There is no doubt that the Primus Nine is displeased with her decision and is pressing her to reassess. Before we left the conference room, I had a vision of Channing and me in *Mercy*'s spaceport as The One departed. You were not there."

"So?"

There was a pained expression on Angeline's face, as if even a child should have understood. "If you were still alive, you would be with Channing and me when The One departed."

Lara pulled back. "Are you saying she's going to kill me?"

"I don't think she's decided yet. But she's coming here to make that decision."

"This is absurd," Lara said as she stood.

Angeline pushed her back down.

"You must control your emotions. The One knows you have the Touch, but what's not in your record is your emotional profile. Channing's reports have likely raised some concerns, and if The One concludes you cannot learn to control your impulses and emotions, she will terminate you."

Lara stood up again, this time deflecting Angeline's attempt to push her back down. "I'll tell you why you don't see me in your vision when your One departs. Because I'm not going to be there. I'm getting off this carnival ride, catching the next shuttle to Earth."

She pushed past Angeline, then pulled her duffel bag from the closet and tossed it on the bed. As she began throwing her clothes inside, Angeline grabbed Lara's arm.

"Don't be foolish! No one can hide from The One."

Lara wrenched her arm from Angeline's grasp and entered the bathroom, returning a moment later with an armful of personal items, dumping them into the duffel bag. Angeline grabbed her again.

When Lara tried to pull from her grasp, Angeline wrapped her arms around her. "Calm down! You're not thinking rationally."

Lara strained against Angeline's hold but couldn't break free. She reacted in a reflex action, ducking and twisting toward Angeline, sliding under her arms. Lara stood quickly and shoved her right hand forward, hitting Angeline in the center of her chest, knocking the Nexus guide backward onto the bed. As Angeline pushed herself to her feet, Lara spotted the clock on her nightstand. She grabbed it and swung toward Angeline, smashing it into the side of her face. The Nexus guide cried out as she fell onto the bed again.

Grabbing her duffel bag, Lara rushed from her room into the passageway, evaluating what to do next. Telling Angeline she was taking the next shuttle to Earth was one thing; how to actually accomplish it was another.

Hoping Captain Townsend would help her, she hurried to his door and pounded on it with her fist. There was no answer. As Lara kept banging, Angeline burst into the passageway, a red welt on the side of her face. Behind her, Channing moved swiftly down the corridor toward them. The berthing passageway behind Lara was a dead end. She would have to make it past both Nexi.

Channing and Angeline stopped a few feet from Lara. As she contemplated her next move, Channing said, "If you want to live, do exactly as I say."

A few minutes later, Lara was standing in *Mercy*'s spaceport between Channing and Angeline, with each Nexus having a firm grasp on one arm, while to her right, Admiral Reynolds stood, accompanied by several Medical Corps captains. During Lara's transit to the spaceport, Channing had explained that her fate would depend on The One's assessment of her propensity to *turn*. Even though the Corvads had been eliminated, the House would not let one of their own turn into a renegade.

Following Channing's advice, Lara tried to calm herself, preparing to display no reaction to anything The One said or did once she arrived. Respond if spoken to, but disengage emotionally to the greatest extent possible.

No anxiety. No fear. No anger.

To clear her mind, Lara focused on what was happening in *Mercy*'s busy spaceport, which ran the entire circumference of the ship's middle level, separated into several dozen bays. The outer hull of each bay was perforated with several access openings, with each spaceport bay protected from the void of space by shimmering force fields across its openings, through which the space shuttles passed. Several shuttles arrived and departed as they waited, until a sleek blue-and-white ship passed through the nearest opening and approached the landing pad where they stood. The shuttle slowed to a hover, then settled onto *Mercy*'s deck.

As the engines wound down, a door in the side of the shuttle slid open. Channing and Angeline released their hold on Lara, sliding their hands into the sleeves of their robes. Lara did the same as five robed figures emerged from the shuttle. The individual in the lead was a slender woman, late forties, with silver hair woven into a circular braid behind her head. She stopped shortly after setting foot on *Mercy*'s deck, and four men took position behind her, forming a human phalanx. The One's eyes moved across the Nexi and military personnel assembled for her arrival, then settled on Lara. Each of the four men accompanying The One also focused on Lara, oblivious to all others. Lara did her best to quell her rising fear.

Admiral Reynolds stepped forward, introducing himself to the Nexus One. After the perfunctory greetings, he stepped aside as The One and her guard moved forward, stopping before Lara. The temperature of the spaceport seemed to drop as The One scrutinized her, goose bumps forming on Lara's skin.

A perplexed expression appeared on The One's face. Turning to Angeline, she noticed the red welt on her cheek. She reached up and touched the mark. After a few seconds, a disapproving frown appeared on The One's face.

She dropped her hand as she said to Channing, "Bring Lara to me when I am finished with McCarthy."

The One headed toward the nearest spaceport exit, accompanied by her guard.

When Admiral Reynolds offered to escort her, The One replied, "Thank you, Admiral, but I can find my way."

21

The One and her four praetorians passed the nurse's station, and when they reached the end of the corridor, she flashed a hand signal. The four men trailing her halted. She continued on, entering Admiral Jon McCarthy's room without knocking. The admiral was conferring with a Fleet captain while two other captains worked at their desks in the converted four-patient hospital room.

McCarthy eyed the robed figure as she stopped by the door, then said to the officers, "Leave us."

The captains departed while McCarthy retreated to the back of the hospital room, turning to gaze through the window at the starships in 1st Fleet. The One moved forward and stopped beside him, likewise examining the white warships resting in space.

After a moment, The One spoke. "It's been a long time."

"Not long enough," McCarthy replied, still looking out the window. When The One did not respond, McCarthy asked, "Why are you here?"

"You know damn well why I'm here."

"Where The One is involved, it is difficult to predict the outcome or her reasoning. Enlighten me."

The One turned toward McCarthy. "I see you haven't changed."

"I do as I have been tasked. Is that not enough?" He faced The One.

"It is a beginning." After a short pause, The One continued, "I'm here for two reasons. The first is to discuss your interactions with Channing and the other Nexi."

"The new guide you sent is untrained," McCarthy replied. "She'll be nothing but a distraction during battle."

"I don't care whether you accept your new guide. That is for you and Fleet Admiral Fitzgerald to decide. I'm here for another reason. Your inability to manage your emotions threatens us all."

"My emotions are well contained."

"Containing them is not enough. There is no place in your life for emotion. You should have learned that after what happened while you were in command of the Normandy battle group."

"I learned my lesson."

"You did not," Rhea replied. "You stand beside me infected with emotion, unable to let go of resentment almost twenty years old. Regina's death has compounded the unresolved issue between us."

"You're right," McCarthy said. "And it will never be resolved, because Nexi are nothing more than commodities to you, to be discarded if defective or used to fill an order if not."

"You oversimplify the situation and my responsibility."

"Do I? You sentenced Elena to death. Is that an oversimplification?"

"I was tasked by the Council to assign one of you to the Army and the other to the Navy. One of you had to go to Darian 3."

"She was *only* sixteen."

"*You* were only sixteen."

"It should have been *me!*"

"We've been through this before," she answered. "It was Elena's decision, not mine."

"No one decides for The One," McCarthy said icily. "It was *your* decision."

There was an uneasy silence between them until The One replied, "You were the one I intended to send to Darian. I told Elena the night before you were to depart. She begged me to send her instead. She pleaded with me, and I acquiesced. The Council directed me to send one of you to Darian, and I complied."

"Sending her to Darian 3 was a death sentence, and you knew it. You should have sent me and spared Elena."

"Elena was convinced that you were destined for greater things. It's difficult to see accurately so far into the future, but Elena said she had seen it. I decided to trust her view."

"You trusted the view of a sixteen-year-old over your own? Elena lied, and you chose to believe her." McCarthy turned away, looking out into space again. "Nothing is resolved."

"Nothing is resolved," The One replied, "because you refuse to accept your guilt. Your new guide, despite her lack of training, discerned in a few minutes what evaded me for eighteen years. Elena is dead not because of me, but because of you."

McCarthy turned slowly toward The One as she continued, "Just as you realize Regina is dead because of your failure at Ritalis, Elena is dead because she cared enough for you to sacrifice herself. She's dead because of you, not me. You know this, yet you refuse to accept it."

McCarthy hesitated, processing The One's assertion. He replied, his voice faltering. "You had the power to save her."

"You're correct, Jon. And I did not. That is why I'm here. This issue has poisoned our relationship, and it's time I did something I should have done long ago." There was a strained silence until she finally spoke again.

"I'm sorry."

She added, "My apology is long overdue, as is your acceptance of your culpability. You, as well as I, are responsible for the loss of many. But while you are culpable, you should feel no guilt. You understand that as a fleet admiral, unaffected by the death of thousands in a single hour, yet you cannot move past the loss of one. Elena and Regina are no different than the faceless men and women you sentenced to death each battle."

After a long moment, McCarthy nodded. "You are correct. I will address this and be ready by the time the Korilians arrive. My mind will be clear."

The One extended her hand. "The future is not set."

McCarthy examined her outstretched hand. Slowly, he reached toward her, and they grasped each other's forearm. "Together," he said, "we will change it."

"Which gets me to the second reason I traveled to *Mercy*," The One said as she released McCarthy's arm. "I came to evaluate your new guide, and she is even more unusual than I expected. Channing and Angeline would not have noticed, but it would have been obvious to you. Why did you not tell me she has no timeline into the future?"

"I found it intriguing," McCarthy replied. "Why would the absence of a timeline warrant contacting The One?"

"Because every living thing has a line. Without one, she cannot exist. How is that possible?"

McCarthy shrugged. "I leave that to you to figure out."

The One replied, "It will soon be irrelevant. This woman has the Touch and is unable to control her emotions. Combined with enormous talent and no line to follow, I have to agree with Ronan. She's too much of a risk and must be terminated."

"You'll attend to the matter personally?"

"I will. In a few minutes."

The One pulled the hood over her head. As she prepared to leave, McCarthy said, "You cannot kill her."

She pushed her hood back. "Why not?"

"I require a replacement guide. Unless there is someone else to send me, she will have to do."

"As you pointed out," Rhea said, "she's untrained and will be of no assistance. Letting her live is not worth the risk."

"It is," McCarthy replied. "Although she will be of little use to me, she will fill an important role. If we engage in battle without a guide, the confidence of my fleet will be affected."

The One countered, "Anyone wearing a blue robe and Nexus uniform can stand on the bridge of your command ship and instill confidence. I will send you another Nexus."

"You said Lara had immense talent. Perhaps she will be of assistance after all, and be the difference between victory and defeat. You cannot follow her line, so you cannot foresee her impact."

"Why the sudden interest in this woman?"

McCarthy shrugged. "Maybe I'd like to save her life, when I failed to save Regina's."

The One didn't respond as she evaluated his words. McCarthy pressed the matter. "I'm asking you to let her live for only a few weeks. If we lose the battle against the Korilians, it will not matter. If we win, you can reassess the situation afterward."

The One pulled the hood over her head again. As she turned and headed for the door, she said, "I will take your *request* into consideration."

22

In the small conference room where she had spent the last two days with Channing and Angeline, Lara awaited word that The One was ready to see her. Angeline sat across from her, periodically closing her eyes, forcing premonitions to appear. However, there was no indication that she had discerned Lara's fate. Channing and Angeline had not spoken since they left *Mercy*'s spaceport, and the silence in the room weighed heavily on Lara as Channing responded to a message on his wristlet. He looked up, eyeing her, but didn't speak or take action. A few minutes later, another message arrived, and after responding, he stood without a word, as did Angeline.

Channing and Angeline stopped at the conference room door, where they both turned to Lara, waiting for her to join them. Prior to The One's arrival, Channing had convinced her that an attempt to flee would seal her fate; the only hope of survival was to undergo The One's scrutiny. Whether The One had completed her assessment in the spaceport or required additional time, Lara didn't know. As Channing and Angeline waited patiently at the door, Lara reluctantly concluded she had no viable alternative. She pushed back from the table and joined them.

Channing led the way through *Mercy*'s passageways, up to the highest level, approaching the entrance to another conference room, where two of The One's praetorians were posted outside. Unlike in the spaceport, the men ignored Lara as she approached, but they followed closely behind as the doors whisked open and Channing led them inside.

Across the large conference room, The One stood beside a large window looking out into space, with Earth encompassing almost the entire view, along with one of the eight immense starship construction yards looming directly ahead. The One turned as Channing, Angeline, and Lara pulled to a stop.

The two other praetorians were just inside the room, and the four men joined The One as she moved toward Lara. The One, flanked by two praetorians on each side, stopped before her. The One said nothing as she stared at Lara, and there was a sudden chill in the room. Lara tried to assess the situation, but The One's face was expressionless. Lara felt Angeline's anxiety slowly climb, while from Channing she sensed subdued resignation.

As the temperature of the room plummeted, Lara's muscles stiffened, and she had trouble breathing. She tried to step away from The One but couldn't move. Her muscles were unresponsive.

When Channing noticed her labored breathing, he spoke to The One. "Lara's reference to The Five should be resolved before permanent action is taken."

The One turned to Channing, then after a short moment, Lara's muscles relaxed, and she sucked in a deep breath.

With her eyes still on Channing, The One finally spoke. "Change your strategy. Our time is short, and she will not learn to control her emotions in the time available. Let her harness them, if she is so inclined."

"That will only compound the issue," Channing replied.

"Her effectiveness during the battle is what matters. Any negative impact on her is irrelevant. I will reassess afterward and take any negative progress into consideration."

"Yes, One," Channing replied.

The One turned to Lara and smiled, but Lara felt no warmth.

"Welcome to the Nexus House," The One said.

She headed toward the conference room exit, the praetorians joining her as she left. As the doors slid shut behind them, Lara almost collapsed from relief. Angeline steadied her with an arm around her waist.

Lara turned to Channing. "Thank you."

Channing replied, "You should thank Admiral McCarthy. He messaged me after his meeting with The One, asking me to do what I could to save your life."

Lara paused to absorb McCarthy's unexpected request, then asked, "Why did he do that?"

"You'll have to ask him," Channing replied. "You'll have plenty of opportunities, though. He has accepted you as his new guide."

23

"Wake up, Lara!"

"Wake up, Lara!"

Lara silenced the alarm clock on her nightstand, then stretched beneath the sheets. As she stared at the ceiling in the darkness, she contemplated her schedule for the day; she had awakened an hour earlier than required to accommodate another unscheduled visit with Admiral McCarthy. He had saved her life, intervening with the Nexus One, and as much as she dreaded meeting with him again, a thank-you was due. She had tried to see him yesterday after The One left, but McCarthy was busy, and she had been turned away by his aide. Perhaps she could catch him first thing in the morning. Lara slid from the bed and headed into the bathroom.

Twenty minutes later, she was dressed in her Nexus jumpsuit, striding down *Mercy*'s passageways. As she made her way toward McCarthy's ward, her trepidation mounted. Their last meeting had not ended well. Her mind swirled with possible ways to begin their conversation, along with the multiple ways McCarthy might respond. The journey through *Mercy*'s corridors passed quickly, and she soon arrived at the nurse's station in the admiral's ward.

"I'd like to meet with Admiral McCarthy," Lara said to the nurse, hoping he was already awake.

The nurse replied, "Admiral McCarthy is no longer in the ward. He received his medical clearance last night and returned to his command ship."

McCarthy's room was selected on the nurse's monitor; the desks had been replaced with beds, returning it to a four-patient configuration, leaving no evidence McCarthy had been aboard.

Without a meeting with McCarthy this morning, Lara arrived early at the conference room to resume her Nexus training. Both Channing and Angeline arrived on time, settling into their chairs across from Lara. Her training resumed, with Channing guiding Lara through mental exercises intended to enhance her ability to force premonitions to appear. After several hours, they took their first break. Lara slumped into her chair, exhausted.

Channing spent the break perusing messages on his wristlet. With Channing preoccupied, Lara turned to Angeline. "Who are the five?"

Angeline answered, "The Nexus House is not always ruled by one person. When it is, he or she is referred to as The One. When two rule, they are called The Two, and so on. There was one time in the history of the House when we were ruled by five masters. They were The Five."

"Why are The Five so important?"

"Because their wisdom is unparalleled. Unfortunately, much of that knowledge, recorded for future generations, has been lost, and we seek to regain it. That you might have a connection with The Five makes you important. We'll explore that relationship when we have time."

Lara was about to inquire further when Angeline added, "You will learn about House lore later, when you study with the Sevens."

Channing scrolled through another message on his wristlet, then looked up. "Change in plans. Admiral McCarthy has directed us to continue our training aboard his command ship, where we'll have access to a battle simulator. A shuttle will transfer us from *Mercy* to the command ship in one hour. Pack up and meet me in the spaceport, bay twenty-one."

An hour later, Lara stood between Channing and Angeline in *Mercy*'s spaceport, duffel bag in hand, as a shuttle passed through the bay's shimmering life-support shield. After the shuttle touched down, a door slid open, and a Fleet officer emerged. Greetings were exchanged, then Lieutenant Commander Bryn Greenwood ushered the three Nexi aboard a small, six-person shuttle, which rose from the spaceport deck and headed toward the exit.

As they passed through the life-support shield, Lara felt lighter, and she realized they were beyond the influence of *Mercy*'s gravity generators. She peered through the cockpit window, watching the shuttle head toward one of the repair yards, where the 1st Fleet command ship was docked. Channing explained what had happened at Ritalis—the Korilian attack on the command ship—and that its bridge and bow shield generator were being repaired. The repair yard, a small speck in the distance orbiting Earth, grew steadily larger until it filled the entire cockpit window. Unlike the construction yards, which were long and thin—ten parallel assembly lines stretching miles into the distance—the repair yard was a flat circular hub with dozens of starships docked along its perimeter, each ship inside a repair bay.

The shuttle passed through a life-support shield into the bay containing the 1st Fleet command ship, then into the command ship's spaceport, where gravity returned to normal. After the shuttle settled onto the spaceport deck, the door slid open. As the three Nexi emerged, they were greeted by a Fleet captain and his aide.

"I'm Captain Altair Priebus, commanding officer of *Lider*, the First Fleet command ship. Lieutenant Commander Greenwood will show you to berthing, then escort Miss Anderson to the admiral's quarters."

Channing asked, "Lara only?"

"Yes," Captain Priebus replied. "Admiral McCarthy wants to talk with Lara privately."

Channing and Angeline exchanged curious looks but did not question Priebus further.

Priebus and his aide departed, and Greenwood escorted the three Nexi to their quarters. As Lara wondered how spacious her berthing would be, Greenwood stopped along a corridor and opened the door to a small eight-by-six-foot room containing a narrow bed and a small desk. With a chair occupying almost half the floor space, there was barely enough room to stand and dress. Greenwood informed Lara there was a bathroom down the corridor, then showed Channing and Angeline to their rooms, adjacent to Lara's.

Lara tossed her duffel bag onto her bed, then Greenwood escorted her to Admiral McCarthy's quarters on the top deck of the starship, entering a small outer office with an adjacent conference room. Greenwood departed, leaving Lara in the care of Commander Howard Cortland, who rose from his desk and introduced himself as McCarthy's executive assistant.

"Admiral McCarthy will be here shortly. You may wait in his quarters." Cortland gestured toward the door.

Lara took a deep breath and let it out slowly. The last time she had seen McCarthy, he'd been standing a foot away from her, his eyes glaring with fury. It would not be long now before she stood face-to-face with him again.

She stepped slowly forward, and the door whisked open.

24

Lara stopped inside McCarthy's quarters, examining her surroundings as the door slid shut behind her. To her left was a twin-sized bed, neatly made up, and to her right was a desk built into the bulkhead. Not far away was a small round table and two contour-chairs. Lara headed toward the table, settling into one of the plush chairs, which automatically adjusted to the contours of her body. While she waited for McCarthy to arrive, she noticed a small videograph display built into the bulkhead above McCarthy's desk. It cycled through several dozen videographs, displaying each one for a few seconds. When it returned to the first video and made a second run, Lara's attention was drawn to four of the short clips. Turning her chair toward the desk, she waited for the pertinent ones to reappear.

The first was a video of a teenage blonde wearing an Army green-and-olive uniform. What was unusual was that she was an officer—a second lieutenant—at such a young age. Although the Army had been forced to enlist recruits as young as sixteen over the last few years due to severe losses during the war, officers were at least twenty-two years old before earning their commission.

The young woman was standing by a troop transport as soldiers in combat gear boarded in two columns. Her hair fluttered in the brisk breeze ahead of an advancing storm; dark, cumulous clouds were approaching in the distance. But what caught Lara's attention the most were her eyes. She could feel the emotion from across the room: emerald-green eyes filled with sadness, as if she had seen a future containing nothing but despair.

The blonde Army officer faded, replaced with a shoulder-and-head image of a woman wearing the crimson-and-burgundy Fleet uniform—a commander. She was a beautiful brunette, early thirties, and in contrast to the blonde, she was smiling. She lifted her left hand to display a diamond engagement ring, and Lara sensed her excitement and pride, with the sparkle in the woman's eyes matching that of the diamond.

The next videograph was one of Admiral McCarthy standing beside a female Nexus Eight on a damaged starship bridge, each with an arm around the other. Their faces and uniforms were smeared with black soot as equipment around them smoldered. There was no expression on McCarthy's face, but the Eight, who Lara surmised was Regina, was smiling as she pulled McCarthy close.

The fourth videograph contained a man and woman standing beside each other, with the woman holding an infant in her arms. The man, who looked strikingly like Admiral McCarthy, wore the old red uniform of the Space Exploration Corps, which had been transformed into the Colonial Navy at the outbreak of the Korilian War. The woman wore a flowing micromesh dress common to the inhabitants of the planet Polermis. Lara assumed the couple was McCarthy's parents, and for some reason she took comfort in knowing he was an off-worlder like her.

The door to McCarthy's quarters opened, and the admiral entered. As the door closed behind him, he noticed Lara was facing his desk. He glanced at the videograph display, then tapped his wristlet. The display went dark as Lara rose to greet him.

McCarthy settled into the chair across from her, then said, "Be seated."

Lara took her seat, deciding to let McCarthy speak first and follow his lead. But he said nothing, staring at her instead. His penetrating gaze almost made her squirm. When she could take it no longer, she spoke first.

"Thank you for interceding with the Nexus One and saving my life."

There was no reaction or response from McCarthy, so she continued, "I want to apologize for my behavior yesterday. I had no right to look into your mind and use that information against you. And I certainly shouldn't have thrown that juice bottle at you."

As Lara wondered what McCarthy was thinking, he said sternly, "If we are to work together, there's one thing you must learn." Lara braced herself for what would undoubtedly be harsh words, then he added, "You're going to have to improve your aim."

As she tried to decipher what he meant, McCarthy grinned. His smile was infectious, and she couldn't keep from smiling in return. The ice between them melted away.

Lara said, "I've never been very accurate with my throws."

"Lucky for me," McCarthy replied. His smile faded as he said, "I'm the one who should apologize. I was upset at my failure at Ritalis. My carelessness not only cost Regina her life but jeopardized everything I and countless others have worked toward these last five years. I took my frustration out on you, unfairly."

McCarthy's stiff military bearing relaxed as he extended his hand. "We need to start over. Welcome to First Fleet and assignment as my guide. We'll be working closely together, and when we're alone, you may call me Jon."

Lara shook his hand, and as she looked into his eyes, her thoughts drifted. McCarthy was an attractive man, but his good looks had made little impression on her up to now because he'd been such a jerk. Now that their relationship had turned amicable, she couldn't deny her attraction to him. Tall, muscular, with deep blue eyes that drew her in. After a moment, McCarthy smiled again, and Lara realized she was still holding his hand. She released it and hoped she didn't blush.

McCarthy stood and went to his desk, where he opened a cabinet and withdrew a liquor bottle and two crystal glasses. He poured two drinks and handed one to Lara. "Here's to the start of a rewarding friendship." He tapped his glass against hers, then settled back into his chair.

Lara sniffed the liquor—cognac—then took a sip, her thoughts dwelling on his proposal.

Admiral Jon McCarthy.

Friend.

She liked the sound of that.

As she pondered her newfound friendship, her thoughts turned to his intervention with the Nexus One. "If you don't mind me asking, why did you ask Channing to save me?"

McCarthy answered, "During my discussion with The One, it became clear she intended to kill you. I felt responsible. If it weren't for my failure at Ritalis, you would not have been tasked as my new guide and become subject to scrutiny from the Nexus One."

"Why do you keep referring to your failure at Ritalis? You couldn't have predicted the Korilian suicide attack on your command ship."

McCarthy examined her thoughtfully, then replied, "Because any time you lose something you aren't willing to concede, it's a failure. Losing Regina at Ritalis was one of the worst possible outcomes. Something I was not willing to concede."

Even though Lara didn't sense his grief—McCarthy's ability to control his emotions was remarkable—she felt the pain in his voice. He forced a smile, then added, "But now I have you, and I'm convinced we'll make an excellent team."

Lara didn't share his conviction, but she appreciated his encouraging words.

"I'm not sure how much you know about me," Lara replied, "but I'm not a standard Nexus. I hadn't even heard of them until a few days ago, when I was tasked to become your new guide. I'm still trying to figure things out, and I'm not sure what to make of these Nexus."

"Nexi," McCarthy said. "The plural of Nexus is Nexi."

"Thanks," Lara replied, then continued. "I don't know how much experience you have with them aside from Regina, but I'm worried. Their goal appears noble, helping us defeat the Korilians, yet at the same time, they seem...ruthless."

McCarthy said, "You're quite intuitive, coming to that realization after only a few interactions."

Lara lowered her voice, even though there was no one else in the admiral's quarters. "Do you trust them?"

McCarthy leaned back in his chair. "I do," he answered. "They have humankind's best interest at heart, even though it doesn't appear so at times, and they are ruthless only when it comes to protecting themselves."

"Protecting themselves from what?"

"I'm not the one to address this issue. When this battle is over and you receive standard Nexus training, I'm sure your questions will be answered."

McCarthy's words reassured her. Like Captain Townsend, he believed they could defeat the Korilians, a stark contrast to the despair prevalent on Ritalis. Plus, he seemed comfortable with the Nexi. That was good enough for her.

25

The day after transferring aboard the 1st Fleet command ship, Lara stood beside Admiral McCarthy on *Lider*'s flag bridge, with Channing and Angeline behind them, as they prepared to run through a battle simulation. The equipment damaged during the Korilian attack at Ritalis had been repaired, and with the exception of final adjustments to the bow shield generator, the 1st Fleet command ship was fully operational.

Aside from McCarthy and the three Nexi, the bridge was unmanned except for several technicians running tests on the repaired consoles. However, the bridge appeared crowded, since the simulator had created fifty holograms manning their stations. At this point, the fake crew members were frozen in place, as the battle simulation hadn't yet started. Although there were two command chairs on the bridge—for McCarthy and his guide—Lara and the admiral were standing at a console containing a three-dimensional tactical display.

It was McCarthy's decision, over Channing's objection, to throw Lara into a battle simulation. Lara wasn't ready, Channing insisted. A full-scale battle would overwhelm her. Lara wholeheartedly agreed.

McCarthy announced, "Computer. Prepare battle simulation, Telemantic scenario."

"Admiral," Channing intervened. "I strongly object. Telemantic is a difficult scenario. I don't need to remind you that in fifteen years, only one person has passed."

"I'm well aware of that," McCarthy replied. "However, I need to see how Lara responds in an unpredictable and high-stress scenario."

Channing nodded his understanding, and McCarthy ordered, "Commence simulation."

The fifty holograms came alive, all working busily at their consoles, and the dozen large video displays mounted across the curved front of the bridge energized.

"Freeze simulation," McCarthy ordered, and he turned to Angeline, who moved forward, stopping beside Lara.

Angeline explained the information presented on each display, with several containing strategic information—the status of the entire Colonial Navy as it engaged the Korilian armada—while other displays contained tactical information about their current location and destination. Lara listened as the data came fast and furious, ending with the pertinent information about 1st Fleet. It was preparing to jump to the Telemantic star system, where two Korilian battle groups were attempting to destroy the star fortress complex guarding a hyper-jump hole.

"Continue simulation," McCarthy said.

After the holograms returned to life, the operations officer announced, "Five seconds to the jump."

As the time counted down, the bridge temperature decreased suddenly, and Lara rubbed her arms as a chill went through her body. McCarthy gave her a curious look, then the bridge went dark for a few seconds, simulating the jump interval.

"Shields up!" the shield supervisor announced as the command ship completed the jump.

Lara's gaze shifted from screen to screen, attempting to digest the information. Angeline whispered in her ear, explaining that 1st Fleet was organized in a hollow cylinder attack formation, one of the open ends aimed at the left flank of the Korilian battle groups.

McCarthy ordered 1st Fleet into motion. "Ahead flank, all battle groups."

1st Fleet sliced into the Korilian formation, destroying the Korilian starships trapped within the hollow cylinder. As 1st Fleet exited the other side of the Korilian formation, McCarthy turned to Lara. "Another pass, or flare?"

Lara gave McCarthy a blank stare, and he halted the simulation. Angeline explained the pros and cons of another pass through the Korilian starships using the hollow cylinder formation, versus flaring out to envelop the Korilian battle groups.

She added, "At each critical decision point, Admiral McCarthy will turn to you for guidance in case you've received a premonition that sheds light on which course of action is preferable. Additionally, you can intervene at any time if you perceive danger. If you have no recommendation when queried, just say so."

Having experienced no premonitions thus far, Lara replied, "I have no recommendation."

McCarthy recommenced the simulation and ordered 1st Fleet to conduct a flare maneuver, shifting 1st Fleet starships from a cylinder to a sphere, trapping the Korilian starships inside. The Korilian formation began to contract, making it easier for 1st Fleet to envelop them, which Angeline explained was unexpected.

McCarthy turned to Lara. "Assessment?"

Lara sensed this was a critical moment. Angeline stared at her, and Channing had stopped taking notes, awaiting her response. Lara closed her eyes and recalled Channing's recommendations on how to force premonitions to occur, selecting a scenario he had tailored for her.

She imagined herself standing on a beach, the waves breaking onto the sand. In the distance, a thick white fog rolled quickly ashore. As the white mist approached and was about to touch her face, the fog spread outward, surrounding her in a circular pattern. The sky darkened, revealing bright stars all around her, and she was startled when she noticed the beach was no longer underfoot; just more stars, as if she were floating in space.

Lara spotted the star fortresses to her left, while to her right was the 1st Fleet formation, surrounding the Korilian starships. She was inside a vision that had transported her to the Telemantic sector. As she wondered what information she could glean from her vision, a sphere of fog formed, surrounding the 1st Fleet ships the same way they surrounded the Korilians.

Angeline nudged Lara. "You must respond quickly," she said. "Tell us what you see."

Lara replied, "I see a sphere of fog surrounding First Fleet."

The 1st Fleet flight officer reported, "Admiral, all carriers are ready to launch."

McCarthy glanced at Lara again. Angeline explained the carriers would have to drop their shields to launch their vipers, and 1st Fleet would be committed.

Lara's vision dissipated, so she replied, "I have no recommendation."

McCarthy gave the order, and the fleet's carriers dropped their shields and launched their viper wings. As the last of the vipers spewed forth from the carriers, bright flashes illuminated the darkness through the bridge windows.

Four Korilian battle groups had jumped into the Telemantic system. McCarthy reacted quickly, ordering 1st Fleet to retreat inside the star fortresses' perimeter, while the Korilians enveloped both 1st Fleet and the star fortress complex. Through the command ship bridge windows, a constant barrage of red Korilian and blue Colonial pulses illuminated the darkness as the two opposing fleets battled. The six star fortresses, which had been trading pulses with Korilian starships, went silent for a moment, then opened fire on 1st Fleet.

"Attempt to override!" McCarthy ordered. "Reset all fortresses!"

The operations officer sent the commands, but the star fortresses fired again, destroying another six Colonial ships. The Korilian starships commenced firing as well, and yellow flares lit up *Lider*'s bridge when Korilian pulses impacted the command ship's shields. Six more battleships disintegrated under the star fortress assault, and shields were weakening throughout the fleet as they endured the onslaught.

"To all ships," McCarthy ordered, "prepare for jump."

The orders went out, and a moment later, McCarthy received a report from the operations officer. "The jump drive isn't spinning up, Admiral. Shield interference from the star fortresses is too high."

McCarthy turned to Lara. "Recommendation?"

Lara closed her eyes and imagined herself on the beach again, watching the fog roll in. However, nothing special happened this time; the fog spread up the beach and inland, surrounding her with cool mist.

"We're trapped," McCarthy said. "I need a recommendation!"

Hearing the urgency in his voice, Lara cleared her mind and reset the image, placing herself back on the beach with the fog offshore, heading quickly inland. Again, nothing unusual happened; the fog rolled ashore and enveloped her.

While still in the vision, she heard McCarthy's voice, his request more urgent. "I need a recommendation. Now!"

Lara began to panic. They were at a critical point in the battle, and she was failing miserably. Suddenly, she was teetering on the edge of a bridge crossing what looked like the Nuvian River on the planet Altaria, with a thick layer of fog between the bridge and the rough water. She lost her balance and fell headfirst through the dense fog, plunging into the cold river. She struggled to right herself, then swam toward the surface, but it seemed impossibly far away. Her lungs began to burn, and she swam harder, rising slowly toward the light.

She finally reached the surface and gasped for air. However, instead of being in the turbulent waters of the Nuvian River, she was treading water in the middle of a tranquil lake framed by a white, sandy shore and surrounded by lush green vegetation. A majestic mountain range rose in front of her, behind which was a rare triple-sunset. A blue-white sun was slipping behind one of the jagged mountain peaks while two sister stars hovered a few degrees above and to the right of the setting sun, their yellow and reddish-orange hues illuminating the ripples spreading across the lake's surface in a dazzling spectacle.

As Lara tried to figure out where she was, she spotted a man and woman walking along the shore. She wiped the water from her eyes and took a closer look. They were her and Admiral McCarthy. As they walked along the sandy shore, she had her shoes in one hand and McCarthy's hand in the other. They approached a trail that began at the edge of the lake, leading up into the dense green vegetation. McCarthy led her onto the path, which wound steadily upward to a pass between two of the towering mountain peaks.

Lara squinted, trying to follow their passage up the trail, and as she concentrated, her vision began to shake, as if she were watching a movie in turbulence. The severity of the shaking increased until the vision was no longer discernable, then it dissolved entirely, leaving her standing on the command ship bridge. As Lara collected her thoughts, she noticed that McCarthy, Angeline, and Channing were staring at her. The battle simulation was continuing, but they were focused solely on her.

Finally, McCarthy spoke. "Terminate simulation."

The fifty crew holograms disappeared, and the bridge displays went black. McCarthy stared at her; she could tell he was assessing something. Meanwhile, Channing's and Angeline's expressions were somber.

"This is most unfortunate," Channing said. "Her latent talent is impressive, but she cannot control it."

"Control what?" Lara asked.

Channing didn't answer. Instead, he spoke to McCarthy. "This complicates things, as if the challenge wasn't great enough to begin with."

McCarthy continued studying her, and Lara sensed disappointment and despair from both Channing and Angeline.

"What's going on?" Lara asked.

McCarthy glanced at the repair yard technicians on the bridge, still running the new equipment consoles through diagnostic tests.

"My stateroom," he directed, then headed aft toward his quarters.

Channing joined him, and Angeline motioned for Lara to follow.

26

Lara and Angeline followed McCarthy and Channing from the flag bridge into the admiral's quarters. As the door slid shut behind them, there was a strained silence in the room. McCarthy leaned back against his desk, facing Lara, while Channing and Angeline stood to the side. McCarthy's eyes were fixed on Lara, but he seemed lost in thought.

McCarthy finally said, "I assume there are no other guide candidates? Not even in the early stages of training?"

"There is one other," Channing replied. "She is a Nine with strong level-eight talent, but The One found her unsuitable. She does not perform well under pressure, and I concur with The One's assessment. Our options are to continue working with Lara, or replace her with a fake guide. I recommend the latter. Engaging the Korilians with Lara on the bridge is perilous."

Lara couldn't follow the conversation. How did she suddenly become perilous? She was about to ask someone to explain when McCarthy replied, "I can work with this. Her first vision was solid. She's not experienced enough to interpret each vision yet, but I can do that for her. Regarding the second vision, she needs to be told. You'll be able to train her more effectively if she knows."

"The directive is clear," Channing said. "Only the Colonial Council and Fleet Admiral Fitzgerald can know."

McCarthy replied, "All Nexi are authorized."

"She was inducted only a few days ago."

"Is she a Nexus or not?"

"She has not been sufficiently indoctrinated."

"Yes or no?" McCarthy asked.

Channing hesitated a moment, then acquiesced. "Yes."

"Then she can be told."

"Told what?" Lara asked.

McCarthy ignored Lara, directing his next question to Channing and Angeline. "What has she been told so far?"

The temperature in the admiral's stateroom dropped suddenly, then he replied, "I see. Lara needs to better understand the higher levels."

As the temperature lowered, goose bumps formed on Lara's skin and she rubbed her arms to warm them. McCarthy cast a curious glance at her, as he had done on the bridge when she got the chills at the beginning of the simulation.

McCarthy looked quickly at Channing, who replied, "I will inquire," then typed a message into his wristlet. McCarthy turned to Lara and gestured her toward the small table and two chairs. "Have a seat."

Lara settled into one of the contour-chairs as the stateroom temperature returned to normal.

Channing spoke next, addressing Lara this time. "I'll expound on what Angeline told you when you arrived on *Mercy*. As she explained, there are ten levels of prescient ability within the Nexus House. The first level is basic intuition, levels two through four pertain to discerning additional information about the present, levels five through seven deal with the past, and those with level-eight through level-ten abilities can perceive the future to varying degrees.

"Angeline and I are Eights. We have occasional glimpses of the future, like looking through a foggy window with small circles of clarity. A Nine's ability is a quantum leap above an Eight's, a clear window into the future. However, a Nine can view the future of only a single prime timeline; he's not omniscient. His view of the future is like listening to the radio. A Nine can hear the radio broadcast clearly, but he can listen to only one frequency at a time. That's why Eights are preferred over Nines as fleet guides. Eights can receive visions of key events about to happen along any timeline. They're not limited to a single prime like a Nine is while viewing.

"Nines are useful in close combat for reasons you'll learn later. However, in battle involving thousands of external decisions, a Nine's view of the future is perilous. Think of the future as a maze, and what a Nine might choose as the optimal path at the first intersection might lead to a dead end and disaster. A Nine cannot see farther down the line and evaluate all the paths. That's what a Ten can do.

"A Ten can look into the future and postulate different actions, each one creating a timeline branching off from the Prime. Each timeline can be followed into the future, postulating additional actions. A Ten's view into the future can be visualized as a tree, with the current future, or prime timeline, being the trunk of the tree, and the alternate futures being the numerous and ever-increasing branches.

"Few have the ability to become Eights, and even fewer become Nines. Those with the ability to achieve level ten are extremely rare; about once a decade someone accomplishes the feat."

Channing paused, then added, "Admiral McCarthy is a Nexus Ten."

Lara was at a momentary loss for words. She finally understood why McCarthy had been so successful in combat.

McCarthy continued where Channing left off. "A Ten's ability is extremely valuable in combat. I can evaluate hundreds of different defense or attack plans, constantly adjusting the tactics to produce the best outcome. Even if there is no way to win the battle, I can minimize our losses while inflicting as much damage as possible before we jump away."

Lara sat at the table in amazement, processing McCarthy's revelation. "If you can see the future, then why haven't we been able to defeat the Korilians?"

"How far I can perceive the future depends on the complexity of the situation and how close I am to the timeline. For battle purposes, I can look about ten minutes into the future."

Ten minutes? She had expected something more grandiose.

"There are some events I can follow years, even decades into the future. But battle is a complicated line to follow, with hundreds of decisions affecting the future every minute. Although ten minutes may not seem like a lot," McCarthy said, seemingly in response to her thoughts, "ten minutes in battle can mean the difference between victory and defeat, between life and death. I can also perceive how the battle will unfold in vague generalities much further, and make critical decisions well before a normal person could.

"My ability has been carefully cultivated for the last eighteen years. At first, I was allowed to participate only in battles we were certain we would win, and then only in the heaviest armed battleship available. Fleet leadership considered me their most valuable asset, and they protected me well as I gained experience. As their confidence in my abilities grew, so did my responsibilities. They also kept my abilities secret, fearing the Korilians would learn of my talent and target me during battle."

Lara asked, "Are there other Nexus Tens in the Fleet or Army?"

McCarthy shook his head. "There are only two Tens remaining in the House. The One and me. There was another, assigned to the Army, but she was killed on Darian 3. It's been eighteen years since the last Nexus achieved level ten, which is a bit unusual. As Channing mentioned, we usually develop one about every decade, so we are overdue for the next one.

"The Council is obsessed with obtaining Tens," McCarthy added, "directing the Nexus House to push all Nines to the Test, whether they are likely to pass or not."

"The Test?"

"You'll learn about that in more detail later. Suffice it to say that if you fail, you go mad, your mind trapped in an alternate reality. They become what we call the Lost Ones. Rhea withholds however many Nines are required to defend the House and perform other required functions, but she has followed the Council's edict otherwise, pushing all Nines in excess to the Test."

"Rhea?"

"The One's name is Rhea. As a Ten, I can talk with her as an equal to some extent and use her first name. However, she is a Placidia Ten, while I am not. Anyone who achieves Placidia Ten status becomes co-ruler of the Nexus House."

"Placidia Ten?"

"A Placidia Ten is someone who can view without creating turbulence, which brings the conversation back to what happened during the battle simulation a few minutes ago.

"When more than one Nexus views the future simultaneously, unless both are Placidia Tens, it creates a disturbance. Think of it as trying to watch two different videos on the same monitor. The two views conflict, creating turbulence, and both views become disrupted. That last vision you had on the bridge was a glimpse of a future timeline. I was viewing at the same time—I view continuously during battle—and our two views created turbulence."

McCarthy leaned forward. "This is why I'm explaining everything to you. You must avoid glimpses of future timelines while you are my guide. General premonitions are okay, but viewing specific events must be avoided."

Lara replied, "I have no idea how to do that. My visions just come to me; I don't know how to control what appears, or even how to determine whether a vision is a general one or is following a timeline."

"I realize that," McCarthy said. "That's why Channing's job just became harder. Under normal circumstances we'd be very excited; your latent talent is impressive, being able to catch glimpses of specific timelines. But you're also a loose cannon right now, as likely to hurt as you are to help. Channing and Angeline will continue working with you, and I'll decide just before the battle begins whether you'll be my guide or I'll take a fake version."

McCarthy looked to Channing, who replied, "I'll inform The One and ensure another Nexus is on standby."

"Finally," McCarthy said, "you cannot reveal my abilities to anyone. Other Nexi know, as well as the Council and Fleet Admiral Fitzgerald. But no one else is authorized. Understand?"

Lara nodded.

"Do you have any more questions?"

Lara was overwhelmed with the revelations, not only about McCarthy's ability, but that *she* could also see into the future. She wondered what she and McCarthy were doing walking along the lakeshore and heading up the steep mountain trail. She debated whether to inquire about her vision, but instead her thoughts went to the beginning of the conversation in his stateroom, when McCarthy had asked Channing and Angeline what they had told her.

"Can you read minds?" she asked. "You asked Channing and Angeline what they had told me, and they informed you without talking."

McCarthy smiled. "No, I can't read minds. What happened is I simply viewed a future in which I continued the conversation and they answered my questions. Once I learned what they told you, there was no need to actually have that conversation."

Lara nodded, starting to gain an appreciation for the extent of McCarthy's power.

"However," McCarthy added, "it's not always that simple. Oftentimes, the conversation must still occur for the benefit of the other person or others in attendance."

Turning to Channing and Angeline, McCarthy added, "There's something else you must know about Lara." He paused, choosing his words carefully. "She has no prime timeline."

Channing's and Angeline's eyes widened. "That's impossible," Channing said.

McCarthy replied, "The One had the same reaction, and I'm sure she's looking into that back at Domus Praesidium. But clearly," he gestured toward Lara, "it's not impossible."

Angeline's eyes widened farther. "That's why I didn't see her in my visions—why I didn't see her in the spaceport when The One departed. Without a line, Lara is invisible in the future?"

"That's correct. I cannot see her in my view." McCarthy turned back to Lara. "Which makes you intriguing. With my ability to foresee the future, imagine how boring it is knowing the answer to every question before the other person responds, or even before I ask them. Imagine how tedious it is knowing how the day will go before I step out of bed each morning."

Lara replied, "But I imagine you're able to pick the perfect birthday gifts."

"There's that," McCarthy said, smiling briefly. "On principle, however, I normally don't view in my personal life. Only during battle or unusual circumstances, like meeting my new guide, which gets me to the final issue I want to discuss. That chill you feel on occasion—you're detecting my view somehow."

Lara recalled the times the room temperature dropped suddenly, and realized each occasion had been in McCarthy's or The One's presence.

McCarthy added, "Only Nines and Tens have the ability to detect when someone is viewing. You have no timeline to follow, plus, without the necessary training, you can detect when someone is viewing." He looked to Channing.

Channing said, "I sent a note, but there's no reply yet."

McCarthy nodded, then turned back to Lara. "Do you have any more questions?"

Lara replied, "If you can see the future, even if it's limited to only ten minutes during battle, how were you surprised by the Korilian dreadnoughts at Ritalis?"

"Trying to predict the future during battle is complicated. There are many timelines to follow, and I failed to check my own frequently enough. There were only a few minutes left in the battle. I got complacent, and it cost Regina her life."

At the mention of Regina, Lara sensed McCarthy's guilt and grief, bleeding through his usually impassive facade.

After a moment, he added, "Normal people often misunderstand the capability of a Ten. Rhea and I are prescient, not omniscient. We don't have thorough and universal knowledge of the future. What we know is obtained by following specific timelines, and there are trillions of timelines to follow; every living thing has one—except you, for some reason. We can evaluate a timeline quickly, but only one line at a time, so our knowledge of the future is very narrow and specific, dependent on which timelines we evaluate.

"I choose which line to follow based on experience. However, while I'm following one line, disaster can befall along another. That's where you come in. Any guidance you can provide during battle that helps focus my attention, choosing which lines to follow, is helpful."

He added, "Do you have any more questions?"

Lara shook her head. She was certain she'd have plenty the moment she left the admiral's stateroom. For now, she was overwhelmed with what she had learned.

27

In the deepest reaches of Domus Praesidium, the Nexus One descended a narrow circular staircase hewn from the hard igneous rock, the white glow from the electronic torch in her hand forcing the darkness to retreat. At the bottom of the long stairway, as Rhea reached the tenth level underground, her torch illuminated a fifteen-foot-diameter antechamber with the stairs on one end and a smooth metal door on the other. Stopping by the door, she placed her torch into a receptacle on the wall, then placed her hand on a palm reader beside the door.

The door slid slowly open, revealing a brightly lit ten-foot-wide passageway, its walls smooth and polished in contradiction to the rough granite walls of the stairway and antechamber. At the far end of the two-hundred-foot-long corridor, three plasma gun turrets, with one turret mounted in the ceiling and one on each side of the passageway, guarded another closed metal door. With three plasma guns, the door was the most heavily defended entrance in the Praesidium. The plasma turrets activated when Rhea entered the corridor, extending from their recessed locations and training their gun sights on her.

As Rhea traversed the passageway, scanners on each side of the corridor examined her silhouette and walking characteristics, comparing them to stored profiles. After a few seconds, the three plasma turrets returned to their dormant positions. Rhea continued down the passageway, her pace quickening as the number of unanswered questions in her mind mounted.

Their new Nexus, Lara Anderson, was quite unusual. With no line to follow into the future, combined with the ability to detect Nexus views, she was an enigma that needed to be explored. Rhea could have gone to Sanctuary and spoken to the holograms of The Three, but the Codex offered a less emotional avenue to the answers she sought. But only if the information she needed resided in the recovered sections of the sacred document.

Five hundred years ago, the Codex had been destroyed during a Corvad attack that breached the Praesidium walls for the only time in three thousand years. The penetration of a Corvad Ten leading half of their Praetorian Legion had been unexpected, superbly hidden from the Nexus views. Once inside the Praesidium, the Corvads gained access to the Nexus computer network and inserted a virus that erased all documents. After infiltrating the north wing where the only paper copy of the Codex was stored, the object of their attack became clear—a suicidal mission sacrificing a Ten and half of their praetorians in an effort to destroy thousands of years of Nexus House wisdom.

It had taken over a century, but the Codex had been rebuilt, some of the knowledge pieced together from remnants of the original, other knowledge reconstituted from excerpts available elsewhere in the House, used for training the various levels. The Sevens had completed the tremendously complex task, and the Codex was once again functional. But there were sections that had not been recovered. Although some of the lost knowledge would be slowly regained over the centuries, the most crucial information would likely be lost forever. Much of the wisdom of The Five had been erased from existence.

Only once in the history of the House had there been five Placidia Tens. The ascension of four Placidia Tens occurred every few centuries, and the unprecedented Five—occurring six centuries ago—was truly wondrous. The exponential ability of multiple Placidia Tens, viewing the same line simultaneously, led to remarkable discoveries and revelations, recorded in the Codex for following generations who were not so fortunate. Regrettably, The Five's wisdom and guidance had been destroyed and only partially reconstituted. The enormity of that loss was reason alone to exterminate the Corvad vermin.

After its reconstitution, the Codex had been moved to a new, impenetrable location deep within Domus Praesidium instead of the small alcove adjacent to Rhea's office. Although the three plasma turrets at the end of the corridor were formidable weapons, the true barrier to passage was beyond the door they guarded.

Rhea reached the end of the corridor, and the door slid open, revealing a ledge overlooking a hundred-foot-wide chasm. On the far side of the dark abyss, another door was inset into the sheer mountain face, and on both sides of the door, a small viewport was carved into the mountain cliff. Behind each portal, protected by two feet of reinforced mountain rock, two Nexus Nines—disruptors—stood duty, only their eyes visible through the opening. Although the disruptors carried no physical weapons, their minds were sufficient to prevent passage. Not even The One could cross if opposed.

She moved onto the ledge, composed of three parallel slabs side-by-side extending partway over the abyss. When Rhea stepped onto the center slab, the ones on each side dissolved. She had selected the correct one. As she continued briskly down the center slab, its end widened and another ten-foot section appeared, likewise with three parallel slabs. Rhea chose the one on the right, and the two slabs on the left dissolved. The process repeated itself, with Rhea selecting the correct slab eight more times until the final section had been put in place, completing the creation of a bridge that spanned the deep crevasse.

The passage across the abyss was protected by simple mathematical probability; the odds of selecting the correct slab in each section was one in three, and of correctly guessing ten consecutive times one in 59,000. But what made the transit even more challenging was that for each passage across the abyss, the path was different; the correct slab in each successive section was random, and thus the path across could not be memorized. However, in the absence of action by the disruptors, determining the correct path was child's play for Rhea.

The door in the mountain face slid open, and Rhea passed between the disruptors into the Repository. At the far end of the ten-by-twenty-foot room, an electronic tome rested atop a pedestal carved from the metamorphic rock wall, protected behind a shimmering blue force field. A palm reader was affixed to the wall on the right, which could be used to deactivate the protective field, but today Rhea would not read. She was pressed for time and would instead use the artificial intelligence interface the Sevens had built during the Codex's reconstruction.

Rhea stopped before the Codex as the door slid shut behind her. "New authorization," she said firmly.

"Ready," a woman's soft voice replied, the glowing force field pulsing with the response.

"Rhea Sidener."

The Codex replied, "Accepted."

"New request—answer question," she announced, selecting the tome's Question and Answer feature.

"Ready," the Codex replied.

"Can an untrained individual detect a Nexus view?"

"No."

Rhea's thoughts were derailed by the response. During her journey from her office to the Repository, she had formulated a series of interconnected questions branching off in various directions. The first question had been asked merely to set the stage as Rhea prepared to work her way toward the answer. There was no possible way Lara was trained, yet the Codex's answer implied she was. But the Codex interface was sometimes too literal, and perhaps Rhea hadn't phrased the question properly. She tried again, hoping to get the only answer that made sense.

"Has any untrained individual ever *suspected* a Nexus view?"

"That is a nonsensical question," the Codex replied. "An untrained individual would not know what a view is and therefore cannot suspect it."

True. It appeared that she again hadn't asked the right question. Changing tack, Rhea selected a different Codex interface. "New request— draw conclusion."

"Ready," the Codex replied.

"A woman detects a Nexus view. What training has she received?"

"She is a Nine or Ten."

Rhea folded her arms across her chest. She wasn't making much progress. Lara clearly wasn't a Nine or Ten. Perhaps she had again improperly phrased the question.

She collected her thoughts, then spoke. "An untrained woman can sense a temperature change from a Nexus view. What latent skill does she possess?"

"She has potent level one and three skills."

Finally, an answer that made sense. And an obvious reason now that Rhea thought about it. The woman's keen intuition had kicked in, telling her something unusual was occurring, and her perception had homed in on the minute physical changes to her surroundings.

With Lara's curious ability to detect a Nexus view resolved, Rhea turned to a more significant issue—Lara's lack of a prime timeline, the phenomenon all house psychics followed into the past or future. Without a line, Lara could not exist.

"New request—Codex search."

"Ready."

"Is there any reference to a person without a prime timeline?"

"There is one reference, contained in the text of The Five."

"Show me."

"*Warning*—the text of The Five has not been completely reconstructed. Inaccurate conclusions may be drawn."

"I understand the warning. Proceed."

The Codex's force field pulsed intense blue, then white words appeared on the shimmering field. Rhea read the inscription.

Harken the arrival of the One with no line...

Rhea sucked in a sharp breath. The Five had foreseen Lara's arrival, deeming it important enough to record for future Nexus generations. Unfortunately, the rest of the passage was unreadable. She decided to examine the actual text.

"Display the passage containing this reference."

The words hovering in the blue force field were replaced with several passages of text. Unfortunately, most of the text—entire paragraphs—was garbled, not yet recovered by the Sevens. Rhea examined the section header, and her eyes widened. The quote came from the final segment of The Five's wisdom, akin to the Bible's Book of Revelations.

Frustration simmered beneath Rhea's thoughts, subdued only in comparison to her hatred of the Corvad scum who had destroyed the Codex.

"End query," she said, and the words disappeared.

Rhea left the Codex Repository, proceeding swiftly across the dark chasm as each section of the bridge materialized before her, others dissolving as she passed by.

A few minutes later, after ascending to the fifth level of the Praesidium, Rhea stopped outside a set of double doors in the south wing. After placing her palm on the identification screen, the doors whisked open, and she entered the laboratory where the Sevens worked on the remaining segments of the Codex. Having messaged the Primus Seven after leaving the Repository, she found Chen Wei waiting inside.

The Corvad attack five centuries ago had erased every electronic copy of the Codex and incinerated the only paper printout, leaving only blackened, burnt pages. Inside the busy laboratory, twenty of the most capable Sevens were interspersed between dozens of small robotic arms. Each arm was working with a section of the damaged Codex, organizing black flakes no bigger than the tip of a pen, attempting to reassemble the charred remains of burnt pages. The pages that had remained intact had been easy to recover, despite being nothing but thin, black sheets. The Sevens could easily decipher the words that had been written on the paper before it had burned.

However, much of the Codex had disintegrated into small fragments, the black ashes commingling. Although individual letters could be recovered, they could be arranged in almost any order—trillions of permutations. The robotic arms were selecting small flakes of the Codex ashes, assembling them in a specific order. The Sevens then went to work, determining whether the hidden letters made sense grammatically in the order arranged and, more important, whether the letters and words they formed had previously existed beside each other before the pages had burned. Painstaking work, with success measured in a phrase a week.

When Chen Wei approached, Rhea said, "Focus all effort on the last section of the text of The Five. Also, search all parts of the Codex for any reference to *the One with no line*."

"Yes, One," Chen replied.

28

Fleet Admiral Nanci Fitzgerald sat with her elbows propped on her desk, rubbing her temples with her fingertips in a slow, circular motion. The pressure in her head had built steadily throughout the day, and the videocon she had just concluded with the Resolute battleship design team had turned a low-level headache into a migraine. With a Colonial Council meeting in five minutes, Fitzgerald retrieved a pill from a bottle in her desk drawer and downed it with a gulp of lukewarm coffee.

At sixty-six years old, lines creased her face, but it was more than age that had taken a toll. The strain of the last five years weighed heavily on her as she had guided the Fleet through its most critical time. It hadn't been easy to watch the Fleet retreat, abandoning planet after planet. But she was convinced the course she had chosen was the right one, conserving the Fleet's assets and buying valuable time in preparation for humankind's final stand.

She had taken command of the Fleet five years ago with the hope she would reverse the tide of steady losses. But she had shocked the Council when she proposed a reversal in strategy—abandon their ground forces. For twenty-five years, the Fleet had provided support to Earth's colonies, keeping the supply lines open while the Army waged battle planet-side. But Fitzgerald instead recommended only token Fleet resistance, saturating the few remaining planets under their control with ground forces, then abandoning them in exchange for lighter Fleet losses. It would be Darian 3 again, a dozen times over.

The Korilians were predictable; they would not advance until each planet had been wiped clean of humanity's presence, and Fitzgerald proposed using that trait against them. Unless the Fleet defeated the Korilian armada, there was no hope for humankind. No matter how strong Earth's defenses were, if the Fleet was destroyed and Korilian starships were in orbit supporting their ground assault, pounding the surface with dreadnought and cruiser pulses, humankind would be eradicated. The only hope was to destroy the Korilian fleet, even if that meant sacrificing billions of men and women on distant planets.

The Council had approved her strategy, and now it was time to make good on her promise. The civilian population was unaware, but the Colonial Ground Forces were depleted, expended over the last five years in the planet-by-planet war of attrition, bogging down the Korilian advance while the Fleet nursed itself back to health. With the new Resolute-class battleships and McCarthy's unique ability, there was finally a chance they could defeat the Korilians.

However, none of the Resolute battleships were operational. The one crucial capability—their new pulse generators—was not yet functional. They needed to capture a Korilian warship intact, but the Korilians were as fanatical about destroying disabled ships as humans were. The Korilians had gained the advantage early in the war after capturing Colonial starships, exploiting their shield and weapon technology. Since then, disabled Colonial ships self-destructed if they could not jump away. Korilian warships did the same.

Time was running out. The best estimate was that the Korilian armada would jump into Earth's solar system in two weeks. Fitzgerald had until then to capture a Korilian warship and analyze its shield design. Despite their best efforts, an intact Korilian starship eluded them. The situation had become critical, and she had developed a risky plan, one that required the Council's approval. Admiral McCarthy would lead a raid into Korilian territory. However, if McCarthy were killed, the war would be lost. Humanity's only chance to defeat the Korilian horde was with McCarthy leading the combined Fleet.

Fitzgerald checked her wristlet. It was almost time. With her head still pounding, she headed to the Fleet communication center and entered a twenty-foot-diameter chamber. At the appointed time, twelve holograms appeared, evenly spaced along the chamber circumference. If it weren't for the occasional static that flickered through the holographic images, a casual observer would have concluded that all twelve regents were present.

The twelve white-robed regents were evenly split between men and women, and three members each held a staff. Council President David Portner wore a red stole around his neck, while the next two highest-ranking members—Regent Morel Alperi and Regent Lijuan Xiang—the directors of personnel and material, respectively, were adorned with orange stoles. The remaining nine lower-ranked regents wore yellow.

"Greetings, Colonial Council," Fitzgerald began. "Thank you for affording me the opportunity to address you."

Portner replied, "I assume you bring good news—that the Resolute-class battleships are now fully operational."

Fitzgerald bit her tongue. She had briefed the Council numerous times on the Resolute-class progress, each time explaining the need to capture a Korilian warship intact. Had one been captured, the Council would have been informed. Portner's comment was a jab at her failure.

"Regrettably, no," Fitzgerald replied.

"Time is running out," Portner said, concern in his voice.

Alperi interjected, "It is as I've said. Fitzgerald is incompetent and should have been fired years ago. Look at the predicament we're in—all of our colonies have been destroyed, and the Korilians are on Earth's doorstep. We should replace her with someone competent before it's too late."

Regent Adriana Sousa replied, "I must remind you that you approved Fitzgerald's plan, while I voted against it. That proves you are the incompetent one and should be removed from your position. Your failure to supply adequate ground forces is why we are losing, just as much as Fitzgerald's ludicrous plan."

"You're the incompetent one," Alperi replied. "You'd be in over your head as the Director of Personnel. I have to supply resources to the armed forces and the factories building starships and other weapons. Lijuan ties my hands with her incessant requests for more personnel."

Lijuan joined the conversation. "I submit the requests; you make the decisions, Morel. Despite you constantly tying *my* hands, we have more starships now than we've had in fifteen years. But we are getting off track. The war is progressing exactly as Fleet Admiral Fitzgerald predicted. We knew it would come to this. We deliberately sacrificed our colonies and ground forces to buy time, and the Fleet has not been stronger since before Telemantic. Let Fleet Admiral Fitzgerald continue."

Portner replied, "Lijuan is wise. Let us hear what Fleet Admiral Fitzgerald has to say. Continue, Fleet Admiral."

Fitzgerald provided an update on Resolute-class construction progress, then broached the sensitive subject. "As President Portner mentioned, we have not yet captured a Korilian warship. The situation is critical, and we need to take aggressive action. With your approval, Admiral McCarthy will lead a small task force into Korilian territory to capture a Korilian warship."

The Council erupted in a cacophony of discord, with all twelve members speaking simultaneously. Fitzgerald drew a deep breath and waited in silence until Alperi pounded his staff on the floor. "Absolutely not!"

The bickering between regents died down, and Alperi continued. "We cannot risk Admiral McCarthy. Without him, our Fleet will be defeated."

Lijuan countered, "Without functional Resolute-class battleships, we will also lose. If Fleet Admiral Fitzgerald believes the only way we can capture a Korilian warship is to harness McCarthy's skill, then we'll have to take that risk."

Alperi replied, "This is a plan from the woman who has led us to the brink of defeat." Alperi pointed to Fitzgerald. "This woman *and* her plans should be scrapped," he said, generating another round of discord until Portner brought the meeting to order by pounding his staff repeatedly on the floor.

"The decision facing us is straightforward," Portner said. "It is time to vote. *Yes* to approve Fleet Admiral Fitzgerald's proposal. *No* to oppose." Portner turned to Alperi first.

"No," he said.

The voting continued in a circular fashion, reaching Lijuan tied five to five.

"Yes," she said.

The decisive vote would be cast by Portner. A tie would result in Fitzgerald's request being disapproved. After a moment, Portner announced, "Yes."

There was silence in the conference room until Portner focused his attention on Fitzgerald. "Do not disappoint us."

Alperi's hologram was the first to disappear, followed by Portner and the others. Lijuan's hologram was the last, and she offered an encouraging smile before fading away.

Fitzgerald returned to her office, then sent a conference request to 1st Fleet command. A minute later, Admiral McCarthy appeared on the video screen mounted on the far wall.

"Good afternoon, Fleet Admiral," he said.

"Hello, Jon," she replied.

Fitzgerald spent a few minutes inquiring on McCarthy's health and 1st Fleet's refit before broaching the critical issue.

"As you're aware, we have not yet captured a Korilian warship, and we're running out of time. You will lead a task force into Korilian territory to capture a cruiser or dreadnought. No one better understands your ability and its limitations, so I leave it to you to develop a plan. Fleet Intelligence is at your disposal, and you can select whatever Fleet assets you require.

"However, time is critical. We need an intact Korilian warship within seventy-two hours so we have enough time to extract the information we need and program the Resolute-class pulse generators before the Korilian armada reaches Earth. Inform me once you have developed a plan and have identified the assets you require."

McCarthy replied, "I understand, Fleet Admiral. I've already started working on it and should be able to brief you by the end of the day."

Fitzgerald smiled. Of course McCarthy would already know he'd be tasked with this mission. "I look forward to the brief," she said, then terminated the videocon.

29

Moments earlier, Lara had been participating with Admiral McCarthy in a battle simulation on the bridge of the 1st Fleet command ship, with Angeline and Channing behind them as usual. As the battle progressed, McCarthy had occasionally paused the simulation to allow for Channing's feedback and Angeline's comments. The focus of this simulation was battle strategy, teaching Lara the critical intricacies in the hope it would help focus her attention during the upcoming battle. Lara did her best to assimilate the information but was sure she was retaining less than half of what was explained.

One of McCarthy's aides had entered and informed him that Fleet Admiral Fitzgerald had requested a videocon. McCarthy froze the simulation and departed, then returned a few minutes later.

"Terminate simulation," he ordered.

Lara felt the chill from his view as he approached.

"We're done for today," McCarthy said. "No training the next few days either. I've been assigned a task by Fleet Admiral Fitzgerald. Lara and Angeline will come with me. It will give Lara an opportunity to experience combat."

"What type of combat?" Channing asked.

"I'm not sure yet. I'm still evaluating various scenarios. I'll provide details later tonight, but be prepared to depart the command ship at zero-five-hundred tomorrow."

"We're not taking the command ship?" Angeline asked.

"It'll be a small task force. A quick in-and-out, hopefully."

McCarthy departed for his stateroom, and Lara, Channing, and Angeline headed toward theirs. As they left the flag bridge, they passed two Fleet captains, stern looks on their faces, inbound toward McCarthy's quarters. Lara sensed their apprehension as they passed, and she wondered what was afoot. When she arrived at her quarters, her thoughts returned to the two Fleet captains, and she wondered if she could eavesdrop on their conversation with McCarthy.

Angeline and Channing had provided more detail on the ten Nexus levels, and she had learned that levels two through four dealt with the present. A level-two Nexus could have out-of-body experiences, but only at the location he or she was at, typically floating overhead and able to observe things that might be missed in the normal course of events. A level-three Nexus could glean information not apparent to an observer, such as the suit and value of a poker card hidden from view. At level four, a Nexus could tap both level-two and level-three skills, but in any location, perceiving what was happening and being said in locations halfway around the world. The farther away and more secretive the meeting, the more difficult the task.

Channing had explained that her dream as a child about the school shuttle plunging from the bridge into the water had been a level-four skill. Wondering if she could conjure a level-four vision on command, she imagined herself floating just above and behind Admiral McCarthy. To her surprise, an image of McCarthy formed in her mind. He was stepping into the conference room adjacent to his quarters.

The two Fleet captains Lara had passed were standing at one end of the conference room. Both officers snapped to attention when Admiral McCarthy entered. The captain on the right was a tall Black woman, and beside her was a man of the same height, with blond hair and skin as pale as hers was dark. Lara's attention was drawn to the female captain. She had cold, almost lifeless eyes. Lara shuddered involuntarily, wondering what kind of experiences produced a person like that.

McCarthy addressed them from across the room, his face darkening as he spoke. "You disobeyed a direct order at Ritalis. Again." McCarthy folded his arms across his chest. "What is your excuse this time, Captain Rajhi? And don't give me any crap about communication difficulties."

The female captain answered, "You were in a different sector and didn't have a clear understanding of the tactical situation."

"The hell I didn't," McCarthy said. "My command ship has access to the sensors on every starship in my fleet. I knew exactly what was occurring in your sector."

"With all due respect, sir, we selected a better course of action."

"No," McCarthy replied. "You selected an *acceptable* course of action."

"It worked," Captain Rajhi replied, "and we saved *Helena*."

Lara recalled the damaged battleship she had seen on her trip from Ritalis to *Mercy*, with the crippled starship flanked by two other battleships ferrying personnel aboard to assist. These two captains must be the commanding officers of the two battleships. They had stayed with *Helena* at Ritalis, defending the ship from the Korilians until it could jump to safety.

"You did save *Helena*," McCarthy said, "but I'm tired of you two disobeying orders. If you were assigned to any other fleet, you would have been relieved for cause long ago. Give me one reason why I shouldn't court-martial both of you."

Rajhi answered, "Because we're the two best battleship commanding officers in First Fleet, sir."

McCarthy didn't immediately reply, glaring at the two officers as he contemplated their fate. "My money is on Townsend. He's just as good as you *and* follows orders."

Rajhi replied, "He's had a more capable ship. One that was heavily damaged at Ruehiri, I might add. And his failure is being rewarded with command of a new Resolute battleship, while Gynt and I remain aboard the two oldest battleships in the Fleet."

"Townsend lost his ship because he followed my order, not because of incompetence. That he and his crew survived is a testament to his ability. Regarding your command of *Athens* and *Sparta*, that is a result of your success. They are the last two first-flight Helena-class starships in service. But they are rugged and durable, and your crews are the most experienced in the Fleet. Do you really want command of a new starship? I can transfer both of you aboard two Atlantis-class battleships coming out of the construction yards, with fresh, green crews. Just say the word."

McCarthy waited for a response, but there was none. Both captains stared straight ahead, their jaws set tightly.

"Getting back to why you are here," he said. "You're excellent starship captains, but doing what you're told is more important than your tactical abilities. If either of you disobey another order, you'll be stripped of command and reduced in rank. Do I make myself clear?"

"Yes, sir," both captains said simultaneously, still standing rigidly at attention.

After an uneasy moment, McCarthy said, "I'm going to give both of you a chance to redeem yourselves. I've been assigned a mission into Korilian territory, and I'll be taking a few battleships with me. Do you happen to know any captains who'd like to join me?"

Rajhi replied, "I can think of one."

A faint smile creased the other captain's face. "I can think of another."

"Excellent," McCarthy said. "Why don't you inform those two commanding officers to rendezvous in sector four-two-five at zero-six-hundred tomorrow."

"Yes, Admiral," both captains replied.

"You're dismissed."

The two captains left the conference room. As soon as they passed from McCarthy's sight, wide grins broke across their faces. Captain Rajhi swung her left arm down while the other captain swung his right arm forward, their palms smacking together by their thighs.

A low five.

They were congratulating themselves on surviving McCarthy's wrath.

After the two captains left, Lara turned her attention back to McCarthy, standing at one end of the conference room, his arms still folded across his chest, a faint smile on his face. He must have been viewing and had witnessed the two starship captains' congratulatory gesture.

Lara realized that McCarthy's stern reprimand of the two captains had been more for show. There was more to Admiral McCarthy than met the eye.

30

It was five a.m. the next morning when Angeline knocked on Lara's door. Having risen a half hour earlier, Lara was ready, and she accompanied the Nexus guide as they strode briskly through the command ship corridors. There was time to stop for breakfast, but Angeline didn't recommend it. They were about to take massive starship jumps, not the puddle-jumps the Nexus shuttle had taken from Ritalis, and it would be best if she had an empty stomach. Lara would have skipped breakfast anyway. Her stomach was tied in knots as she prepared to engage in battle for the first time.

They arrived in the command ship's spaceport and waited by the designated shuttle. Channing stopped by, offering Lara encouraging words and advice. Hopefully, useful premonitions would occur. If Lara viewed a future timeline by accident, creating turbulence with McCarthy's view, the admiral would instruct her to terminate her vision. If she could not, Channing had given Angeline a handheld tranquilizer cartridge that would incapacitate Lara and terminate her view. It was just a precaution, of course. Channing was hopeful the mission would be uneventful from a Nexus perspective.

McCarthy arrived and boarded the shuttle without a word. Angeline and Lara followed, and the door slid shut behind them, sealing them in a small transport that lifted off and passed through the spaceport life-support shield. They sped away from the repair yard, but instead of heading toward 1st Fleet, the shuttle turned toward white blips in the distance. As they approached, the specks grew larger, and soon another fleet took substance—hundreds of gigantic white starships resting in space.

Angeline pointed out one of the shuttle's windows. "That's my fleet," she said. "Third Fleet. The next best after McCarthy's."

Lara sensed Angeline's pride; she no doubt had something to do with 3rd Fleet's success.

"How many ships are there in each fleet?" Lara asked.

"Four hundred when they're at full strength, organized into four battle groups. Each battle group normally contains forty-eight battleships, the same number of cruisers, and four carriers. That's a battleship," Angela said, pointing to the nearest starship, a formidable spacecraft with a large portal in the ship's bow and weapons rippling down its sides.

"Pulse generator up front, defense batteries along the sides, and engines in the stern. Your basic battleship and cruiser configuration. Those ships," Angela pointed toward two ships half the size of the battleship, "are cruisers, faster than battleships but packing only half the punch."

As the battleships and cruisers passed down the port side of the shuttle, Lara spotted a starship she hadn't seen before, dwarfing even the battleships, with the name *Medusa* on its side. Angeline provided the details: *Medusa* was a Pegasus-class carrier, with twenty runways exiting the ship's bow in a circular pattern, giving the ship a resemblance to the Gatling guns of the Old West. *Medusa* could launch its wing of five hundred vipers in four minutes.

"The carriers' small vipers can't damage a starship while its shields are up," Angeline said, "but they can tear one apart after one of its shields fails and its hull armor is penetrated."

The shuttle pilot, who sat only a few feet away in the small shuttle, said, "My son is assigned to *Medusa*." The pilot paused before continuing, glancing at McCarthy over his shoulder. "He's survived as a viper pilot for three years. Must be some sort of record."

Lara recalled the conversations she'd had with injured Fleet officers at Camden Colonial Hospital. Assignment as a viper pilot was considered a death sentence. The average life span was three battles, which amounted to six months. Less than twenty percent of viper pilots lasted a year, and only a miniscule number survived two.

"That's remarkable," McCarthy said. "He must be incredibly skilled."

"He is," the pilot answered. "He's a fine young man," he added, his voice cracking with emotion.

The shuttle sped past 3rd Fleet, heading into an area seemingly devoid of ships. Slowly, eight ships materialized from the darkness: six battleships, a seventh ship that looked like an armed troop transport, and a small gray ship identical to the one that had towed *Helena* to a repair yard using its tractor beam. The shuttle approached one of the battleships, which had *Atlantis* written on its hull, then entered the ship's spaceport, settling onto the deck.

As Lara and the others exited the shuttle, an alarm rang throughout the spaceport, and as Lara wondered what it meant, she spotted the large spaceport doors in the ship's hull slide slowly shut. Angeline explained the crew was preparing for battle, shutting the spaceport doors instead of relying on the force field across the opening. The doors closed with a heavy thud, and the alarm stopped, which coincided with the approach of a Fleet captain. Lara recognized Jeff Townsend, who had helped rescue her from Ritalis.

Townsend saluted McCarthy. "Welcome aboard *Atlantis*, Admiral."

After McCarthy returned his salute, Townsend added, "Thank you for selecting me to accompany you on this mission, not to mention giving me temporary command of *Atlantis* again while *Europe* receives her final weapon modification. It'll be like old times, heading into battle by your side when you were in command of the Normandy battle group. You'll see many familiar faces among the crew. They're looking forward to seeing you."

McCarthy smiled. "I'm looking forward to seeing them as well, not to mention heading into battle aboard *Atlantis* again. I could think of no better ship or captain."

Townsend turned his attention to Lara. "It's good to see you again, Lara. I hope your training is going well."

After shaking Lara's hand, he greeted Angeline. "Allow me to introduce myself; I didn't get a chance when I arrived aboard *Mercy* with Lara. It's an honor to have the Third Fleet guide aboard my ship. Admiral Goergen has nothing but glowing things to say about you. I look forward to your guidance during this mission."

Angeline replied, "Thank you for your kind words, Captain. However, I will not provide assistance during this mission." Townsend responded with a confused look, to which Angeline replied, "Lara will provide guidance. I'm here to continue her training."

Townsend turned back to Lara. "Your training must be coming along nicely, then?"

Instead of answering his question, Lara simply nodded. It was probably better if Townsend didn't know how little assistance she would likely provide.

Townsend escorted McCarthy to the starship's bridge, with Angeline and Lara following behind while the two Fleet officers talked. As they progressed through the battleship's passageways, Angeline explained quietly to Lara that McCarthy had commanded the Normandy battle group several years ago from the starship *Atlantis*, and Townsend had been the ship's captain. *Atlantis* was damaged and Townsend injured a few months ago during the engagement at Ruehiri, and the battleship was repaired and given a new commanding officer while Townsend healed. Instead of returning to *Atlantis* when medically cleared, Townsend had been assigned to the new Resolute-class battleship *Europe*, which was completing its shakedown operations and crew training cycle.

They entered the battleship's bridge, which was similar in layout to the 1st Fleet command ship, except smaller, with only one-third as many consoles and personnel. Unlike most starships, Angeline explained, *Atlantis* and a few other battleships had a second command chair on the bridge: one for the ship's captain, and another for a battle group commander or deputy fleet commander.

When McCarthy arrived on the bridge, about half of the bridge crew approached, greeting him with handshakes and smiles. Their affection for him was obvious, and Lara sensed they were excited to have him aboard again. She also sensed subtle emotions from McCarthy—his pleasure returning to *Atlantis* and seeing his former shipmates.

After everyone returned to their workstations, Townsend informed

McCarthy, "All commanding officers are standing by for the operations brief. Whenever you're ready, Admiral."

"Let's begin," McCarthy said.

Seven officers appeared on the display: five Colonial Navy captains and a lieutenant commander, plus one Marine colonel, each with their ship name in the bottom right corner. Two of the captains were the officers McCarthy had reprimanded aboard the 1st Fleet command ship. Angeline whispered in Lara's ear, informing her that those two officers commanded older Helena-class battleships, *Athens* and *Sparta*, which for some reason McCarthy had selected over the newer Atlantis-class battleships. The three other captains commanded Atlantis-class starships— *Crimea*, *Odessa*, and *Sochi*—like Townsend, who commanded *Atlantis* herself. The Marine colonel was aboard the planetary assault ship *Venomous*, while the final officer, a lieutenant commander, was in charge of the Fleet tug *Hercules*.

"Good morning," McCarthy began. "Most of you are aware that the Resolute-class battleships are not yet operational, undergoing final weapon adjustments. What you probably don't know is that those adjustments require the capture of an intact Korilian warship so that its shield design can be exploited. You've been selected to participate in a mission that will take us behind Korilian lines to capture that warship. It'll be a quick in-and-out—a two-jump trip with an eight-hour hold at the first jump, and no jump hold after the engagement. The Korilians will respond quickly, so we can't afford to linger.

"Each ship will be assigned a specific mission. Four will take out one of the Korilian starship shields, the fifth will target the jump drive, and the sixth will target the Korilian ship's self-destruct mechanism. This needs to occur in rapid succession, taking out the self-destruct mechanism before it can be activated. Once that's accomplished, *Hercules* will tractor-beam the disabled ship, and we'll make the first jump home.

"At the first return jump point, Colonel Kratovil will be waiting aboard *Venomous* with four companies of Marines, who will board the Korilian starship to ensure its shield generators are not sabotaged before we return to Earth."

McCarthy nodded to Townsend, who gave an order to his operations officer. Another display energized, showing a map of the nearby solar systems.

"Recon probes have detected Korilian forces gathering at Ritalis, Dolranus, and Natari. We've identified several of their supply routes, and recon probes have discovered a solo Korilian cruiser en route to Ritalis. We're going to intercept it."

A yellow line appeared on the map, showing the mission's ingress and egress routes. "We'll be jumping past Ritalis by way of Proxima in an attempt to avoid detection by Korilian probes, targeting the Korilian jump point at Zulu-4037. Any questions?"

Lara sensed the tension on the bridge rise with the mention of Proxima, and one of the battleship captains interjected, "Proxima is a dangerous jump to make. The gravitational fields are strong and unpredictable. We could get trapped."

"That's a risk we're going to take," McCarthy said. "The Korilians have recon probes across their entire front and along their supply lines. Proxima is the only unmonitored approach. Any more questions?"

There was a short silence before Captain Rajhi spoke. "Admiral, how will we know where to target the Korilian ship to take out its jump drive and self-destruct mechanisms? We don't have internal diagrams of Korilian ships to guide our shots."

McCarthy answered, "The cruiser we're targeting is a Sierra class, and intelligence has obtained data that pinpoints those critical locations."

Lara sensed McCarthy was lying; there was no such intelligence. He must have viewed the cruiser attack in his mind hundreds of times, with the Colonial battleships targeting different sectors of the ship until the desired outcome was achieved. However, he could not reveal that to the starship captains.

McCarthy added, "During the jump hold at Proxima, you'll be advised on how to target the cruiser's jump drive and self-destruct mechanism. Do you have any more questions?"

When no one responded, McCarthy said, "Between the truncated jump hold at Proxima and no hold after capturing the Korilian cruiser, it's going to be tough on your crews, but we don't have a choice. This is the best, and perhaps only, opportunity we have to capture a Korilian warship intact."

After a short pause, he added, "Prepare to jump to Proxima in fifteen minutes. Coordinates will be provided shortly. Set shields for auto-generation once the jump is complete."

The screens went dark as each starship captain and the colonel signed off.

Townsend began final preparations for the jump, and Lara sensed the temperature plummet; McCarthy, who stood with his arms folded across his chest as he stared out the bridge windows, had started viewing.

Angeline pulled a plastic container from her pocket, which opened to reveal several anti-nausea pills. While the short shuttle jumps from Ritalis to Earth hadn't been rough, Angeline explained that the physiological effects of long-distance jumps were much more severe. People almost always vomited after their first jump, and it took a while to recover. Although the standard jump hold was normally twelve hours, starship crews could jump faster if they were willing to endure more severe physiological effects, which compounded upon each jump if there was insufficient rest time. Successive jumps without adequate delays could result in disoriented crews, even unconsciousness and death if the jumps were conducted too rapidly.

Angeline handed Lara a pill, then placed another one in her mouth and directed Lara to do the same. As the pill dissolved on Lara's tongue, Angeline pointed toward the nearest console, where a slot contained several *jump bags*, the colloquial name for vomit bags. With this being Lara's first long-distance jump in ten years, since the trip from her home planet of Altaria to Ritalis as a teenager, the bag would likely come in handy.

The orders and reports between the watchstanders died down until there was silence on the bridge. When the jump timer reached two minutes remaining, Townsend settled into the captain's chair. McCarthy remained standing with his arms folded across his chest, then motioned Lara toward his seat.

When she hesitated, not wanting to take his chair, McCarthy said, "You'll need the seat more than I will."

He gestured to the chair again, and this time Lara took it. At the one-minute point, five deep tones reverberated throughout the ship, followed by the computer's female voice over the ship's intercom system.

"One minute to the jump."

As the time counted down, Angeline moved beside McCarthy. Lara felt a twinge of jealousy; McCarthy would make the jump with Angeline at his side.

At the ten-second mark, five deep tones reverberated throughout the ship again. When the time reached zero, Lara's vision went black as she tumbled down a spiraling hole.

31

Lara tumbled through the darkness, emerging on the brightly lit starship bridge again, but the turbulent, swirling sensation didn't cease. As the bridge kept spinning, Lara's stomach rose in her throat, and she stumbled toward the slot containing the jump bags. She opened one just in time and was surprised at how much she vomited, considering she hadn't had anything for breakfast.

Lara braced herself on a console, waiting for the deck to stop spinning as urgent reports echoed in her ears.

"Shields are up!"

"No Korilian warships in this sector."

"Gravitational field is at ninety-three percent of maximum allowed for jumps. Highly volatile. Fluctuating plus or minus four percent."

Lara heard Townsend's calm voice. "Inform me at each one percent increase in average gravitational field."

As the bridge's spinning slowed and her nausea faded, Lara looked around. *Atlantis*'s crew sat at their consoles, attending to their duties. Townsend was moving about, conferring with watchstanders, while Admiral McCarthy stood nearby with Angeline at his side. The Nexus Eight moved toward Lara.

"How do you feel?" she asked, rubbing Lara's back.

"Awful," Lara replied. "How long do the effects last?"

"About an hour, as long as there's adequate time between jumps. If you make subsequent jumps too quickly, the effects are more severe and last longer. We'll be jumping in eight hours instead of the standard twelve, so the next jump will be worse. With the third jump only a few minutes later, let's just say—the effects of this jump are pleasant in comparison."

Lara's stomach started to settle, and the spinning deck stabilized. She sealed her jump bag and dropped it into a disposal slot, then looked out the bridge windows. A large, rocky planet loomed ahead, framed by a blue-white star behind it. The six battleships, Marine assault ship, and Fleet tug had changed positions during the jump. The battleships were now arranged in two lines—three over three—with *Atlantis* being the middle starship in the top row. Behind the battleships were the assault ship *Venomous* and Fleet tug *Hercules*.

Despite the calm demeanor of *Atlantis's* crew, Lara sensed tension on the bridge, which dissipated when the sensor supervisor reported, "No Korilian recon probes in this sector."

McCarthy asked Lara, "Any premonitions?"

Lara shook her head. "Aside from being pretty sure I'm going to get sick again after the next jump, I've got nothing."

McCarthy offered an encouraging smile. "The first few jumps will be tough, but you'll get used to it after a while." Turning his attention back to the battleship's crew, he ordered, "Launch communication pods to Earth and Zulu-4037."

The shield supervisor reported, "Dropping shield four."

A few seconds later, six objects shot from the port side of *Atlantis*, streaking away from the battleship formation. They looked like small specks on the display, but Angeline explained each was the size of a two-story house. Although the communication electronics could fit into the palm of her hand, the jump drives were immense, dictating the communication pod size.

The shield supervisor announced, "Restoring shield four."

"Where are the pods headed?" Lara asked.

Angeline replied, "We're establishing communication links. Data transmissions would take thousands of light-years to reach us, so we have to set up a three-pod relay system. The pods pick up the transmissions, then jump back and relay the data in a round-robin fashion. The recon probe at Zulu-4037 is already communicating with Fleet Command, but we're establishing a direct link to the probe, plus another link to Earth to communicate with Fleet Command."

One of the pods in the first three-pod set disappeared in a flash of white light, with a second pod vanishing a second later. The third pod disappeared just as the first one returned. The other set of pods began jumping in similar fashion.

The communication supervisor announced, "Direct communication with Fleet Command has been established," followed by a similar report from the reconnaissance supervisor, announcing that communications had been established with the probe at Zulu-4037.

"We're maintaining the asteroid between our communication pods and the Korilian ships to prevent detection."

Six Korilian starships appeared on one of the bridge displays: two dreadnoughts and four cruisers. They were dark gray starships of similar design to Colonial ships—pulse-generator portal on the bow, with weapon batteries rippling down the sides of the hull until they reached quad engines at the stern. Angeline explained the weapons along the hull were suppression-fire batteries, which served a dual purpose: destroy vipers and slow the pulse-generator recharge of opposing warships by forcing them to divert more energy to their shields.

The reconnaissance supervisor followed up, "Six Korilian warships in jump hold at Zulu-4037, plus one Korilian surveillance probe. Our recon probe is embedded in a nearby asteroid and does not appear to have been discovered."

Townsend acknowledged the report, then the sensor supervisor called out, "Average gravitational field has increased to ninety-four percent. Fluctuations remain plus or minus four percent."

"I understand," Townsend replied. "Continue monitoring."

McCarthy returned to his seat and was joined by Townsend, who settled into the captain's chair beside him. After the orders and reports died down, silence descended on the bridge again. There was nothing more to do at the moment except wait for the six Korilian warships to depart Zulu-4037, followed by the arrival of the lone cruiser.

Angeline spoke to McCarthy. "With your permission, Admiral, Lara and I will continue training during the jump hold."

McCarthy nodded his approval, and as the two Nexi left the bridge, Angeline said to Lara, "Let's get something to settle your stomach."

Angeline led the way through the battleship's passageways and decks, arriving in the senior officers' wardroom, where a culinary specialist was preparing the next meal.

She whispered in Lara's ear, "The Navy gives fancy titles to their cooks."

Angeline asked for coffee, while Lara asked if the culinary specialist had any navarro-root brew, the Altarian version of Earth's green tea, used to calm upset stomachs. The starship had none, but the man recommended and prepared a cup of chamomile tea, which Lara gladly accepted.

As they sat at the table in the otherwise empty wardroom, with a cup of warm tea in Lara's hands, she decided to ask a few questions before resuming her Nexus training. Her thoughts turned first to McCarthy. His firm control of his emotions and the overarching Nexus fear of them hadn't been explained.

"Why are Nexi so concerned with emotion?"

Angeline eyed Lara as she took a sip of her coffee. Placing her cup on the table, she said, "There are several reasons, most related to the Corvads and the House War."

"The House War?"

"There were originally six major houses, but they split three millennia ago into the six true, original houses and six new, false houses. For three thousand years, the true houses battled the false houses. Over the centuries, ten of the houses were destroyed, leaving only our House, the last true house, battling the Corvads, the last false house. Thirty years ago, just before the outbreak of the Korilian War, we finally defeated the Corvads."

"Why did the six original houses split?"

"Primarily over O'Lorun's mandate that tasked the original six houses with guiding humankind throughout the ages, providing guidance discreetly without revealing their existence. Some within the houses resented O'Lorun's mandate, which limited the houses' influence on the general population. Instead, they wanted to use their prescient abilities and unique powers to rule humanity."

"Who is O'Lorun?"

Angeline replied, "She is the Mother of us all. The six bloodlines—houses—sprang from her womb eons ago. She was also the only one able to wield the Krystalis."

"The Krystalis?"

Angeline nodded. "The Krystalis was a gem that imbued whoever held it with immense power. The exact nature is unclear, as the Krystalis was destroyed, shattered when the houses split. But during the House War, each side attempted to obtain all of the fragments. There were some who believed the Krystalis could be reforged if the fragments were brought together, and the original Nexus masters made it clear—the Krystalis could never fall into Corvad hands."

"What do the Corvads have to do with emotion?" Lara asked.

"Corvads harnessed emotion to propel their views farther," Angeline answered. "But their Tens became addicted to emotion like a drug, requiring stronger and stronger doses. The strongest emotions are the negative ones—hatred, jealousy, and fear—and one of the strongest emotions is the fear created by the certainty of death. Corvad Tens slaughtered innocent men and women, feeding on the intense emotion to fuel their views. They were cruel and despicable.

"To avoid becoming addicted like the Corvads, emotion has been banned from Nexus views for three thousand years. Emotion is such an inherent part of human nature, however, that we train Nexi to manage their emotions from a young age, and any Nexus who cannot control them is not allowed to proceed past level eight. As we say in the House, *Emotion is the source of all evil.*"

"Why did The One almost kill me?" Lara asked. "Why not just stop me at level eight if she was worried about my ability to control my emotions?"

Angeline eyed her thoughtfully. "If we were still at war with the

Corvads, we would not be having this conversation. You would be dead; I would have killed you myself."

The Nexus Eight's words surprised Lara. By Nexus standards, Angeline was as warm and fuzzy as they came, yet there was a hardness in her voice when she spoke of Corvads.

Angeline continued, "You would have been killed because you are the ideal Corvad recruit. You have immense latent talent, and you're on the volatile end of the emotional spectrum. Add the Touch to your liabilities, and there's no doubt that Ronan is frothing at the mouth at The One's decision to let you live."

"Ronan?"

"Ronan is the Primus Nine, one of the few Nines who survived the final battle with the Corvads, and is now in command of the Praetorian Legion —level nines who are trained for combat. The praetorians take their responsibility seriously; for three thousand years they defended us from the Corvads." Angeline smiled. "But don't worry about Ronan. Let's focus on your prescient training for now. When you finish your tea, we'll begin."

Lara's cup was almost empty, and she took one final sip. The chamomile had worked as hoped, settling her stomach. Pushing her cup aside, she said to Angeline, "I'm ready."

Angeline spent the next few hours refining the techniques Channing had developed for Lara, which would help her invoke a premonition on command. It was clear that Lara was a synesthesian, which was critical to being a fleet guide. However, Lara's synesthesia revolved around fog, which Channing had never encountered, and they had not yet built a Rosetta Stone that would allow Lara to readily translate her premonitions into tactically relevant information.

Additionally, Channing had never been in battle, while Angeline was the most seasoned guide even before Regina was killed, and she tweaked the techniques Channing had developed, simplifying them where possible. For a new fleet guide, the processes could not be overly complex. With adrenaline flowing in the heat of battle, Lara would be distracted by real-time events and needed processes she could easily slip into and complete in a short time.

After a few hours, officers began filtering into the wardroom to eat, forcing Angeline and Lara to retreat to a small conference table at the back of the wardroom. When offered food by the culinary specialist, Lara declined, fearing her body's response after the next jump, which would occur four hours earlier than normal, not to mention another jump only a few minutes later. Lara's stomach was rumbling from hunger, and she eyed the cornbread muffin Angeline nibbled on as they continued their training.

The wardroom eventually emptied, and as they approached the eight-hour point in the jump hold, Angeline wrapped up the training session and led the way to the bridge. As they traversed the passageways, the air suddenly felt heavy, and Lara's knees went weak. She stopped and placed a hand on the corridor bulkhead, trying to make sense of what was going on. Angeline inquired, but before Lara could reply, waves of emotion rolled over her, almost suffocating her with their intensity. The emotions were ones Lara knew well: despair and fear.

The sensation was coming from the corridor ahead. Lara pointed a finger. "Something's happening."

There was nothing down the hallway except a sealed door. Lara slowly regained her strength and accompanied Angeline down the passageway, and the emotions intensified as they approached the door. Angeline stopped and examined the markings.

Intelligence Center.

Angeline placed her wristlet against the security scanner. The door unlocked and slid open, revealing men and women manning several dozen consoles. But instead of focusing on their console displays, they were standing and facing a large video monitor, watching events unfold. Lara read the information on the bottom of the screen.

Ritalis.

Lara's home planet for the last ten years.

The video was a feed from the planet's surface, near 10th Army head-quarters in the mountains. The two women slipped inside the intelligence center, and Angeline queried the nearest watchstander, who explained that this was the last video feed from the planet. The Korilians were attacking the 10th Army mountain complex, and its shield had just collapsed.

Under other circumstances, the video on the display would have been serene. It was sunset, and the red Ritalian sun, twice the size of Earth's, was slipping toward the horizon, illuminating a thin layer of cirrus clouds a gorgeous orange-reddish hue. But instead of appreciating the beautiful sunset, Lara watched in dismay as the Korilian assault unfolded.

Red pulses from dreadnoughts and cruisers in orbit rained down on the mountain range. The jagged peaks had been reduced to rubble, pulverized into smaller chunks by successive pulses as the Korilian starships blasted away at the mountains. Reinforced sections of the Army complex had become unearthed, and the Korilian pulses blasted holes through the fifty-foot-thick walls. When the ten-mile-long fortification had been breached in several dozen places, the pulses stopped.

The video swiveled skyward to capture the next phase of the Korilian assault. Descending from the starships and piercing the thin clouds like a swarm of black insects were thousands of Surface Assault Vehicles. The Army defense batteries at the base of the mountains opened fire from their recessed, hidden locations, targeting the descending SAVs. However, as the defense batteries fired, they were targeted by the starships. The defense batteries had shields, but they quickly weakened under the Korilian onslaught, and each battery took out only a few dozen SAVs before it was destroyed.

Thousands of SAVs reached the surface. As the SAV ramps lowered and the Korilian ground troops inside prepared to assault the 10th Army complex, the video went black. There was a somber silence in the intelligence center for a long moment, with the men and women staring at the dark display until they slowly settled into their console seats. Lara realized she had just witnessed a preview of what would happen on Earth if the Fleet was defeated.

An alarm sounded throughout the ship. Alternating low and high tones echoed from speakers in the ceiling, accompanied by the lights shifting from white to a pulsating red. The ship's female computer voice followed.

"Man Battle Stations. Prepare for jump in five minutes. Man Battle Stations."

Angeline and Lara hurried back to the bridge, arriving three minutes before the jump. McCarthy was seated, staring ahead, while Townsend moved about, checking with supervisors before returning to his command chair. On one of the bridge displays, sitting motionless in space, was a lone Korilian cruiser.

McCarthy stood and approached a curved console in front of the two command chairs, which provided access to the battleship's sensors and communication systems, where he activated a three-dimensional display. Holograms of two different sectors appeared: Proxima, with blue icons representing the six Colonial battleships, a green icon denoting the assault ship, and a light blue icon representing the Fleet tug. In the second sector, a single red icon glowed.

With a flick of his fingers, McCarthy expanded the red icon, and it transformed into a miniature replica of the Korilian cruiser. With the tip of his finger, he pinpointed three locations along the port side of the starship, then sent the coordinates to the fire control systems aboard *Atlantis* and the other battleships. Angeline explained that the attack had to be carefully coordinated, collapsing one of the Korilian cruiser's shields, then immediately disabling the starship's jump drive and self-destruct mechanism. A clean shot on the jump drive was critical. Partial damage would result in jump drive implosion and the loss of the Korilian cruiser.

Five deep tones reverberated from the ship's speakers, followed by the announcement over the ship's intercom.

"One minute to the jump."

McCarthy motioned Lara toward his chair and she accepted, while Angeline took position alongside him again. At the ten-second mark, five deep tones reverberated throughout the ship, and the shield supervisor announced, "Dropping all shields."

When the clock reached zero, Lara fell into a dark spiraling hole again.

32

After a brief bout of darkness, the bridge reappeared. Intense nausea swept over Lara again, and the urge to vomit was uncontrollable. Fortunately, her stomach was empty, and she dry-heaved instead.

Urgent orders and reports began flowing between Townsend and his crew the instant they completed the jump. The Korilian cruiser loomed directly ahead, the faint glow of its surrounding shields visible to the naked eye. On one of the tactical displays, Lara noted that the six Colonial battleships and Fleet tug had made the jump, while *Venomous* remained at Proxima.

The Korilian cruiser responded immediately, targeting *Odessa*, the top left Colonial battleship before its shields formed. A bright red pulse shot from the cruiser's bow, but it inflicted no appreciable damage against the heavily armored battleship, even without shields. McCarthy touched an icon, and four of the six battleships fired simultaneously, their pulses collapsing the center shield on the cruiser's port side. *Atlantis* fired next, breaching the cruiser's hull armor and carving a hole into the center of the Korilian cruiser, while the battleship on *Atlantis*'s starboard side fired last, its pulse melting through several forward compartments.

"Shields are up!" announced the shield supervisor.

The six Colonial starships targeted the Korilian cruiser again, this time with their suppression-fire batteries, while the cruiser fired at *Odessa*, its pulse absorbed by the warship's shield. Meanwhile, one of *Atlantis*'s weapon batteries destroyed the Korilian surveillance probe before it could jump away with its data.

Although the deck was still spinning, Lara pushed herself to her feet and joined Angeline, asking her a question that hadn't occurred to her until now—how did their pulses and suppression fire pass through *Atlantis*'s shields, but the Korilian pulses could not?

Angeline explained that their pulses were designed with a specific frequency and modulation that allowed the energy to pass through the shield. That was why they needed to capture the Korilian cruiser—so they could determine the settings that allowed pulses to pass through Korilian shields.

With the Korilian cruiser outgunned by six Colonial battleships, the exchange didn't last long. The cruiser's shields collapsed and its weapons fell silent, its hull gutted with pockmarks instead of gun mounts. Another tap on the three-dimensional display from McCarthy, and *Hercules*'s engines ignited, pushing the Fleet tug toward the Korilian cruiser.

As *Hercules* headed toward the warship, closing to within range of its tractor beam, the orders and reports on the bridge died down. The Korilian cruiser and Colonial warships hung motionless in space, with the only detectable activity being *Hercules*'s trek toward the cruiser.

Lara felt a tingling sensation and looked around, attempting to determine the reason. As the tingling increased, she closed her eyes and attempted to invoke a premonition using one of the techniques Angeline had tweaked a few hours earlier. Instead of standing on a deserted beach, she was standing in an abandoned starship bridge with every display and console dark, waiting for something to occur. One of the bridge displays energized, and she spotted *Hercules* on the display heading toward the disabled Korilian cruiser. Suddenly, the Fleet tug dissolved into a cloud of white fog. Lara opened her eyes and pointed to the Fleet tug on the display.

"*Hercules*."

"I'm aware," McCarthy replied. "The Korilians are responding. They've detected our attack somehow."

His hands moved quickly, sending orders to all six battleships. Their main engines ignited and thrusters fired, and five Colonial battleships moved toward *Hercules* while *Odessa* headed toward the Korilian cruiser. As Lara wondered what McCarthy was doing, six bright flashes illuminated the bridge.

The sensor supervisor called out, "Korilian warships! Two dreadnoughts. Four cruisers."

Atlantis's weapons supervisor reported, "Pulse generator still recharging. Fifteen seconds remaining."

Shields formed around the Korilian warships before the Colonial pulse generators completed their recharge, and the Korilians fired first, targeting *Odessa.* The six-pulse onslaught collapsed one of the battleship's shields and penetrated its armor, with the pulses melting a trench down the port side of the battleship's hull. Thrusters on the wounded battleship ignited, rolling the starship 180 degrees, placing its operational starboard shields toward the Korilians.

The Colonial battleships completed their pulse-generator recharge, and McCarthy directed them to engage the nearest Korilian dreadnought. All six Colonial ships fired simultaneously, targeting the same shield. Like *Odessa*, the dreadnought's shield collapsed and its armor was penetrated, with the six-battleship barrage melting a passage deep inside the Korilian warship. Explosions rippled through the starship, then the dreadnought exploded, a red fireball almost instantly quenched by the void of space. The warship disintegrated into thousands of fragments hurtling outward in every direction.

McCarthy examined a tactical display that showed the status of the Korilian warships. It wasn't long before the remaining dreadnought and four cruisers were ready to fire. They didn't attack, beginning radical maneuvers instead.

Lara felt *Atlantis's* bow and stern thrusters kick in, altering the mammoth battleship's course. The other Colonial battleships also maneuvered aggressively, each in different directions. Lara wondered what was going on, then finally understood. The Korilians had deciphered the Colonial Fleet plan, and the cruisers were maneuvering for a clear shot at the Fleet tug *Hercules*, which had no shields. McCarthy was maneuvering the

Colonial battleships in response, placing them between *Hercules* and the Korilian warships' lines of fire.

McCarthy's eyes flicked repeatedly toward *Hercules* as it closed on the disabled Korilian cruiser. Although Lara detected no emotion from McCarthy, she picked up concern from Captain Townsend. The Korilian cruisers were smaller and nimbler than the Colonial battleships and would eventually gain a clear shot. It was a race against time, with the Korilians attempting to destroy the Fleet tug before it could tractor-beam the cruiser and jump away.

While five of the Colonial battleships maneuvered to stay between the Korilian warships and *Hercules*, *Odessa* closed on the wounded Korilian cruiser, halting only a few hundred meters away. As Lara wondered why, the remaining Korilian dreadnought fired on *Odessa*. With a shot at *Hercules* blocked by the Colonial battleships, the Korilians were implementing plan B: destroy their own cruiser. *Odessa* had moved into the way just in time.

However, *Odessa*'s maneuver had exposed a small gap in its down shield. The Korilian pulse slipped into the gap, carving a hole deep into the Colonial battleship. Shortly thereafter, *Odessa*'s remaining shields failed and her main engines extinguished.

The pulse generators on the other Colonial starships completed their recharge, and they targeted the remaining Korilian dreadnought. Its shield collapsed under the onslaught of five close-range battleship pulses. The bow of the Korilian warship evaporated as the pulses tore through the ship. Seconds later, the dreadnought disintegrated, folding in on itself like a sheet of paper wadded into a ball. It compressed until it was a tiny speck, then the dreadnought remnants disappeared altogether in a flash of orange light, its jump drive imploding.

Lara focused on the Korilian cruisers, which were still maneuvering aggressively, attempting to gain a clear shot on either *Hercules* or the disabled Korilian cruiser. McCarthy's eyes shifted between displays, studying the starship maneuvers and pulse-regeneration progress while continually sending new commands to every Colonial starship except *Odessa*.

The damaged battleship was a dark hulk drifting in space beside the Korilian cruiser, with the only light coming from periodic explosions inside the crippled warship. Faint lights finally reappeared throughout the battle-ship, although there was no indication of shields or propulsion.

The communications supervisor reported, "*Odessa*'s aft reactor is back online. Reestablishing data links." A moment later, the supervisor reported, "Bow and port shield generators damaged. Forward reactor offline. Pulse generator and jump drive are down hard."

Lara sensed resignation in the supervisor's voice. *Odessa* could not jump to safety, and they were in no position to evacuate the crew. Other Korilian warships were undoubtedly on their way, and McCarthy had to jump away with the Korilian cruiser before reinforcements arrived.

Hercules slowed and turned, pointing its stern toward the disabled cruiser and *Odessa*. But no tractor beam appeared.

The communications supervisor announced, "*Hercules* reports they cannot jump with the Korilian cruiser and *Odessa* in the tractor beam. Too much mass."

As McCarthy evaluated his options, Lara realized time was running out. The Korilian cruisers were outmaneuvering the Colonial battleships, with one of the cruisers on the verge of gaining a clear shot on the Fleet tug. *Odessa* needed to move out of the way but had no propulsion. And there wasn't enough time for the Fleet tug to tractor-beam *Odessa* out of the way and return for the Korilian cruiser. As Lara wondered how the situation would be resolved, she heard McCarthy's calm voice.

"Inform *Hercules* that *Odessa* will be destroyed. Tractor-beam the Korilian cruiser once sufficient remnants have cleared."

To the weapons supervisor, McCarthy ordered, "A four-ship crossfire on *Odessa*, avoiding the Korilian cruiser. Calculate trajectories."

The supervisor acknowledged, then reported a moment later, "*Crimea*, *Sochi*, *Athens*, and *Sparta* are best positioned."

As McCarthy manipulated the three-dimensional display, sending orders to the four battleships, Lara couldn't believe what he was doing—destroying one of his own ships, killing over one thousand men and women aboard. She turned to Angeline, but the Nexus Eight stared dispassionately at the screen, giving no indication she found fault with McCarthy's order. Likewise for the starship's bridge crew, which processed the order to destroy their sister starship without any hint of reservation.

"*Crimea* and *Sochi* acknowledge," the supervisor reported. "Awaiting *Athens* and *Sparta*."

While they awaited the response from the two Helena-class battleships, Lara's eyes went to *Odessa* as three of the Korilian cruisers fired on the disabled battleship. The fourth cruiser withheld fire. It was on the verge of outmaneuvering *Sochi* and would have a clear shot at the disabled Korilian cruiser in less than a minute.

Three more Korilian pulses cut into *Odessa*, initiating a cascade of explosions inside the battleship. Faint lights and burning fires illuminated the interior of the crippled starship, and she imagined the crew was frantically fighting the fires and repairing damaged systems. All for naught. As the seconds ticked away with no response from *Athens* and *Sparta*, Lara felt the tension mount.

Finally, the weapons supervisor reported, "*Athens* and *Sparta* have acknowledged the order. All ships report ready to engage."

"Fire," McCarthy ordered.

Lara watched the Colonial battleships fire on one of their own. The pulses cut *Odessa* into four sections, which spiraled away from the Korilian cruiser. It wasn't long before *Hercules* had a clear path, and a sparkling beam shot out from behind the Fleet tug. Seconds later, both ships disappeared in a flash of white light.

McCarthy announced, "All ships jump immediately." He sent commands via his three-dimensional display while the operations officer also relayed the order.

The operations officer announced, "Thirty seconds to the jump."

His report was followed by the ship's alarm—five deep tones, then the ship's computer announcing the pending jump.

The time counted down slowly, and Lara followed McCarthy's eyes as he compared the pulse-recharge timers on the Korilian cruisers to the jump countdown.

Twenty seconds to the jump, but only seventeen seconds until all four Korilian cruisers completed their pulse recharge. Lara wondered whether a four-pulse cruiser attack could penetrate a Colonial battleship's exterior armor once shields were dropped for the jump.

Atlantis's pulse generator was charged, and when the jump clock reached five seconds, McCarthy issued an order and the battleship fired on one of the Korilian cruisers. The starship's shields absorbed the pulse, illuminating in a bright flare of sizzling energy. When the Colonial warships dropped their shields for the jump, the other three Korilian cruisers fired at *Atlantis*, their pulses impacting the battleship's armor.

Lara's vision went black again as she was buffeted by the now-familiar tumbling sensation.

33

"Armor intact. No penetration!"

The dark void was replaced with orders and reports, along with a spinning starship bridge. The strength seemed to have been sapped from Lara's body, and her legs gave way.

As she collapsed, strong hands caught her fall, and she looked up to see Admiral McCarthy swimming above her. Another set of hands took her from McCarthy and lowered her to the deck, and Angeline's face replaced the Admiral's. The Nexus Eight knelt on the deck, holding Lara's head in her lap. A migraine pounded in Lara's temples, and the pressure was so intense she thought her head might explode. With every heartbeat, pain shot through her body.

"Back-to-back jumps only a few minutes apart," Angeline said, "and you don't have your jump-legs yet. It'll take a few hours for the symptoms to subside this time."

Lara couldn't respond. Her mouth was dry and her tongue swollen, and she could barely blink; it felt like her eyes were about to pop out of her head.

Angeline seemed to read her thoughts. "The eyes are the most vulnerable from the pressure buildup. But don't worry. If you lose an eye or two, the Fleet hospital ships have plenty of replacements." She smiled. "You can even change the color of your eyes, if you'd like."

The spinning bridge slowed enough for Lara to assess her surroundings, and only then did she notice Angeline's face had paled and she was bracing herself on the starship deck with one hand while she held Lara's head in her lap with her other. Other crew members had suffered from the back-to-back jumps; many rested their heads in their hands as they sat at their workstations, and two watchstanders were slumped over their consoles. Less affected crew members replaced them while medics attended to the incapacitated personnel.

A ship's medic was soon by Lara's side, and the young man gave Lara a shot in her arm. The pain throbbing throughout her body faded, but the nausea and pressure inside her head remained.

Angeline helped Lara to a sitting position, where she examined the displays. They had returned to Proxima, with the blue-white sun burning behind the rocky planet again. *Atlantis* hadn't sustained any notable damage from the Korilian three-pulse attack, and the other four Colonial battleships had also successfully made the jump.

Hercules was nearby with its captive Korilian cruiser. The tractor beam had disappeared, and two dozen assault vehicles were speeding from *Venomous* toward the disabled cruiser. Angeline explained the vehicles carried boarding parties of Marines, who would take control of the cruiser. Thankfully, Korilian starships carried no combat troops, but the fighting would still be ferocious. Lara watched as the assault ships blew holes in the ship's exterior to provide access for the Marines, then attached to the cruiser's hull.

McCarthy had deactivated the three-dimensional display and taken his seat beside Townsend, with both men watching the progress of the battle aboard the Korilian cruiser. On one of the screens, an outline of the cruiser appeared, with green blotches indicating how much of the starship the Marines controlled. Another screen displayed the status at Zulu-4037, with the information relayed from their recon probe. The four Korilian cruisers had been joined by eight dreadnoughts; the Colonial starships had jumped away just in time. Remnants of *Odessa* spiraled slowly outward, and one large chunk passed near their recon probe. On the side of the white remnant were five black letters: *ODESS.*

On *Atlantis's* bridge, it was quiet. There had been no cheers from the starship's crew celebrating their successful mission. A somber silence prevailed instead as the men and women reflected on the loss of *Odessa* and her crew, as well as the part they played in the battleship's demise. They had undoubtedly experienced similar scenarios in previous battles, but this was Lara's first time, and a lump formed in her throat. She hadn't known anyone aboard *Odessa* but felt the pain of their deaths nonetheless.

From McCarthy, Lara sensed nothing. No elation, no pride, no sorrow, no remorse. From the short but intense starship battle, Lara gained an appreciation for the Nexus House approach to emotion. McCarthy had done what was required to accomplish the mission, sacrificing *Odessa* in the process, unencumbered by emotion. But although McCarthy superbly controlled his emotions, he wasn't bereft of them. Lara couldn't imagine dealing with the guilt that came with ordering the battleship's destruction.

As Lara's nausea slowly subsided, she returned her attention to the display, watching the Marines make steady progress aboard the Korilian cruiser; the green color spread slowly outward from the two dozen insertion points. The cruiser schematic eventually turned solid green, and shortly thereafter, the Marine colonel appeared on one of the screens, informing Admiral McCarthy that they had complete control.

McCarthy rose from his command console and stopped by several of the bridge watchstanders. Lara couldn't overhear the conversations but noted how their faces brightened when they talked with him. After a few minutes, he stopped by Angeline and Lara, who were still sitting on the deck.

"How do you feel?" he asked Lara.

"Like I've been hit by a shuttle."

"Can you walk yet?"

Lara wasn't sure, and with McCarthy's and Angeline's help, she got to her feet. When she stood on her own, however, her legs gave way again. She couldn't stand, much less walk.

McCarthy looked around, spotting four medics, but they were assisting the two incapacitated crew members, who had regained consciousness, off the bridge. He turned back to Lara and in a swift, effortless move, lifted her into his arms, cradling her with one arm beneath her knees and another under her back. The bridge spun even more, and Lara pressed her face against McCarthy's chest, wrapping her arms around his neck.

"I'll take Lara to Medical," he said to Angeline. "Are you okay?"

The Nexus Eight smiled. "Never better."

McCarthy headed aft toward the elevator, and it wasn't long before they arrived in Medical. One of the medics directed McCarthy to an empty bed, where he laid Lara gently on the mattress. The medic placed a diagnostic clip on her finger, then gave her another shot, this time in her neck. The nausea faded, and pressure inside her head eased. The tension left her muscles, and her eyelids became heavy.

"You'll sleep for a few hours," the medic said as he examined her diagnostics again, then moved to another patient.

McCarthy remained by her side, and as she closed her eyes, he said, "You did well."

She hadn't done much, simply pointing at *Hercules*, but she appreciated his compliment. Whether it was from the medication or McCarthy's kind words, a warm glow spread through her body as she drifted off to sleep.

Lara woke to find a Nexus Eight sitting beside her bed. But it wasn't Angeline. The woman, who was about Lara's age and looked vaguely familiar, was a brunette with an unusually pale complexion.

"Hello, Lara. How do you feel?" the woman asked.

"Much better." The headache and pressure inside her head had dissipated, and her body no longer ached. The room was stable, and there was no hint of nausea. Wondering how long she had slept, she checked her wristlet, but it had been removed. She searched for a clock but found none. Oddly, Medical was otherwise deserted—no other patients or staff, the beds empty.

"How long did I sleep?" she asked.

"I'm not allowed to answer that question." The woman smiled, her pale-blue lips framing white teeth.

"Why not?" Lara asked, her senses beginning to sharpen. Something was amiss.

"You won't let me."

The woman's answers weren't making sense. Lara sat up to continue the conversation, and only then did she see the red stain in the center of the woman's uniform and a shard of glass protruding from her stomach. Blood trickled off the end of the shard onto the floor, creating a red puddle spreading slowly outward.

It was then that she recognized the woman. She was Regina, the Nexus Eight in the videograph on McCarthy's desk—the fleet guide he had held in his arms as she died. Lara realized she was either dreaming or having a vision.

She searched for an appropriate question for the dead guide. "Why are you here?"

"To help you."

"Help me do what?"

"Like Jon said, you did well today. But in the upcoming battle against the Korilians, you will need to do more."

"Can you be more specific?"

"To some extent," Regina answered. "As you will learn as a Nexus, the future is fluid, changed whenever critical decisions are made. To properly shape the future, you must do more than advise Jon on your visions."

"What must I do?"

Regina stood and leaned toward Lara, touching the side of her face with an ice-cold hand. Blood ran off the shard onto Lara's bed, spreading as the sheets absorbed the cold, red fluid. Regina leaned closer, whispering in her ear. "Finish what others start. After all, isn't that why you're here?"

"What do you mean, *why I'm here*?"

Regina didn't answer. Instead, she examined the floor and bed, both of which had become covered in blood. The fluid warmed rapidly, becoming so hot that steam rose from the blood.

"You're comingling your futures," Regina said. "Stay focused."

The Nexus Eight dissolved into a white mist, but just before she dissipated, she said again, "Finish what others start."

As Regina faded, Admiral McCarthy appeared, walking toward Lara.

She was about to warn him of the slick blood-covered floor when she noticed Regina's blood was gone; there was no indication she had been present.

McCarthy stopped beside Lara's bed, cocking his head slightly as a confused expression appeared on his face. "What's wrong?"

"I had a vision," Lara replied. "A conversation with Regina."

He raised an eyebrow. "Regina? What did she say?"

"She told me to finish what others start. Do you know what she meant?"

McCarthy contemplated the matter for a moment, then replied, "I don't. Did she say anything else?"

Lara considered mentioning that Regina wouldn't tell her how long she'd slept, and her odd reference to some purpose—*why she was here*—then opted to tell McCarthy only about the former. "She wouldn't tell me how long I slept."

McCarthy replied, "You don't need a vision for that. Seven hours. How do you feel?"

"Good. Back to normal."

"Are you hungry?"

Until this moment, Lara hadn't noticed the rumbling in her stomach. She was famished, which wasn't surprising, since the only thing she'd had all day was a cup of tea.

"I'm starving."

McCarthy looked around, capturing the attention of a nearby medic. "Let's get you checked out of here. Dinner is in a half hour. Townsend and I are looking forward to your company."

The medic stopped by, and it wasn't long before Lara was released.

Dinner was a twelve-person formal affair with the battleship's senior officers, with four courses prepared and served by the starship's culinary specialists. The food was quite good, as was the company, and four hours later, Lara stood on the bridge of *Atlantis* as the Colonial task force prepared for the jump to Earth. The Fleet tug had tractor-beamed the Korilian cruiser again, and the one-minute jump alarm and verbal warning echoed throughout *Atlantis's* compartments. Angeline offered Lara another anti-nausea pill, which Lara eagerly accepted, considering she'd eaten a large meal only a few hours earlier.

McCarthy and Townsend were seated on the battleship's bridge, and Angeline stood beside Townsend's chair, so Lara moved beside McCarthy, the two Nexus guides serving as bookends to the Fleet officers. Lara turned toward the bridge displays as the jump clock reached ten, followed by the deep-toned alarm. As the clock approached zero, Lara braced herself for the now familiar dark and disorienting jump.

The darkness faded more quickly this time, and the nausea wasn't as severe. One of the tactical displays updated, showing the Colonial ships and the Korilian cruiser near a repair yard and close to one of the massive defense stations orbiting Earth. On another display, the image of Fleet Admiral Nanci Fitzgerald materialized, with the admiral seated behind her desk.

"Well done, Admiral McCarthy," she said. "The Fleet owes you and your task force a debt of gratitude." There was no mention of *Odessa* or of McCarthy's decision to destroy the crippled battleship.

McCarthy acknowledged Fitzgerald's compliment, then asked if she had any additional instructions.

Fitzgerald replied, "*Hercules* will tow the Korilian cruiser to a repair yard, where we'll begin working on it. You and your task force are released for further duties."

The display went black, then Townsend turned to McCarthy. "A shuttle will take you and the Nexus guides back to your command ship at your convenience, sir."

"How about fifteen minutes?" McCarthy said. He stood and shook Townsend's hand.

"Another successful mission together," Townsend said. He bid farewell to Lara and Angeline, then McCarthy departed the bridge with the two Nexus guides.

34

Ten days later, on the otherwise deserted bridge of the 1st Fleet command ship, Lara stood beside Admiral McCarthy during a battle simulation, with Angeline nearby and Channing behind them, as usual, taking notes. Since their return from Proxima, time had raced by with two-a-day simulator sessions, and Lara was slowly getting the hang of things from a premonition perspective. Yesterday, however, they had shifted to Fleet tactics. Basic formations and tactics had begun to gel, but the more advanced maneuvers eluded her.

Angeline sensed Lara's frustration. "I know this is overwhelming," Angeline said. "But we're teaching you tactics so you'll understand what's going on. The most important trigger for premonitions is your intuition, and having an idea of what the Korilians are up to helps."

Channing looked up from his wristlet. "Admiral, two Nexus shuttles are en route to your command ship, due to arrive in twenty minutes."

"Who's aboard, and what's the purpose of their visit?"

Channing scrolled down the message on his wristlet. "That's odd," he said. "There is only one person per shuttle, and no reason is provided for their visit. An Eight named Harindar Kapur is aboard one." At the mention of Harindar, Angeline brightened. As Channing scrolled farther down the message, his eyebrows furrowed. "Ronan is aboard the other."

Angeline's and Channing's anxiety flared, and Lara remembered her discussion with Angeline during the jump hold at Proxima; Ronan was the Primus Nine, responsible for defending the House, and was displeased The One had let her live. Lara's pulse quickened as the temperature dropped suddenly. McCarthy was viewing.

"Why is Ronan coming?" Lara asked.

"It's unclear," McCarthy answered. "I can't follow your line into the future. I tried following Ronan's, but it dissolves as soon as you interact with him."

"I'll meet with him?"

"Currently, yes. But that can be changed."

Angeline offered, "Why don't Channing and I meet Ronan and Harindar when they arrive and find out why they're here?"

"Good idea," McCarthy said. "Lara and I will wait in my quarters."

The two Nexi departed the bridge, and although Lara could tell both were concerned for her safety, there was a spring in Angeline's step. McCarthy headed toward his quarters, past the commander at his desk who greeted him, and Lara followed into his stateroom.

"Have a seat," McCarthy said, gesturing toward the small table and two chairs.

Pulling a crystal bottle from a cabinet by his desk, he poured two drinks, offering one to Lara as he settled into the chair across from her. "You deserve this," he said. "You're doing well. Especially considering how... *old* you are." He offered an uncharacteristic grin. "It's standard practice to induct children into the House at the age of five. Like learning a new language, adults have trouble picking things up as quickly, compared to children."

She thanked McCarthy and took a sip. There was still a chill in the air as McCarthy continued viewing. He sat across from her, quiet. While they waited, Lara checked the videograph display on his desk, hoping it was energized. During her previous visit, four of the videographs had garnered her attention. One in particular stuck in her mind—the brunette showing off her engagement ring.

Lara glanced at McCarthy's left hand. He wore no ring, and Captain Townsend said he wasn't in a relationship. So, who was the woman with the engagement ring? The question had popped into her mind repeatedly over the last three weeks, and she could no longer contain her curiosity.

"Tell me about yourself," she said. "I know you're a Nexus Ten and an admiral, but not much else."

"What do you want to know?"

"The personal stuff. Your family, ever been married, any children, et cetera."

"That won't take long, then," he said. "I was born on Polermis, I'm thirty-four years old and an only child. My mom and dad were both killed in combat, my dad during the first year of the war and my mom when I was seven. I'm single and have never been married. I was inducted into the Nexus House when I was five and tasked to the Fleet when I was sixteen. I have but one goal in life, and that is to lead the men and women in my command to victory, sparing as many of their lives as possible in the process."

Like McCarthy, Lara had lost both parents to the war. But they weren't alone; the casualty rates during the war were high, and many had lost one or both parents at an early age.

McCarthy said, "Now it's your turn. I've read your file. Time to fill in the blanks."

"Well, there's not much to tell. Single, no kids, married to my work. I'm also an only child and orphaned by the time I was thirteen, so we're petty similar on most counts. Except..." She stared at her wedding ring, and her throat constricted.

She gathered her thoughts and continued. "I was married to a wonderful man. But he died three years ago aboard *Vancouver*. In the Tindal system."

McCarthy was silent for a moment, then replied, "I was there. We lost a lot of good men and women in that battle. I'm sorry for your loss."

Lara managed a smile, though her lips quivered at the thought of Gary's death. As she stared at her wedding ring, she was suddenly overwhelmed with guilt. She realized she no longer thought about Gary each night before bed. Over the last three weeks, she'd barely thought about him at all. However, there *was* someone she thought about each night and when she awoke, and it wasn't Gary. It felt like she had betrayed him. She felt heat in her face as emotion overwhelmed her.

She lashed out. "What do you know about loss? You only know how to kill Korilians and sacrifice innocent men and women, like what you did to *Odessa*." No sooner had she spoken the words, she regretted them.

McCarthy looked away.

"I'm sorry," Lara said. "That was uncalled for."

McCarthy didn't respond, and the room slowly warmed. Lara searched for additional words to offer, to better apologize. Then he turned and stared at her for a long moment.

"Her name was Teresa," he said finally.

"Who?"

"Commander Teresa Davis. She was my chief of staff when I was in charge of the Normandy battle group. We fell in love, and there was nothing I wouldn't have done for her."

Lara noted the past tense. "What happened to her?"

"Her tour of duty ended, and I arranged for her to relieve an executive officer of one of the ships in my battle group so I could protect her. A few months after she transferred, we were involved in a fierce engagement, and the situation deteriorated. We needed to jump away, but Teresa's ship was damaged, its jump drive temporarily disabled. I had to choose between leaving her behind or sacrificing other ships to save her."

"What did you do?"

"I couldn't leave her. I delayed the battle group's departure until her jump drive was repaired. I lost five battleships. Thousands dead, sacrificed to save one woman. When I told Teresa what I'd done, she was horrified. She requested a transfer to another battle group to ensure I'd never be tempted to sacrifice anyone for her again. Her ship was destroyed three months later." McCarthy paused, then added, "So, yes, I do know something about loss. And also how to kill, as you pointed out."

Lara felt no emotion from McCarthy, but there was no doubt her words had hurt him. As they sat in silence, Lara searched for a segue to continue their conversation and put the awkward encounter behind them, finally latching onto a question no one had satisfactorily answered.

"Why do the Korilians hate us so much?"

McCarthy replied, "They never offered an explanation. They just began attacking us. The most prevalent belief is that they perceive us as a threat to their plan to rule the galaxy."

"Why haven't we been able to defeat them?"

"From a Fleet perspective, the Korilians have a slight advantage in numbers, gained during the early years of the war. Since then, Earth's construction and repair yards have kept pace. However, Korilian command and control abilities are much more sophisticated than ours. They're a tele-pathic species and have the ability to coordinate their attacks at a level we can only dream of. When our fleets are evenly matched, they win, unless they're facing me. The other fleets, however, need a substantial numerical superiority for victory. Unfortunately, the Korilians usually manage to engage at even or better odds."

Responding to a vibration, McCarthy checked his wristlet. After reading the message, he looked up. "Ronan is delivering something to me and wants to meet you."

"Do you think it's safe?" Lara asked. "If Ronan tries to kill me, can you stop him?"

"No," McCarthy said. "I cannot defeat Ronan. He's a praetorian, trained for combat, especially hand-to-hand. I have some close-combat training, but Ronan is the most lethal Nine in House history."

"What about your view? Wouldn't you be able to predict his attacks and defeat him?"

"Ronan is a Nine, which means he's also prescient; it's a prerequisite to become a praetorian, since their opponents are also Nines. You can imagine the advantage a prescient combatant would have over a normal adversary, being able to predict his opponent's every move. But when faced by another praetorian who is viewing, both views dissolve.

"When two Houses engage in battle, the praetorians close their oppo-nents quickly. Their competing views cause turbulence, destroying their views. At that point, physical skill takes over. Tens, on the other hand, are usually too rare and valuable to engage in close combat. A Ten stays back where he can view and provide direction. A good analogy for House warfare is that a Ten is the general and the praetorians are his soldiers.

"Praetorians train thousands of hours each year, honing their combat skills, while Tens focus on manipulating their view, learning how to split the timelines more efficiently—being able to follow more branches farther into the future. I haven't had the kind of combat training that Ronan has had, nor could I match his skill even if I had.

"However, I think you're safe. He won't go against The One's direction, and there's nothing I'm aware of that would have changed her mind. Your training is progressing nicely, and you haven't created more turbulence, so everything is pointing to you being an asset in the upcoming battle. Saving humanity will take precedence over protecting the House.

"In case my assessment is wrong, however..." He tapped his wristlet, and a man answered. "Yes, Admiral?"

"Have the master-at-arms bring a pistol to my stateroom."

"Aye, Admiral," the man replied.

A minute later, the stateroom intercom activated. "Admiral, Chief Suarez is here."

"Let him in," McCarthy replied.

The stateroom door slid open, and Suarez entered, carrying a holstered pistol.

"As requested, Admiral," he said.

McCarthy dismissed the chief, then pulled the weapon from its holster. "Standard Fleet-issue pulse-pistol," he said. "Some admirals and all battleship and cruiser captains are armed during battle. At full power, it'll vaporize a three-inch-wide hole through anyone not wearing armor or protective fabric. The Nexus uniform you're wearing is a normal garment, but there are soft-armor versions that will stop anything but the most powerful pulse-rifle."

He adjusted a dial on the side of the pistol, selecting the *Stun* position. "This will produce a wide area beam and hit Ronan's exposed flesh, incapacitating him for a few minutes.

Lara asked, "Since Ronan's a Nine, won't he be able to see the future and compensate for anything you do?"

"Not if we're within twenty feet and I start viewing. I'll disrupt his view, leaving physical skill as the deciding factor. Or a pulse-gun," McCarthy added, "which Ronan won't be able to defend against, since he's not outfitted for combat."

"Outfitted for combat?"

"An armor suit, like soldiers and Marines wear in combat against the Korilians, plus deflector shields on his forearms. Nines dressed for combat carry lots of interesting offensive and defensive weapons. But Ronan is wearing only a standard Nexus jumpsuit today. Of course, he could kill both of us bare-handed unless adequate precautions are taken."

McCarthy stood and fastened the belt around his waist, then slid the pistol into its holster.

Looking down at Lara, he said, "Time to introduce you to Ronan."

35

As they stepped from the elevator into the spaceport, Lara's eyes were drawn to the two blue-and-white Nexus shuttles, contrasting with the Fleet burgundy-and-crimson vehicles. One of the Nexus shuttles appeared to be a standard executive transport, while the other was much bigger. Lara suddenly recognized the larger shuttle. It was the one used to rescue her from Ritalis.

Channing and Angeline were standing between the shuttles, talking with two Nexi: Angeline was with Harindar, who had been aboard the rescue shuttle with Captain Townsend, while Channing conversed with a man with short, gray-flecked hair and a muscular build, who she concluded was Ronan. With McCarthy unable to determine the future, she probed for emotion.

Angeline was clearly attracted to Harindar, and the feeling was mutual. However, in the three weeks working with Angeline, she had said nothing about a love interest. But then again, with a guide's average life span being only two years, Angeline and Harindar had probably concluded there wasn't much point to starting a relationship.

Focusing on Ronan, she felt nothing, and Lara recalled the lack of emotion she had detected from The One and her praetorian guard. When it came to controlling emotion, there seemed to be a different degree of training above Level Eight, required to ensure emotion didn't impact a Nine's or Ten's view.

The four Nexi turned toward McCarthy and Lara as they approached, and Ronan extended his hand to McCarthy. But instead of shaking hands, they clasped each other's forearm.

McCarthy said, "It's good to see you again."

"Likewise," Ronan said as he released McCarthy's arm. "You've filled out nicely from a gangly sixteen-year-old. You'd make an excellent praetorian. If you decide to drop down a level, let me know and I'll finish your training."

McCarthy replied, "I became a Ten because I got tired of you beating the crap out of me. I'm happy where I am."

Ronan grinned. "All in your best interest. Your training might come in handy one day." His eyes went to the pulse-pistol strapped to McCarthy's waist. A confused expression formed on his face, and then his eyes widened slightly. He turned to Lara, and she felt the temperature drop as the Nexus Nine viewed. When the chill passed, his confused look was replaced by displeasure, and he chose not to greet her, keeping his hand to his side.

Lara took an instant dislike to Ronan; if he distrusted her, there was no reason to consider him a friend. On an impulse, she extended her hand, hoping to make him uncomfortable, rubbing into his face the fact that she had the Touch and The One had let her live.

Instead of being offended, Ronan reciprocated, his hand stopping an inch away from hers, his eyes hardening. "Do you really want to look into my mind?"

Lara recalled her mother's advice—*Looking into someone's mind is perilous; you might not like what you find.*

She hesitated, then withdrew her hand.

Ronan lowered his hand and stepped forward, stopping uncomfortably close. His voice dropped a notch as he spoke. "The first rule in combat is to never engage unless you plan to follow through." Lara stared at him dispassionately, then he added, "You need not fear me. I protect all Nexi. You are one of us now, and no harm will come to you unless you turn against us."

He stepped back, turning to McCarthy. "I need a few minutes alone with you. We can talk in the shuttle."

McCarthy accompanied Ronan into the sleek Nexus executive transport, and after the door closed behind them, Lara turned to Channing. "Is Ronan always this pleasant?"

Channing replied, "Ronan is one of the few praetorians remaining from the Corvad years. His views are shaped by a different time, when Nexus blood was spilled often. You should respect him."

Lara hadn't expected Channing's rebuke. After absorbing his words, she decided to give Ronan some slack. Protecting the House was no doubt a significant burden, and it was prudent that the person assigned that task maintain a wary eye.

There was an uneasy silence, broken when Harindar extended his hand. "Lara, it's a pleasure to see you again."

Inside the shuttle, Ronan turned to McCarthy. "I bring word from The One. She queried the Codex about Lara's lack of a line. There is a reference in the text of The Five."

McCarthy's eyebrows rose as Ronan continued, "The quote is, 'Harken the arrival of the One with no line.' Unfortunately, the rest of the passage has not been recovered. The Five foresaw Lara's arrival, but we don't know if they considered her an ally or a threat. The One has focused the Sevens on the issue, but we haven't learned anything more yet."

McCarthy nodded his understanding, and Ronan added, "If I were you, I'd be careful. Watch her closely. There are too many things...*wrong* with her."

"I understand," McCarthy said. "I'll take your advice under consideration."

"One more thing," Ronan said. He reached into his pocket, withdrawing a small blue envelope, which he handed to McCarthy. "From The One."

McCarthy examined the envelope. On the front was the Nexus House symbol—an intricate circular design with an eye in the center. McCarthy pressed the symbol with his thumb, and the envelope and symbol turned transparent. A handwritten note appeared.

A token, inside the gift.

He studied the words, trying to decipher the message. "Do you know what this means?"

Ronan replied, "It has something to do with the other shuttle. She said you'd understand."

"The other shuttle?"

"It's a gift from The One. We've been working on it for some time; she believes it might come in handy during the upcoming battle."

"How can a shuttle help in battle?"

"It's not a normal shuttle. Harindar will explain."

Ronan extended his hand, and the two men grasped each other's forearm again. "The future is not set," Ronan said. "Be careful, and good luck."

Lara spotted McCarthy exiting Ronan's shuttle, slipping an envelope into his pocket as he approached. Harindar introduced himself to McCarthy, explaining that he worked in the Engineering Design department.

"Ronan and I are dropping off this shuttle, Admiral. She's a one-of-a-kind, four-person transport, built just for you."

McCarthy surveyed the large vehicle. "It looks like it can carry forty people, not four."

Harindar patted the side of the shuttle. "That's because this baby can jump."

McCarthy was taken aback. Jump drives were enormous, with the smallest drives being the size of a two-story house. The entire shuttle was less than half that size.

"Not only can she jump, but due to the more compact drive, she can jump in smaller increments. If a battle is large enough, you can make tactical jumps between ships."

"Does it have a shield?"

"Unfortunately, no," Harindar said. "Lots of reasons why, all complicated, but the easiest answer is that having a shield generator so close to the jump drive is problematic. That's one of the reasons Fleet starships are so large. The shield generators need to be a sufficient distance from the jump drive."

"Without a shield," McCarthy said, "this shuttle's going nowhere during battle."

"We just do what we're told," Harindar said. "The One told us to build a shuttle that can jump and deliver it to you, so..."—he gestured to the shuttle—"she's all yours."

Harindar called out, "Shuttle, open."

The door slid aside.

"She's fully automated and responds to voice commands. Tell her where you want to go, and the autopilot will take you there. If necessary, you can deactivate the autopilot and take manual control."

McCarthy said, "I received a note from The One, which said there was something for me inside the shuttle. Do you know what she meant?"

Harindar cocked his head. "There's nothing unusual inside. Just your standard four-passenger layout. The artificial intelligence is very sophisticated for a shuttle, however—as advanced as the Cyborg Laws allow—and is programmed to respond only to your voice. Or an administrator." Harindar pointed to himself. "I took the shuttle through its paces, including an unplanned trip to Ritalis to rescue yours truly." He gestured toward Lara.

Lara took a moment to explain to McCarthy how she had been rescued from Ritalis.

When Lara finished, Harindar added, "She's a nice little ship."

Lara sensed Harindar's pride in the shuttle and found it comforting for some reason to learn that the House was populated not only with fleet guides and combat-trained Nines but with geeky engineers.

"Also," Harindar added, "tap your wristlet on the sync pad inside, and you'll be able to communicate with it remotely."

McCarthy gave Harindar an odd look, wondering why he'd have to communicate remotely with a shuttle, and the Nexus Eight shrugged. "Added feature. We just do what we're told." He broke into a grin, then said, "Ronan is waiting. Message me if you have any questions." He extended his hand to McCarthy, and the two men gripped each other's forearm.

He did the same to Lara, and she followed McCarthy's example. Harindar bid farewell to Angeline, and their grip lingered.

"The future is not set," Harindar said.

Lara sensed both hope and despair in his words, and she keyed on the identical phrase—*The future is not set*—that Channing had used with Angeline just before The One arrived on *Mercy*.

Angeline said, "I'll escort Harindar to his shuttle, if that's all right with you, Admiral."

"It's quite all right."

Angeline and Harindar walked slowly toward Ronan's shuttle, talking along the way, and Lara could tell they were prolonging their meeting for as long as possible.

Channing chimed in. "I have a few things to attend to while you get acquainted with your new shuttle." He turned to Lara. "Why don't you stay with Admiral McCarthy." It was more of an order than a question.

Before Channing departed, McCarthy unfastened the pulse-pistol belt from his waist and handed it to Channing. "Return this to the master-at-arms."

Channing took the pistol and departed, and McCarthy began examining his new shuttle, studying the exterior design. After a moment, he headed toward the shuttle door, and Lara joined him.

"Admiral McCarthy," she said. "I have a question. Is there something special about the phrase, 'The future is not set'?"

"It's a standard Nexus farewell," McCarthy answered, "usually used in times of concern or uncertainty. Additionally, when two Tens exchange the farewell, the second Ten responds, 'Together, we will change it.'"

He answered almost absentmindedly, still focused on the shuttle. He stepped into the transport, and Lara followed, finding herself inside the vehicle that had rescued her from Ritalis. McCarthy settled into one of the front seats and Lara sat beside him as they examined the controls, which didn't amount to much—a few small displays in the console, plus a three-dimensional map that McCarthy activated by pressing a console button. He manipulated the map with his hands, determining it could be rotated in any direction and expanded or contracted, then he deactivated it by voice, testing the shuttle's artificial intelligence.

"Map off."

The map deenergized.

McCarthy pressed one of two identical buttons on the console, one in front of him and another in front of Lara, and the console in front of him opened, revealing manual controls for the shuttle. He pressed the button again, and the controls disappeared behind the console again.

He tapped his wristlet against a sync pad on the console, and his wristlet beeped, confirming the sync.

"Shuttle, do you have a name?" McCarthy asked.

A woman's voice replied, "I do not, Admiral. The One said you would name me."

A blast of emotion hit Lara, sensations so intense that she flinched. She turned to McCarthy, whose face had paled. Lara sorted through the feelings —affection, anger, and guilt.

He had recognized the woman's voice, and Lara's thoughts turned to the conversation she'd had with McCarthy in his stateroom.

"Is that Teresa's voice?" she asked.

McCarthy shook his head.

"You recognize it?" she asked.

He nodded this time, then closed his eyes and leaned back in his chair. The intensity of his emotions ebbed as he slowly gained control. They dwindled to a flicker, then were extinguished, and the color returned to his face. But his eyes remained shut.

As McCarthy sat there, almost in a trance, Lara wondered who the woman was. Clearly, it was someone important. But if it wasn't Teresa, who was it? Lara's thoughts went to the videographs on McCarthy's desk and the four that had captured her attention. Teresa was the brunette with the diamond ring, Regina was the Nexus Eight, and the couple holding the infant was McCarthy's parents. That left the young female Army officer.

"Who is she?" Lara asked.

"Elena," Jon answered. "She was another Nexus Ten. We were inducted into the House when we were five years old. We grew up together and became like brother and sister."

"What happened to her?"

"I was tasked to the Fleet and Elena to the Army. In an effort to bleed the Korilians dry on Darian 3, the Army sent her to that forsaken planet with an entire army group. But then the Korilian fleet severed our supply lines, and no one made it off the planet. When the Korilians moved on, we sent recon probes in. The Korilians left no one alive. The Army lost its most valuable asset, and I lost my closest friend."

Their conversation was interrupted by flashing red lights throughout the spaceport, followed by an announcement over the starship's intercom.

"Set Defense Alert One. Set Defense Alert One."

Red lights flashed again, and as the normal white lighting returned, Lara observed personnel scurrying throughout the spaceport, converging on the supply shuttles being off-loaded. McCarthy's wristlet pulsed, and he read a short message.

"Operations brief in one hour at Central," he said, referring to the sprawling complex on the moon. He tapped a message into his wristlet, then added, "Channing and Angeline will join us, and we'll take my new shuttle."

They waited in silence for Channing and Angeline, and Lara could tell McCarthy was deep in thought. Finally, he spoke.

"Shuttle, I've decided to name you Elena."

"Elena," the shuttle repeated. "I like it. Thank you, Admiral McCarthy."

McCarthy replied, "You may call me Jon."

Channing and Angeline appeared in the doorway and climbed into the shuttle. After taking their seats, McCarthy said, "Elena, take us to Central."

"Yes, Jon."

After the door slid shut, the shuttle rose from the deck and sped toward the spaceport exit. As they passed through the repair yard's shimmering life-support shield into the void of space, McCarthy said, "We don't have much longer now. Ritalis has fallen, and the Korilians will jump to Earth within the next few hours. We'll learn more during the operations brief at Central."

___

36

As they traveled to their destination, Earth's moon grew quickly in the shuttle window. *Elena* adjusted the vehicle's trajectory as they approached the lunar surface, skimming just above the flat gray landscape. In the distance, a white facility grew steadily larger. McCarthy was silent during the transit, responding to a few messages on his wristlet, glancing at Lara after receiving one of them. Angeline broke the silence as they approached the end of the flight, providing Lara with a few details about their destination.

"Central isn't the actual name of the base," she said. "Its official name is the Deep Space Exploration Control Facility. But that's a mouthful, and since it's no longer used for that purpose, most people call it Central. You can see why."

The center of the lunar base was a large semi-spherical hub, like a half-buried ball. Three concourses stretched out from the hub like a three-pointed star, each ending in a launchpad. On two sides of each launchpad, metal frames rose several hundred yards. Lara listened as Angeline explained the reason for Central's unique design.

"Humankind's first attempt at deep space exploration was the Prometheus Project—space stations creating wormholes for instantaneous travel, controlled from Central. But the project was plagued with problems and was eventually abandoned.

"Fortunately, jump drives were developed shortly afterward, and the three concourses and launchpads were added. Early jump drives were rudimentary, and in addition to low gravity, high-velocity and acceleration vectors were required. The metal frames on the launchpads are magnetic rails, used to accelerate early spaceships to the required acceleration and velocity values. Central was modified again after the outbreak of the Korilian War and now serves as a major military facility."

Angeline paused when *Elena* informed McCarthy that Central had provided docking instructions, and the shuttle angled toward an open portal in the side of Central's hub. The shuttle passed through a shimmering life-support shield, and Central's gravity generators took effect. Lara shielded her eyes from the bright spaceport lights, noting several dozen shuttles docked in the multilevel spaceport. *Elena* settled into an empty bay in the highest level, where Captain Townsend and a four-star admiral awaited. Angeline provided a few details about Admiral Liam Carroll.

Carroll was Fleet Admiral Fitzgerald's right-hand man, serving as her deputy fleet commander while she was in command of 1st Fleet. When she was promoted to Fleet Admiral, Carroll was promoted as well, serving as Fitzgerald's deputy commander again, this time for the entire fleet.

The shuttle touched down, and the door slid open. The four Nexi exited the transport, and Carroll shook McCarthy's hand as Central's intercom blared, *"First Fleet, arriving,"* announcing Admiral McCarthy's arrival at the lunar base.

"Welcome to Central, Jon," Carroll said. "I take it First Fleet has received adequate replacements and has refitted satisfactorily?"

"We're back to full strength," McCarthy answered, "both in capital ships and vipers. We completed our supply loadout yesterday."

"Good. Everyone is assembling in the ready room. After the brief, Fleet Admiral Fitzgerald will see you in her quarters."

Carroll departed, and Townsend escorted McCarthy through Central's passageways while Lara, Angeline, and Channing followed behind, listening to the conversation.

"How's your new ship?" McCarthy asked.

"She's performing well. The Resolute class is quite an improvement, especially the pulse generator. We received the weapon upgrade two days ago."

"I take it you've been briefed on the new pulse capability?"

"Yes," Townsend replied. "So far only the eight Resolute-class commanding officers know, plus Admirals Fitzgerald and Carroll. I didn't realize you were aware."

"Admiral Fitzgerald and I have discussed the battle plan in detail, and as you've probably realized, the performance of the Resolutes will be critical to our success."

"I can see that," Townsend said. "The one thing that concerns me is the pulse regeneration time. Five minutes to recharge is a long time. The Korilians will get off five pulses to our one."

"That's why Fitzgerald handpicked the eight commanding officers. Shield management will be crucial, and we need experienced officers in command."

As they proceeded through Central's passageways, filled with men and women hustling between compartments, Lara sensed the tension that permeated the air as the Colonial Navy made final preparations for battle. She also noticed how their faces brightened when Admiral McCarthy passed by.

"It's good to hear First Fleet has been returned to full strength," Townsend said. "How about Second Fleet? I heard Denton lost sixty percent of his ships."

"He did," McCarthy answered. "Second Fleet has been reconstituted to two battle groups."

"Is that going to be a problem?" Townsend asked. "Second Fleet at half strength?"

"No. We estimated we'd lose almost three battle groups at Ritalis between First and Second Fleet. The battle plan assumes First Fleet at full strength and Second Fleet at half strength. So, we're right where we thought we'd be. With your ship and the other seven Resolutes assigned to Second Fleet, it will be a potent force."

"We might still have a problem," Townsend said. "Denton isn't taking his losses at Ritalis well. He lost over two battle groups while you lost only one half. He's blaming himself—second-guessing his ability."

"It's not his fault," McCarthy said. "And he'll realize that soon enough."

"How's that?" Townsend asked.

"The capability of the Resolute-class battleships isn't going to be the only revelation today."

Townsend shot McCarthy a curious look as they reached the entrance to Central's ready room. McCarthy stopped outside the closed doors, turning toward Channing. "Take Lara and Angeline to the flag conference room. Two Council regents are here for the brief, and they've asked to meet Lara."

Lara's heart skipped a beat. Regents were reclusive, rarely leaving their lofty Council towers. Public appearances were unheard of and an audience seldom granted. In a few minutes, Lara would meet two of the most powerful persons in the colonies.

After McCarthy and Townsend stepped into Central's ready room, Channing led Lara and Angeline up four decks to a large conference room with floor-to-ceiling windows overlooking the ready room. Inside were a man and woman, each wearing a white robe with an orange stole identifying them as the two most important members of the Council aside from the Council president.

The two regents—a man in his fifties with a gray goatee and an Asian woman in her late forties—were surrounded by Fleet personnel. As Channing waited patiently for an opportunity to introduce Lara, he leaned toward her and explained who the man and woman were.

"Regent Morel Alperi is the Director of Personnel, responsible for assigning a profession to every person on Earth when they reach the age of sixteen. That authority makes him the most powerful member of the Council, arguably more influential than the Council president himself. Regent Lijuan Xiang is the Director of Material, responsible for manufacturing ships for the Fleet and weapons for the ground forces."

An opening presented itself, and Channing strode forward with Lara and Angeline. "Regent Alperi, Regent Xiang, I am Dewan Channing, Nexus Deinde Eight. Lara Anderson and Angeline Del Rio are two of our fleet guides. Lara is the new guide assigned to First Fleet."

Regent Alperi shook Channing's hand. "It's a pleasure to meet the man responsible for training our fleet guides." After greeting Angeline, he turned to Lara. "How is your assignment to the Nexus House coming along? I must admit that I was reluctant to approve your new tasking. Rhea was most insistent, however, and I chose to defer to her judgment." Alperi added, "I hope you understand how important your tasking is. Do not disappoint me."

Lara quickly determined that Alperi was a pompous man impressed with his self-importance. She fixed a smile on her face, then replied, "I'll do my best."

Lijuan interrupted. "It's a pleasure to finally meet you." She greeted Lara with a warm handshake that lingered. Despite Lijuan's friendly facade, an uneasiness crept over Lara. Lijuan released Lara's hand and caressed her arm as she continued, "If we are victorious in the upcoming battle, Morel is going to take all the credit"—she flashed a mischievous smile at Alperi— "for tasking you as McCarthy's new guide and, of course, for saving humanity."

As the conversation continued, the other four Nexus fleet guides arrived, and Channing and Angeline excused themselves to join them. Alperi eventually drifted off, engaging other Fleet officers while Lijuan remained focused on Lara. She seemed genuinely interested in her as a person and not just a resource to be tasked, asking questions about her parents and childhood. Lara's uneasiness soon faded.

A Fleet officer politely interrupted them, informing Lijuan the operations brief was about to commence. The regents took their seats in the first row overlooking the ready room, and Lara and the other Nexi settled into the second row. While they waited for the brief to begin, Lara scanned the ready room, an amphitheater sloping down to a stage displaying a large floating hologram of the Colonial Navy emblem. Seated in the amphitheater were two hundred admirals, neatly organized into their battle groups and fleets. There was a conspicuous gap of empty seats, representing the missing commanders from 2nd Fleet's two destroyed battle groups. In addition to the admirals, there were eight captains in the 2nd Fleet section, and Lara spotted Captain Townsend.

The six fleet commanders sat at a long, thin table curving across the front of the ready room, each officer in front of their respective fleet. As Lara's gaze settled on McCarthy, Admiral Liam Carroll entered the room.

"Attention on deck!" he announced.

Everyone rose to their feet, waiting for Fleet Admiral Fitzgerald's arrival.

37

Fleet Admiral Nanci Fitzgerald stood alone in the darkness outside Central's ready room, reviewing in her mind the meticulous plan that would determine humanity's fate. When she had taken command of the Fleet five years ago, she had convinced the Council to adopt a new strategy, one that would nurse the Fleet back to health at the expense of the ground forces. However, the seed for that plan had been planted almost two decades earlier.

It was eighteen years ago when she first met Jon McCarthy deep within the Nexus House conclave in the Ural Mountains. As she escorted him to her battleship, Fitzgerald told the sixteen-year-old Nexus that he had a long journey ahead of him, one that would take many years. McCarthy had learned quickly under her tutelage, and as both were promoted up the ranks, she continued to provide guidance to the young man.

Eighteen years later, she now knew him better than anyone else did, even the Nexus One. Despite his allegiance to the House, McCarthy was no less dedicated than the next Fleet officer. There was no doubt in Fitzgerald's mind that McCarthy would sacrifice his life if the order was given. In a few hours, she would have to decide whether to issue that order.

Fitzgerald heard Admiral Carroll's voice echo through the ready room, calling her officers to attention. She took a deep breath and exhaled slowly, then strode into the ready room, stopping beneath the Colonial Navy symbol towering above her. "As you were," she announced as she faced her two hundred admirals and eight handpicked captains.

She assessed her officers as they took their seats. Their mood was somber; they knew the upcoming battle would be a fight to the death for every starship crew in the Fleet, and if they did not prevail...every man, woman, and child on Earth would be exterminated. As she stood facing her fleet commanders, she sensed their determination to succeed. They'd defend Earth tenaciously and somehow find a way to defeat the Korilian Empire.

Fitzgerald surveyed Admiral James Denton, commander of 2nd Fleet. He sat with slumped shoulders, a hollow look in his eyes. Denton blamed himself for his substantial losses at Ritalis. But it wasn't his poor command of 2nd Fleet that had produced the disparate losses between his and McCarthy's fleets. In a few minutes, he would understand. But she would explain the battle plan first. With the Korilian armada about to jump into Earth's solar system, it was time to reveal *everything*.

"Good evening," she said. "You know why we're here, so let's get down to business. Intelligence reports Korilian strength at just over two thousand cruisers and dreadnoughts, with approximately one hundred carriers. This means we are on a roughly one-to-one capital ship and marauder-to-viper ratio with the Korilian fleet. Past experience has shown that we require a thirty percent advantage to obtain a favorable outcome due to their superior command and control, so we have our work cut out for us.

"The Korilians are predictable in one way. They'll attempt to locate and destroy our command ships. We'll use this knowledge against them and set a trap, which, if successful, will destroy the entire Korilian fleet. It won't be easy, but this is how we're going to do it."

The Colonial Navy symbol towering above her was replaced with a three-dimensional display showing the disposition of the six fleets during the upcoming battle, illustrating every aspect of the planned operation as she explained.

"As you can see, every fleet except Second Fleet will be organized into a planar defense with a cylindrical flank, with the axis opposing the Korilian advance. To withstand the Korilian assault, two battle groups from every fleet except Second Fleet will be transferred to First Fleet, effective immediately. This will give First Fleet twelve battle groups to oppose the main Korilian thrust."

Fitzgerald knew the transfer of eight battle groups to 1st Fleet would raise valid objections, and she observed the murmuring throughout the ready room. She ignored it for the moment and continued.

"As the Korilian attack progresses, First Fleet will retreat in the center, forming a funnel aimed at its command ship, making it appear that a breakthrough is imminent. However, this is exactly what we want, because lying in wait will be Second Fleet's two battle groups. Both battle groups will be under a zero-emissions order, with no shields, weapons, or propulsion energized."

Fleet Admiral Fitzgerald paused before disclosing the first of two major revelations.

"Second Fleet will be reinforced with eight Resolute-class battleships. I realize the new Resolutes have not yet been tested in battle, for good reason. They have a new pulse-generator design, and ten days ago, a Korilian cruiser was captured intact. We've adjusted the pulse generators aboard the Resolute-class battleships, and we believe a single pulse will penetrate not only the Korilian shields, but even a dreadnought's exterior armor."

A buzz broke out in the ready room as the admirals commented to each other. Fitzgerald waited a moment for the conversations to die down before continuing.

"At the appropriate time, First Fleet will open the end of their funnel. Second Fleet will then commence operations and destroy the Korilian forces breaking through, then begin a thrust of its own, directly into the heart of the Korilian fleet. Their objective is the Korilian command ship.

"We've confirmed that the Korilian armada has only one command ship, as expected. Their advantage in command and control stems from coordinating their operations from a single ship, and their combat effectiveness is significantly impaired if this ship is destroyed. It is critical that

Second Fleet penetrate the Korilian defense and eliminate their command ship.

"Once the command ship is destroyed, the four fleets on First Fleet's flanks will shift from defensive to offensive operations. Your goal will be to overrun the Korilian flanks, forming a sphere around the entire Korilian fleet. You will then contract the sphere, destroying every capital ship and marauder along the way.

"To prevent the Korilian starships from jumping away once the outcome becomes clear, our orbiting defense stations will play a role. Although they'll be too far away to engage, they'll launch mines into the battlefield. But these won't be ordinary mines. Instead of ordnance, they'll carry shield generators. They'll remain dormant until the appropriate time, and once we gain the advantage, we'll activate enough to disable all Korilian jump drives within the sphere. The Korilians will destroy the shield generators, of course, but we'll continue to activate dormant mines and insert new ones until we are able to destroy every Korilian ship."

Fitzgerald waited, allowing the admirals to absorb the battle plan and its obvious shortcomings. The first flaw in Fitzgerald's plan was that Korilian command ships were well protected and the Colonial Navy had never destroyed one unless the Korilian force was significantly outnumbered. That wouldn't be the case in the upcoming battle. The Resolute-class battleships gave them a fighting chance, but the 2nd Fleet juggernaut would be significantly outnumbered once they penetrated the center of the Korilian fleet and their objective became clear.

The second flaw concerned 1st Fleet's ability to withstand the Korilian assault, letting forces through only where 2nd Fleet awaited. If the planar defense was breached elsewhere, Korilian forces would pour through the opening and envelop the Fleet's flanks. There were two related problems with this plan. The first was that the Korilians could throw the equivalent of twenty-two battle groups, minus whatever forces were positioned on the flanks, at 1st Fleet's planar defense. To reinforce 1st Fleet, eight additional battle groups had been assigned to McCarthy's command, which addressed one problem while creating another.

While Korilian command and control seemed unaffected by the number of ships involved, human command and control was not. There were four battle groups per fleet for a reason. Experience had shown that satisfactory command of more than four battle groups could not be achieved. Yet twelve had been assigned to McCarthy. He had demonstrated an extraordinary ability to coordinate his fleet's actions, undoubtedly due to his prescient abilities, and Fitzgerald gambled that he could coordinate the actions of twelve battle groups well enough to give the rest of the plan a chance to succeed.

Fitzgerald wasn't the only one who understood the flaws in the proposed battle plan. Every admiral seated before her had an appreciation for the Herculean task assigned to 1st Fleet. The commander of one of 2nd Fleet's two remaining battle groups stood to address Admiral Fitzgerald. His fleet had been mauled by the Korilians three weeks earlier, and he had watched two battle groups disintegrate under the Korilian onslaught.

He began by identifying himself and his command. "Vice Admiral Reinhardt, Commander, Tarawa battle group, Second Fleet."

"Proceed," Fitzgerald said.

"After the Ritalis campaign, I can offer a realistic assessment of this battle plan."

Fitzgerald had seen this coming the moment the plan was conceived. "Your *opinion* is...?"

"My opinion," Vice Admiral Reinhardt replied, "is that this plan is ludicrous!"

Shouting broke out in the ready room as some admirals echoed Reinhardt's sentiment and others admonished him for the disrespectful tone and lack of faith in the Fleet's ability. Yet everyone in the room knew there was a kernel of truth in the vice admiral's assertion. Fitzgerald stood with her hands clasped behind her back, waiting for the fervor to abate. The discussions slowly faded as the fleet commanders realized she hadn't responded.

Finally, she replied, "Well stated, Admiral."

Her response took everyone by surprise. She'd been under considerable stress to develop a strategy that at least offered the hope of victory, and everyone expected her to defend the battle plan vehemently. Instead, she had agreed her plan had no chance to succeed.

She continued, "I assume you're referring to the prospect of First Fleet absorbing the Korilian assault without breaking."

"I am," Vice Admiral Reinhardt replied. "There's no way twelve battle groups can withstand an attack by the entire Korilian fleet. And the assignment of twelve battle groups to one admiral compounds the problem. I respect Admiral McCarthy's abilities. Everyone does. But the effective coordination of twelve battle groups by one fleet commander is not possible."

"Again, well stated," Fitzgerald said. "Under normal circumstances, your assessment would be correct."

Fitzgerald glanced at McCarthy as she paced across the front of the ready room. His abilities had been kept secret long enough. What the Fleet needed now was hope. For the battle plan to succeed, they must first believe it could. Fitzgerald stopped and turned, facing her admirals. It was time for the second revelation of the night.

"First Fleet was given this assignment for a reason." She paused, then disclosed the long-held secret. "Admiral McCarthy is a Nexus Ten."

The ready room broke out into a frenzy of conversation. Most were aware of the supposed abilities of a level-ten prescient. Many things fell into place in the minds of the admirals there today. The reason for McCarthy's success. His penchant for personally evaluating all sensor data. His direct control of his fleet's operations during battle.

Fitzgerald surveyed Admiral Denton. He no longer sat with slumped shoulders and defeat in his eyes. He now understood that 2nd Fleet fared far worse than 1st Fleet at Ritalis not because of his failure, but because of McCarthy's extraordinary abilities. And now he'd have a chance to exact revenge for the savage beating his fleet had taken. It was his task to destroy the Korilian thrust and then ram it back down their throats. He looked at Fitzgerald and nodded, his confidence returning.

Vice Admiral Reinhardt settled into his seat, no longer considering 1st Fleet's task impossible. Fitzgerald waited for the conversations to subside, then wrapped things up with the last important piece of data.

"In addition to the Resolute class's new pulse generators, we've determined that it's possible to modify older pulse generators for a single shot that will penetrate the Korilian shields and armor. However, the creation of this pulse will destroy your pulse generator, so use this option as a last resort. The specifications will be sent to each ship's fire control system shortly.

"Make no mistake," she said. "This is a fight to the death for every member of the Fleet. We cannot retreat. We cannot fight another day."

Fleet Admiral Fitzgerald drew herself to attention and uttered the time-honored naval farewell to those going into battle.

"Good hunting!"

38

Alone in her quarters after the operations brief, Fleet Admiral Fitzgerald poured herself a drink, then slumped into a chair in her sitting room. She took a sip as she stared out the window, paying no attention to the gray landscape or the steady stream of shuttles departing the lunar base, returning the admirals to their ships. Her mind raced through a multitude of final details as the Fleet prepared for battle, reviewing the critical decisions she would have to make in the next twenty-four hours. She was pulled from her thoughts by the door intercom informing her that Admiral McCarthy had arrived.

"Open door," she said as she stood. The door slid open, and McCarthy entered. "Jon, it's good to see you."

She smiled warmly, offering a firm handshake. She gripped his hand longer than normal, for there was no one besides McCarthy who understood what she was going through. Additionally, none of her children had survived the war, and Jon was the closest thing to a son that she had left.

"Drink?" she asked.

"No, thanks."

Fitzgerald settled into a chair, as did McCarthy. "How's your new guide?" she asked.

"She's inconsistent but has flashes of useful insight."

"I understand you're considering not taking her. I don't understand the Nexus intricacies, but have you decided?"

"Not yet. I'll make the decision soon, though, as we don't have much time."

"What's your assessment?"

"The Korilians will make the jump within the hour, then close to within range in five."

Fitzgerald nodded. "That's consistent with Fleet intel. Additional warships flowing to the Korilian staging points have slowed to a trickle."

"The Fleet is ready," McCarthy said, "but how are you doing?"

"Our final stand against the Korilian Empire will begin in a few hours, and I'm second-guessing every decision I've made over the last five years."

"You've made the right choices," McCarthy said. "The Fleet hasn't been this strong since before Telemantic."

"Yes, but is it strong enough?"

McCarthy didn't respond.

There was a long silence, then Fitzgerald continued. "You're like a son to me, Jon. I've tried to provide the guidance you've needed through the years, and you've developed into a fine young man and the best tactician the Fleet has ever known."

McCarthy accepted her compliment as she continued.

"You did well at Ritalis. We gained valuable time while inflicting heavy casualties. Second Fleet took heavy losses as well, but the important point is that Ritalis was the first time we've gone toe-to-toe with the Korilians with equal forces using more than your fleet. You deserve the credit for that. I'm convinced that had you been in command of both fleets, we would have prevailed. In this next battle, you'll have command of over half of the Fleet. Your prescient abilities have served us well, and now we must put your talent to the ultimate test."

She paused, then focused on the critical issue. "First Fleet must hold. If the Korilians break through the center, the battle will degenerate into a dogfight we cannot win." She leaned forward, fixing her eyes on his. "The fate of humanity rests on your shoulders. I have no doubt that you will do what is required and succeed."

Her last words were deliberately vague. During battle, McCarthy could see ten minutes ahead with certainty, and Fitzgerald wondered if he could see enough of the future to discern what she was contemplating. Either way, it would all come down to McCarthy.

39

Staring out the window overlooking the deserted ready room, Lara listened as Channing and Angeline talked beside her in the otherwise empty conference room, waiting for Admiral McCarthy. After the operations brief, Alperi and Lijuan had bade farewell and headed to their Council shuttle, returning to Earth. The Nexus guides—all except Angeline and Lara—had also departed, joining their fleet admirals as they returned to their command ships. It was time for Angeline to leave as well, and she turned to Lara.

"You have done well," Angeline said. "Much better than I imagined a few weeks ago. Just tell McCarthy what you see, and he'll interpret it for you."

Lara sensed emotion building within Angeline, and the Nexus Eight hugged her tightly and whispered in her ear, "The future is not set."

Angeline pulled back with tears in her eyes. Without another word, she departed, leaving Channing and Lara alone.

Channing said nothing, studying Lara in a way that made her uncomfortable. His wristlet pulsed, and after checking it, he announced, "Admiral McCarthy is on his way."

He was silent for another minute, probing Lara with dark eyes, then spoke again. "I have only a few words to add. The future is difficult to predict, even for a Ten, especially in battle where so many decisions are made in a short period of time. I fear that McCarthy leaned on Regina more heavily than he realizes, and that support is now gone. You have done well, as Angeline said, but you are far from a seasoned fleet guide."

Lara swallowed hard. If this was Channing's idea of a pep talk, it was failing miserably.

"Do you have any guidance?" she asked.

"I do," Channing said, "from The One. She told me to pass along one piece of advice. *Trust your instinct.*"

"Did she say anything more specific?"

"She did not," Channing answered. "However, the phrase is a bit unusual. The standard Nexus wording is *Trust your intuition.* I have contemplated the difference between instinct and intuition, hoping to offer additional advice, but I have nothing concrete to offer. I leave it to you to determine what she meant. Assuming, of course, McCarthy takes you into battle."

"What?" Lara asked. "I've done well and haven't created any more turbulence. I thought he had already decided to take me."

"He has not," Channing replied. "But he'll decide soon, and you will either head to the command ship with him or Domus Praesidium with me."

As Lara absorbed Channing's words, she realized how different things were now compared to three weeks ago. At the beginning of her Nexus training, she wanted nothing more than to return to her tasking as a counselor somewhere. Now, her heart was set on accompanying McCarthy into battle.

Lara asked, "Is there anything I can do to influence his decision?"

Channing shook his head. "The die will be cast in the next few minutes."

The conference doors opened, and McCarthy appeared. Channing and Lara approached as he said, "Come with me to the observation deck."

He led them to a nearby elevator, and they ascended to Central's top level, entering a circular lounge. Lara was awestruck by the sight. The circumference was lined with twenty-foot-high windows offering a 360-degree view of the lunar surface. A glass dome capped the observation deck, with the stars and Earth shining brightly through.

The reaction to McCarthy's arrival rippled across the observation deck, as conversations ceased and men and women rose from their chairs. After a moment of hesitation, they approached him. Lara recalled that McCarthy didn't get out much, refitting his fleet as quickly as possible before returning to battle. She and Channing stood to the side while McCarthy greeted those eager to meet the admiral who had led 1st Fleet to so many victories. It wasn't until this moment that Lara realized how special her relationship with McCarthy was, spending hours with him each day.

When McCarthy finished greeting everyone, he led Lara and Channing to the observation deck perimeter, stopping to gaze across the lunar surface. Central was in its last few hours of daylight, preparing to pass into its two-week-long night, and a mountain range in the distance cast long dark shadows across the barren landscape.

"The Apennine Mountains," McCarthy said, seemingly in response to her thoughts. "When we started exploring our solar system, Apollo Fifteen landed not far from here, at the base of the Apennine Mountains. Our exploration of the galaxy began here at Central, with the launch of the first ship with a jump drive."

As Lara stood in the facility where humans had begun their journey to the stars, she wondered what those pioneers had thought as they engaged a jump drive for the first time.

Will we like what we find?

Then she realized there was a more important question they had failed to ask:

Will what we find...like us?

The answer was clear. Humanity was on the brink of extinction, being exterminated by a species that for some reason did not like humans.

McCarthy said nothing more as he stared beyond the horizon, prompting Lara to ask, "Why did you bring us here?"

"I wanted you to see what we are up against."

Lara didn't understand and was about to ask him to explain when white flashes appeared in the distance. She had watched Colonial fleets return from battle before but had never seen so many flashes. Her entire field of view was filled with the bright white announcement of starships jumping into Earth's solar system.

The bright flashes continued—hundreds and then thousands—announcing the arrival of the Korilian armada. Men and women along the perimeter of the observation deck, their eyes wide and hands to their mouths, stepped back from the windows, as if the extra few feet could somehow protect them.

McCarthy said nothing more, eyeing Lara carefully as Central's alarms activated: alternating high and low tones, followed by an announcement.

"General Quarters, General Quarters. All hands report to assigned stations. Compartments will be sealed in fifteen minutes."

The announcement was repeated, followed again by the two-toned alarm.

McCarthy remained at the observation deck perimeter, and Lara watched the engine plumes on 1st Fleet starships ignite as they began to reposition between Earth and the Korilian armada. Lara glanced at her wristlet as the time counted down to the fifteen-minute mark. Once the compartments were sealed, she assumed no one could leave Central. They needed to get back to the 1st Fleet command ship.

"We need to go, Admiral. They're locking everything down in five minutes."

McCarthy started toward the elevator without a word. Channing and Lara joined him, and they descended to the bustling spaceport, with transports lifting off and speeding toward the exit. After reaching the Nexus shuttle, McCarthy turned to Lara.

"You have a choice," he said. "A shuttle to the command ship, or a transport to Earth with Channing."

Lara replied without hesitation. "The command ship."

McCarthy nodded, then turned to Channing. "Thank you for your assistance, Dewan."

The Nexus Eight gripped McCarthy's wrist in the standard Nexus farewell, then headed toward one of the awaiting transports.

McCarthy and Lara boarded their Nexus shuttle. "*Elena*, take us to my command ship."

The shuttle lifted from the deck and passed through the spaceport's life-support shield, then accelerated quickly upward from the lunar surface.

40

The Nexus shuttle sped toward the repair yard where the 1st Fleet command ship, *Lider,* was docked, the small transport threading its way through 6th Fleet. The steady stream of supply shuttles entering the starships over the last few weeks had ended, and Lara watched the spaceport doors in the sides of the battleships and cruisers slowly close in preparation for battle. *Elena* kept the shuttle farther from the ships than during their last journey, and as Lara wondered why, she spotted hazy outlines appearing around the starships; they were bringing up their shields.

The repair yard grew in size as they approached, with *Elena* adjusting course to accommodate the departing warships as they undocked. The starships were backing slowly from the repair yard bays, then turning toward their respective fleets. *Elena* entered *Lider*'s bay and eased into the command ship's spaceport. As they stepped from the shuttle, alarms sounded and the ship's spaceport doors began closing.

Lieutenant Commander Bryn Greenwood, who had escorted them from *Mercy,* approached, saluting McCarthy as the ship's intercom announced, *"First Fleet, arriving."*

"Captain Priebus is on the command bridge, Admiral," Greenwood said, "preparing to undock. Is there anything I can assist you with?"

"I'm fine," McCarthy said.

McCarthy and Lara made their way to the flag bridge, entering to find it fully manned and bustling with activity. McCarthy settled into the right chair, and Lara sat to his left. A few minutes after their arrival, Lara felt the ship's bow thrusters activate, and the starship slowly backed out of the repair bay. When the bow cleared the repair yard, the starship twisted around, and Lara felt a vibration as the main engines were brought online.

As *Lider* accelerated toward 1st Fleet, Lara examined the flag bridge personnel. In addition to the starship crew, there were two Marines, each wearing a sand-colored armored suit—standard Marine battle armor—which offered protection from pulse blasts and razor-sharp Korilian limbs. Each Marine had a pulse-pistol on his waist and a heavy pulse-rifle strapped to his back. Only their eyes were visible through the helmet shield, and Lara watched in fascination as information scrolled down the transparent facepiece, which the Marines' eyes followed.

Lara leaned toward McCarthy and asked quietly, "Why are Marines aboard?"

McCarthy replied, "All Fleet starships carry a Marine detachment in battle in case they get boarded by Korilians. It doesn't happen often these days, as crews are quick to self-destruct disabled ships, but if the Korilians try to take control of a disabled starship while there is still a chance to repair the damage, Marines come in handy. We have a few dozen Marines on *Lider*."

Lara nodded her understanding, reflecting on the Marines' purpose. She wasn't sure which fate was preferable—facing a Korilian boarding party or self-destructing.

The 1st Fleet command ship slowed, and Lara turned her attention to the bridge windows. A squadron of twelve Atlantis-class battleships loomed ahead, organized in a spherical formation, and ahead of them lay 1st Fleet's twelve battle groups. *Lider* slowed to a stop in the center of the twelve-battleship sphere, and the command ship's shields were raised. McCarthy then ordered the squadron of Atlantis-class battleships to bring their shields up as well, joining them together in an outer protective bubble, providing *Lider* with an extra layer of protection.

McCarthy approached the console in front of the command chairs, activating the three-dimensional display. Lara joined him as he manipulated the icons. The display morphed into a flat circular grid with ninety hexagonal sectors, joined by another seventy sectors in the cylindrical flank, which wrapped back toward Earth, melding with the orbiting defense stations.

The formation resembled a soda can, with one end merging with the defense stations and the other end—the flat planar field—facing the Korilians. The formation was quite flexible, Lara had learned; the planar field could be expanded and contracted, bent inward to absorb a heavy assault, tilt its axis to meet the trajectory of the Korilian attack, or even split into several mini-planar fields—like multifaceted eyes—if the Korilians attacked in more than one area.

Within this protective cylinder and behind the orbiting defense stations were the Fleet's most valuable resources—the eight starship construction yards and eight repair yards. If the Korilians broke through and destroyed those shipyards, the war would be lost even if the Korilians were repelled; it would take years to rebuild the shipyards, during which time the Fleet would receive no replacement starships. The Fleet would be quickly overwhelmed.

McCarthy sent orders to his battle groups, and they began to populate each hexagonal sector with five battleships and five cruisers. Behind the planar grid, McCarthy held two battle groups in reserve, plus forty carriers waiting to launch their viper wings.

After the fleets maneuvered into position, two thousand warships populated the Colonial defense: one thousand in the planar grid with two hundred in reserve, plus eight hundred along the circular flank. Conspicuously missing, however, was 2nd Fleet. The icons in McCarthy's display were colored based on their fleet. 1st Fleet ships were blue, and the other ships were green, orange, purple, and brown. There were only five fleets displayed in the defense grid.

"Where is Second Fleet?" Lara asked.

McCarthy pointed out the sides of the bridge windows. Lara looked but saw only the starships from the other four fleets in the distance, forming the cylindrical flank.

"You can't see them," McCarthy said, "and neither can the Korilians. All detectable systems are offline: shields, sensors, communications, and transponders. Even lighting is deenergized, with Second Fleet operating in darkened-ship status."

McCarthy tapped several controls on his console, configuring the monitors curving along the front of the bridge. One of the displays zoomed in until the advancing Korilian ships became visible: dark gray hulks with faint red lighting inside, growing steadily larger as they approached.

Admiral McCarthy returned to his command chair, monitoring the sensor data. The orders and reports on the bridge dwindled to silence, and McCarthy and *Lider*'s crew waited.

"How much longer?" Lara asked.

McCarthy replied, "They'll close to effective weapon range in an hour."

During one of Lara's training sessions on *Lider*'s bridge, Angeline had explained that pulses lost strength as they traveled, interacting with interstellar matter. The closer the starship was to the target when it fired, the stronger the pulse. For example, at long range, a starship shield could absorb a ten-pulse barrage, while at very close range, a double-pulse could collapse a shield. Although a starship's tyranium coils held enough energy to recharge the pulse generator during a battle lasting several days, starship crews tended not to waste energy on attacks yielding little damage. Instead, they typically waited until the ships got fairly close before engaging.

McCarthy sat silently beside Lara, examining the displays. The two fleets were evenly matched, as Fleet Admiral Fitzgerald had predicted during her operations brief. That meant the odds were in the Korilians' favor due to their superior command and control, and they would likely prevail unless their command ship was destroyed.

Five years of preparation and thirty years of conflict were about to culminate in humankind's final stand against the Korilian Empire.

41

On *Lider*'s flag bridge, with the crew sitting silently at their consoles, the tension rose steadily as the Korilian armada closed on the Colonial Fleet. Lara monitored the sensor data on the various displays, with the most important factor—time to engagement range—counting down on the bottom right corner of each screen.

With thirty minutes remaining, McCarthy broke the silence. "Flight officer. To all First Fleet carriers, launch wings."

The order went out, and one of the displays reconfigured, showing forty carriers behind the command ship. Each starship began launching vipers from the twenty runways exiting the bow. Each carrier completed a twenty-viper launch cycle every ten seconds. In just over four minutes, twenty thousand vipers spewed forth, forming up into forty wings.

As the Korilians closed, McCarthy waited patiently, his starships sitting motionless in their assigned sectors, with the viper wings behind the 1st Fleet command ship.

"*One minute to ten-pulse engagement range,*" announced *Lider*'s computer.

Everything was in automatic for the time being. The combat systems of all one thousand 1st Fleet starships in the planar grid were tied together, with the computers calculating how many pulses were required to collapse a Korilian starship shield. At this range, it would take ten battleship or

twenty cruiser pulses—or various combinations of cruisers and battleships
—to collapse a Korilian shield, and the combat systems colluded to assign
the requisite number of ships to a single target.

When the Korilians closed to within nine-pulse range, the 1st Fleet
combat systems would automatically retarget, assigning only nine battleships per target, and so on, increasing the shield-collapse rate for the first
barrage as the Korilians closed. The Korilians, however, were doing the
same. McCarthy had explained earlier that he would let the Korilians fire
first, with the Colonial Fleet counterfiring milliseconds later.

"Ten-pulse engagement range."

The Korilians did not attack; their armada continued closing.

"Nine-pulse engagement range."

The Korilians closed to within eight-pulse range and still didn't engage.

Seven-pulse range and still no attack.

Lara leaned toward McCarthy. "Why aren't they engaging?"

McCarthy replied, "The Korilians are disposing with finesse in this
battle, closing more than normal before their first barrage to maximize the
damage. They have the advantage and plan to destroy our Fleet as rapidly
as possible to reduce the possibility we might get lucky."

When the Korilians closed to within six-pulse range, McCarthy stood
and approached his control console. Lara moved beside him.

Immediately after the ship's computer announced, *"Five-pulse engagement range,"* *Lider's* sensor displays lit up with the images of humankind's
final stand against the Korilian Empire. Explosions filled the displays and
bridge windows as thousands of capital ships fired their pulse generators,
blue pulses speeding outward while incoming red pulses impacted the
Colonial ships, their shields illuminating as they absorbed the pulse
energy.

Korilian pulses collapsed the shields of over one hundred Colonial
battleships, with Colonial pulses penetrating an equal number of Korilian
shields. None of the pulses penetrated the battleship armor, however,
although some damage was inflicted.

Colonial ships with collapsed shields turned sideways, presenting beam
shields while their bow shields regenerated. Damaged Korilian warships
slipped behind fully operational warships until their bow shields reformed.

The Korilian armada continued its advance as their pulse generators recharged.

At the one-minute point—fifty-seven seconds to be exact—the Korilians fired again, with the Colonial starships counterfiring so quickly that their pulses appeared simultaneous. On McCarthy's three-dimensional display, the sectors became colored, and Lara deduced that green meant the sector had five fully operational battleships, yellow meant four, orange—three, pink—two, red—one, and black—zero. The Korilians were targeting the middle of the Colonial Fleet formation; the center sector and the six around it had turned various colors.

Lara examined the colored grids on the bridge consoles, which would provide additional information as the battle progressed: how many battleships and cruisers had been lost in each sector and battle group, plus the status of the remaining warships—how many had a shield down, main engines inoperative, one or two reactors down, or inoperable jump drives, although the latter wouldn't matter in this battle; no Colonial warship would jump away.

McCarthy touched various sectors on his display, with a two-finger tap selecting a supplying sector and a one-finger tap identifying the receiving one. The sector colors changed as battleships flowed in toward the center, with outlying sectors turning from green to yellow while the central sectors returned to green. Starships continued sliding into adjacent sectors until the yellow sectors were dispersed evenly throughout the ninety-sector planar grid.

The Korilian and Colonial ships continued firing at fifty-seven-second intervals until they finally closed the distance, with the white and dark gray starships exchanging pulses at almost point-blank range as they passed each other. The starships began maneuvering, turning and rotating as they attempted to hit their adversary on the same shield while presenting a different shield to their opponent. The Colonial Fleet formation gradually retreated as the Korilians advanced, ensuring that each Korilian ship remained engaged, that none slipped cleanly through.

McCarthy manipulated the three-dimensional display with his hands, zooming in for more detailed looks by spreading his hands apart, shrinking the display by pushing it together, and turning it by grabbing the sides and twisting. His hands moved with amazing speed; in one ten-second period, he zoomed the display out to examine the top right sectors in the planar grid, dropped down to the left, twisted the display ninety degrees to examine the left flank, then did a one-eighty to examine the right flank. Another twist and squeeze of his hands and the display returned to its normal size and orientation.

His hands never stopped moving, constantly directing the flow of Colonial battleships and cruisers. Some of the ship movements were in response to Korilian attacks, directing replacements into weakened sectors, while other redeployments were Colonial offensives, temporarily overwhelming enemy forces in various sectors before the Korilians could respond.

Shortly after the two opposing fleets engaged, sensors detected incoming Korilian marauder wings headed toward starships with down shields and penetrated armor. It took five minutes to regenerate a collapsed shield, during which time the armor could be penetrated by additional pulses and significant damage inflicted by marauders. A shield generator going down permanently was a death sentence unless the starship could jump away.

In response to the incoming marauders, McCarthy tapped several of the Colonial wings stationed behind *Lider*, and several thousand vipers streaked by the command ship, en route to engage the inbound marauders.

After the initial Korilian assault, Lara's tension began to ease. 1st Fleet had absorbed the main Korilian thrust and held. Although 1st Fleet was arranged in what looked like a simple planar formation, Lara had learned that the starships were organized in several complex ways. The first was that the battleships and cruisers worked independently of each other: two grids superimposed on each other, with each hexagonal sector assigned a five-battleship fire group and a cruiser team of five. The *really* complicated part, however, was the maneuvering.

Instead of entire fire groups moving to adjacent sectors, sometimes one or two battleships or cruisers would shift and join an adjacent fire group, which enabled the quick concentration of firepower in a sector. In response, the Korilians would shift starships to match the Colonial fire-power while maneuvering in countless other sectors in an effort to over-whelm Colonial forces elsewhere. To Lara, it felt like the planar defense grid was a living entity, its surface writhing as starships moved back and forth.

Lara's attention was drawn to a Korilian buildup near the center of the Colonial Fleet formation. The Korilians had slid two extra dreadnoughts into the six sectors bordering a central sector. Lara had been through enough simulations to know what the Korilians were up to. With another shift, the two extra dreadnoughts in the adjoining sectors would converge on the center sector, increasing the number of Korilian dreadnoughts to seventeen, facing only five Colonial battleships.

McCarthy seemed oblivious to the threat, and Lara was about to say something when wisps of fog appeared on the display, winding their way toward the center. But they stopped short, circling the two sectors to the left and right of the center. Lara examined the Korilian forces more closely, then realized the Korilian movements were a ruse; they weren't planning to attack the center at all.

Instead of pivoting toward the center, the Korilians were waiting until McCarthy shifted battleships inward, then the Korilians would pivot outward instead, attacking the weakened border sectors. If McCarthy took the bait, expecting the Korilians to attack the center, he wouldn't be able to reinforce the true targets of the Korilian attack in time.

"Admiral," Lara said, "the center pivot is a feint. They're going to attack the sectors on either side."

"I know," McCarthy said.

His hands never stopped moving, and Lara watched in surprise as he took the bait, sliding battleships in adjacent sectors toward the center. As Lara predicted, the Korilians pivoted outward instead.

McCarthy sent additional orders, and the entire center of the Colonial Fleet formation writhed with motion, with battleships and cruisers moving in multiple directions. When the movement ceased, Lara assessed the situation: McCarthy had not only shifted enough battleships into those two sectors to maintain even odds, but he'd also sent starships into the sectors the Korilians had just pivoted out of, obtaining a two-to-one advantage in four sectors. Whether through experience or his prescient ability, McCarthy had seen through the Korilian ruse and outmaneuvered them.

The Korilians responded, routing additional starships to the affected sectors to reestablish even odds, but not before the Colonial warships destroyed four Korilian dreadnoughts.

And so it went as minutes turned into hours, each side attempting to outmaneuver the other, concentrating starship firepower in various sectors in unpredictable ways. The bulk of the Korilian armada was concentrated in the center, and despite McCarthy's prowess, Colonial losses began to mount. Slowly, Colonial forces in the center began to retreat, buying time for McCarthy to reroute his dwindling forces. A funnel in the center of 1st Fleet's planar grid began to form, retreating deeper and deeper toward the 1st Fleet command ship.

42

The battle continued as Colonial ships handed Korilian warships off to each other while they waited for their pulse generators to recharge, pounding and collapsing Korilian shields while the Korilians did the same. Lara periodically attempted to summon a vision, imagining she was standing on a deserted starship bridge as Angeline had advised her to do. The characteristic fog that was present in all of her visions formed each time, but it simply flowed along the starship's deck, swirling gently at her feet. She received the same vision repeatedly and told McCarthy, but the information didn't seem to affect his actions.

On one occasion, she touched McCarthy's hand to gain his attention and immediately became dizzy, her mind filling with hundreds of visions, each advancing forward at breathtaking speed. She hadn't meant to use her Touch, but she had seen into McCarthy's mind, giving her an appreciation for his prescient ability as he simultaneously analyzed hundreds of futures based on different actions in the present. Lara refrained from touching his hand again.

The hours began to accumulate as the Korilians pressed their attack, pushing forward in the center toward the 1st Fleet command ship. Colonial ships continued their retreat, increasing the funnel depth to keep the Korilian forces in front. As the Korilians advanced, McCarthy kept *Lider* in place, tapping into his two reserve battle groups to reinforce depleted sectors. The defense grid stabilized, preventing a Korilian breakthrough. Additional Korilian starships flowed into the funnel, matched by Colonial reinforcements. Another hour of battle and the funnel held, with the intensity of the battle escalating.

White flashes suddenly illuminated the bridge, forcing Lara to shield her eyes, but not before she saw over a dozen Korilian dreadnoughts directly ahead. Lara's heart leapt to her throat when she realized the Korilians were attempting the same tactic that had almost worked at Ritalis. Only this time, fourteen Korilian starships were attacking, and *Lider's* protective ring of Atlantis-class battleships could take out only six of them.

The Colonial battleships fired, and Lara was surprised when blue double-pulses carved through ten of the Korilian dreadnoughts. As she wondered how twelve battleships had fired twenty pulses, an additional eight Atlantis-class battleships appeared on McCarthy's display as they brought up their shields and transponders. McCarthy had either foreseen the Korilian attack or prepared well, keeping the extra battleships off the grid like 2nd Fleet, waiting to surprise the Korilian ambush.

The remaining four dreadnoughts fired simultaneously, their pulses penetrating the outer protective bubble and *Lider's* bow shield. The command ship's armor prevented the pulses from penetrating the starship's hull, but the pulses vaporized the communication equipment mounted below the bridge.

The shield supervisor called out, "Bow shield at three percent and recharging."

Alarms flashed on several consoles, and the communications supervisor reported, "Loss of primary communication antennas. Shifting to starboard auxiliaries and backup channels."

After *Lider's* battleship screen completed their pulse generator recharges, the remaining four Korilian dreadnoughts were destroyed.

McCarthy muttered under his breath, "I predicted ten, not fourteen. The Korilians changed their mind just before executing, without cause." He turned to Lara. "Can you sense anything?"

Up to now, it seemed the battle was in hand. But the Korilians had suddenly become unpredictable. She closed her eyes and did her best to summon a vision. But like Angeline predicted, it was more difficult during battle, especially after the surprise Korilian attack; Lara's heart raced, and she found it difficult to concentrate. Instead of standing on a deserted bridge, her mind was filled with visions of *Lider*'s bridge, with its displays of information and personnel diligently carrying out their duties. She tried to calm herself, slowing her breathing.

Fleet Admiral Fitzgerald's image suddenly appeared on one of the displays. "Admiral McCarthy, what is your status?" she asked. "We've lost tactical communication with First Fleet."

"My apologies, Admiral," McCarthy said. "We took a quad-pulse, which caused some damage. We had to switch to backup communication channels. We'll send the new frequencies to the command center now."

"I understand," Fitzgerald said. "Inform me of any deviations from the plan."

The display went black, and McCarthy returned his attention to the battle. But then fog began seeping from the display and it flickered to life again, only this time Fitzgerald's image was replaced with a destroyed command center. A layer of gray smoke floated between twisted support beams that had fallen from the ceiling onto personnel and equipment, and the command center staff lay either sprawled on the floor or collapsed onto consoles that smoldered beneath them. Fleet Admiral Fitzgerald was slumped over one of the data fusion tables, her head turned to the side. Thin rivulets of blood ran from her nose and the side of her mouth, and a pool of blood had coagulated under her face. Her steel-blue eyes were frozen open.

Lara's vision began shaking, and McCarthy reached over and grabbed her hand, squeezing it so hard she thought her bones might crack. As pain shot up her arm, the vision of Fitzgerald in the destroyed command center dissipated into fog. After the fleet admiral's image faded, McCarthy released Lara's hand.

Lara realized she must have been viewing the future. If so, it didn't bode well for the battle's outcome. She explained to McCarthy what she had observed on the display, then asked if the Fleet command center would be destroyed.

"One possible future," he answered. "If we fail to destroy the Korilian command ship, what you saw will come to pass."

He returned his attention to the monitors and tactical displays, then resumed sending orders to various sectors.

The battle raged on; four hours, then eight, then twelve. McCarthy had initially engaged the Korilians with ten battle groups, keeping two in reserve. By the twelfth hour, both reserve battle groups had been fully committed, shoring up weakened sectors. McCarthy maintained the steadily deepening funnel in the center intact, carefully redeploying his dwindling forces, drawing the Korilian onslaught toward the 2nd Fleet ambush. But 1st Fleet had no more reserves as additional Korilian starships surged into the funnel. 1st Fleet would be overwhelmed by the next assault.

43

Admiral James Denton stood on *Telemantic*'s darkened bridge, watching the faint illumination of explosions in the distance, evidence of the approaching battle. Denton observed McCarthy's deft command of 1st Fleet in silent admiration as the younger admiral steadily drew the Korilians toward an unwelcome surprise. *Telemantic*'s bridge crew was quiet, waiting pensively for the order to commence operations. To ensure 2nd Fleet's presence went undetected, each ship remained under a darkened-ship status, with shields down and main engines offline, and a strict electronic emissions restriction.

In addition to two battle groups at full strength, 2nd Fleet's offensive would be spearheaded by eight new Resolute-class battleships: the lead ship—*Resolute*—six more named after Earth's inhabited continents, and the final ship christened *Telemantic* in honor of the men and women who had died in that fateful planetary system—an entire Colonial fleet annihilated. Denton had chosen *Telemantic* as his flagship, as he could find no better ship from which to orchestrate the destruction of the Korilian horde than the namesake that represented the sacrifice of so many brave men and women.

Denton was the most experienced fleet commander, having commanded 2nd Fleet for over eight years. Fleet Admiral Fitzgerald had selected 1st and 2nd Fleets to defend Ritalis because they were led by the two best fleet commanders. Denton had demonstrated his abilities countless times over the last eight years, and McCarthy had achieved tremendous success in the two years he had commanded 1st Fleet. Following his severe losses at Ritalis, however, he had questioned his abilities.

Have I been at it too long? Have I lost my edge? Is it time to step aside and let the next generation lead?

But after learning that McCarthy was a Nexus Ten, Denton's confidence had returned. He would lead 2nd Fleet one more time.

And he would have his revenge.

At sixty-one, Denton was the oldest fleet commander, almost ten years older than the other five. He had been thirty-one at the outbreak of the war, when the Space Exploration Corps had begun transforming into the Colonial Navy. He had served on numerous Colonial warships, learning much from their crews and commanding officers. But he learned the most from Captain Victoria Bergman, commanding officer of the battleship *Valiant*. She was a brilliant tactician, always knowing how the Korilians would coordinate their next attack, which shields to reinforce and how to maneuver her ship.

Not only did Bergman lead her ship in battle—she led her crew. She knew how to inspire those who served with her, whether by a subtle compliment to a crew member on watch, the exacting standards she demanded during training sessions, or her tours through the ship late at night, talking to the crew about their families and about what they would do when the war was over.

Denton was Captain Bergman's executive officer during their last battle aboard *Valiant*, when they had found themselves hopelessly outnumbered four to one. Bergman and her crew fought well, destroying one of the opposing Korilian dreadnoughts. But there were no Colonial ships available to assist *Valiant*, and one of her shields finally failed and her armor was penetrated. Korilian suppression fire tore through *Valiant*, and both reactors went offline. With all shields down and no propulsion, *Valiant* drifted in space, waiting for the coup de grace that would come as soon as one of the Korilian pulse generators completed its recharge.

But the pulse never came. The Korilians decided to board *Valiant* instead. Five insertions along the starboard side.

Bergman ordered Denton to get one of the reactors back online. Whatever it took. *Valiant* needed power.

Denton made it to the first reactor; damaged beyond repair.

He headed to the second.

The reactor compartment had taken structural damage. The injectors were misaligned, and the fusion reaction would sustain itself for only a few milliseconds. They had to cool the reactor below the minimum allowed, giving the reaction a chance to reach self-sustaining. But if they cooled the reactor too much, the reactor containment could fracture as soon as the fusion began—consuming *Valiant* in a mini-nova.

They had no choice. Denton gave the orders.

Sub-cool the reactor.

Commence the fusion sequence.

It worked. The aft reactor came online. All shield generators were initializing, and *Valiant* would have shields in five minutes. They would be safe.

From the outside.

But not within.

Five Korilian boarding parties—one hundred assault troops. *Valiant* had a crew of several hundred, but they were untrained in hand-to-hand combat. Only the Marines could effectively fight the Korilians, and there were only two platoons on board. Forty Marines.

Denton called the bridge for new orders from Captain Bergman.

No response.

He headed back to the bridge, running into the remainder of a squad of Marines along the way. Three alive. They joined Denton and made their way forward, finally reaching the bridge. The Korilians had already been there.

The bridge crew was dead, lined up and executed along the starboard side of the ship.

All except for Bergman.

She sat with her back against the forward bridge railing, her legs sprawled out before her and her arms wide apart, holding onto the bridge railing at shoulder height, her chest a bloody pulp from a pulse blast. The holster around her waist was empty, her firearm at her feet. Denton's eyes were drawn to Bergman's hands, holding onto the railing.

No, she wasn't holding on.

The bastards.

They had fused her hands to the railing.

Crucified her.

The physical pain must have been excruciating, but the emotional torment must have been worse. They made her watch while they executed her bridge crew.

Then her.

Admiral Denton relaxed his grip on *Telemantic's* forward bridge railing, his white knuckles slowly returning to their normal pink color. He would have his revenge. For Captain Victoria Bergman. For the crew of *Valiant*. For all the men and women slaughtered by the Korilians.

He had waited twenty years. He could wait a few more hours.

44

When the battle entered its sixteenth hour, Fleet Admiral Fitzgerald's image appeared on one of McCarthy's displays.

"Yes, Admiral McCarthy?" she asked.

"I can't hold the Korilians off any longer. We have to open the end of the cone now or risk a breach somewhere else in the defense grid."

"I agree. You've done a superb job and given our plan a chance to succeed. Open the cone. I'll send orders to Second Fleet at the appropriate time."

Fleet Admiral Fitzgerald's image disappeared, and McCarthy issued new orders to 1st Fleet. The center bridge display shifted to a sector with two Colonial battleships and four cruisers opposed by a half dozen dreadnoughts. One of the Colonial battleships had a collapsed shield, and its crew was desperately trying to keep it away from the Korilian dreadnoughts as the shield regenerated.

A captain appeared on one of the bridge displays, the data on the bottom identifying him as Captain Jim Rushing, commanding officer of the battleship *Georgia*.

"Admiral, we're outnumbered in this sector and require reinforcements."

Lara had learned enough about the sensor displays to realize there were Colonial battleships in the adjacent sectors that could assist *Georgia*.

However, instead of ordering starships into *Georgia*'s sector, McCarthy replied, "We're opening the funnel."

Rushing grabbed onto one of the bridge consoles as *Georgia* jolted from a Korilian pulse. "I take it you're opening the funnel in my sector."

"Unfortunately."

Rushing nodded. "I was hoping it wouldn't be us." He looked around the bridge at his crew fighting for their survival, then turned back to McCarthy. "It's been an honor serving under you, Admiral."

"The honor is mine, Jim."

The display went black, and Lara watched the Korilians destroy *Georgia* and the remaining Colonial ships in that sector. Korilian starships began pouring through the hole in the Colonial Fleet defense, headed toward the 1st Fleet command ship.

And 2nd Fleet.

45

Seated in his command chair on *Telemantic's* bridge, Admiral Denton had monitored the exchange between McCarthy and *Georgia's* commanding officer. When McCarthy's image faded from the display, he glanced at *Telemantic's* captain, who took his cue.

"Man Battle Stations," the captain ordered.

Denton stood, knowing that the commanding officers throughout 2nd Fleet were also monitoring 1st Fleet communications and were ordering their ships to full manning as well.

Three minutes later, *Telemantic's* commanding officer approached Denton. "*Telemantic* is at Battle Stations. Awaiting your orders, sir."

Denton examined the ship's sensor displays, watching dozens of Korilian ships speed through the breach in 1st Fleet's defenses in an attempt to destroy the fleet's command ship and envelop the Colonial formation. He watched patiently, waiting for Fleet Admiral Fitzgerald's order. The nearest display flickered to life.

"Admiral Denton. Engage the Korilians." After Denton acknowledged, Fitzgerald added, "Good luck, James."

Denton turned to *Telemantic's* commanding officer. "Directional comms to the carriers. Launch all vipers."

The order was relayed, and 2nd Fleet's eight carriers began launching their viper wings. Five minutes later, four thousand vipers had formed into eight wings behind 2nd Fleet.

Denton turned to his communications officer. "Order Second Fleet to commence operations."

The officer relayed the order, and two hundred battleships and cruisers simultaneously energized their shields, main engines, and weapon systems, while eight viper wings surged forward to engage the Korilian marauder escort. The lead Korilian ships slowed when 2nd Fleet materialized before them.

Denton ordered, "All ships, ahead flank."

2nd Fleet, spearheaded by the eight Resolute-class battleships, surged forward in a phalanx formation. The lead Korilian ships opened fire, with several pulses hitting *Telemantic* on the bow shield, inflicting only minor damage. Denton noted that the new Resolute shields held up better than the ones on older battleships.

Next came the test of the Resolutes' new pulse generators. The weapon engineers had guaranteed the new pulses would penetrate Korilian shields and armor, with the pulse energy reacting in a way that would destroy the entire warship. A major drawback, however, was the five minutes it took to recharge Resolute-class generators. This wouldn't be a problem if the pulses destroyed a Korilian ship with each firing. But if they merely damaged the ships instead, allowing them to pound the Resolute battleships in the interim five minutes, the odds of victory would swing drastically in favor of the Korilians.

Denton watched intently as *Telemantic*'s weapons officer monitored the status of the pulse charge and selected the desired target. The ship's fire control operator loudly announced, "Contact assigned," and the weapons officer tapped the *Fire* icon.

An intense blue pulse sped from *Telemantic*'s bow toward the nearest Korilian dreadnought, illuminating the starship's forward port shield in a spectacle of sizzling electrical charges. The pulse penetrated the shield and melted a hole through the warship's amor, then carved a path through the dreadnought. Dozens of internal explosions rocked the starship in the ensuing seconds, culminating in an explosion that obliterated the dreadnought. Loud cheers erupted around Admiral Denton as *Telemantic*'s crew celebrated. Their new weaponry had worked as advertised.

The eight Resolutes eliminated eight Korilian dreadnoughts, and the rest of 2nd Fleet quickly destroyed the several dozen Korilian ships that had broken through 1st Fleet's defense. As 2nd Fleet surged forward, it was met by additional Korilian ships. 2nd Fleet pressed the offensive, methodically destroying the enemy. An hour later, the entire 2nd Fleet had passed through the funnel opening practically unscathed and had commenced its counterattack into the Korilian center.

46

In the Fleet command center on Earth, Fleet Admiral Fitzgerald stood beside Admiral Liam Carroll at the back of the dimly lit facility, monitoring the displays lining the front wall. So far, 2nd Fleet was surging forward as planned. As Denton advanced, Admiral McCarthy reversed the funnel in the center of the planar grid, moving forward in support of 2nd Fleet's flanks.

The command center supervisor approached. "Ma'am, the Korilian fleet is redeploying."

"To what extent?" Fitzgerald asked, without shifting her gaze.

"They're routing thirty percent of their capital ships from the flanks to the center and committing their dreadnought reserve."

"How much of their reserve?"

"All of it, ma'am."

Fitzgerald glanced at Admiral Carroll. The Korilian response wasn't a surprise, but its timing was. She had hoped they would be slow to grasp the danger 2nd Fleet presented and be reluctant to commit their entire reserve this quickly. 2nd Fleet would now face an overwhelming Korilian force undoubtedly focused on destroying the Resolute-class battleships.

Fitzgerald instructed the supervisor, "Order Third through Sixth Fleets to press forward. Tie down as many Korilian ships as possible to keep them from reinforcing the center."

Standing on *Telemantic*'s forward bridge, Admiral Denton assessed the status of 2nd Fleet, having finally eliminated the last Korilian starships in their sector. Denton's losses had been minimal while overwhelming the Korilian resistance. But as 2nd Fleet surged forward, the redeploying Korilian fleet came into view. Arrayed before them were hundreds of densely packed dreadnoughts and cruisers, awaiting the 2nd Fleet offensive.

"Slow to ahead standard," Denton ordered, "and restore formation."

A few minutes later, *Telemantic*'s commanding officer reported, "Sir, the fleet has returned to a phalanx."

"Very well," Denton said. "Order the fleet to ahead full."

Denton felt the rhythmic vibration of *Telemantic*'s main engines through the ship's deck as *Telemantic* and the rest of 2nd Fleet surged toward the Korilian warships.

47

As 2nd Fleet sped forward, Lara remained by McCarthy's side while he issued orders to 1st Fleet, ensuring his ships kept pace with the circular trailing edge of the 2nd Fleet phalanx, protecting its flanks. It wasn't long before 2nd Fleet slammed into the center of the redeployed Korilian armada, initiating a battle more intense than anything Lara had witnessed thus far. McCarthy cycled through sensor screens and tactical displays, monitoring the status of both 1st and 2nd Fleet operations.

An image of a Resolute-class battleship suddenly appeared on one of the displays on McCarthy's console. The Resolute on the display—Captain Townsend's *Europe*—was engaged by eight Korilian dreadnoughts, four on each side, and the starship was in distress. Engine plumes were visible from only her port main engine, and dozens of Korilian marauders swarmed around her starboard side. McCarthy tapped one of the console controls, and Lara heard voice communications.

"...number three shield has collapsed and the shield generator is down. Request immediate assistance."

Lara watched intently as the eight Korilian dreadnoughts waited for their pulse generators to recharge, with the four ships on *Europe's* starboard side engaging *Europe* in the meantime with suppression-fire batteries, bombarding the Colonial battleship's starboard side in a brilliant array of explosions. The Korilian suppression fire detonated harmlessly on *Europe*'s shields, except in the forward sector where she was missing her number three shield. The suppression fire tore gaping holes into the ship.

Two Korilian dreadnoughts disintegrated in intense blue flashes, and not long thereafter, two Resolute-class battleships, *North America* and *Asia*, pulled up near *Europe*, engaging the remaining Korilian dreadnoughts. Additionally, *Varna*, an Atlantis-class battleship, arrived, placing itself between the Korilian dreadnoughts and *Europe*'s vulnerable starboard side. The Korilian suppression fire impacted harmlessly on *Varna*'s shields.

However, while *Varna* did an excellent job defending *Europe* from the Korilian dreadnoughts, she could do little to protect the Resolute battleship from the small Korilian marauders. They made swift attack runs between *Europe* and *Varna*, easily evading the battleships' self-defense batteries, their effectiveness impaired by the ship's own shields. McCarthy had explained that in order to penetrate outward through their shields, the self-defense battery pulses traveled at relatively slow speeds compared to the small marauders. The agile marauders evaded the self-defense fire most of the time, making the capital ships dependent on viper support in critical situations like this.

The marauders continued their strafing runs between *Europe* and *Varna*, focusing their attacks on *Europe*'s self-defense batteries left unprotected by its missing number three shield. The exposed batteries were quickly destroyed, and the marauders concentrated their attacks on *Europe*'s exposed starboard side. Lara watched as *Europe* was hit with a continuous barrage of strafing runs, and she listened intently to *Europe*'s call for assistance.

"Request status of viper support. Urgent priority. Repeat, *urgent priority*."

The marauder weaponry was only a fraction as powerful as the dreadnought and cruiser pulses, but the combined effect of hundreds of attacks on *Europe*'s unprotected section was significant. Lara watched as compartment after compartment collapsed under the marauder onslaught.

Several marauders exploded in fireballs as four squadrons of Colonial vipers approached, streaming between *Europe* and *Varna*. The marauders ceased their attack on *Europe* and engaged the vipers. Four more viper squadrons arrived, and the marauders were soon destroyed.

On *Europe*'s bridge, Captain Townsend reviewed his ship's battle damage with concern. The Korilians had been concentrating on *Europe* and the other Resolute battleships, targeting a single shield, and it had finally collapsed. Even worse, the shield generator had been damaged, and they had been unable to reinitialize the shield. *Europe* would not survive this battle with a shield down, nor could she keep up with 2nd Fleet with only her port main engine operational.

Townsend looked up as *Europe* was hailed by Admiral Denton, who appeared on Townsend's display. "What's your status?" Denton asked.

"Number three shield and starboard main engine are down. All other systems fully operational."

"What's the prognosis for repair?"

"No determination yet, sir."

"How long before you have an estimate?"

"Unknown, sir."

Denton paused, and Townsend knew what he was thinking. The success of 2nd Fleet's attack rested largely on its speed of advance, breaking through the Korilian defenses and destroying their command ship before 2nd Fleet was annihilated. 2nd Fleet couldn't afford to slow down, even if it meant leaving one of its Resolute-class battleships behind. Also, Denton couldn't afford to leave additional battleships behind to defend *Europe* from stray Korilian ships; every operational battleship would be needed as 2nd Fleet pressed forward.

Europe would be left behind, but Denton decided to give Townsend a temporary reprieve from destruction.

"You have thirty minutes, Captain," Denton finally said. "*North America* and *Varna* will remain as your escort during that time, then rejoin the Fleet."

Townsend knew what would happen if *Europe* didn't restore propulsion and shields and was then abandoned. "We can maintain ahead standard on the port engine."

"Not good enough," Denton replied. "Second Fleet will remain at ahead full."

"I understand, sir," Townsend replied, realizing *Europe*'s fate would hang in the balance for the next thirty minutes.

48

As 2nd Fleet continued its assault into the Korilian center, McCarthy frequently shifted one of his console displays to a sector where there was no activity, just dark space. Lara wondered why he spent so much time evaluating this area, and then one of the main bridge displays also shifted to this seemingly uneventful sector.

McCarthy stared intently at the display, and Lara took a closer look. At first, it seemed that the center of the screen was out of focus, as if there were a large circular smudge on the monitor. When she examined the image more closely, she discerned thousands of the small vipers and marauders engaged in a fierce, swirling battle.

Fleet Admiral Fitzgerald's image appeared on McCarthy's console. "Go ahead, Admiral McCarthy."

"Ma'am, we have a large melee forming in sector two-one-eight."

"We've been watching it," she said. "What's your assessment?"

"The Korilians have committed ten thousand marauders so far, which I've matched. The problem is the Korilians have another fourteen thousand inbound. I'm going to reduce First Fleet to a defensive viper load, but that will still leave us at a four-to-three disadvantage. I'm going to need another six thousand vipers to maintain one-to-one odds."

"Should we allocate Second Fleet's vipers to the melee?" Admiral Fitzgerald asked.

"No, ma'am. That's exactly what they want. The Korilians created the melee just off-axis to the Second Fleet thrust, hoping we'll divert Second Fleet assets. That's because they have another six thousand marauders waiting directly ahead of Second Fleet. We'll have to divert vipers from the flanks to reinforce the melee and Second Fleet."

"Will they arrive in time?"

"Yes. Most of the Korilian marauders are inbound from their flanks as well, so if we start now, we'll be fine. Request you send six thousand vipers to the melee, and another two thousand to Second Fleet."

Fitzgerald replied, "I'll reassign assets. Is there anything else?"

"That should do it for now."

The console screen went dark, and McCarthy focused again on the bridge display. Streams of vipers and marauders were pouring into the melee as the Korilians attempted to win the immense battle by allocating overwhelming forces, while 1st Fleet steadily matched their numbers.

The bottom of the display tracked the number of marauders and vipers engaged, as well as the losses. Each side was losing fighters so rapidly that the numbers never stopped changing. Lara estimated that each side was losing a fighter every second; almost four thousand per hour. She reflected on the shuttle pilot's comments during their trip to *Atlantis* and finally understood why assignment as a viper pilot was a virtual death sentence.

"Admiral," Lara asked, "do you remember the shuttle pilot who took us to *Atlantis*?"

"Yes."

"He said his son was a viper pilot on the carrier *Medusa*. Is he in there?"

"Probably. *Medusa* was in one of the battle groups reassigned to First Fleet."

McCarthy tapped his console and said, "Locate *Medusa*'s wing commander. On-screen."

The display telescoped in toward the battle, and the distant blur of battle was replaced with a single viper in hot pursuit of a marauder, diving and weaving around dozens of others engaged in battles of their own. The viper followed closely, firing rapid bursts from its forward gun mounts. The

marauder finally made a fatal error and its path cut through the viper
tracer fire.

The marauder disintegrated in an explosion, which was pierced
seconds later by another pair of Colonial and Korilian fighters engaged in
their own battle for survival, exiting the fireball and streaking past the original viper on both sides. The first viper slowed and turned, and Lara read
the inscription on the side of the ship, just below the cockpit window:

COMMANDER DAN METZGER – MEDUSA WING COMMANDER

Through the dimly lit cockpit, Lara caught a view of the pilot as the
ship turned in the direction of the two fighters that sped by, his face faintly
illuminated inside his helmet. The young man was the spitting image of the
shuttle pilot they had met on the way to *Atlantis*. Lara hoped Commander
Metzger would defy the odds again and survive yet another battle.

McCarthy zoomed the display back out, and Lara watched four new
streams of vipers begin pouring into the battle, as 3rd through 6th Fleet
reinforced the 1st Fleet contingent, matching the influx of marauders.

What Lara initially mistook as complete chaos inside the melee, with
thousands of uncoordinated battles, was actually a well-organized and
executed process. While McCarthy returned his attention to the main
battle, Lara watched the display as surviving vipers repeatedly reformed
into squadrons, which were directed by their wing commanders to engage
lesser Korilian forces in an attempt to overwhelm and eliminate their
outnumbered counterparts.

The other side countered, vectoring in reinforcements to maintain even
odds there while at the same time gaining a temporary advantage elsewhere. Each battle eventually degenerated into dozens of individual
dogfights, with the survivors reforming with incoming reinforcements,
repeating the scenario again and again.

Lara's attention was drawn back to the fate of 2nd Fleet when Captain
Townsend appeared on one of McCarthy's console displays, which had
remained configured to monitor 2nd Fleet communications. The display
was currently split-screen between *Europe* and *Telemantic*.

"...unable to repair our number three shield generator." Townsend
stood on *Europe*'s bridge, delivering the unwelcome news.

"Understand all," Admiral Denton said. "Return to a repair yard. What's your estimated repair time?"

"We need a complete generator change out, Admiral. That'll take four days."

Admiral Denton's video flickered as *Telemantic* was hit by a Korilian pulse, ardent reminder of the difficult task facing 2nd Fleet, now with only seven Resolute-class battleships.

One of Denton's aides approached. "Admiral," he said. "We've lost *Australia*."

Six Resolutes left.

49

In the Fleet command center, as the 2nd Fleet assault entered its sixth hour, Fleet Admiral Fitzgerald stopped beside one of the three-dimensional fusion tables, examining the green symbols representing friendly forces and the red icons indicating Korilian warships. She had moved from the back of the facility, where she had a view of the entire battle, to the fusion table displaying the only sector that mattered. Admiral Carroll stood beside her, likewise assessing 2nd Fleet's progress.

2nd Fleet had destroyed over three hundred Korilian dreadnoughts, double the rate of its own losses. But the Korilians had diverted ships from their flanks and committed their formidable dreadnought reserve, maintaining a two-to-one advantage despite the tremendous casualties inflicted by the Resolutes and the rest of 2nd Fleet.

The Korilians had realized the Resolute battleships were the most serious threat and had focused on their destruction, and there were only three Resolute-class battleships remaining: *Telemantic*, *North America*, and *Asia*. Fitzgerald's anxiety had risen steadily as 2nd Fleet losses mounted, her concern growing after each loss of a Resolute-class battleship.

One of the leading green symbols flickered, then disappeared, and the command center supervisor reported, "We've lost *Asia*."

Fitzgerald didn't acknowledge the report, her eyes instead going to the slightly delayed video of the sector, noting the unusual purple flash that accompanied the demise of each Resolute-class battleship, presumably related to the design of the new shields or pulse generators.

She returned her focus to the green symbols representing 2nd Fleet. There were only two Resolute-class battleships now, plus another twenty Colonial battleships. Opposing them were forty-two Korilian dreadnoughts.

They were still on the wrong end of two-to-one odds.

Fitzgerald said nothing while she studied the display, her attention focused on the green diamonds representing *Telemantic* and *North America* and the numerous red symbols converging on them.

50

Aboard *Telemantic*, Admiral Denton stood beside the ship's commanding officer, both men overlooking a data fusion table, focused on the red Korilian icons. *Telemantic* and *North America* were teamed together at the tip of the 2nd Fleet offensive, with both ships being pounded by surrounding Korilian dreadnoughts. *Telemantic* and *North America* rolled after each attack, presenting shields from the other side of the ship toward the Korilians while the weakened shields regenerated. However, the Korilians had achieved a critical attack ratio, and *Telemantic*'s and *North America*'s shields were gradually draining.

Telemantic completed its latest pulse recharge, and its fire control locked onto the nearest Korilian dreadnought. Denton keyed on the fire control operator's report.

"Contact five-two-three assigned. Pulse ready."

The weapons officer announced, "Fire!" and *Telemantic*'s pulse sliced cleanly through the center of the Korilian dreadnought, causing explosions throughout the ship. The dreadnought broke in half, with the two halves spiraling slowly away.

Denton no longer savored the destruction of Korilian ships. Instead, he and *Telemantic*'s crew braced themselves, knowing the Korilians would attack aggressively during the five minutes between pulse recharges. Four

Korilian dreadnoughts advanced toward *Telemantic* while another four moved toward *North America*.

A moment later, the four Korilian ships engaging *North America* fired simultaneously, and a bright purple flash illuminated *Telemantic's* bridge, almost blinding Denton with its intensity. He turned toward the sensor supervisor.

"Status report," Denton asked, but he already knew the answer.

"We've lost *North America*," the supervisor replied.

They were down to one Resolute-class battleship. But as long as *Telemantic* survived, they had a chance.

Telemantic rocked violently to starboard as it was hit with a quad-pulse, and shield warnings cascaded across the console displays. The four nearest Korilian dreadnoughts had fired simultaneously, hitting *Telemantic's* forward port shield.

"Shield two has collapsed!" announced the shield supervisor.

"Minor hull breach in compartment eight," the damage control coordinator reported. "All systems operational with the exception of shield two."

"Five minutes to minimum shield," the shield supervisor announced. "We can then power share with the other shields."

They didn't have five minutes; the four Korilian dreadnoughts would complete their pulse recharge in only one. Without their forward port shield, the Korilians would carve *Telemantic* into pieces.

The watch officer addressed *Telemantic's* commanding officer, standing beside Denton. "Sir, we have to reverse course and present our flank shields while the forward shield regenerates."

Telemantic's commanding officer hesitated as he assessed the situation. *Telemantic* was an extremely large ship and did not turn rapidly. "There's not enough time," he said. "The Korilians will fire again before we complete the turn. What about a one-eighty roll?"

"No, sir. A roll to starboard would expose us to the four dreadnoughts that destroyed *North America*, and their recharges will be completed even sooner."

Telemantic's commanding officer froze, unable to latch onto a solution to their predicament. Time was of the essence, and *Telemantic* had to do something or she would be destroyed. Denton quickly formulated a plan but didn't have time to explain it.

He turned to *Telemantic*'s officer of the deck. "I have the conn," Denton announced loudly so all bridge personnel heard. He took operational command of *Telemantic*, as was his prerogative as the senior officer aboard.

"All ahead flank!" he ordered. "Come left to course two-three-zero, down four!"

The helm did as ordered, and crew members looked up from their consoles with concern. Denton had ordered *Telemantic* directly toward the four Korilian dreadnoughts on its port side.

Denton had realized the shield supervisor was correct; *Telemantic* had to quickly present its flank shields to the opposing Korilian dreadnoughts. But the way to do that wasn't by turning the ship. Instead, *Telemantic*'s only hope was to thread the needle between the four Korilian dreadnoughts. Once past them, *Telemantic*'s rear shields would protect her long enough for her missing shield to regenerate. The critical question was—would *Telemantic* pass the Korilian dreadnoughts before their pulse generators completed their recharge? If the answer was yes, Denton's plan was brilliant.

If not, *Telemantic* was on a suicide run.

Denton turned to the weapons officer. "Suppression fire on all four port contacts."

The weapons officer relayed the order, and *Telemantic* opened fire on the four Korilian dreadnoughts, draining their shields and delaying their pulse-generator recharge.

"Time to intercept?" Denton asked.

"Forty seconds," replied *Telemantic*'s navigator.

Telemantic sped forward at ahead flank speed. Two of the Korilian warships began to fall to starboard, and Denton modified his original order. "Suppression fire on contacts five-four-three and five-four-four only!"

Only the two dreadnoughts to port, which still had a clear shot through *Telemantic*'s missing shield, mattered now.

"Twenty seconds to intercept!" announced the navigator.

Denton gripped the bridge railing as the first Korilian dreadnought passed *Telemantic* on its port side and began falling astern. He turned his attention to the remaining dreadnought, which exchanged suppression fire with *Telemantic*, the two ships lighting up each other's shields in a cascading series of detonations. The Korilian suppression fire tore gaping holes into *Telemantic's* unprotected port bow, and reports flowed steadily into Damage Control Central, yet no major system had been affected thus far.

"Ten seconds!"

Telemantic's commanding officer placed his hand on Denton's shoulder. "You've done it," he said as they watched the last Korilian dreadnought through the forward bridge windows.

Then the Korilian ship's pulse generator doors opened, and Denton and *Telemantic's* bridge crew watched in horror as the Korilian dreadnought fired at point-blank range, targeting *Telemantic's* nonexistent shield two. The pulse sliced through *Telemantic's* weakened armor, and the battleship shuddered as a series of explosions rippled throughout the ship.

Seconds later, an intense light illuminated the remaining 2nd Fleet ships as *Telemantic* disintegrated in a purple flash.

51

Admiral Carroll was standing beside Fleet Admiral Fitzgerald in the command center, both officers studying the disposition of Korilian and 2nd Fleet forces on the fusion plot, when the green diamond representing *Telemantic* disappeared. The command center grew quiet as personnel realized the last of the Resolute-class battleships—and the 2nd Fleet flagship—had been destroyed; that their carefully developed plan had just disintegrated with *Telemantic*.

All eyes turned to Fitzgerald, whose gaze remained fixed on the fusion plot displaying the remnants of 2nd Fleet and its Korilian counterparts. The watchstanders waited for new orders from the admiral, but she seemed lost in her thoughts, unaware that subordinates awaited her direction.

Admiral Carroll broke the uneasy silence. "Fleet Admiral."

Fitzgerald turned her head slightly, then looked back at the fusion plot. "What is the Second Fleet order of battle?" she asked.

The fusion plot supervisor replied, "Zero Resolute-class battleships, eighteen battleships of various classes, and thirty-three cruisers. Deployed against them are forty Korilian dreadnoughts and sixty-seven cruisers."

Fitzgerald stared at the fusion plot as silence hung over the command center.

Carroll spoke again. "Admiral Fitzgerald, we must fall back and regroup."

"No," Fitzgerald said firmly. But she offered no insight into what she was contemplating.

Admiral Carroll continued, "Second Fleet is significantly outnumbered. Without Resolute-class battleships, it cannot continue the attack. We'll have to shift to a defensive posture, and it won't be long before the Korilians break through. We need the firepower from our orbiting defense stations. We should fall back and redeploy around Earth. Form a defensive perimeter integrated with our defense stations and wear the Korilians down."

Fitzgerald spun toward Carroll. "We've simulated that battle plan, and it's failed every time! The Korilians will eventually break through, destroying our construction and repair yards. That will seal our fate, as we will have no way to replace our losses while the Korilians replace theirs. The Korilians will eventually wear *us* down."

"We don't have a choice," Carroll replied. "It will buy us time to develop an alternate strategy."

"An alternate strategy!" Fitzgerald's eyes blazed with intensity. "We've spent years honing our plans for today's battle, and you think we can develop an alternate strategy in a matter of hours, on the run, with an exhausted Fleet!"

Carroll knew Fitzgerald was right. But retreating and redeploying around Earth was the only option that held promise. Fitzgerald turned away and studied the sensor displays, staring at the hundreds of Colonial and Korilian symbols.

After a long moment, she said, "First Fleet will continue the attack."

No one moved while Admiral Carroll and the command center supervisors processed the impossibility of Fitzgerald's order.

"First Fleet cannot continue the attack," Carroll said. "Any attempt to do so will result in the collapse of the center and the destruction of the entire Fleet. The offensive has failed, Admiral. We must regroup."

Fitzgerald swiveled toward Carroll. "It was supposed to happen this way!"

Her words took Carroll by surprise. "What do you mean?"

"Second Fleet was supposed to fail!"

Silence gripped the command center until Carroll asked, "What are you talking about?"

"Second Fleet did what they were supposed to: force the Korilians to commit their reserves and weaken the center. They succeeded. Now it's time for First Fleet to finish the job."

Carroll replied, "I've reviewed every facet of the operations plan, and this was never an option."

"That's because I'm the only one who knew."

"Why is that?"

Fitzgerald surveyed the men and women in the command center. Operations had ground to a standstill as they watched the encounter between the two admirals.

Finally, she answered, "Do you think I was going to tell Second Fleet their offensive was doomed to fail? That they would be annihilated? It had to be this way." She paused, then said calmly, "Things are proceeding exactly as planned."

Admiral Carroll had been Fitzgerald's deputy fleet commander during her five years as Fleet Admiral and before that when she had been in command of 1st Fleet. She was a brilliant officer, but ruthless as well. She had convinced the Council to sacrifice almost a billion ground troops over the last five years, gaining time for the Fleet to rebuild. Now, she had sacrificed 2nd Fleet, weakening the Korilian center in the hope that McCarthy could finish the job.

It was either that or she was lying, desperately grasping onto a sliver of hope.

"I understand, ma'am," Carroll said.

Fitzgerald turned and spoke loudly, so everyone in the command center could hear. "First Fleet will continue the attack. Hail Admiral McCarthy."

52

A moment later, Admiral McCarthy's image materialized on one of the command center displays. Fitzgerald informed him of 2nd Fleet's status, then ordered him to continue the attack.

"This is not unexpected," McCarthy said. "I've had my two strongest battle groups standing down while the Korilians were focused on Second Fleet. They're rested and ready for the offensive."

"That's excellent news," Fitzgerald replied, and Carroll sensed relief in her voice. She added, "Sensors indicate First Fleet is at a numerical par with the remaining Korilian forces in the center. However, you have no Resolute-class battleships to aid you. I'm relying on you to give us the edge we need."

McCarthy didn't reply, awaiting further instructions.

Admiral Fitzgerald ended their discussion. "That's all, Jon. Except... good luck."

The display went dark, then she turned to Admiral Carroll. Neither said a word, as they both understood the daunting task facing 1st Fleet. Maybe McCarthy's abilities would give them a chance to succeed.

As Admiral Fitzgerald's image disappeared from *Lider*'s display, it was silent on the bridge. Lara wanted to offer encouragement but didn't know what to say. As she searched for appropriate words, two admirals appeared on one of the displays, which was divided in split-screen mode. Their unit IDs identified them as the commanders of the Okinawa and Normandy battle groups.

McCarthy explained 1st Fleet's new assignment; the destruction of the Korilian command ship was their goal at any cost. After the admirals' images disappeared from the screen, McCarthy focused on his three-dimensional display. His fingers moved quickly, sending orders to his reserve forces. Seconds later, the Normandy and Okinawa battle groups surged toward the center sectors as McCarthy set the 1st Fleet offensive in motion.

53

As the 1st Fleet offensive entered its fifth hour, sweat beaded across McCarthy's forehead. Lara's body had reacted in an opposite manner; it seemed the bridge had become colder during the conflict, whether from McCarthy's view or from the mounting tension. Her hands were ice cold and her fingers felt like icicles. Throughout the battle, she had done what she could to assist, attempting to force premonitions, but had failed miserably. Either due to stress or insufficient talent, she had provided no insight since the 1st Fleet offensive had begun.

McCarthy's prescient ability had proved valuable, however, allowing 1st Fleet to concentrate superior forces in critical areas. But 1st Fleet suffered losses where McCarthy was unable to evaluate the battle in detail and provide direction. As a result, 1st Fleet losses matched those of the Korilians. Less than half of the ships in the Okinawa and Normandy battle groups remained, leaving only forty battleships and a handful of cruisers. The smaller ships had been decimated by the dense concentration of Korilian dreadnoughts in the hotly contested center.

As the Korilian and 1st Fleet losses mounted, McCarthy's attack had degenerated from a centralized thrust into numerous small engagements. McCarthy had modified his original plan, breaking his force into several forays, hoping one would break through. The entire 1st Fleet didn't need to puncture the Korilian defense; it would take only two battleships to take out the Korilian command ship. As Lara hoped one of the attacks would be successful, her attention was drawn to the two battleships that had penetrated the deepest into the Korilian center.

Captain Nesrine Rajhi stood on the bridge of her Helena-class battleship as a pulse impacted *Athens*'s bow shield, the flash reflecting off her ebony-colored skin. *Athens*'s sister ship, *Sparta*, was deployed on her starboard side as they engaged two enemy dreadnoughts. Rajhi sensed the death knell of both Korilian starships, which *Athens* and *Sparta* had been pounding for the last fifteen minutes.

Athens's and *Sparta*'s pulse generators completed their recharge, and Rajhi's weapons officer announced, "Fire!", initiating a simultaneous *Athens-Sparta* attack. The dual-pulse hit the Korilian dreadnought's bow shield, which flashed brightly as it collapsed. The pulse pierced the warship's already compromised armor, passing deep into its internal compartments.

The inside of the Korilian dreadnought lit up with a series of explosions, and it began to spiral out of control. The ship's remaining shields soon failed, and *Athens*'s suppression fire tore through the Korilian hulk until the dreadnought went dark, drifting away.

After the next pulse-generator recharge was complete, Rajhi turned her attention to the dreadnought on *Athens*'s starboard side. Another dual *Athens-Sparta* pulse collapsed their adversary's bow shield, targeting a trench in the dreadnought's armor that had been cleaved during a previous attack. The dual-pulse penetrated the weakened armor, and the Korilian dreadnought exploded into a thousand pieces hurtling through space.

Rajhi examined the bridge displays, vacant of any visible Korilian ships.

"Sensor report," she commanded, waiting for the next wave of Korilian warships that always appeared as *Athens* finished off one, then another, and then another.

"Sector clear," the supervisor announced. "No Korilian ships detected."

Rajhi reflected on the supervisor's report.

They had broken through.

No Korilian ships remained to oppose their pursuit and destruction of the Korilian command ship. Rajhi turned to the watch officer. "Status report."

"Shields at seventy-three percent and recharging. All weapons and propulsion are fully operational. We're in good shape, ma'am."

"What about *Sparta*?"

The sensor supervisor reported, "Some minor issues, but no showstoppers. You've got two fully operational Helena-class battleships at your disposal, ma'am."

Rajhi smiled. "Inform Admiral McCarthy we've broken through and are proceeding on an intercept course with the Korilian command ship."

She followed up with, "Helm, ahead flank. Bring *Sparta* up on the starboard beam."

54

As *Athens* and *Sparta* surged deeper behind the enemy lines, Rajhi scanned the sensor displays, searching for Korilian dreadnoughts being vectored their way. But it appeared that all Korilian warships were tied down in battles with other Colonial forces. Ten minutes passed without any sighting of additional starships as *Athens* and *Sparta* sped toward the Korilian command ship. Rajhi monitored its response on *Athens*'s sensor display; the command ship sat motionless in space, directly ahead, giving no indication it had detected the two Colonial battleships closing to within firing range.

Athens's bridge crew was quiet as they scanned the surrounding area. Rajhi put the transit time to good use, spending a few minutes with each supervisor, reviewing her ship's status in detail, along with a cursory review of *Sparta*'s condition.

Rajhi was pleased that it was *Athens* and *Sparta* that had broken through. She had taken command of *Athens* five years ago, and her counterpart, Gynt Salukas, had assumed command of *Sparta* a few days later. The two battleships had fought alongside each other and had developed into a finely tuned team. Each crew had an intuitive sense of what the other crew would do in battle, able to anticipate the tactics the other would employ and what they would do in extremis.

Athens and *Sparta* had been in their squadron longer than any other ship, surviving while the other ten ships in their squadron were destroyed, only to be replaced, and those ships destroyed in turn. *Athens* and *Sparta* fought together, and when the fleet stood down from battle, the two crews enjoyed their time off together. Over the last five years, the commanding officers and their crews had developed a close rapport.

Rajhi examined the combined seal for the two battleships, etched onto the starboard bridge bulkhead. Every Colonial Navy ship had an official seal, but *Athens* and *Sparta* had designed one together—a pictograph of *Athens*'s and *Sparta*'s ship emblems side-by-side. In the center was their unofficial dictum, in Latin, as was customary for all Colonial ships. As Rajhi read those words, she recalled the night they were first spoken.

Rajhi sat across a small table from Gynt Salukas, both officers wearing the rank of captain on their Colonial Navy jumpsuit collars, along with the Trident insignia of major command gleaming above their right breasts. Empty shot glasses littered the table, and the din of their crews' festivities almost drowned out their conversation. Rajhi tilted her head back and downed the last full shot glass in front of her, and Gynt did the same.

The two crews were enjoying a well-deserved break on Seldane IV after six long months in battle and were making up for lost time. Rajhi watched an Athens *crew member lift a Spartan onto his shoulder in a fireman's carry, both of them still holding a drink in one hand. A dozen others gathered around in a circle, shouting and clapping, forming a rhythm that slowly increased in pace. The* Athens *crew member began spinning around, slowly at first, picking up speed as the tempo of the group's shouting and clapping increased.*

Rajhi returned her attention to the officer across from her. From dark, frigid Iceland, Gynt was the antithesis of Rajhi, at least in background. Blond hair, blue eyes, and pale white skin, he'd have suffered on the burning-hot plains of Tunisia. Yet despite their disparate backgrounds, they shared a common goal and had forged a commitment between them.

"So, it's agreed, then?" Rajhi said.

"It is," Gynt replied.

Rajhi reached down and retrieved a knife from her calf pocket and snapped open the blade with a flick of her wrist. She looked at Gynt, who nodded. She placed the blade against her right palm, then sliced across the width of her hand. Blood oozed from the four-inch-long cut, and Rajhi handed the knife to Gynt, who did the same. Rajhi rested her elbow on the table and extended her hand toward Gynt, who grasped it.

"Macto Pariter," he said.

Rajhi grinned, her white teeth contrasting with her pitch-black skin.

Fight together.

Athens and Sparta were a formidable team. They had faced two-to-one odds on many occasions and had always triumphed. Rajhi relished the challenge of combat and looked forward to returning to battle with Sparta at her side. But she knew what the inevitable outcome would be, despite the advantage their experience and commitment to each other gave them.

Shortly before arriving at Seldane IV, one of the crew members noted that Athens and Sparta had survived together almost five years to the day, and mentioned that the odds of a battleship lasting five years in battle was less than one percent. Athens and Sparta had defied the odds. But Rajhi knew it was only a matter of time before their ships were destroyed. Each of the eight construction yards in Earth's orbit completed a starship every five days. Almost six hundred battleships and cruisers every year, to replace Fleet losses.

The smile faded from Rajhi's face as she acknowledged the inevitable.

"Abeo Pariter," she said.

Die together.

Rajhi flexed her fingers around Gynt's hand, and she felt the warmth of their commingled blood collect at the base of their palms. She watched the red droplets fall from their hands, almost in slow motion, splattering onto the table.

"I will never abandon you, Nesrine."

Rajhi squeezed Gynt's hand firmly.

"Nor will I."

Rajhi turned away from the seal etched into the starboard bulkhead, refocusing on the combat displays. As *Athens* and *Sparta* surged forward, side-by-side, Rajhi relished their accomplishment. The two ships had defied the odds again. And together, they would destroy the Korilian command ship.

Aboard *Lider*, Lara studied the sensor display, watching the two blue symbols representing *Athens* and *Sparta* speed toward the Korilian command ship, while McCarthy masterfully manipulated the dwindling icons on his three-dimensional display, ensuring all Korilian ships within range of *Athens* and *Sparta* remained engaged. The Korilians were attempting to divert dreadnoughts toward the center, but McCarthy kept moving ships inward, reengaging and slowing down the Korilian ships each time they tried to slip away.

As *Athens* and *Sparta* closed on the Korilian command ship, Lara felt the tension on the bridge build. Another ten minutes and the Korilian ship would be in range. Sensor operators selected the two battleships and reviewed their offensive and defensive weapons status. The warships were in good condition.

As Lara studied the sensor display, fog formed at the sensor technician's feet, spreading quickly across the bridge deck. It swirled around her and McCarthy's feet, and once the deck was completely covered, the fog swept up the bulkheads and overhead, completely encapsulating the bridge, then flowed inward until the entire bridge was filled with fog.

Lara couldn't see more than a foot in front of her, and the bridge went eerily quiet. The fog quickly dissipated, leaving Lara standing not on *Lider*'s bridge but on a deserted battleship bridge. She studied her surroundings, trying to determine which ship it was and make sense of the premonition.

A tendril of fog formed at her feet and rose slowly, swirling before her face for a moment. It flowed back down to the deck, then snaked toward the starboard bulkhead where it circled an emblem: two battleships, side-by-side. Beneath each ship, she read the names.

Athens and *Sparta*.

Lara's vision vanished, leaving her back aboard the 1st Fleet command ship. Her heart beat rapidly as she tried to make sense of the premonition.

McCarthy must have noticed her reaction, because he asked, "What did you see?"

"I was on an abandoned starship bridge," she said.

"Could you tell which ship it was?"

"There was an emblem on the bulkhead with pictures of *Athens* and *Sparta*."

"Did you notice anything else, or have any insight into why you were there?"

Lara scoured her memory of the vision, searching for additional details. Recalling nothing noteworthy, she said, "There was nothing else. I have no idea what the vision means."

A cloud of fog suddenly coalesced in front of Lara, taking the form of Captain Nesrine Rajhi. She grabbed Lara by the throat with one hand, squeezing with an impossibly strong grip, almost lifting Lara from the deck. Lara realized that Rajhi was an apparition, but this was the first time a vision had produced a physical effect on her.

The battleship captain said, "You are denser than I suspected. The One gave you excellent advice, but you have neither intuition *nor* instinct. Let me spell it out for you as clearly as I'm allowed. *Hey diddle diddle, the cat and the fiddle, the cow...*"

Rajhi vanished, and Lara gasped for air, her reaction gaining McCarthy's attention. After she caught her breath, she explained what Rajhi had done and said.

McCarthy didn't respond as he sent additional orders to his fleet, but Lara could tell he was attempting to interpret her premonition. Finally, he said, "I don't know what it means. You need to decipher it."

"Do you have any advice?"

"Regina was an excellent guide, and I always followed her guidance."

His response didn't help. "What does Regina have to do with my vision?"

"In the vision you had with Regina after the Korilian cruiser mission, she told you to 'Finish what others start.'"

Lara recalled her vision aboard *Atlantis*, when Regina appeared beside her bed in Medical, offering the advice—*Finish what others start*. Lara had assumed Regina was referring to the Korilian War, but maybe Regina's advice was more literal.

Rajhi's last words echoed in Lara's mind, and she decided to finish the nursery rhyme.

Hey diddle diddle,
The cat and the fiddle,
The cow jumped over the moon.

She couldn't remember the other lines but knew it finished with—*And the dish ran away with the spoon.*

Lara focused on the third line, which Rajhi had cut off. *The cow...jumped over the moon.* Suddenly, it clicked. *The cow...jumped over the moon.*

She turned to McCarthy. "We need to take your new shuttle and jump."

"Where to?"

"In my earlier vision, a tendril of fog circled an emblem representing *Athens* and *Sparta*. I think the outcome of this battle is going to hinge on what those two battleships do. If we're supposed to jump, that means you need to be on one of those battleships, providing direction."

McCarthy didn't reply.

Lara added, "I know you said you wouldn't jump in a shuttle without shields during battle, but there are no Korilian starships near *Athens* and *Sparta*. Can we make the jump?"

"We?" he said.

"Of course. I'm your guide, and I belong by your side."

"That you do," McCarthy said.

He said nothing more for a moment, his hands manipulating the icons in his display, and Lara could tell his mind was churning. "Computer," he said, "which commanding officer is senior—*Athens* or *Sparta*?"

When battleships or cruisers operated as fire teams, the senior officer had authority over the other captains.

The computer replied, "Captain Nesrine Rajhi, commanding *Athens*, is senior."

McCarthy tapped his wristlet and spoke.

"*Elena*, can you jump to sector two-seven-seven from here?"

McCarthy's shuttle replied, "Yes, Jon."

He pressed a control on his console, and a vice admiral appeared on the display.

"Vice Admiral Mendoza. I'll be boarding *Athens*. Don't ask how. I'm transferring operational control of all First Fleet ships except *Athens* and *Sparta* to your command until further notice."

After Vice Admiral Mendoza acknowledged the order, McCarthy terminated the communication and hailed Captain Priebus on *Lider*'s command bridge, one deck below.

"Lara and I are jumping to *Athens* in my shuttle. Drop shield as soon as we're ready to exit the spaceport."

A few minutes later, Lara and McCarthy were seated in his shuttle. The life-support shield formed, then the spaceport doors began opening. *Elena* waited until *Lider* dropped shield four, then the shuttle lifted from the deck and passed through the opening.

55

As *Athens* and *Sparta* sped toward the stationary Korilian command ship, *Athens*'s sensor supervisor continued to scan the current sector, reporting no other Korilian contacts. Rajhi was surprised by the Korilian command ship's lack of evasion; it should have begun retreating at maximum speed as the Colonial battleships approached. The command ship couldn't outrun *Athens* or *Sparta*, but it could gain valuable time as reinforcements were vectored in.

The sensor supervisor announced, "She's got an escort! Six Victor-class dreadnoughts."

Rajhi cursed under her breath. It had seemed too easy. Of course the Korilians wouldn't leave their command ship undefended. And six Victor-class warships—the newest and most capable dreadnought class, with weapons and shields that slightly outmatched those of *Athens* and *Sparta*. Even so, in a two-on-two engagement, *Athens* and *Sparta* had a chance. But six against two?

"Slow to ahead standard," Rajhi ordered.

Rajhi assessed the situation, watching the dreadnoughts form up into two rows of three ships each, protecting the command ship behind them.

"Time to within weapon range?" Rajhi asked her weapons officer.

"Six minutes," he replied.

"Man Battle Stations," Rajhi ordered, having stood down the crew only fifteen minutes earlier for a short break. A moment later, the watch officer reported that Battle Stations were manned.

"Ma'am," the communications specialist called out, "we're being hailed by First Fleet."

"On-screen," Rajhi ordered.

Admiral McCarthy's image appeared on the display. "Well done, Captain Rajhi. Come to all stop. I'm coming aboard."

Rajhi wasn't sure she heard McCarthy correctly. "Admiral, did you say you were coming aboard?"

"That's correct. I have a shuttle that can make the jump. I'll arrive in one minute." McCarthy's image disappeared.

"Helm, all stop," Rajhi ordered. "Relay the order to *Sparta*." Turning to her shield supervisor, she gave an order she'd never before given in combat. "Drop shield four and open the spaceport doors. Bring the shield back up as soon as the admiral is aboard."

A moment later, Rajhi was informed of McCarthy's appearance alongside *Athens*, followed by the announcement throughout the ship—*First Fleet, arriving*. McCarthy entered the bridge not long thereafter, accompanied by his Nexus guide.

"Welcome aboard, sir. Your orders?"

"None for now, Captain. Hold your position."

"May I ask for how long? The Korilians will vector in additional forces to ensure the threat to their command ship is eliminated. I realize the situation is bleak, but if we have any hope at all, we must strike while we have the opportunity."

"I understand, Captain. But we'll hold our position for now, and wait."

"For what, sir?"

"For them to come to us."

56

Rajhi glanced over her shoulder, examining Admiral McCarthy and his guide, who stood at the back of *Athens*'s bridge. He had said nothing since he directed *Athens* and *Sparta* to hold their positions, and Rajhi and her crew tensely awaited orders. The two Colonial starships rested in space, opposed by the six dreadnoughts, which likewise seemed content to do the same. The inaction grated on Rajhi's nerves. The seconds turned into minutes; the wait seemed like hours.

Suddenly, the dreadnoughts accelerated toward *Athens* and *Sparta*.

"All Victors advancing at ahead standard," the sensor supervisor announced.

Rajhi turned to McCarthy. "Request permission to engage."

"No," McCarthy said. "Hold your position."

McCarthy's response took Rajhi by surprise. It was a standard tactic to maneuver aggressively during combat, turning and rotating the ship to protect weakened shields as they regenerated, bringing secondary weapon systems into play as the pulse generator recharged. Rajhi's request had been only a formality, since McCarthy's last order was to hold position.

Rajhi replied, "We'll be destroyed if we don't maneuver."

"Hold your position," McCarthy repeated.

Rajhi stood in disbelief for a moment, then turned to the shield supervisor. "Maximum power to the forward shields."

Athens and *Sparta* lay motionless in space, minutes away from certain destruction. Rajhi had experienced McCarthy's strategic brilliance firsthand numerous times but couldn't fathom what he had in mind. This situation was tactical, not strategic, and the tactics to be employed were straightforward. Yet McCarthy refused to allow her to employ the most basic tactic of all—maneuverability.

The ship's sensor supervisor announced quizzically, "Ma'am, the Korilians aren't maneuvering either. They're coming right at us."

Interesting, Rajhi thought. The Korilians seemed overconfident in their superiority, not bothering to maneuver either. But they had reason to be confident. The odds were unquestionably in their favor.

"One minute to engagement range," the weapons officer announced.

McCarthy spoke, "Lay down a planar suppression field on the forward axis."

Rajhi replied, "Sir, a suppression field won't do us any good. The Korilians are outside suppression-fire range, and their pulses will penetrate the field. It's pointless."

"Do as you're ordered, Captain. Suppression fire from both ships."

Rajhi was again stymied with the tactics being employed but gave the orders to *Athens* and *Sparta*. Seconds later, both crews commenced firing with all forward batteries, laying down a suppression field between the Colonial and Korilian warships.

"Thirty seconds to pulse range," the weapons officer announced. "Locked onto contact seven-two-six. So is *Sparta*.

"Twenty seconds."

Rajhi glanced at McCarthy again, wondering what he had in mind. But he gave no hint of what he was thinking.

"Ten seconds."

Just before the weapons officer's count reached zero, all six dreadnoughts fired on *Athens* and *Sparta*, three targeting *Athens* and three attacking *Sparta*. *Athens* rocked with the combined impact of the three Korilian blasts.

"Return fire!" Rajhi ordered.

Athens and *Sparta* fired simultaneously on the top center Korilian dreadnought, the two pulses impacting the target's bow shield. Rajhi immediately turned her attention to *Athens*. "Shield status?"

The shield supervisor reported, "Bow shield down to sixty-eight percent. Power-sharing with all forward shields."

Not bad, Rajhi thought. But how many more attacks could *Athens* withstand?

The next minute passed slowly as Rajhi waited for *Athens*'s pulse-generator recharge, knowing the Korilian recharges would complete first. The Korilian warships continued their advance, finally halting just beyond the suppression field laid down by *Athens* and *Sparta*.

"Fifteen seconds to recharge," announced the weapons officer.

Seconds later, all six Korilian dreadnoughts fired again on *Athens* and *Sparta*.

"Shield holding," the shield supervisor announced.

"Fire!" Rajhi ordered.

Athens and *Sparta* fired again on the same dreadnought, scoring a direct hit on its bow shield. Seconds later, a Korilian dreadnought on the right flank of the formation exploded in a blinding blue flash.

"What the hell?" Rajhi muttered as she tried to understand what happened. *Athens* and *Sparta* had targeted the top-center warship, but the dreadnought on the right had been destroyed.

Her eyes shifted to the nearest sensor display as a yellow starship icon appeared, then its color changed to blue. A unit identification tag flickered to life.

The sensor supervisor called out, "It's *Europe*! Coming in at three points off the starboard stern. At ahead flank! She's bringing up her shields now. She's been in secured emission status!"

The sensor supervisor shifted one of the displays to video. *Europe* was on an intercept course with the Korilian dreadnoughts, her engine plumes white hot from extended operation at ahead flank. A resounding cheer echoed through *Athens*'s bridge; the tactical picture had changed dramatically. A moment ago, the odds were overwhelmingly in favor of the Korilians. Now, with one of the Korilian dreadnoughts destroyed and a Resolute-class battleship in play, the Colonial ships had a chance.

"It's all yours now, Captain," McCarthy said.

Excitement coursed through Rajhi's body as she turned to the helm. "All ahead flank! Come left to course zero-four-zero, up fifteen!"

57

Rajhi approached one of the consoles to review *Europe*'s status, skimming the messages the battleship had sent to Fleet Command. *Europe* had been unable to repair her starboard engines by the deadline set by Admiral Denton, and *North America* and *Varna* had abandoned her, rejoining 2nd Fleet as ordered. But *Europe* continued her repair efforts, finally bringing the starboard main engine online. They had been too far behind to rejoin 2nd Fleet before *Telemantic* was destroyed, and operational control of *Europe* had passed to 1st Fleet. McCarthy had ordered *Europe* to proceed to specified coordinates, with shields down and under a strict communications restriction. Even her unit ID transponder had been secured.

Without shields or radio transmissions, *Europe*'s approach would have been difficult to detect. However, the battleship's engine signature would have been noticeable at close range. Rajhi now understood why McCarthy had directed *Athens* and *Sparta* to lay down a suppression field. It had interfered with the Korilian sensors and allowed *Europe* to approach unnoticed. The plan had worked flawlessly, and now *Europe* was speeding past the five Korilian dreadnoughts while *Athens* and *Sparta* approached the dreadnoughts head on.

Rajhi returned her attention to the nearest Korilian starship, the one that *Athens* and *Sparta* had already pounded twice with dual-pulses. She instructed her weapons officer, "Prepare for straddle shot, contact seven-two-six, *Athens* as master."

The weapons officer entered several commands into *Athens*'s fire control system, then replied, "*Sparta* acknowledges."

Rajhi examined the sensor and weapon displays closely, then announced, "Prepare to execute straddle sequence in twenty seconds."

Conversation on the bridge ceased as the seconds counted down on one of the displays. When the time reached zero, Rajhi issued the first set of commands. "Helm, hard right, steady course zero-eight-five, down thirty. Port bow thrusters, full power."

Athens veered to starboard, and the bow tilted toward the Korilian dreadnought until *Athens* was at a thirty-degree down angle. *Sparta* simultaneously executed a similar maneuver to port. As *Athens* steadied on course, the Korilian ship loomed directly ahead, caught between two Colonial warships in a pincer maneuver. The dreadnought turned down in an attempt to avoid the two inbound battleships.

Athens closed rapidly on the Korilian warship, and it soon filled the bridge windows; *Athens* and *Sparta* were on a collision course with the dreadnought. A yellow flash illuminated *Athens*'s bridge as two Korilian pulses hit one of her port shields, and seconds later the weapons officer announced, "Recharge complete!"

Rajhi ordered, "Fire!" and *Athens* and *Sparta* fired simultaneously at point-blank range.

The two pulses collapsed the weakened Korilian shield, then penetrated the dreadnought's armor at the same spot, on top of the ship just behind the bow compartment. The pulses continued into the starship, crisscrossing in opposite directions. Fiery explosions jetted outward from almost the entire circumference of the Korilian dreadnought, and the bow broke from the rest of the ship.

Immediately after *Athens* fired her pulse generator, Rajhi altered course to avoid collision with the aft end of the dreadnought. "Helm, hard left! Secure port thrusters. Starboard bow thrusters, full power!"

As *Athens* turned away from the Korilian starship, the shield supervisor shouted, "She's spiraling toward us!"

The dreadnought's starboard main engine had failed, leaving only the port main engine operational. The stern began tilting up and twisting sideways, and the red-hot exhaust plume exiting its port main engine swung slowly toward *Athens*.

Rajhi yelled, "Down sixty! Port roll!"

Athens pitched downward and rolled to port, trying to evade the Korilian engine plume. Although shields protected ships from pulses, they didn't stop heat. More than one starship had been severely damaged due to passing too close to an adversary's main engines.

Athens contact coordinator announced, "Closest point of approach in fifteen seconds."

The Korilian ship twisted toward them, and soon the dreadnought's stern was perpendicular to *Athens*, its main engines pointed directly at them. The two-thousand-degree plume melted through *Athens*'s hull.

"Loss of starboard main engines!" the helm announced. The outline of the ship's starboard main engines on the Engineering status display flashed red, while the port main engines remained green.

The damage control supervisor reported, "Hull breach, starboard engine room. Loss of starboard primary fuel injectors. Bringing backup injectors online."

Athens twisted to starboard due to the uneven thrust from her port main engines. "Compensate with bow thrusters!" Rajhi ordered.

The starboard bow thrusters fired, slowing *Athens*'s swing to starboard. A few seconds later, the starboard main engines turned yellow on the status board, then green. The starboard main engines reignited, and *Athens* steadied.

"Up ninety, steady course zero-four-zero."

Athens tilted upward and swung left, returning to her original course toward the Korilian command ship. Rajhi looked up and noted that *Sparta* had also returned to her original course, slightly ahead of *Athens*, a short distance behind *Europe*.

The tension on the bridge dissipated once they cleared the dreadnought, and the crew's attention turned to damage control reports from the engine room. Rajhi focused on the four remaining dreadnoughts, which had reversed course and were now pursuing the Colonial ships.

"Captain Rajhi," McCarthy said, "order *Sparta* to fall in behind *Europe*. Ten degrees off her starboard stern."

Rajhi acknowledged McCarthy's order and relayed it to *Sparta*, which adjusted course and fell in behind *Europe*.

58

As the three Colonial warships sped toward the Korilian command ship, it began retreating at maximum speed but slowly lost ground to the faster battleships. *Europe* was in the lead, her engine plumes burning brightly, with *Athens* and *Sparta* close behind, side-by-side. The three battleships would eventually close to within weapon range; the question in Rajhi's mind was whether the pursuing dreadnoughts would destroy them first.

"Ma'am," the sensor supervisor said with concern. "*Europe* is missing a shield."

Rajhi cocked her head. "Say again."

"She's missing shield three."

During her brief review of *Europe*'s status, Rajhi hadn't bothered to check for shields. She stopped by the operations console and reviewed the data.

Unbelievable!

Europe had repaired her starboard main engines but not the damaged shield generator. She had engaged six Korilian dreadnoughts with a missing shield.

A death sentence.

Rajhi realized now why Admiral McCarthy had ordered *Sparta* to fall in behind *Europe*'s starboard stern—to protect her from the pursuing dreadnoughts. However, *Sparta* couldn't maintain station there for long, and *Europe*'s vulnerable starboard side would soon be exposed. The result was a foregone conclusion.

Athens's starboard bridge windows lit up with a yellow flash. The four dreadnoughts had completed their pulse recharge, firing simultaneously on *Sparta*'s stern shield. It seemed the Korilians had also noticed *Europe*'s missing shield and were intent on removing the obstacle between them and the powerful but vulnerable Resolute-class battleship.

Rajhi stopped beside her sensor supervisor. *Sparta*'s stern shield had been reduced to fifteen percent. It was power-sharing with the other aft shields as it recharged, but it would reach only fifty percent before the dreadnoughts fired again. The next quad-pulse would collapse or buckle *Sparta*'s stern shield, and the following attack would destroy her. *Sparta* had to turn away to bring fully charged shields into play. Rajhi looked to McCarthy for direction.

"All ships will remain on course," he said.

"Sir," Rajhi replied, "*Sparta* cannot take two more quad-pulses on her stern shield. If she doesn't turn away, she'll be destroyed."

McCarthy looked through *Athens*'s bridge windows, not bothering to meet Rajhi's gaze. "*Europe* must be protected while her pulse generator recharges. *Sparta* will stay on course."

"Sir, at our current closure rate, *Europe* will be within range of the command ship in nine minutes. We don't have nine minutes. *Sparta* will be destroyed in two, and if we take *Sparta*'s place, we'll be destroyed three minutes later, and *Europe* a minute after that. The only viable option is for *Athens* and *Sparta* to turn and engage."

McCarthy locked his eyes on Rajhi. "Doing so is pointless. They'll ignore any ship that turns to fight, attacking the ships pursuing their command ship instead. *Sparta* will maintain position behind *Europe*."

Rajhi gritted her teeth. When she replied, she was unable to restrain the emotion. "*Europe* is finished! She cannot maintain course once *Sparta* and *Athens* are destroyed, nor can she engage four dreadnoughts with any chance of survival. Our only hope lies in *Athens* and *Sparta*. We must engage!"

"*Sparta* will maintain course, Captain."

A yellow flash illuminated *Athens*'s bridge windows as another quad-pulse hit *Sparta*.

The sensor supervisor announced, "*Sparta*'s stern shield has buckled. Minor damage to aft compartments, main engines are still operational."

The communications officer reported, "*Sparta* requests permission to turn away."

Rajhi glanced over her shoulder at *Athens* and *Sparta*'s joint motto, emblazoned on *Athens*'s starboard bridge bulkhead.

Fight together.

Die together.

She had sworn an oath and would not abandon *Sparta* to pointless destruction.

Rajhi turned to McCarthy. "I will not stand by while you needlessly sacrifice *Sparta*. *Athens* and *Sparta* will turn and fight." She turned to her communications officer. "Direct *Sparta* to maneuver as required."

"Belay that order!" McCarthy shouted.

The communications officer froze as he reached toward his panel.

McCarthy stepped toward Rajhi, stopping an arm's length away. "I gave you a direct order, Captain. You will either follow it, or I will relieve you of command."

Rajhi ignored McCarthy, repeating her order to the communications officer. "Direct *Sparta* to maneuver as required."

"Stop!" McCarthy ordered. The communications officer froze again. His eyes darted between the battleship's captain and the four-star admiral as his hand hovered just above *Sparta*'s symbol on his console.

To Rajhi, McCarthy said, "You are relieved of command."

"The hell I am!" Rajhi replied. "I will remain in command until the end of this battle, then suffer the repercussions."

It was McCarthy's turn to ignore Rajhi. He turned to *Athens*'s executive officer, standing beside Rajhi. "You are now *Athens*'s commanding officer. You will keep *Sparta* in her current position."

The executive officer shifted uneasily on his feet, his eyes moving between Rajhi and McCarthy. Throughout the bridge, personnel cast furtive glances between them as they watched the tense confrontation. Finally, the executive officer replied.

"I respectfully decline, Admiral. Our crew has served under Captain Rajhi and survived longer than any crew in the Fleet. She will remain our captain."

McCarthy surveyed the bridge crew, seeking the next most senior officer. As his eyes swept the bridge, Lara probed the crew's emotions, trying to ascertain the probability a senior officer would relieve Rajhi, or if the crew would follow McCarthy's orders if he attempted to take command himself. She sorted through a mixture of emotions, identifying one more dominant than the other. *Loyalty.*

No officer would relieve Rajhi of command; they would follow her orders as long as she gave them. As far as the crew was concerned, McCarthy was a brilliant officer who knew how to move ships around on a three-dimensional chessboard. But he didn't know how to command a ship in combat. Rajhi did, and under her leadership, *Athens* had repeatedly defied the odds and prevailed over their opponents, even when outmatched. They owed their lives to her.

As Lara assessed the situation, she wondered why Rajhi questioned McCarthy's orders. Surely, she understood that he'd analyzed numerous scenarios, and as distasteful as it was, there was no other choice. Then it dawned on Lara—*Rajhi didn't know!*

Rajhi didn't know McCarthy was a Nexus Ten. Only the Fleet admirals and the eight Resolute commanding officers were at the operations brief when Fleet Admiral Fitzgerald had revealed McCarthy's ability. The battle began a few hours later, and word of McCarthy's ability hadn't yet spread throughout the Fleet.

Lara interjected, "Captain Rajhi. You must listen to Admiral McCarthy. He's a Nexus Ten."

"I don't care if he's a twenty," Rajhi replied. "I will not let him sacrifice *Sparta* and doom *Athens* to the same fate, leaving only *Europe*, which has no chance of success."

Rajhi's reasoning seemed sound, yet McCarthy seemed intent on sacrificing *Sparta*, so Lara wondered what he saw. She reached over and touched his hand.

Unlike earlier in the battle, Lara saw only one future instead of multiple visions, one where *Sparta* turned away as Rajhi desired, along with *Athens*.

Europe was destroyed before her pulse generator completed its recharge, while *Athens* and *Sparta* combined to destroy one of the dreadnoughts. But while they attempted to close on the Korilian command ship, they were repeatedly forced to maneuver to protect their weakened shields. This delay was the critical issue, because there were four more inbound dreadnoughts that would join the remaining three. *Athens* and *Sparta* would never reach the command ship.

Lara pulled her hand away, and the image disappeared. Rajhi stood before them, her eyes blazing defiance. It was clear that she wasn't going to follow McCarthy's order.

A wisp of fog materialized at Rajhi's feet, weaving as it rose up her leg, then swirled around the pulse-pistol on her hip. As Rajhi turned to address her communications officer again, the Nexus One's words of advice flashed in Lara's mind.

Trust your instinct.

Lara acted without thinking, pulling the pistol from Rajhi's holster and swinging it up toward Rajhi's head. The battleship captain froze as the muzzle halted an inch from her temple. Her fists clenched, but her face betrayed no emotion.

Lara said, "Maybe the admiral can't relieve you of command, but I can."

Nesrine Rajhi calmly assessed her predicament. McCarthy's guide had a pulse-pistol aimed at her head. Around her, the bridge personnel stood frozen at their stations.

As Rajhi contemplated her options, the communications officer announced, "Ma'am, *Sparta*'s hailing again. Placing on-screen."

"No!" Rajhi shouted.

She would not let *Sparta* see what was occurring on her ship: *Athens*'s commanding officer with a gun to her head. But *Sparta* needed orders, and soon. The deadlock on *Athens*'s bridge had to be resolved. Rajhi's mind worked quickly—she was trained for battle and analyzed the situation in only a few seconds.

Rajhi spun toward Lara, grabbing the pistol barrel. But instead of wresting the weapon from Lara's hand, she pulled the muzzle firmly against her forehead. Rajhi glared at Lara, defiance and disdain smoldering in her eyes. Then she reached up with her other hand and started prying Lara's hand away from the pistol grip, one finger at a time.

Lara's pulse raced as she realized Rajhi was forcing her to make a decision: either let go or squeeze the trigger. Rajhi pulled three of her fingers away, then bent them backward to force Lara to release her index finger from the trigger. As sharp pain shot up her hand, she tried to reason with the starship captain.

"I know you don't understand," she said, "but it's the right decision. Admiral McCarthy has analyzed all possible futures. Believe me when I tell you...if *Sparta* turns away, we will all die, and the command ship will escape."

Her words went unheeded; Rajhi continued bending Lara's fingers backward. In a few seconds, her fingers would snap if she didn't release the pistol or pull the trigger. She looked to McCarthy for direction.

"Let go," he said.

Lara released the pistol, flexing her hand as Rajhi placed the weapon in her right hand. Then the starship captain leveled it at Lara's head.

With rage burning in her eyes, Rajhi said, "That's the last time you'll pull a stunt like that."

McCarthy suddenly stepped forward, thrusting his right palm into her chest. Rajhi flew backward onto the deck, sliding to a halt on her back. There was a dazed look in her eyes as McCarthy approached, extracting the weapon from her hand.

He aimed it at her head.

"You will follow my orders, or I'll kill you. Do you understand?"

Rajhi hesitated, then replied, "Yes, Admiral."

She pushed herself to her feet, then glared at Lara before turning to her communicator.

"*Sparta* on-screen," she commanded.

Captain Salukas appeared on the display. "Nesrine! Request permission to turn away!"

Rajhi forced the words out. "Permission denied. *Sparta* will maintain position behind *Europe*." She stood there rigidly, then added, "I'm sorry, Gynt."

Salukas said nothing for a moment, then the screen went black.

Lara examined the display showing *Sparta* and *Europe*, wondering if Salukas would follow Rajhi's order. *Sparta* maintained course, holding its position behind *Europe*.

A few seconds later, the quad-pulse came.

Sparta's stern shield blazed bright yellow, then collapsed. The battleship's main engines exploded in an orange-and-black-tinged fireball, sending shards of metal in all directions. *Sparta* slowed, falling behind *Athens*, then lost all shields. As the four Korilian dreadnoughts passed by, they targeted *Sparta* with suppression-fire batteries, engulfing the wounded ship in hundreds of detonations. As the dreadnoughts pulled away, *Sparta* exploded in a bright blue flash.

It was silent on *Athens*'s bridge as the crew watched *Sparta*'s remnants disappear into the darkness. After a moment, Rajhi ordered her ship to take *Sparta*'s place, just off *Europe*'s starboard stern. Lara examined the distance to the Korilian command ship. Still seven minutes away from weapon range.

They didn't have seven minutes. After three quad-pulses, *Athens* would share *Sparta*'s fate.

59

Athens and *Europe* maintained course, slowly closing on the Korilian command ship. Rajhi turned her attention to the four Korilian dreadnoughts behind *Athens*, seconds ticking away as their pulse generators recharged.

The sensor supervisor announced, "All four contacts are targeting our stern shield."

"Shield status?" Rajhi asked.

"Stern shield at one hundred percent. Power-sharing with shields six and seven."

Seconds later, the dreadnoughts fired, and Rajhi's skin tingled as *Athens*'s stern shield absorbed the quad-pulse.

"Stern shield holding," the shield supervisor reported. "Shield at twenty-one percent."

"Estimated strength before the next pulse?" Rajhi asked.

"Sixty percent," the shield supervisor replied.

Not strong enough.

At sixty percent, the shield would buckle or collapse when hit by another quad-pulse, with potential damage to the main engines. Either way, *Athens* would be destroyed during the third quad-pulse unless Rajhi maneuvered to bring another shield into play.

"Admiral," Rajhi said, "we must turn and fight. We cannot take two more hits on our aft shield."

"No," McCarthy said. "Drop all forward shields."

"Sir?"

"Drop the forward shields and send all power aft."

"Sir, once we drop the forward shields, they'll take five minutes to regenerate if we need them."

"You won't need them."

McCarthy's proposal was innovative but would doom *Athens*. Without forward shields, the ship could not turn away, and its stern shield would soon collapse. With the Korilian command ship six minutes from weapon range, both *Athens* and *Europe* would be eliminated before they achieved their objective. Rajhi could think of no scenario where either ship survived and reached the command ship.

"Trust me," McCarthy said. "Drop the forward shields."

"Yes, sir," Rajhi said reluctantly, then turned to the shield supervisor. "Drop all forward shields."

The shield supervisor acknowledged and announced, "Dropping shields one, two, and three. Routing maximum power to the aft shields. Mid shields at minimum power."

The next minute passed quickly as *Athens* prepared for the next Korilian barrage. As the anticipated recharge time approached, the sensor supervisor counted down the time.

"Ten seconds."

The shield supervisor added, "Stern shield at eighty percent." The shield had recharged faster than normal now that extra power was being routed aft.

"Five seconds."

The Korilian dreadnoughts fired, and Rajhi's skin tingled more sharply this time as the quad-pulse hit *Athens*'s weakened stern shield.

"Shield holding," the shield supervisor reported. "Twelve percent."

Rajhi did the math in her head, estimating the strength of *Athens*'s stern shield after a minute of regeneration. "Admiral," she said, "we won't be able to take another quad-pulse."

McCarthy gestured toward the forward display. "You won't have to."

Europe had completed its pulse recharge and was turning to bring its pulse generator to bear on the Korilian dreadnoughts behind her. *Europe* turned to port, protecting her vulnerable starboard side. One of the dreadnoughts was soon within weapons arc, and *Europe* fired. The pulse penetrated the ship's forward shield, piercing through every compartment from bow to stern. The Korilian ship's jump drive, damaged by the pulse, imploded, destroying the ship in a blinding orange flash.

The three remaining dreadnoughts maneuvered to gain a clear shot on *Europe's* starboard side, while *Europe* attempted to reverse her port turn. But *Europe* was an immense starship and did not turn quickly. *Europe* eventually stopped her port turn and started swinging to starboard. But not soon enough.

The Korilian dreadnoughts completed their recharge, and all three fired on *Europe*. One of the Korilian starships had a desirable shot, and its pulse skimmed along *Europe's* starboard bow, clipping the bow shield before penetrating through *Europe's* missing number three shield and compromised armor. *Europe's* bow shield absorbed part of the pulse's energy, but not enough. Explosions rippled aft along *Europe's* starboard side.

Rajhi watched as explosions cascaded inside the battleship. She had watched the death throes of starships many times and knew *Europe* had received a fatal blow. It was only a matter of time before more shields failed or the ship's pulse generator or jump drive imploded.

Europe adjusted course, turning back toward the Korilian dreadnoughts, confusing Rajhi. Instead of turning away, presenting the ship's operational shields to the Korilians, the battleship's captain was giving the Korilians a clear shot at *Europe's* exposed starboard side. In less than a minute, once the Korilian pulse generators recharged, *Europe* would be destroyed. Then Rajhi realized what *Europe's* captain was doing.

The Korilians didn't have another minute.

In their haste to gain a clear shot on *Europe's* starboard side, the Korilians hadn't thought through the implications. *Europe* and one of the Korilian dreadnoughts were headed almost directly toward each other. As the dreadnought turned to avoid the Colonial warship, *Europe* adjusted course to maintain an intercept course.

Europe was going to ram the Korilian warship.

60

Captain Jeff Townsend stood on *Europe*'s bridge, gripping the forward railing. Beneath his feet, the deck shuddered as explosions tore his ship apart. Townsend knew it was only a matter of time before *Europe* was destroyed, but he hoped his ship held together long enough to repay the Korilian dreadnought looming ahead for what it had done.

Townsend had been pleased when he had been selected to command one of the Resolute-class battleships. Despite his failure at Ruehiri, Fleet Admiral Fitzgerald still held his ability in high regard. But Townsend had again been disappointed with his performance, allowing the Korilians to disable *Europe* early in the battle. The crew had been demoralized as well, but McCarthy had given them a chance for redemption, routing them to the crucial encounter. *Europe* had destroyed two of the Korilian dreadnoughts protecting their command ship, and if *Europe* was successful in this final endeavor, they will have destroyed a third, all while missing a shield. *That* was redemption.

Even as the ship shuddered from explosions, each one stronger than the last, the crew remained focused, damage reports flowing in and orders going out.

Forward reactor down.

Shifting to the aft power grid.

Pulse generator, still recharging. Four more minutes.

The watch officer ordered continuous course adjustments, keeping *Europe* aimed at her target as the dreadnought tried to evade. The Korilians activated their suppression-fire batteries, hoping they could destroy *Europe* before the starship rammed them. Explosions rippled inside the Colonial battleship, and her remaining shields failed. The dreadnought's suppression fire tore into *Europe*, but she held together, her main engine plumes burning brightly as she closed the remaining distance.

Europe collided with the Korilian starship almost bow on bow, and the forward compartment of *Europe* began disintegrating as it impacted the dreadnought's forward shield. But *Europe*'s immense mass and speed overwhelmed and collapsed the dreadnought's bow shield, and both ships crashed into each other. *Europe* and the Korilian warship morphed into a mass of buckling compartments amid hundreds of explosions as the two ships became one, and it wasn't long before *Europe*'s pulse generator imploded, consuming both starships in a bright purple flash.

61

Rajhi watched as *Europe* and the Korilian dreadnought disintegrated, with fragments of the two ships ejected by a final explosion of streaking comets that disappeared into the darkness. Only *Athens* remained now, surging toward the Korilian command ship with two dreadnoughts in pursuit.

The warship's lighting dimmed momentarily as a double-pulse impacted *Athens*'s stern shield.

"Shield strength?" Rajhi asked.

"Forty-three percent."

McCarthy's plan finally made sense. He had factored in *Europe*'s ability to destroy one and perhaps two of the pursuing dreadnoughts, and *Athens* would not have to endure another quad-pulse. *Europe* had bought *Athens* valuable time, but her stern shield would still fail after enough double-pulses. The question was—how long before they failed, and would they close to within weapon range of the Korilian command ship before then?

"Time to within weapon range?"

"Five minutes, twenty seconds."

Rajhi did the mental calculations. Starting shield strength: forty-three percent; four double-pulses from seven klicks away.

They weren't going to make it.

The shield supervisor confirmed her conclusion. "Stern shield will fail on the fourth double."

Then Rajhi realized the shield supervisor was wrong. The shield would hold due to the extra power being sent aft. The ship's algorithms weren't designed to account for no forward shields on the power grid. But the stern shield would buckle on the fourth double and collapse shortly afterward once the dreadnoughts began bombarding the weakened shield with suppression fire.

The end result was the same. *Athens's* stern shield would collapse just before they would close to within weapon range of the Korilian command ship. But after the shield fell, Rajhi hoped *Athens* would hold together long enough to get one pulse off.

The tactical picture was now clear. Her sole goal was to reach the command ship intact and destroy it in a single pulse.

Rajhi announced, "Reconfigure the pulse generator per tactical order six-four-two."

The weapons officer repeated back the command, then began adjusting the frequency and modulation of *Athens's* pulse generator per the directions provided by Fleet Command prior to the battle so *Athens's* pulse could penetrate Korilian shields like the new Resolutes.

According to the directive, they would be able to take one shot, but their pulse generator would be destroyed in the process.

What then?

Athens would have no pulse generator and no forward or stern shields, pursued by two fully operational dreadnoughts.

The situation was hopeless.

Rajhi thought about Gynt and the sacrifice he and his crew had made. It looked like she would fulfill their pact after all.

Fight together. Die together.

Still, Rajhi wasn't ready to give up, and a desperate plan formed in her mind.

"Bring up the forward shields!"

"Ma'am?" the shield supervisor asked. "That will drain power from the stern shield."

"Bring up the forward shields. Now!" Rajhi didn't have time to explain. Every second was crucial. Even now, it might be too late.

The shield supervisor entered the required commands. "Forward shields regenerating."

"On the third double-pulse, slow to ahead full," Rajhi ordered.

The helm acknowledged, but the shield supervisor again questioned Rajhi's order. "Ma'am, if we slow, the Korilians will close, and their fourth double-pulse will be stronger."

"I realize that," Rajhi replied. "But we're going to lose the stern shield after the fourth pulse anyway, regardless of what distance they fire from."

She wanted the Korilians closer.

Rajhi stood quietly, her hands clasped behind her back as everyone waited for the next double-pulse. The stern shield flared at the expected time.

"Stern shield strength, thirty-two percent."

Athens continued toward the Korilian command ship, slowly recharging its stern shield. Behind her, Admiral McCarthy and his guide stood silent. Had they discerned her plan, or had they given up? The situation, after all, appeared hopeless.

Rajhi smiled.

The stern shield was hit with another double-pulse. The shield held but was reduced to twenty-two percent.

Over the next minute, the shield slowly recharged again. *Athens* was hit by the third double-pulse, and Rajhi heard the expected reports.

"Slowing to ahead full."

"Stern shield at twelve percent."

"Ma'am, the pulse generator has been reconfigured per tactical order six-four-two. I must remind you that the pulse generator will be permanently disabled after the next pulse."

"Understood," Rajhi said.

The stage was set.

Athens's stern shield would fail after the next Korilian double-pulse. They could begin the five-minute regeneration, but it'd be pointless. No matter which way *Athens* maneuvered, one of the dreadnoughts would obtain a clear shot through *Athens*'s missing stern shield.

The Korilian command ship was finally visible on-screen. It was over five times the size of a dreadnought, bristling with antenna spires and transducer spheres. Rajhi glanced at Admiral McCarthy and his guide, wondering if the admiral would offer reassurance that everything would turn out okay. But there was no response from McCarthy, who stared out the bridge windows while the Nexus bitch beside him glared at her.

Finally, the double-pulse came, and instead of the calm assessments that followed previous pulses, Rajhi sensed the tension in her crew's reports:

"Stern shield at two percent and buckling. Attempting to stabilize!"

"Both Korilian ships targeting stern shield with suppression fire!"

Rajhi examined the aft camera; the stern shield glowed as it was bombarded by the suppression-fire batteries, with the shield's illumination steadily weakening. It wouldn't hold much longer.

"Time to weapon range?"

"Twenty seconds."

Athens continued closing on the Korilian command ship.

"Stern shield failing!"

"Fifteen seconds."

Not much farther now...

"Stern shield has collapsed!"

"Secure the starboard fuel injectors! Make it look like a flameout!"

Athens's starboard main engine plume sputtered, then extinguished.

"Ten seconds."

Rajhi felt tremors beneath her feet as the Korilian suppression fire tore into *Athens*'s unprotected stern.

"Five seconds."

"Secure the port fuel injectors!"

Athens's port main engines went dark.

"Within weapon range!"

"Fire!"

Athens shuddered as its pulse generator ejected a pulse it hadn't been designed for, and its tyranium coil shattered the instant the pulse was generated. But the pulse left *Athens* and sped toward the Korilian command ship. Rajhi and the rest of her bridge crew watched as the pulse hit the command ship's forward shield, which lit up in a bright yellow flash. The pulse passed through the shield, then bored into the center of the Korilian ship.

62

The Korilian command ship exploded in a giant red fireball, accompanied by a bright white impulse ring speeding outward, rocking *Athens* as it passed by. But Rajhi and her crew had little time for celebration, as the two closing dreadnoughts ravaged *Athens* with suppression fire while their pulse generators recharged.

Immediately after giving the command to fire, Rajhi ordered, "Starboard bow and port stern thrusters, full power!"

The thrusters activated, and *Athens* twisted slowly to port, turning broadside in front of the incoming dreadnoughts. Rajhi stood at the forward bridge railing, unfazed by the Korilian suppression fire tearing into the unprotected bow and stern, watching as the dreadnoughts continued closing on *Athens*.

That's it, you cretins.

The dreadnoughts had maneuvered close beside each other during their pursuit of *Athens* to increase the intensity of their double-pulses and had remained at ahead flank when *Athens* slowed to full. As a result, they were close together and almost directly behind *Athens* when Rajhi secured the main engines and began twisting her battleship to port. *Athens* was a large ship, over five times longer than she was wide, and the Korilians realized what Rajhi was doing too late. They were now both on a collision course with *Athens*, one aimed directly at *Athens*'s stern and the other at its bow.

The dreadnoughts turned away, one to port and the other to starboard, and also maneuvered vertically in an attempt to pass over or under *Athens*'s bow and stern.

Rajhi watched the evasive maneuvers. Everything hinged on how the two dreadnoughts avoided *Athens*, with a fifty-fifty chance they would fall into the trap. As one turned down and the other up, she smiled.

"Bow thrusters ninety up, stern thrusters ninety down, full power!"

Athens's bow tilted upward, directly toward one dreadnought, and her stern down toward the other. Both Korilian starships targeted *Athens*, their suppression fire tearing gaping holes into the battleship's outer compartments. Damage control reports streamed into *Athens*'s bridge, but Rajhi didn't respond. There was one report she was waiting for.

Finally, it came.

"Forward shields restored!"

Athens had twisted broadside by now, with a thirty-degree up angle. The dreadnought approaching *Athens*'s bow had maneuvered sufficiently to evade *Athens*. But not far enough away to avoid *Athens*'s forward shields, which hadn't existed until now.

"Shield impact in fifteen seconds!"

"Drop all mid and aft shields!" Rajhi ordered. "Send all power to the forward shields!"

Rajhi grabbed onto the forward bridge railing, bracing herself. A few seconds later, the dreadnought's and *Athens*'s forward shields collided.

"Shields holding!"

The starships' powerful shields intertwined, illuminating the bridge windows in a dazzling electrical firestorm as the shield interaction sent sizzling arcs in every direction. *Athens*'s and the dreadnought's forward shields grew brighter and brighter, almost blinding Rajhi with their intensity.

A bright yellow flash lit up the bridge windows, and the shimmer around the dreadnought's bow disappeared.

The sensor supervisor announced, "Korilian bow shield has collapsed! Our shields holding strong!"

Rajhi glanced at the sensor display, noting that the dreadnought on *Athens*'s stern had modified its course to pass directly behind *Athens* so it could target its suppression fire directly into the opening of *Athens*'s main engines. But the Korilians had made one fatal assumption. Rajhi had turned off one main engine when the stern shield collapsed, and the other one a few seconds later, giving the appearance that the main engines had failed. A glance at the Engineering status display confirmed both were fully operational.

She turned to the helm. "Reset all fuel injectors. Main engines, ahead flank!"

Both engines ignited simultaneously, with two-thousand-degree plumes jetting three hundred yards behind *Athens*. The dreadnought was only a hundred yards away, and red-hot plumes passed through the Korilian ship's shields unabated, searing through the dreadnought's hull. As the warship passed astern, *Athens*'s main engines burned a black trench deep into its side.

With both main engines firing at ahead flank, *Athens* surged forward, directly into the Korilian warship ahead, no longer protected by its bow shield. The dreadnought began disintegrating, melting inward as compartment after compartment was vaporized by *Athens*'s shields.

"Secure the bridge!" Rajhi ordered.

Heavy metal shield doors slid quickly over the bridge windows. Seconds later, the dreadnought's pulse generator met *Athens*'s bow shield, and the Korilian starship was consumed in a powerful detonation. The blast rocked *Athens*, shoving the battleship's bow down so violently that the deck fell away from Rajhi and the rest of the bridge crew, suspending them temporarily in mid-air before they came crashing down to the deck.

Athens's crew picked themselves up, returning to their stations. The deck had buckled, creating a fifteen-degree down slope midway through the bridge.

"Open the shield doors," Rajhi ordered.

The damage control coordinator carried out the order, but only half of the heavy metal enclosures retracted, with the others jammed in place. Rajhi turned her attention to the Korilian dreadnought behind them. Suppression fire continued to pour into *Athens*'s stern, and the Helena-class battleship shuddered from a powerful explosion as one of the main engine fuel lines was breached by the suppression fire. *Athens*'s starboard main engines disintegrated, and the port main engines were torn apart by the debris from the exploding starboard side.

But the main engines had done their job. As the dreadnought cleared *Athens*'s stern, dozens of explosions outlined the deep black scar seared into the dreadnought's side. Its shields and then main engines failed, and the ship began drifting away. A moment later, the warship was sheared in two from an explosion, and the two halves of the ship spiraled slowly away in opposite directions.

As Rajhi watched the demise of the second dreadnought, the lights and consoles on the bridge flickered, then went dark. Emergency lights activated seconds later, bathing the bridge in yellow light, and the essential bridge consoles returned to life. *Athens* drifted in space, her bow compartment bent downward at a fifteen-degree angle, her engineering compartment ripped open, with only the twisted steel of the port main engine remaining. On the ship's damage control display, red symbols lit up the entire stern and bow sections.

"Status!" Rajhi ordered.

The ship's crew reported in a predetermined sequence, as they had done in countless battles.

"Both main engines destroyed. Stern thrusters inoperable."

"All shields down. Forward generators destroyed. Mid and aft shield generator evaluation in progress."

"Pulse generator destroyed."

"Containment breach in aft reactor, evacuating aft reactor compartment. Forward reactor down hard, loss of primary cooling. Emergency cooling in progress."

"Seventeen fires in engineering. Severe structural damage in bow compartment, frames twenty-three through twenty-nine."

Silence gripped the bridge after the reports ended. Solemn faces turned to Rajhi, awaiting her response. *Athens* was crippled. No propulsion, no weapons, no shields. She couldn't even defend herself from the small marauders.

"Jump drive?"

The look in the navigator's eyes told Rajhi the answer before she spoke. "Inoperable."

Rajhi examined the crew who had fought beside her for five long years. She glanced at the consoles, which displayed the status of the ship that had protected them in countless battles.

Rajhi's executive officer broke the heavy silence. "Ma'am, *Athens* is..." His voice trailed off, unable to complete the sentence.

"I know," Rajhi said.

She looked at each member of the bridge crew before giving the necessary orders.

"Abandon ship. Initiate the self-destruct sequence."

Rajhi approached one of the consoles, joined by her executive officer. She entered the destruct code, and her executive officer did the same. A red blinking triangle appeared in the center of the console, and Rajhi slowly reached over and pressed her palm onto it. The ship's computer made the necessary announcement throughout *Athens's* compartments:

"The ship will self-destruct in fifteen minutes. All personnel proceed to evacuation stations."

Red lights began flashing every few seconds.

After the announcement was repeated, Rajhi spoke to her bridge crew. "You have done well and should be proud of what we accomplished, both today and over the last five years." She wanted to say more, but nothing followed.

Her executive officer took his cue and announced loudly, "All personnel proceed to evacuation stations."

The bridge crew departed, leaving only Admiral McCarthy and his guide alone with Rajhi. She stood next to the forward bridge railing, looking out through the bridge windows, half of them still covered by the damaged shield doors.

McCarthy approached, stopping behind her. "Nesrine," he said. "We have to leave."

Rajhi slowly turned and walked down the starboard side of the bridge, pausing when she reached the emblem of *Athens* and *Sparta* etched into the bulkhead. She placed a hand on the emblem and held it there for a moment before continuing on. After they exited, Rajhi turned and looked into the battleship's bridge for the last time as the door slid shut.

Rajhi proceeded to her evacuation station while McCarthy led Lara back to his shuttle in *Athens*'s spaceport. As they sped away from the crippled ship and prepared for the jump back to his command ship, Lara counted down the time, watching *Athens* behind them on one of the shuttle displays. At the fifteen-minute mark, the battleship was consumed in a bright green detonation, and a few seconds later, the shock wave jolted the shuttle as it prepared to jump.

63

Moments earlier, when the Korilian command ship was destroyed, cheers erupted throughout the Fleet command center, accompanied by congratulatory handshakes and hugs. As the celebration died down, Fleet Admiral Fitzgerald stood proudly at the front of the facility.

"Implement phase three," she announced. "Envelop the Korilian armada."

The command center personnel activated the shield mines that had been stealthily launched over the last twenty-four hours, and the orbiting defense stations began launching hundreds more, which would interfere with the jump drives and prevent the Korilian warships from jumping away. Orders went out to all Colonial Fleet forces, with 3rd through 6th Fleets advancing while 1st Fleet consolidated its position in the center, engaging the Korilian ships as they retreated.

Personnel waited tensely for an indication that the shield mines worked. After no Korilian starship disappeared in a white flash, the tension gradually eased. The Korilians either couldn't jump away or had decided to stay and fight. Either way was fine with Fitzgerald. Due to the losses inflicted by 2nd Fleet and her Resolute battleships, Colonial forces now outnumbered the Korilians. Additionally, the Korilian flanks had been significantly weakened as they diverted starships into the center to oppose the Colonial offensive. 3rd through 6th Fleets surged forward, overrunning the Korilian forces.

Two hours after the destruction of the Korilian command ship, lead elements of 3rd and 5th Fleets met, joined shortly afterward by 4th and 6th Fleet cruisers, marking the successful envelopment of the entire Korilian armada. The five fleets began contracting their sphere, methodically destroying every Korilian ship.

Aboard the 1st Fleet command ship, Lara stood beside McCarthy again on the bridge, where he had resumed command of his fleet. He had just issued another set of orders when the Nexus One's image appeared on McCarthy's wristlet display.

"Well done, Jon," she said. "Humanity owes you a debt of gratitude." Without waiting for McCarthy's response, she added, "Return to Domus Praesidium as soon as possible, and bring Lara with you."

After Rhea's image disappeared, McCarthy contemplated her order for a moment, then contacted Fleet Admiral Fitzgerald, informing her of The One's instructions.

A few hours later, the last Korilian warship was destroyed, accompanied by resounding cheer in *Lider*'s flag bridge. McCarthy praised his staff for their superb performance, then turned over command of 1st Fleet to Vice Admiral Mendoza.

As McCarthy led the way to his shuttle, Lara's thoughts turned to her pending meeting with The One. During their last meeting, The One said she would assess Lara again after the battle, determining her fate. Lara said nothing as they headed toward the spaceport, and McCarthy must have sensed her anxiety mounting with each step.

"She hasn't decided yet," McCarthy said.

Lara replied, "But she will soon."

Upon reaching the spaceport, they entered McCarthy's Nexus shuttle.

"*Elena*," McCarthy said, "take us to Domus Praesidium."

"To the plateau pad or one of the tactical hangars?"

"The plateau pad."

The spaceport doors opened, *Lider*'s port shield was dropped, and the Nexus shuttle exited the spaceport and turned toward Earth. As the planet grew larger in the shuttle's window, the tension in Lara's body began to ease —the battle was over, and the Colonial Fleet had prevailed.

Despite her reservations about being assigned as a fleet guide, she had not only contributed to the battle, but her assistance had been crucial, leading to the destruction of the Korilian command ship. Then there was the personal aspect—she and McCarthy had survived.

As the shuttle entered Earth's atmosphere, descending toward Domus Praesidium, Lara reflected on what the future might hold and how much her life had changed in the last three weeks. As her mind drifted to the past, she realized she still wore her wedding ring. Without hesitation, she removed the ring and placed it in her jumpsuit pocket. If The One let her live, she would begin a new life in more ways than one.

64

At the outer reaches of Domus Praesidium's west wing, deep beneath the Ural Mountains, The One's footsteps echoed off granite walls as she wound her way through the maze of passageways, eventually treading down a desolate, dusty hallway. As she passed beneath widely spaced sodium lamps, her shadow on the blue marble floor gradually grew and then receded. It had been ten years since she had visited Sanctuary, consulting with the holographic images of the three Placidia Tens who had ruled the Nexus House before her, obtaining guidance from their memories.

The holograms of The Three could recall events and information from the past, but they could not remember new discussions. During her previous visits to Sanctuary, The Three had objected to the same issue each time. She could no longer face them. Tonight, however, she would endure their piercing disapproval, for she had questions the Codex could not answer. Perhaps The Three could provide insight into the enigma of Lara Anderson.

Harken the arrival of the One with no line...

The rest of the sentence was garbled, and there were too many ways to complete it. The Corvad attack had erased much of the wisdom of The Five, and it was finally clear why the Corvads had sacrificed half of their Praetorian Legion in the effort. It seemed the Codex contained guidance crucial to the Nexus House's survival, and that guidance had been erased, leaving her unable to discern the appropriate response to this unusual woman. Perhaps one of The Three could provide the insight required. Even though the discussion might open a wound sealed by ten years of avoidance, she would enter Sanctuary.

Rhea reached the end of the passageway, stopping at a dead end, staring at the rough-hewn granite wall where construction on this passageway had halted three millennia ago. Then she took a step forward, passing through the imaginary wall. She didn't understand the technology that had been developed long ago to conceal Sanctuary's location, and only she and Ronan knew of the chamber's existence.

Before her was another wall—this one real—with a three-foot-diameter bronze House seal affixed at chest height. She touched the eye in the center of the emblem, and the seal began rotating. Ronan had previously tried to open the chamber entrance, but the seal responded only to Rhea's touch, as if it somehow knew that she, and she alone, ruled the Nexus House.

After the seal turned ninety degrees, a vertical seam appeared through the middle of the wall and seal. The two halves of the wall and seal split and pulled slowly apart, creating an opening into a twenty-by-thirty-foot chamber. After Rhea entered, the walls slid shut behind her.

At the front of the room was a podium made of quartz, and at the other end of the chamber were five circular daises. On the wall behind the daises was a six-foot-diameter Nexus House seal, but instead of the ordinary bronze symbols that adorned the rest of Domus Praesidium, this seal was fabricated from precious metals and jewels, with a single transparent orb in the center of the Nexus eye that began to glow with a diffuse blue light when she entered the chamber.

She stopped behind the podium, placing her hands on both sides, mustering the courage to proceed. Reaching forward, she selected one of the crystals stored on the podium and placed it into a slot. A hologram of an elderly man wearing a flowing blue robe appeared on the center dais.

The apparition stared at Rhea as she approached and stopped before him. After a long silence, the elderly man spoke. "I see you are upset. Tell me, Rhea, what troubles you?"

There were many things that troubled her, but she would try to keep the conversation focused on the reason she entered Sanctuary. "Master Tanner," she said, bowing her head in respect. "Are you aware of a Codex reference to *the One with no line*?"

"I am," Tanner replied. An anxious expression formed on his face. "Has this person arrived?"

"Yes," Rhea replied. "A woman in her twenties."

"What is the status of our conflict with the Corvads?" Tanner asked quickly, his calm tone replaced with urgency. "That you speak to me here tells me I did not return. What of Valeriya and Angus?" he asked, referring to the other two Nexus Placidia Tens who had led their legion into battle. "And were we successful in eradicating the Corvads?"

"Valeriya and Angus also did not return. But you were successful. Every Corvad compound was seized and the Corvads killed. We obtained their registry listing every Corvad hidden within the civilian population, and our Nines hunted them down. The Corvads are no more."

The apparition smiled as he tilted his face toward the ceiling, spreading his arms out to his sides, palms up. After a moment, he dropped his hands and looked at Rhea.

"Finally! Three millennia of conflict brought to an end." His smile slowly faded as he continued. "As far as this woman with no line goes, we have nothing to fear now. There has been much debate about her purpose —whether she would be a weapon used against us or an ally in our defense. But with the Corvads destroyed, our House is safe. Nothing can threaten us."

As Rhea absorbed Tanner's words, she knew he was wrong; the Nexus House and humanity had never been more threatened. The Three had never mentioned the Korilian War, and Rhea thought it peculiar that such a significant issue would go without mention. Even now, Tanner seemed unaware of the threat. It suddenly dawned on her that The Three had never seen the war—their views had been altered.

"There is a significant threat. Humankind has been at war with the Korilian Empire for thirty years, and its outcome is unclear."

Confusion worked across Tanner's face. Her assumption had been correct; he had not seen it.

"The Korilian War?"

Rhea went on to explain what had occurred over the last thirty years, with her update culminating in humankind's final stand against the Korilian Empire. They had won the battle, but the war was far from over.

When she finished, Tanner asked the critical question. "What is the status of the Praetorian Legion?"

"We have only one cohort, and the other Nines are at the minimum quantity required to support House functions."

Tanner's face turned pale, the color draining from his holographic image. "How is that possible? Why is the legion at only ten percent, thirty years after our last battle with the Corvads?"

"The Council desired Tens to support the war against the Korilians, demanding I push all Nines to the level-ten Test. I have retained the minimum required to support the House but have otherwise complied."

A disapproving frown formed on Tanner's face. "Why did you not discuss this with me sooner, when I could have given you appropriate guidance?"

"I did not consider the Korilian War to be a House matter."

Tanner's eyes lit up in anger, his voice rising as he spoke. "You acquiesce to the Council's demands, forcing all Nines to the Test, leaving the House defenseless, and didn't consider this a House matter?"

Anger smoldered inside Rhea. For thirty years she had shouldered the burden of shepherding the House through its most trying time. She hadn't asked for the responsibility but had accepted it and done her best after The Three led their praetorians into battle and never returned. The future of the House had been placed in the hands of a seventeen-year-old left with no mentors—just a few crystals. It wasn't her fault. It was theirs.

Rhea snapped at the hologram, jabbing her finger into the ethereal man's chest as she spoke. "It was *your* views that were faulty! *You* left this House and humanity defenseless, pursuing the Corvads when an even greater threat existed! If there is anyone to blame, it is *you* and not *me!*"

Tanner remained silent as Rhea vented her frustration. When she finished, he stared at her for a moment. Then his eyes softened, the anger fading from his features. "You are correct," he said softly. "We should have seen this war. Something has gone very wrong, and unfortunately The Three can no longer resolve it. That is your task now."

Rhea bowed her head. "Tell me what to do."

"First, tell me about our Tens, and do we have any Placidia Tens besides you?"

"The war has taken its toll. We have a single Ten remaining, and he is not capable of placidia views."

"Tell me more."

"His name is Jon McCarthy. He has trouble following the more distant lines but is extremely proficient analyzing proximal lines; I dare say the best ever in the history of the House. Better even than you."

Tanner cast a skeptical glance at Rhea until she added, "Several hundred alternate views simultaneously."

The doubt faded from Tanner's face. "If he is this talented, perhaps we will defeat the Korilians after all. However, although the outcome is unclear, humankind's fate is sealed. The game pieces have been selected and placed on the board. Except..."

He paused a moment before continuing, "This woman whose line cannot be followed. Perhaps we misread the guidance from The Five. We always interpreted her to be a factor in our conflict with the Corvads. Maybe her arrival is related to the war against the Korilians. Does she have any latent power? Has she been trained?"

"She has enormous latent talent," Rhea replied. "And I am considering training her. However..." Rhea paused, bracing herself for Tanner's reaction. "She has the Touch."

Tanner drew back, and a cold, hard look settled on his face. "Why did you not tell me at the beginning, when you first mentioned this woman?" Before Rhea could reply, he said, "This woman is a Corvad. You must kill it. Swiftly and without warning. Its abilities may be hidden, and you cannot give it the opportunity to defend itself."

Rhea didn't notice Tanner's use of the pronoun "it" to refer to Lara. She had long ago gotten used to the Nexus habit of referring to Corvads as "its" —*things* to be destroyed.

She replied, "This woman is in her twenties, born after your final battle with the Corvads. She can't be one, unless a cell survived and trained her. I'm confident that all cells were destroyed, and there's no indication she was trained. The Codex says it's possible to learn the Touch on one's own."

"It is," Tanner conceded, "but rare." He paused for a moment, then asked, "Is Chernov still the Primus Seven?"

"No," Rhea replied. "He is almost a hundred years old and retired. But he still lives."

"Excellent," Tanner said. "Bring this woman before him."

"Why?"

"Before Chernov became Primus Seven, he was the lead interrogator at Sentinel."

At Tanner's mention of Sentinel, an image formed in Rhea's mind of the towering rock prison rising from the Black Sea, where those suspected of being Corvads were interrogated.

Tanner continued, "Chernov is very talented. He can detect Corvads by their subtle mannerisms and linguistic tendencies, the turn of a phrase or reactions to various situations. Bring this woman before Chernov, and he will tell you what you need to know."

Tanner added, "If Chernov has any doubt that she is a Corvad"—hatred burned in his eyes, his voice lowering as he spoke—"you *must* kill it."

65

Streaking through Earth's atmosphere, the Nexus shuttle plunged through white cumulus clouds, descending toward its destination. Lara observed one of the displays, annotated with geographic markers, as the shuttle pierced the clouds above the Caspian Sea, then sped northeast toward the snowcapped Ural Mountains. The shuttle gradually turned eastward, angling down between two jagged mountain peaks, slowing to a hover over a landing pad at the apex of green slopes carpeted with meadow grass and mountain clover. A gentle bump announced the end of their transit.

The shuttle door slid open, and McCarthy led the way up a winding path between steep granite walls. Forty-foot-tall metal doors swung outward as they approached, and Lara entered Domus Praesidium, taken back by the beauty of the rotunda's architecture. Beneath her feet, twisting veins of gold were encased within a translucent quartz floor, offering a view of several levels below them, and her eyes followed fluted marble columns upward over a hundred feet, where an epic battle between medieval knights looked down upon her. She sensed the emotion in the paint—the hatred of the antagonists and the gloating of the victor. As she took in the grandeur of the rotunda's construction, McCarthy led her toward the right-most of three sets of doors, passing between two guards as the doors opened.

Lara accompanied McCarthy down a dimly lit hallway, the entrance doors closing slowly behind them, walking in silence for the next few minutes. As they approached a darkened alcove on the left, the Nexus One and Ronan suddenly appeared before them, flanked by four other Nines, two on each side. The four Nines stood tensely, poised for action. The One said nothing as she stared at Lara.

Despite the Nexi's ability to control their emotions, Lara sensed the tension in the corridor. As she wondered whether The One had already made her decision, an elderly man emerged from the shadows and stopped beside The One. His eyes squinted as he focused on Lara.

After a long moment, he asked Lara, "What is your name, my child?"

"Lara Anderson."

"Do you have a middle name?"

"Taylor."

"A boy's name. Why?"

"It's not a boy's name," Lara replied defensively.

"Perhaps," Chernov said. "And perhaps not."

He studied her for another moment, then said, "The Touch is a very powerful ability. How did you learn it?"

"I don't know. I've always had it."

"You were born with it?"

"Maybe. All I know is that I've had it as long as I can remember."

"Did your mother or father have it?"

"Not that I know of."

Chernov's eyebrows furrowed, then he said, "I'm going to ask you two more questions, and I want you to choose your words carefully. Understand?"

Lara nodded.

"How do you like being a Nexus?" Chernov spread his arms apart as he added, "What do you think of our House?"

Lara hesitated. She had reservations about the Nexus House, some of which she had voiced to McCarthy in his stateroom: an underlying Nexus ruthlessness she found disconcerting. But what did Chernov mean when he said to choose her words *carefully*? Did he mean truthfully, or tactfully?

She examined The One, who was unreadable, as were the Nines beside her. Lara returned her attention to Chernov. After carefully contemplating her response, she decided to answer both truthfully and tactfully. "I don't know yet. First impressions are not always correct, and I have much to learn about our House."

Chernov studied her for a moment. "This is true. Very true," he replied, his voice trailing off as he spoke.

"Come closer," he said, the strength returning to his voice.

Lara stepped forward as directed, stopping an arm's length away. As she approached Chernov and Rhea, Ronan inched closer.

Chernov extended his hand. "Welcome to the Nexus House."

Relief washed over Lara; it seemed she had passed the inquisition, and Chernov was willing to shake hands despite her Touch. However, as she reached forward, Chernov raised his hand a few inches. Lara stopped, debating whether to raise her hand as well. After a moment of indecision, she withdrew her hand.

Chernov turned to The One. "May I have a moment with you?"

The two Nexi stepped back, disappearing into the darkness. Lara heard a whispered conversation in the distance but couldn't discern what they were saying.

"Your assessment?" Rhea asked.

"She is peculiar," Chernov answered. "Like a canvas freshly painted, the colors still drying. However, to stick with a painting analogy, I detect no Corvad pigments or brush strokes."

Chernov paused, contemplating something.

"What is it?" Rhea asked.

"I sense something else," he replied. "A confluence of time and power. What you detect as latent *talent* in this woman..." Chernov shook his head. "It is latent *power*. If you decide to train her, I suspect she will learn quickly because you will not be teaching her, you will be unlocking her power."

Chernov added, "To what extent this power extends and where it came from, I do not know. However, you *must* be careful. Master Tanner's concern could be warranted for different reasons. Perhaps it is best not to train this woman, or even wiser to eliminate her."

As Rhea absorbed his words, Chernov said, "I wish my insight was clearer."

Rhea replied, "You've been helpful."

Chernov nodded, then ambled down the corridor, disappearing in the darkness.

The One reappeared before Lara.

Rhea stared at her for a moment, then said, "Into my office."

She led Lara and McCarthy, with Ronan behind them, into a dark alcove along the corridor, then into a small room.

"Sit," she said, gesturing to three chairs in front of her desk.

Lara and McCarthy obliged, while Ronan stood behind them. After Lara settled into her chair, she glanced around the room. Behind the desk was a credenza against the wall, above which hung a painting of five men and women sitting behind a crescent-shaped table, a strange seal embedded in the wall above them. In addition to the large painting, additional portraits of men and women, usually individuals but occasionally groups of two, three, or four persons, hung from the walls.

The One said nothing as she stood behind her desk, staring at Lara, who felt a chill in the room. The One was viewing. Lara wondered if Rhea could foresee her future; after all, she had no timeline to follow. While she waited, she focused on The One's eyes; they were cold and hard.

Lara lost track of time. Finally, The One spoke.

"You will continue your training here. You will become a Nexus Ten."

66

Moments earlier, in a darkened room atop the one-hundred-and-twenty-floor Terran Council building, Regent Lijuan Xiang watched the display as McCarthy's shuttle descended through the clouds, landing outside the entrance to Domus Praesidium. After the House gates swallowed McCarthy and his new guide, Lijuan released control of the military satellite, allowing it to return to its pre-assigned tasking, looking outward into space.

As she stared at the display, she found it fitting that the satellite settled on *The Three Marys*—the stars in Orion's Belt—symbolizing the three women who visited the sepulcher of Jesus after his resurrection. Lijuan lamented what had become of her House, wondering when its power would be restored. For thirty long years, the remnants of the Corvad House lay hidden, waiting for the catalyst that would spark its resurrection.

Their powerful House had almost been destroyed by the despicable Nexi; only Lijuan and a few disciples had survived. Since then, the Nexus House, with access to the entire population of Earth and its colonies, had harvested the best talent, leaving the Corvad House to the rejected and the offspring of their own. Still, a few promising students had emerged. And although the Corvads had been decimated, the Nexus House was also weak. The Nexus One, in her arrogance, had not reconstituted her Praetorian Legion and had allowed her Tens to be siphoned off to support the war. There was only one Ten remaining and only a single legion cohort.

The Nexus arrogance was infuriating but would be used against them. The Nexus One had stood before Lijuan many times and never suspected she was a Corvad Ten. The Nexi deliberately hindered themselves, excluding emotion from their views instead of harnessing it, using it to propel them through the darkness. Lijuan could not comprehend how the Nexi had prevailed over the Corvad House; the Nexus views were so limited.

Lijuan's view told her the Korilian War was far from over. The Colonial Navy had prevailed in this battle and would push forward, regaining most of the lost territory. But in three years, Korilian resistance would stiffen, and the Fleet would be forced to strike deep into Korilian territory. With Earth no longer threatened, Lijuan would finally have the opportunity to eliminate McCarthy, stripping The One of her last remaining Ten.

But what filled Lijuan's heart with hope was something far more significant. Centuries ago, the Corvad House had been blessed with six Placidia Tens, and they had seen what would occur and had carefully prepared. What they had done was out of Lijuan's hands, but she would soon learn if their unusual preparations, made centuries ago, would bear fruit.

The Nexi could not predict what awaited them; their Codex had been destroyed and the wisdom of their Five vanquished. In a few years, if things went according to plan, the Corvad House would regain its former power, and the Nexi would pay dearly for what they had done. Lijuan intended to be there, in the bowels of Domus Praesidium, as the Nexus One, her disciples slain and her House in ruins, paid the ultimate price. She would look in The One's eyes and relish the horror and despair strangling Rhea's mind as the Nexus One realized her House had been exterminated.

Lijuan smiled. The Corvad House would have its revenge and take back what was rightfully theirs—the Krystalis. And then, there would be no one to stop them.

The Corvad House would fulfill its destiny.

Descent into Hellios: A Colonial Fleet Novel
Nexus House Book 2

From beyond her grave, a hero's final transmission could turn the tide of a galactic war.

Three years after humanity's Final Stand against the Korilian Empire, the Colonial Defense Forces have largely reclaimed the lost colonies. However, as the tide of war shifts against the Colonies again, Admiral Jon McCarthy and Lara Anderson discover a message from a long-dead prescient Nexus Ten amid the ruins of Darian 3. This startling discovery creates the potential to alter the course of the war with the Korilians, tilting the outcome toward humanity's favor.

Admiral McCarthy and Lara accompany 2nd Fleet and a Marine Expeditionary Force on a mission deep inside Korilian territory. Their target is Hellios, a dark planet hosting a Korilian facility shrouded in mystery. The mission to penetrate and neutralize the complex is perilous, and as a hand-picked Marine platoon descends through each level, the stakes escalate. But when they reach a dark chamber in the heart of the enemy stronghold, no one is prepared for what they find.

Get your copy today at
severnriverbooks.com

COMPLETE CAST OF CHARACTERS

<u>NEXUS HOUSE</u>
Rhea Sidener Ten (Placidia) / Nexus One (The One)
Elias Tanner Ten (Placidia) / one of The Three (ruled Nexus House prior to Rhea)
Elena Kapadia Ten / Colonial Army Guide (Darian 3 campaign)
Noah Ronan Nine (Primus) / Legion Commander / Department Head - Defense
Emanuel Kohler Nine (Deinde) / Legion Sub-Commander
Camila Theissen Nine (Centurion) / 1st Cohort Commander
Brandon Dargel Nine / Praetorian trainee
Dominic Zamora Nine / Department Head - Engineering Design
Siella Salvos Nine / Ten trainee
Eugenio Tabarzadi Nine / Pilot
Jina Hong Eight (Primus)
Dewan Channing Eight (Deinde)
Regina Caine Eight / 1st Fleet Guide
Arjun Sarja Eight / 2nd Fleet Guide
Angeline Del Rio Eight / 3rd Fleet Guide
Harindar Kapur Eight / Engineering Design technician
Chen Wei Seven (Primus)

Denys Chernov Seven (Primus) (retired)
Lara Anderson Grief Counselor / Inductee - 1st Fleet Guide

COLONIAL COUNCIL
David Portner Inner Realm Regent / Council president
Morel Alperi Inner Realm Regent / Director of Personnel
Lijuan Xiang Terran (Earth) Regent / Director of Material

COLONIAL FLEET
Nanci Fitzgerald Fleet Admiral / Fleet Commander
Liam Carroll Admiral / Deputy Fleet Commander
Jon McCarthy Admiral / 1st Fleet Commander
James Denton Admiral / 2nd Fleet Commander
Natalia Goergen Admiral / 3rd Fleet Commander
David Reynolds Admiral / Hospital Ship *Mercy* Commanding Officer
Heinrich Mendoza Vice Admiral / 1st Fleet Deputy Commander
Altair Priebus Captain / 1st Fleet Command Ship *Lider* Commanding
Officer
Nesrine Rajhi Captain / Battleship *Athens* Commanding Officer
Gynt Salukas Captain / Battleship *Sparta* Commanding Officer
Jeff Townsend Captain / Battleship *Europe* Commanding Officer
Jim Rushing Captain / Battleship *Georgia* Commanding Officer
Victoria Bergman Captain / Battleship *Valiant* Commanding Officer
Dan Metzger Commander / *Medusa* Viper Wing Commander
Howard Cortland Commander / McCarthy's Aide
Bryn Greenwood Lieutenant Commander / McCarthy's Aide
Duane Suarez Chief / 1st Fleet Command Ship *Lider*'s Master-at-Arms

COLONIAL MARINE CORPS
Brad Kratovil Colonel / *Venomous* Assault Team Leader

OTHER CHARACTERS
Cheryl Anderson Lara Anderson's mother

AUTHOR'S NOTE

I hope you enjoyed the first book in the Colonial Fleet / Nexus House series! If you did, I hope you're looking forward to reading the sequels, which are divided into several series. The first is the six-book Colonial Fleet series, and all six books are already written. Rather than publish each book after it was finished, I decided to hold onto the first five until all six were done. Since these books are science fiction with a decent amount of world-building, I wanted to ensure I didn't paint myself into a corner in previous books with inadequately thought-through aspects of this future. That turned out to be a good decision.

The next novel begins three years after humanity's Final Stand against the Korilian Empire, during which the Colonial Defense Forces have largely reclaimed the lost colonies. However, as the tide of war shifts against the Colonies again, Admiral Jon McCarthy and Lara Anderson discover a message from a long-dead prescient Nexus Ten amid the ruins of Darian 3. This startling discovery reveals information that could alter the course of the Korilian War, tilting the outcome toward humanity's favor.

Admiral McCarthy and Lara accompany 2nd Fleet and a Marine Expeditionary Force on a mission deep inside Korilian territory. Their target is Hellios, a dark planet hosting a Korilian facility shrouded in mystery. The mission to penetrate and neutralize the complex is perilous, and as McCarthy and Lara guide a handpicked Marine platoon into the depths of the facility, the stakes escalate. But when they reach a dark chamber in the heart of the enemy stronghold, no one is prepared for what they find.

I hope you enjoy *Descent into Hellios*!

ACKNOWLEDGMENTS

Many thanks are due to those who helped me write and publish this novel:

First and foremost, to Ned Steele for the inspiration to pick up the pen, to my wife Lynne and my children for their support through the long hours, to Nancy Coffey, without whose assistance I would not be a writer, and to my agent, John Talbot, for his belief in my first book and for taking a chance.

To the many wonderful people at Severn River Publishing. First, to Andrew Watts and Amber Hudock for offering a contract for the first six books in this series, to Cate Streissguth for guiding me through the process, to Julia Barron for her insightful summaries of each book, to my wonderful copyeditor, Kate Schomaker, and to Damonza for the fantastic cover. Thank you all so much.

To my friends in the Crossroads Writers Group: Michael Williams, Adelaida Lucena-Lower, and the Schwartz cousins, John and Rick, thank you for your support on this journey—six long years to write the first six novels in this saga. Your edits and comments have made each book better, and your encouragement kept me going. Thanks again for all your help!

ABOUT THE AUTHOR

RICK CAMPBELL, a retired Navy Commander, spent more than thirty years in the Navy, serving on four nuclear-powered submarines. On his last submarine, he was one of the two men whose permission is required to launch its nuclear warhead-tipped missiles.

Upon retirement from the Navy, Rick was contracted by Macmillan / St. Martin's Press for his novel The Trident Deception, which was hailed by Booklist as "The best submarine novel written in the last thirty years, since Tom Clancy's classic - The Hunt for Red October". His first six books became Barnes & Noble Top-10 and Amazon #1 bestsellers.

Rick lives in the Washington, D.C. area and continues to work on new books across the submarine and science-fiction genres.

Sign up for Rick Campbell's newsletter at
severnriverbooks.com